CW01192679

CATNAPPED

A Magical Romantic Comedy (with a body count)

R.J. BLAIN

Catnapped
A Magical Romantic Comedy (with a body count)
By R.J. Blain

When someone steals Diana's cat, a former lab animal rescued from death's door, she calls on one of the most dangerous beings in the universe for help. Cutting a deal with the devil isn't the smartest move, but there's no way in hell she'll abandon Mr. Flooferson the Magnificent to his fate.

Teaming up with the son of a demon, an angel, and one hell of a woman might push Diana to the limits of her courage and sanity. Unless she wants to sell her soul to the devil, she must cope with her new partner, make the most of a bad situation, and find out who stole her cat and why.

What she learns will forever change humanity--and lead to a battle destined to forever change the heavens and the devil's many hells.

Copyright © 2021 by R.J. Blain

All rights reserved.

No part of this book may be reproduced in any form or by any electronic or mechanical means, including information storage and retrieval systems, without written permission from the author, except for the use of brief quotations in a book review.

Cover Design by Rebecca Frank of Bewitching Book Covers.

ONE

Mr. Flooferson should have been on the couch waiting for me.

SOMEONE HAD TAKEN Mr. Flooferson the Magnificent, and when I got my hands on the culprit, they would know the true meaning of fear. As my cat was terrified of the outdoors, strangers, and anything that reminded him of his former life as a lab animal, there was no way in hell he would've left the comforts of home without the use of force. I couldn't even convince him to meet me at the door. He cried pitifully from the safety of the couch, some ten feet away, until I came into his domain and he could reassure himself I hadn't left him like every other human in his life.

No, unlike every other human in his life, I showed him love without pain. In the shelter hosting the retired lab cats, he'd been the saddest of the lot, so terrified of everyone and everything that the shelter operators had considered putting him out of his misery. No one wanted the scared ones, the ones who couldn't charm unsuspecting humans into adopting them.

Mr. Flooferson should have been on the couch waiting for me, but my door had been kicked in, the lock broken beyond repair. Worse, someone had torn the place apart and left with my cat and his fleece-lined carrier.

Had the bastard left my cat's carrier, I might have believed my baby had run out of fear.

I cracked my knuckles one by one, scowled, and considered my options. The police would need to come and check everything over. After the police flailed about and accomplished little, for they had more important things to do than investigate the loss of my cat, I would begin using every contact I could. While I was only a secretary within the CDC, secretaries held power.

Every day, I talked to the big wigs, the wealthy, and the powerful, and I earned their respect so I could smooth paths for my bosses, who needed to work with people all around the world.

I had the Devil on speed dial, and I wasn't afraid of using his wife to get what I wanted. While I wouldn't cut a deal with the

Devil, I'd find a way to make him do my bidding.

Well, maybe I'd cut a deal with the Devil, but I wouldn't bargain away my soul.

Nobody, and I meant nobody, would hurt *my* cat and get away with it.

I retrieved my cell from my purse and called the non-emergency line for the police, explaining that my home had been broken into and the thieves had stolen my cat and his carrier. My concern about my pet made the cop laugh, but he said he'd send a patrol over as soon as there was one available.

I'd been around the block often enough to understand nobody would be available any time soon.

All right. If the cops wanted to play games, I'd play.

I dialed the Devil, and if Satan gave me a hard time, I'd go straight to his wife and show him his little layer of hell had a new owner until my cat was safely home.

"Good evening, Diana. It's after hours, and you never work from home unless the world is at a literal risk of ending. We aren't scheduled for the End of Days at this moment. As I'm far too lazy to peek right now, what can I do for you?"

"You can help me find who stole my cat, flay the flesh from their bones, toss them into the nastiest pit of your hells, and give me a fiery whip so I can have some fun with the fuckers."

Silence.

I gave the Devil as much time as he needed to realize he spoke to a crazy cat lady on a mission to murder some thieving assholes.

"Have you forgotten who I am, Diana?"

"I absolutely called you fully aware of who and what you are, and if you could put Darlene on the line if you're not willing to help me find my cat, it would save me making a few other phone calls and knocking on your door in an hour. If I have to knock on your door in an hour, I'm going to redefine misery through hellfire for you. And if someone, and by someone I mean you, says it'll be a cold day in hell first, I'll come there and break all of your windows."

Thanks to Darlene, I'd learned the Devil enjoyed his air conditioning, his hells followed a disturbing number of scientific rules, and only some serious magic on his windows and walls kept the heat outside where it belonged.

"That's harsh for my electric bill."

"As if you actually pay it. Assistance or put Darlene on the phone, Lucifer. Jack shit is up for negotiation today. Someone stole my cat."

"This is the most fun I've had in a week.

Since I call my daughter Cupcake, you're just going to have to be Cookie."

"No. I will have Darlene kill you if you start calling me Cookie. And once I send Darlene after you, I'm going to call Kanika and tell her. Once I'm done with her, I'll go through every single one of your brothers until one of them agrees to help me put you in your place."

"Don't ruin my fun," the Devil complained. "I need some fun today. Darlene made me clean up the dungeon this morning."

"I will ruin every part of your life if you don't help me find my cat." I meant it, too. Maybe I was only a secretary, but I had three of the Devil's brothers on speed dial, and I'd play hardball. I would play so hard the entire planet tilted on its axis if necessary.

Nobody fucked with my cat.

The Devil laughed at me. "You know the rules, Snickerdoodle. I can't fiddle much with mortal affairs, and the thieves are mere mortals. I'm sure you can handle them."

Well, Snickerdoodle beat Cookie, so I'd ignore his idiocy in favor of rescuing my missing cat. "Does it look like I give a flying shit about the rules? The cop I called laughed at me and claimed he'd send someone over if they had somebody available. I live in fucking Miami. Do you know what that means? There's nobody available, and there'll be nobody available until the End of Days, and we'll all be fucking dead then. They aren't going to do jack shit about my trashed house, they aren't going to investigate my missing cat, and Mr. Flooferson the Magnificent will be gone forever. I want my cat!"

"Mr. Flooferson… the Magnificent?"

I gave credit where credit was due; the Devil didn't outright laugh at me. "Yes. That is my cat's name."

"Why did you name your cat that?"

"He's a former lab animal, and the shelter was going to euthanize him because he was scared of people. He had good reason to be scared of people. That's not his fault. He's a beautiful long-haired cat, and it took me six months, but he lets me hold him now. He's terrified of large spaces, and he won't go within ten feet of the front door. I have to bring a vet to the house because I can't stand the thought of taking him somewhere that might remind him of a lab. They could be torturing my baby. Why would they break into my house and take my cat?"

I didn't give a shit if the Devil thought less of me for the waver in my voice. Focusing on my breathing, I lifted my chin and prepared to wage war against the ruler of some ridiculous number of hells.

"I would suggest you look into what sort

of lab studies he was involved with. If they were testing new drugs, for example, someone might want to recover him to observe long-term consequences of exposure to their drugs. There are many reasons why someone might want to recover a former lab animal. Alternatively, why might someone want to steal *your* cat? You have many contacts, myself included. It could be less about your cat and more about manipulating you because you love your cat."

"Damn fucking straight I love my cat, you cat-spanked devil!"

"I would accuse you of leveling a low blow at me, but I do very much enjoy being spanked by my cat. She's a most lovely feline, and one of my favorite hobbies is playing with her spots. If I'm really good, she might even come out as her natural form."

"I will beg her to never let you see one of her prized spots ever again."

"I should recruit you to become one of my generals. You would whip the chaos right out of my hells within a week. My hells would be immaculately run. I should demand you run my hells for a while in exchange for recovering your cat."

"I have no interest in going to hell as a resident or a visitor, thank you. Now, about Mr. Flooferson the Magnificent. Which is more probable? That someone wants him because of what he went through as a lab animal or that someone wants to manipulate me?"

"In my most humble opinion, I believe that either is equally probable. Was your cat part of a reputable lab?"

Since when did the Devil think of himself as humble? I almost laughed. Instead, I cleared my throat to buy myself a moment to regain my composure. "I have no idea. I just saw there were lab animals in need of loving homes, and I decided my home would be the most loving of homes. I will hurt you if you disagree with me."

The Devil laughed at me. "If someone took your cat because of his history as a lab animal, he would have been rescued from an illegal operation. The legal operations are under regulations to keep the animals happy —and as healthy as possible. Those labs would not try to reclaim an animal. The government has been phasing out animal testing in favor of cutting large checks to humans with the appropriate conditions. They have also been clearing off criminal records in exchange for some pain and suffering, too."

"This is an excellent reminder to maintain my record of being a law-abiding citizen."

"You're disgustingly law-abiding, yes.

You should indulge in some evil. We'd have a great time."

"No, but thank you for your most generous offer, Lucifer."

"Are you sure? Your soul would provide me with decades of entertainment. I would convert you into one of my most prized devils. A general who would take over most of my hells by storm and sometimes answer to me when it's truly necessary."

I considered his offer. "What do you call a female devil, anyway?"

"A devil."

"That's lame. Demonesses are better named."

"I'm sure I could come up with an appropriately feminine title for your enjoyment."

"I'm sure you could, but I must refuse your most generous offer at this time. Now, about my cat. Are you going to help, or am I going to be having a long talk with Darlene?"

The Devil heaved a sigh. "You're almost as bad as my daughter. Must you, Diana?"

"I must. Someone stole my cat, the police aren't taking me seriously, and if I don't figure out what I need to do to get my cat back, I'll take over your realm, and then I'll storm the heavens if I must." It would take more work to access the heavens, but I could make use of some other contacts—or twist the Devil's arm into helping me somehow.

"I'll beg, but please storm the heavens. It would be spectacular. My darling thought about storming the heavens once, but then *He* got the bright idea of inviting her for tea and dainty little sandwiches, and she loves it. Worse, she makes me go with her."

"It's not like I want to keep the heavens. I don't even want to go there. Come on, just get your ass over here and make the police take me seriously. Bring Darlene, so when I start crying, she can yell at you while I'm coming to terms with my inability to kill you or get my hands on the fuckers responsible for taking my cat and destroying my house."

"Any other requests?"

"My cat!"

"I can't do that, Diana. You know I'm not permitted to interfere with mortal matters outside of a bargain, and I have no bargain allowing me access to this matter. You would have to bargain with me."

I loved my cat, but I also didn't want to lose my immortal soul for my cat. "Can bargains be for something other than my soul? I like my soul, Lucifer."

"I'm very aware of your possessiveness over your soul. You would deny even *Him*."

That I would. "I like my soul precisely where it is, in my possession, where no nasty beings, yourself included, can meddle with it. But I'll bargain if you can come up with something that does not result in the loss of my soul."

"You will accept a partner of my choosing for this venture. For however long it takes you to recover your cat and bring the catnappers to justice, and we'll define precisely what justice means as a part of our bargain. Until I have declared justice has been secured, you will work with this individual of my choosing. You will spend a minimum of two hours a day with this individual, who likewise owes me a favor and was wise enough to safeguard his soul from me and my rather evil activities."

I rolled my eyes, as the Devil talked loud and often about his evils but rarely dished them out. I'd met convicts who'd sinned far worse than the Devil on a bad day.

"Rude," the Devil complained.

"But true. Why do you want me to spend time with this individual?"

"Both of his fathers have severely annoyed me, and it will be highly entertaining if I can force him to live up to a bargain."

Shit. The Devil had bargained with the son of a triad? Trouble was the Devil having anything to do with a triad at all. "Demon?" I asked, contemplating tossing up a few prayers to mitigate some of the issues the child of a triad brought around when they showed up.

"Nope."

Damn it. "You seriously let one of your devils out to go on a fling with an angel?"

"Archangel."

I already regretted calling the devil. "You have got to be fucking kidding me."

"If only. The devil in question, who happens to be one of my generals, begged. I hate when they get to the point of begging. The archangel, well, that was a poorly chosen promise in a moment of weakness."

"A poorly chosen promise in a moment of weakness?"

"He claimed if that specific general happened to ever be brought low by a woman, that he would demand proof. Somehow, that became the foundation of a triad." The Devil laughed. "I've stopped worrying about when the heavens and my hells mix. We're one big, demented family. *He* approved, so that's that. Watching one of my generals be brought low by a woman? Truly delightful—especially after he'd spent time mocking *me* about Darlene. To sweeten the deal? He fell for his bride shortly after Darlene stormed my gates. The best of women storm gates to places, I've noticed. Their son is younger than you are, but not by much, and thanks to his genetics, he matured early."

I snorted at that, almost pitying the son of a high-ranked devil, an archangel, and someone who likely classed as one hell of a woman. "Only an idiot mocks you *or* your wife."

"I thought about putting him in time out for a few thousand years, but him being brought low by a woman worked out for the better. And anyway, he likes Darlene, but he does enjoy when he gets to be a pest. He's become even bolder, as Darlene likes him. Darlene would prefer if he stuck to a humanoid form while wearing a suit, which has basically become his dress code. Darlene being happy means everyone has a much higher chance of being happy. Anyway, your partner is thirty-two, he takes after his human mother too much for your good, and he's rather determined."

"The last thing I need is a determined man in my life, Lucy."

"I'm aware, which is part of what makes this so much fun. Will you bargain, Diana?"

"I will discuss the idea of a bargain with you, but I will not agree to any bargain until I hear all the details. And I'm expecting a bribe of you making the police take this seriously in order to open negotiations once you're here."

"Excellent. Do expect company within an hour, and I will bring your new partner with me so you have all of the fine print you so love in front of you—and if you're particularly unfortunate, I'll bring his parents as well."

"You're an asshole, Lucifer."

"I really am. Wear something nice." The Devil hung up on me, leaving me all by myself to scream my frustration over the situation.

After screeching a few curses, I drew in some calming breaths, decided to ignore his commentary about my clothes, and waited for trouble to come knocking at my door.

TWO

"Next time, I'll listen when you warn me about something."

I SHOULD HAVE WORN something nice.

It was one thing to face off against the Devil, who'd opted to show up as a tanned white man in a black suit, while I wore wrinkled work clothes. It was another to face off against the Devil, one of his brothers, and one of his top generals while wearing wrinkled work clothes. Unfortunately for my peace of mind, the archangel proved to be Raguel, best known for pursuing justice with unrelenting determination. To further complicate matters, the devilish general proved to be Belial. How the devil in charge of ruination of all things tolerated the archangel in charge of justice baffled me, but they accompanied a dark-haired woman in designer clothes, who contained the forces of heaven and hell with a single glare.

Even Lucifer behaved at the first sign her attention would fall on him.

How interesting.

The young man with them did take after his mother, and he gave Lucifer a run for his money in the tall, dark, nicely tanned, and handsome department.

Damn.

I pinched the bridge of my nose and questioned my life. It'd been so long since I'd been on a date that I couldn't remember what I was supposed to do when a tall, dark, and handsome crossed my path. If the tall, dark, and handsome kept his mouth shut, spending two hours with him a day would not test my patience in the slightest.

Unfortunately, I'd learned long ago that the tall, dark, and handsome men of the world tended to talk, and their often inane prattling rendered them tall with deliciously dark hair but otherwise removed their appeal.

No, his hair wasn't just deliciously dark. It was pitch black, long and thick enough I could tangle my fingers in it.

How dare the Devil bring temptation into my home when my cat was missing?

"Next time, I'll listen when you warn me about something, Lucifer," I said instead of a proper greeting.

He understood me, even when I abandoned being polite in favor of not strangling someone.

"You look fine." Lucifer stepped into my house, clucking his tongue at the wholesale destruction of just about everything I owned. "It's not like you could have changed into other clothes with your place like this anyway. You weren't kidding. They tore everything apart." Without bothering to ask for permission, he headed for my bedroom. "Not even your panties escaped unscathed. How utterly tragic."

"Yes, Lucifer. I'm aware." My panties had been flung across the entire room, and a fortune of lace, satin, and silk would need to be replaced. Did I even need to replace them? Why had I thought it was a good idea to buy panties that often cost twenty dollars a pop, and the less actual fabric used, the more it cost? Oh, right. I'd been thinking I might want to show them off to some man. In reality, my schedule didn't have room for a man in it, and I wasn't sure where I'd find two hours every day to spend with the tall, dark, and handsome son of a triad. "After I got off the phone with you, I saw my bedroom, sat on what is left of my mattress, and cried. For at least ten minutes. I spent the rest of the wait contemplating murder. I'm paid well, but I'm not paid well enough to replace my entire wardrobe in one fell swoop."

The woman in designer clothes checked out my bedroom, crossed her arms, and tapped her foot. "While you'd told me there'd been a robbery and a stolen cat, you had not told me how severe the situation truly is, Lucifer."

"I'd been too busy coming to see you to poke around to see the level of damage, and I didn't want Diana calling Darlene or Kanika. She would, too. I thought you'd be happy with me for a change. I'm giving your son a chance to finish paying his part of that bargain he struck with me, and I'm not even doing anything terribly nefarious. I could have done something far more nefarious than make him do a good deed." The Devil made a show of shuddering. "I'm going to have to go corrupt my soul after being involved with the doing of a good deed. My reputation might be ruined. Me, the Devil, doing a good deed? Impossible."

I rolled my eyes at the ridiculous number of lies the Devil told in such a short period of time.

"I find that to be disturbing," the woman admitted, and she shot a glare at her son. "You and I will be discussing why you'd entered a bargain with the Devil. You could have at least bargained with your dad instead."

My unwanted partner shrugged, and his grin had a crooked edge to it. "I could have, but talking to Lucifer made my father go home for a while. That let Dad go home for a while, too. I was being a good son for a change. That plus Lucifer suggested it was a good idea for Father and Dad to head home for a while. Don't even try to lie, Mom. You enjoyed having the house to yourself for a few weeks."

"God, yes," the woman replied. "That's the only reason you're getting away with that stunt. I like these louts too much for them to become sickly because they hadn't gone home for a while. I'm banned from both the heavens and the hells because you all think I'll take over."

Lucifer chuckled. "You would try, and I don't want you fighting with Darlene. It's bad enough Darlene goes upstairs often. One of these days, she'll tell me she's taking it over, and then we'll have to rewrite how the world ends. There has to always be an End of Days on the horizon, else we screw up the universal rules. And at least our End of Days has a new beginning at its conclusion. The other options lead to nothing."

The woman shrugged. "Introduce us, Lucifer. Let's see what I have to work with here."

Dealing with the rich and influential on a daily basis made me well aware I courted trouble with the woman. Considering she had an archangel and a devil up her sleeve, I would need to step lightly. "I'm Diana. I'm a secretary."

"She's employed by the CDC, and she works for the upper management dealing with interspecies monitoring and evaluation. In her case, they make her work with the various species as a representative as much as a secretary, as she's naturally talented at resisting various influences. As such, your husbands and son won't bother her. Diana, this is Claudine. She's a high-level practitioner, and she wanted to tame a demon, but she accidentally summoned Belial instead. Then she panicked, and because she didn't know what to do with a devil, she made the same mistake twice, thus summoning Raguel. She then decided she wanted to keep both of them, and every time they left, she summoned them again until she convinced them they should stick around," the Devil informed me.

For someone dubbed the Lord of Lies, the Devil often spoke the truth, and I considered Claudine with interest. "How do you accidentally summon a devilish general? The circles used to summon demons are drastically different from the ones you would use to summon a devil. Also, it's just better to call in favors if you want a demon *or* a devil. They're readily accessible nowadays. Calling them doesn't run the risk of sudden and unexpected death like performing a circle summoning." Was the woman a genius? An idiot? A little of both?

I had several summoning circles up my sleeve, and I'd even created one with the potency to summon Lucifer if needed. The Devil's amusement at my daring entertained us both, and I figured he liked audacious go-getters around rather than sheep ripe for the picking.

"I really do," the Devil agreed.

Claudine shot the Devil a glare. "Could you not snoop on people's thoughts for a single conversation?"

"I possibly could, but that day is not today. Diana might take over Earth if someone isn't keeping an eye on her. She really does love her cat. Anyone fortunate enough to earn her affection gains an unparalleled ally."

"If the Earth can't defend itself from a crazy cat lady, it deserves to be conquered. Anyway, I have ADHD, and I got bored partway through making the circle, so I changed it, and then the next thing I knew, I'd summoned Belial." The woman shrugged. "I was off my meds."

"Please stay on your meds unless I need a summoning done," I informed the woman, who laughed.

While I wouldn't act on it, I acknowledged my curiosity over which one of us could make the better circle. For her to have accidentally summoned Belial, she'd honed her practitioner arts. I'd honed mine, too—but I had made certain to cover my tracks better.

"Yes," the Devil agreed. "Perhaps too well."

Claudine grumbled. "Would you stop that?"

"No. She's far too entertaining. Do continue. I'll try to mitigate my interruptions to the bare necessities."

The woman huffed. "I do try to stay on my meds. Mostly, Raguel shoves them at me and stands around until I take them. Last time I was off them, I wandered all the way to Bermuda before these louts caught up with me. I get distracted by bright, shiny objects. I had never been to Bermuda before, so I just kinda wandered out of the house and went to Bermuda."

I needed to be a little less responsible one day, after my cat was safely recovered, and wander out of the house to some foreign land.

That sounded like the right type of excitement for me.

Belial sighed and straightened his blue tie, which contrasted against the black of his suit and shirt. "Diana, I am impressed you don't doubt Lucifer's claim. Most do."

"Lying is too much work when he's already on track to get the bargain he wants, so he's better off remaining honest, as he knows lying to me over something like that will just piss me off. I'm in no mood for his stupid little games. I'll just call Darlene and have her take over the show. He knows I'll do just that, so he's acting in his interest. Now, here's the deal. Some fucker busted my place up and stole my cat. I want my cat back, and while I won't bargain away my soul, everything else is up for debate, but if someone suggests I bargain off my body, you better make it worth my while."

The archangel laughed, stretched his wings, and rolled his shoulders, something I always found to be disconcerting. The lack of a head did me in every damned time, and that was even with the general understanding of why angels shrouded their true visages from mortal eyes. He said, "You are surprisingly well educated for a human. Where did you learn of the shroud?"

"A book." Of course, the book I'd been poking my nose in fell into the forbidden text category, but I hadn't spent years learning how to read several dead languages to not use my knowledge when an opportunity presented itself.

Raguel circled me, and he tucked his white wings, which were banded with shimmering silver, close to his back. "Is this your doing, Lucifer?"

"Oh, no. I would never do anything as

unscrupulous as to teach some mere mortal forbidden lore. Come on, Raguel. I have a little more class than that. It's more fun to drop hints about where the forbidden lore is at and have them get themselves in trouble all on their own. In this case, I had nothing to do with her acquisition of the book *or* her ability to read it. She was bored. I've learned there is nothing more dangerous than permitting Diana to become bored. The CDC has learned this, as they keep her busy for as many hours of the day as possible. I'm trying to convince her she could become a devilish general of my army."

"No," the archangel replied.

"Well, that's rude. She'd make a fantastic devilish general."

"The answer is still no."

I observed the pair with interest. "Are they always like this, Belial?"

Belial shrugged, and his expression turned thoughtful. "Of Lucifer's angelic siblings, Raguel has the most robust understanding of his role in the many hells, and he is supportive in his own way. Raguel would prefer if his brother finished being rebellious and went home, but that would leave an unfortunate gap in the power structure. Lucifer will not leave Darlene, so the heavens would be taken over by a rather troublesome feline."

"You're stuck ruling hell, Lucifer," I informed the Devil. "But perhaps we should set up some familial visitations, as it seems you benefit from exposure to your angelic family. I obviously need an excuse to call you every single day until my cat is found. Alive and well, mind you. I would be satisfied with sufficient clues to help me locate the culprit, as it does not seem I will be getting any real assistance from the police."

"No, you won't. Enough for insurance purposes," the Devil replied, shaking his head. "But they have no interest in learning the fate of an unwanted cat."

"He is not unwanted."

"He is unwanted by anyone other than you."

The Devil's words hurt, and I considered popping him in the nose for daring to wield the truth like a weapon. I pointed at the unnamed tall, dark, and handsome son of the triad destined to turn my life upside down. "How does he help me find my cat?"

"He's a wayfinder," he replied. "His specific bag of tricks isn't often useful, but he has the ability, and while he can't locate living things, he *can* lead you to the clues you need to find your cat. If you enter another bargain with me, I can take some steps to safeguard your cat's life."

Every bargain with the Devil came with consequences, and I turned to the one being in my house who could help me negotiate without paying too steep a price for what was on offer. "Is there a reason I shouldn't enter this bargain with your brother, Raguel?"

The archangel's laughter reminded me of chimes dancing in the wind. "However strong your affection is for your pet, who has seen much hardship in his life, he is but a small, fragile beast in the grand scheme of things. Such a bargain would be a small thing for my brother. Part of the price would be understanding my brother would know of your pet's fate and would be unable to speak of it to you, but he can persuade those who have him to do no harm to the animal upon striking the bargain. It is a door you can open if you wish. Your soul will not be in peril."

I eyed the Devil with interest. "What is so special about me or my cat that you would enter such a bargain with me?"

The Devil's dark smile chilled me even more than the moment I'd realized someone had stolen Mr. Flooferson. "Much like my little cupcake, you're the kind of woman who changes the world when properly motivated. For her, it took the right man at the right time. Don't tell her this, but I'm quite fond of her man. He suits her, much like my darling suits me. You're an odd one, as you'll change the world for a cat, but you were always an odd one. It would be foolish to expect you to change."

"Well, he's *my* cat. That's reason enough for me."

"Belial? Try to convince your boy he needs to keep Diana from taking anything over. The instant she decides something is hers, that's it. You may also want to keep a close eye on your boy. If she decides she's taking him home with her, that's it. He'll be lost. You'll be out a kid, and then your wife will get upset, and then you'll have to have another child."

Belial regarded his son with narrowed eyes. "I never liked this one all that much anyway. You live here now, boy. Be gone with you. You may visit at the appropriate holidays to appease your other father and your mother."

Well, I could guess Belial had a healthy interest in having another child, which left the archangel. I turned my attention to Raguel.

"As I don't want my feathers plucked for a pillow, I do as the wife wants."

Well, that left Claudine. "I don't know much about you, but I want to be like you one day."

She grinned. "I figured I had a choice in life to make: lead or follow. And while the view is spectacular when I follow those husbands of mine, I generally prefer holding their leashes and enjoying my power for the duration of my mortal life. I've been informed I'm not allowed to exit life any time soon, but they're not clear on how mortality works. They've been trying to convince me we should have another brat for years, but this one refuses to fledge properly. He doesn't live at home, mind you, but he visits every day and tries to pretend he's just checking on his poor beleaguered mother. In reality, he knows if he takes his eye off me, I'll probably show back up with a brother or sister he has to babysit when I have work. When I have work, the overprotective husbands like to hover. Do yourself a favor, Diana. Limit your number of husbands to one. One is bad enough to manage. Two? Two will drive you to the limits of your sanity. And while feathers are a perk of keeping an archangel around, he tends to get really fucking miffed when I start cursing like I really mean it."

Raguel's pained sigh made me grin before I said, "I'm thinking it isn't the number of the men that's causing you problems, but their type. A devilish general and an archangel sharing the same house? I'm honestly impressed the End of Days hasn't started yet."

"Me, too. I've gotten good at managing these two, but they test my patience some days. Today is one of those days. The amount of whining when Lucifer called! You would have thought the world was ending. Lucifer, asking us for a favor? Oh, no. Not a favor. Calling in the payback for a bargain." Claudine turned her glare onto her son. "Darian, I still can't believe you. I swear, if your father didn't have issues with taking the whip to your ass, I'd be stealing from your uncle and giving you something to cry about."

For a being without a head, Raguel did a damned fine job of snorting. I needed some alcohol and a chance to sit down and contemplate the nature of the shroud and how angels operated, their heads essentially located in a different dimension or plane of existence to keep mere mortals such as myself from being eradicated from an accidental peek. The book I had read left a great deal to the imagination.

Curiosity might one day become my undoing.

The Devil, probably in an effort to appease the irritated woman capable of reining in one of his generals and his brother, lifted his hands. "You wouldn't have to steal the whip. I'm sure Darlene would loan you hers without complaint. She got it from Belial as a wedding gift. Just ask him to make you one. He delights in making his toys hurt more. I'm sure he'd find the appropriate balance for your son."

Lucifer's general chuckled. "To my amusement, Claudine has managed to maintain order with the boy through the artful use of a raised brow. We bred a smart one, and he knows not to push his mother's buttons. He's only gotten a spanking a few times, and Raguel holds the honor of being the one to dish out the punishment."

"I just love how my entire family talks about me like I'm not here." Darian met his mother's glare with one of his own. "If my paternal idiots hadn't been making themselves sick staying home for so long, I wouldn't have had good reason to deal with the Devil. Blame them if you want to blame anybody. I made a good bargain, too."

"He really did," Lucifer agreed. "I'm quite proud of him. Darian is a good little nephew. It was a balanced bargain, and he set it up with the intent to keeping it balanced even throughout the negotiation process. Much like Diana here, he is very possessive of his soul, probably due to living most of his life under the same roof as two idiots and his mother. You can come home with me, Darian. Darlene would love to baby you for a while, and after dealing with your parents? My home would be fairly normal."

I wondered who would die first at the hands of the disgruntled devilish general and archangel: Lucifer or Darian.

Claudine frowned, but after a moment, she shrugged. "Go ahead and take him. He's a pain in the ass, he eats through money, and I'm wondering if Raguel was more of a voyeur than a participant in his conception. Did any of your genes actually make it to our son?"

Darian's grin widened. "He's the reason I did such a good job with the negotiations, Mother. Without his influences, I would have probably been just like Dad, super greedy and a lot selfish."

Belial sighed. "I rule over ruin, not greed, you little shit. And how can you call me selfish? I share your mother."

"You do share her, but there is so much bitching and complaining and moaning and groaning. And displays of jealousy you have over how she panicked and complicated everything by involving Father."

"I really shouldn't have panicked," Claudine replied. "That said, I'm very pleased with how it worked out. Darian, stop trying to goad your dad into being annoyed with you. I realize you're on the bandwagon for a sibling, but you do not need to instigate."

Darian stared at his mother, and he raised a brow. "Whether you have another kid is none of my business, but when Dad and Father are happy because they made you happy, I'm happy, and my happiness is very important. Go home and be happy. I can handle the Devil on my own."

I regretted my lack of popcorn. Would Darian emerge from challenging his mother unscathed? Would Raguel or Belial rescue their son from his imminent demise? Were all triads insane?

I'd never looked much into triads, especially the powerhouses between devils and archangels, more than the acknowledgment angels really liked getting it on—more than the CDC's records liked to claim. The initial records claimed a few happened every *generation*.

In reality, it was every few years, and without fail, the offspring of triads caused many problems.

The Devil winked at me. "That's Belial's way of showing his affection. He's a work in progress. I've found my generals become more effective once they've been corrupted by mortals a little. That whole love thing makes them so much more effective at punishing the fucking assholes and making sure they're properly prepared for their eviction back to the mortal coil. Claudine's corruptions are rather extensive, but she's done good work with both these louts. I'll play easy ball with you regarding the safeguarding of your cat. As your home is a mess, you must agree to allow me to handle the repairs and renovations, at my dime, and you must share living space with Darian until I have completely handled the repairs and renovations. To my standards."

Well, as far as bargains went, the one the Devil offered could be much worse. My house would need a lot of work after the damage done to it. "Nothing weird, and you're responsible for replacing any furniture that can't be salvaged. Or you don't want to salvage. I don't care either way. Darlene has to approve all of the renovations and interior design purchases, and this place has to be suitable for business meetings, which I'm sometimes forced to host. Don't lose me my job being a dick. Also, remember cats have a finite lifespan, and you must be finished within my cat's natural lifespan. There will be no soul-stealing of my feline, as your sense of time is twisted due to your severe case of immortality."

"How ruthless, bringing my wife into this."

"You would turn my house into a sex dungeon and get me fired." He'd also take decades doing the job because time bloomed in a rather different fashion for those who had an unlimited amount of it.

"I really would. Can I turn a room into a sex dungeon? You'd like it."

"No."

"How about your basement?"

"I live in Florida, where floods are real

and happen yearly. I do not have a basement."

"I could add one for you."

"I live in Florida, where floods are real and happen yearly," I repeated. "I do not want a basement. It's bad enough doing hurricane repairs just about every year."

The Devil frowned. "Perhaps I should be kind and arrange for your transfer to the Washington offices."

"Which also floods. I do not want to live in the political swamp that is Washington."

"How about New York?"

"An island. What happens on islands?" I countered.

"Infrequent but probable flooding," the Devil muttered. "What is wrong with a little water? It won't hurt you. Usually."

"I live in Florida. I've had enough floods for one lifetime." I sighed. "At least try to be reasonable, Lucy."

"Being reasonable is so challenging. I don't like being reasonable. Raguel, tell her being reasonable is overrated."

"Are you *trying* to lose this bargain, Lucifer?"

Lucifer crossed his arms and sulked. After a few moments, I realized his wife likely went out of her way to make him sulk or pout, as it brought out his softer side. "I'm attempting to butter her up for future endeavors. If I'm really nice to her in this bargain, she may lower her guard on the next. It is a viable strategy."

I sighed, as that was something the Devil would do. "It is a viable strategy, as I have a rather strong and unreasonable desire to engage in fair dealings. In that, I suppose your desire to have me as one of your minions makes a great deal of sense. I am very good at balanced negotiations."

"See, Raguel? Diana is very easy to negotiate with. If I give her a fair bargain out of the gate, she will close the loopholes she considers to be of importance, and we both win and lose some. As I want her to consider future bargains, I will make certain we equally benefit from this bargain, although she will not understand how I benefit until later. I will also make certain how I benefit does not put her at a disadvantage, as it would make her less likely to bargain with me in the future. She's a logical and sensible creature most of the time. Darian, I will consider us even should you do your best to stay with Diana for two to three hours every day. Important responsibilities and other work causing separation is permitted, but if it is a viable option, you must adhere to this. As long as you two are sleeping under the same roof at the same time, I will view the conditions of our agreement to be met."

Darian shrugged. "I have a place, and while I don't have a guest bedroom, there is a couch. It's not like this place is habitable. I don't mind having a roommate, and I suspect this will encourage my parents to force me to move into a proper house rather than an overpriced apartment none of them like."

That caught the attention of all three of his parents.

Ah ha. I bet the Devil had some form of unbalanced agreement with Claudine, Belial, or Raguel, and forcing Darian to upgrade his living arrangements using me would restore the balance. Amused, I waited to see who would crack first: the trio of parents or the Devil with an ace up his sleeve and goals to fulfill.

The Devil glanced my way, lifted a finger to his lips, and winked at me.

Claudine bowed her head and sighed. "When does your lease expire?"

"I'm month-to-month, Mom. You know this. You also know the only reason I haven't gotten a house is because I can't afford to pay for it in cash and refuse to get scalped on a mortgage."

"We can afford to buy a house for you," she muttered.

"But then I wouldn't have earned the house on my own. You're the one who thought it was a good idea for me to be independent. You're also the one who told me women were attracted to capable men who can tie their own shoes without the help of his mommy."

My parents had done the same with me, and whenever I called them, I made a point of reminding them they'd done a good job of molding me to be an adult determined to drive them to the brink of their sanity. "My mortgage only lasted three years because I worked hard to grab every bonus from the CDC I could get my hands on, and I dumped it all into accelerating my payments. I bet after the Devil is done with his renovations, this place might actually be worth more than I paid for it. And your mother *is* right. Women like a capable man who can tie his own shoes without the help of his mommy."

Men who could tie their shoes, cook, clean, and hold a job didn't tend to last long on the singles market, so what was wrong with Darian?

Wait. I considered his parents. Right. He was the son of a triad. Few women met the standards of an archangel, and Belial would bring ruin to anyone who hurt his baby boy.

Poor Darian, doomed to be single until the perfect woman for him came along.

"I could tolerate a three-year mortgage," Darian stated. "Thirty years? Not a snowball's chance in hell."

"Snowballs have a shockingly good chance in my hells, surprisingly enough. I married a snow leopard. She has a seasonal room, as I've learned she loves all of the seasons and not just snow. So, if you're around during the winter season, there's definitely a solid chance for a snowball's survival in the right place."

Darian sighed. "How are the snowball's chances right now?"

"Not good," the Devil admitted.

"My point stands. No more than a three-year mortgage, and it can't bankrupt me."

Claudine snagged Raguel by the arm and Belial by his ear and dragged both of her men towards my front door. "Don't let the woman get away, do what your uncle says, and try not to cause more trouble than you can contain without assistance. I'll discuss this with your fathers and get back to you. Diana, charge the Devil for a week at a nice hotel in the meantime. That couch will kill your back, and the boy's bed is no better. He needs a new one."

"I can afford a hotel," I said.

"It's better if you make the Devil pay for it. It makes him feel useful, and for all he's the Devil, he's really a grouchy angel in disguise, and doing good things makes him feel wanted and useful. Darlene gets bitchy if he doesn't feel wanted and useful."

Without another word, Claudine left with her husbands, and Raguel managed to get the door closed behind him.

What a strange family. I sighed. "Add a reasonable condition to the bargain for a week at a good hotel, Lucifer."

"An hour where you're forced to listen to life advice from me. I will give you a week notice to set up the appointment unless I'm already scheduled to be in your domain. You'd never stop a guest from lecturing you."

Ugh. What a shitty bargain, but it was something I could afford to pay. I could survive through an hour of torture and anguish at the Devil's hands. "Fine." It would be a pain in my ass, but I could deal with an hour of listening to the Devil. "Bargain made, even though I suspect I will regret this."

"You'll find out soon enough," the Devil promised.

THREE

"Why are we discussing my panty situation?"

THE NEXT TIME I bargained with the Devil, I needed to remember to specify the hotel's location. When the Devil called the CDC and informed them that he needed me for a week, I realized I'd gotten played. Worse, the CDC tended to jump at Lucifer's order. The half of the conversation I could hear implied I'd be the Devil's bitch for at least a week.

I waited for him to hang up before I announced, "If you lose me my job, I'm bringing Darlene into this."

"I pay better for the same work."

Narrowing my eyes, I considered him. "It's not losing me my job if I quit, that's true. You can pitch me the benefits, and I'll even listen."

"Two guaranteed days a week off, where I won't disturb you unless the world is at literal risk of ending or my wife makes me, is only the beginning of the benefits I can offer you. You'd also only have to work eight hours a day, and thanks to my wife's wicked influences, I pay my salaried minions overtime, as a salary does not give me rights to blatantly abuse my minions. I have to save the abuses for the fucking assholes in residence." The Devil smirked. "That would give you time to actually make use of your pretty panties in the future."

"Why are we discussing my panty situation?"

"You gave me rights to handle everything in your house. That includes your panties. It would be a shame for such a wonderful selection of sinful panties to go to waste. As such, my job offer must include opportunities to make use of your pretty panties."

I tilted my head in Darian's direction. "And is there a reason we're discussing my panties in front of your nephew?"

"As a matter of fact, yes. First, once I have my way with your wardrobe, you will be highly desired by most men. A little competition is good for him, especially as his overbearing parents do a fairly good job of curtailing his ability to meet women. I have high expectations for my nephews and nieces. Belial provided him with a lot of good gene markers, but it takes a certain amount of cultivation to turn them on. Usually, the triad's grandchildren get the highly potent magic, but Darian has the right gene combinations to put on a good show if I cultivate him a little."

"Why do I want to be cultivated?" Darian asked, his tone more curious than concerned, something I found intriguing.

Wise men became concerned when the Devil came around wanting something.

"You'll be great with women, you'll make an excellent father, and you'll have your father's tendency to bring general ruin to those who cross you and your family. Because of your other father's influences, you'll only ruin those who really deserve it and be generally more of a protector. But since I'm being honest today, as lying does tend to annoy Diana, I want you two to have a child so I can move forward with some of my other plans."

Right. The Devil played the long game, and my life meant little in his general plans. "How delightful. Had I known you view me as a gene donor in your general plans, I would have added additional conditions to the initial bargain."

"That is why I neglected to tell you that until after you'd struck the first bargain with me. But aren't I a generous being? I am giving you an opportunity to negotiate with me using that knowledge."

"How generous of you." When I got my cat back, I hoped Mr. Flooferson the Magnificent realized how much I loved his furry ass. Dealing with the Devil might do me in, but why did he think I wanted a man *or* children?

Okay. I could use two or three children under foot, but in what universe did I have time for even one?

"Well, if you worked for me, you'd have the time," Lucifer informed me.

With my house in shambles, my wardrobe's days long over, and everything I owned either broken or damaged, I could understand why someone might cut a deal with him. "Does your job offer include sufficient compensation to deal with some amorous man trying to convince me I should settle down and have kids? Because if it doesn't, it should—and you should lay out all of the benefits parents might enjoy while in your employ. Don't forget the healthcare. Kids are not cheap, nor are the health bills involved with having kids." I gestured to my house with a sweeping motion of my hand. "And this house? This house is not suitable for children *or* a husband, so you better put some thought into that aspect of things."

Having been around when the Devil tricked his poor daughter into putting up with him, I acknowledged I'd likely somehow fall into his plans one way or another.

The matchmaking abilities of the Devil, frankly, scared me a lot more than any of his hells.

"You should see what I had done to my other nephew. I may have informed him just how much work I'd put into making certain he'd be suitable for the precious seed I'd cultivated just for him. Be grateful you're not part of my plans to protect my unicorns."

Right. One of his poor nephews worked as a police chief in New York, and he'd married one of the Devil's favorite creations, a cindercorn. "How are the cindercorns doing, anyway?"

"The last of the wild herds didn't survive the winter, although I saw to it they passed peacefully. But she'll be the first of the next line, and they'll be much more robust and better suited for modern life. I have all the seeds of my cindercorns, but they've earned some rest. They'll be back one day, though. With those two as the starting of the new line, the cindercorns will be even randier than my standards, so they'll become stable within a few generations, and my nephew's contributions will make it easier for them to convert mates. That's part of why the cindercorns ultimately failed. They simply weren't driven enough to convert a mate, so their numbers dwindled. That will not be a problem in the future."

I winced, as the Devil's file made it clear he had an unreasonable interest in unicorns. "Dare I ask what your next unicorn project is?"

"There's one celestial left. She's from a rather proud line of unicorns. Her parents were old when they had her—in unicorn years, mind you. Unfortunately, her parents died before teaching her the trick of converting a stallion, so I'll have to take some steps. I think she'll be all right otherwise. She has a very healthy interest in children, although she has some issues she'll have to work through first. I almost pity the stallion who'll tame her. She'll keep him busy."

Somehow, I kept from rolling my eyes. "Let me guess. You've already picked her stallion for her."

"I haven't, actually. It's a real problem. Are there even any men worthy of my last celestial?"

"Obviously, as there was one worthy of your cindercorn," I muttered.

"I cultivated that seed very specifically for my cindercorn, thank you very much. I'm debating a lycanthrope for her, although I'm not sure how the virus and her unicorn genetics would interplay. It could be an interesting experiment."

"No."

"Don't ruin my fun."

"You do not need to play matchmaker for her if she does not want a man."

"She wants a man, but she has no idea what to do with one. She's shy. The poor little thing is an introvert, and she works as a waitress."

I winced at the thought of an introvert struggling through day-to-day life working as a waitress. "I've changed my mind. Do your matchmaking, but partner her with someone who can help her develop a career she actually *likes*. And with someone who will treat her well, is a good match for her, and doesn't just meet your genetics standards."

"I'm blaming you when I get into trouble for matchmaking again," the Devil warned me. "And I never just match based on genetics. Well, usually. Having the right genetics is no good if I can't convince the couple they want to procreate. Nothing puts a kink in my plans quite as much as a pair absolutely hating each other and refusing to share the same room. The refusal to share the same room with each other puts a damper on any potential children. And while I'm the Devil, I do play fair. In that regards. Getting the right seed planted does no good if I can't cultivate a nurturing environment for it. Well, mostly. Some seeds require adversity to thrive, and in those cases, I just toss them at two amorous humans who opt against using birth control."

The Devil operated by really strange rules. "You're already in trouble for trying to play matchmaker for me. What's a little extra trouble? Be serious. When are you *not* in trouble with somebody?"

"I don't know. Have I ever not been in trouble with somebody? That's a really good question, one I don't have the answer to."

Heaven help me. "I need to get clothes for tomorrow, and I'm sure Darian likewise needs to pack for a week at this hotel. Also, you need to make arrangements for his work as necessary."

"He has a flexible schedule."

I twitched. "If that means unemployed, I'm going to be rather irritated, Lucifer."

"Oh, no. His mother would never let him get away with unemployment. He wishes he could some days, though. Your new companion is a money-grubbing thief."

I considered the various jobs that might fit that bill. "That doesn't really narrow the field all that much, Lucy. Give me something a little more concrete than that."

Darian laughed. "I ruin businesses for a living, and I'm very good at it. I target the ones Father dislikes, use Dad's advice and general inclinations to bring them down, and once I've done the dirty work, I buy the companies out before I restructure and reorganize them or plunder them for profits. I'm between jobs right now, as I haven't picked my next target. Father makes that sort of thing easy, as he'll complain to my mother when he sees anything particularly unscrupulous. He does it knowing I'll go on a hunt to see if I can add them to my trophy collection. It's a good way to get rich in a hurry."

My eyes widened, and I could see several ways a wayfinder could make a fortune digging out intel on nefarious businessmen. "You use your wayfinding tricks to get dirt on the company, and then you put them in a position where you can take them down or buy them out to either hide the evidence of their misdeeds *or* you shut them down because of their misdeeds and purchase the dissolving company?"

Darian dipped into a bow. "And neither of my fathers can really get upset at me for doing it because justice is served with a hefty dose of ruination—and I take steps to take care of the employees caught in the fallout. And while I bitch about the mortgage on a house, the reality is, I could afford to buy a house, but I need the liquid funds to handle the buyouts, so I make sure to live within my means. I don't want to end up one of those adult men living in his mother's basement."

Well. I could make use of his skills in the hunt for my cat, which elevated the Devil for providing someone who might be able to help me find my poor cat. "It's not a big corporation destined to make you a lot of money or bring you prestige, but I'd be appreciative if you used those skills on whatever sleazebag cockgoblets stole my cat."

"Sleazebag… cockgoblets?"

I shrugged. "It seems appropriate to me. Only a sleaze would steal a traumatized former lab cat, and I'd totally stuff the asshole's dead body into a bag and chuck it into the drink."

"But cockgoblet?"

Well, he hadn't run away yet, which was a point to him and the Devil's meddling ways. "It has a nice ring to it."

"Just don't put a ring on it unless they're specially constructed for that purpose," Lucifer stated, and he dared to leer at me in my house.

As everything in my home was already damaged or broken, what was adding to the carnage? I spun, grabbed hold of the lamp, which had lost its shade somewhere along with half of its bulb, and flung it at the Devil's head. The glass and metal made a rather satisfying crack-thunk when it connected with his thick skull. "I said cockgoblet, not cock ring, you steaming pile of monkey feces."

The lamp thumped to the floor, and the Devil shook his head. To my disappointment, I hadn't made him bleed. "Did Darlene tell you to do that?"

Had she? I considered my past phone calls with her. As I couldn't remember, I grabbed my phone, dialed her number, and listened to the ring tone, hoping she'd answer.

Sometimes she did, sometimes she didn't. If in a mood, she'd play voicemail tag with me for a few days, toying with me because she could.

"What did that husband of mine do now?" the woman answered.

I smiled at her correct assumption her husband had done something. "I've had a long and bad day, but have you ever told me I should hit your husband in the face with a lamp before? He wants to know, and I can't remember."

"I told you to smack him around if he bothers you, which is basically the same thing."

I nodded. "Lucy, she says she told me to smack you around if you bothered me. That counts. Thank you, Darlene."

"How do you like your new suitor? I remembered you'd been complaining how hard it was to find a tall, dark, and handsome the last time Satin strutted his stuff in a designer suit. When I heard about his latest ploy, I didn't stop him because you deserve your own tall, dark, and handsome—

and your suitor has got decent genes to go along with his nice ass."

I frowned, as I hadn't gotten a look at Darian's ass yet. "I haven't had an opportunity to fully admire the local scenery. What grade are we talking about?"

"If the cranky succubi who aren't allowed to play with him are any indication, he's just about a match for my husband. Belial made it clear his little boy was not available for the amusements of a bunch of perverted succubi. Since he's a young, fresh stud, this is very annoying for them. You already have Belial's approval, as you can deal with my idiot husband with little difficulties. You already have the other father's approval because you're straitlaced, and he appreciates that. As for his mother? I've given up trying to guess what she thinks. Honestly, I'm not sure she thinks hardly at all, but that's their problem rather than mine." Darlene sighed. "Why did you throw a lamp at my husband?"

"I didn't just throw it, I hit him in the face with it," I said, unable to keep the pride out of my voice. "He made fun of one of my curses."

"Oh? Which curse?"

"I called the people who stole my cat sleazebag cockgoblets, and then he started in on cock rings, so I threw the lamp to shut him up. It mostly worked."

The Devil sighed.

Darlene laughed. "His sense of humor is a little twisted. If you haven't already, bargain with him for the safety of your cat. He has tricks up his sleeve, and he has a soft spot for felines."

"We came to an agreement about that already."

"Excellent. Once you're done with my husband, send him on home, and I'll reinforce why he'll keep an exceptionally close eye on your pet. In the meantime, there's nothing in the books stating I can't send Mistoffelees over to help keep an eye on your furry friend. She's an excellent scout, and she enjoys when she can get her paws dirty for a good cause. If there are any problems, she'll let me know. I'd offer her sister, too, but Bellsiebubble prefers when she dirties her paws for a naughty cause."

"And I thought Mr. Flooferson the Magnificent had a weird name." I hesitated, but curiosity got the better of me, so I asked, "Do your cats try to kill you in your sleep?"

"No. They love their names, as it makes that lout of mine twitch. They love tormenting him. It is one of their joys in life. And after they're done tormenting the lout, they charm him and make him share his pillow. It drives him insane."

"He shares?" I blurted.

Darlene laughed long and hard. "Surprisingly, yes. I'll leave you to your business. Don't let Lucifer annoy you too much, Diana. Call me back if he gives you trouble." Without wasting any time on goodbyes, she hung up.

I regarded the Devil with a raised brow. "Bellsiebubble?"

Lucifer bowed his head and heaved a sigh. "Two of my brothers encouraged her, so she named our cats in ridiculous fashions. I say ours as though I have any say over her cats, which I do not. Bellsiebubble is a little devil of a kitten. Mistoffelees is more on the angelic side, but she's still a damned cat. Though, that said, I love when Mistoffelees tries to cause trouble with my wife. She tends to faint when caught, as though passing out will somehow spare her from my wrath." The Devil wrinkled his nose. "To be fair, thus far, she's gotten away with it because she's a devilishly cute fluffball."

"So, she said I should bargain with you regarding Mr. Flooferson the Magnificent, and that once you're finished making my day a clusterfuck, that you're to return home to her. She mentioned potentially sending Mistoffelees to keep an eye on the situation." I took a few moments to think through the Devil's commentary over the fainting tendencies of his cat. "I don't want her to faint and get hurt helping my cat, though."

"Oh, don't worry about that. She's a

fierce huntress. She just gets excessively startled when *I* catch her in the act of being naughty. She likes to think I'm not going to catch her, so I enjoy doing just that. That, plus even when she faints, I catch her. I'm not going to let her get hurt during one of our games, so don't you worry yourself over that. And anyway, Mistoffelees is immortal, and about as close to a true immortal as it gets. She and her sister were gifts from *Him* to my wife, and *He* can't stand the damned crying when the pets pass away from old age. I have more immortal fish than I know what to do with at this stage, because the first and last time one of my wife's favorite pet fish passed away from old age, she didn't stop crying for a week. As such, we have a general agreement with *Him*. We fish shop in pairs, and one is angelic while the other is devilish or demonic depending on the current state of affairs. Pets are serious business in our household, because it's not for life. It's until the End of Days. But in good news, they stay in their prime of life until the End of Days, too, so we get to skip the slow decline."

"That's all poor Mr. Flooferson has left," I muttered.

"The future is a fluid thing, Diana, and the longevity of a cat is something easily bargained for. Let us see how the cards of fate are played out before you become overly sentimental. First, you must retrieve your feline. After your feline is retrieved, bargains can be made. But perhaps not a bargain as ruthless as the one in my household, as you do not have an extended lifespan."

I refused to think about meddling with my cat's lifespan, especially after he'd been experimented on in a lab. "Death is a part of life, Lucifer."

"Darlene tried telling me that, while sobbing her heart out. Some days, I think she's too gentle for my many hells, but then she threatens to put my balls in a vice if I slack on torturing the latest fucking asshole to annoy her."

Ouch. "She does not make idle threats."

"No, she doesn't."

"Not to derail your absolutely fascinating discussion, but a police car has just arrived. Are you planning on staying for this part of things, Lucifer?" Darian regarded the Devil with a raised brow.

"Absolutely. I've found when I say they should investigate something, they should investigate, and it will limit the nonsense and petty bullshit significantly. After that, I will abuse my teleportation abilities so you can acquire everything you need for the next week. I recommend you pack enough for two weeks. I'm not very good at returning mortals to their appropriate places on time, and it's not like your parents want you back anyway."

Darian shrugged. "I'm not really sure what I did to deserve that this time, but the list of potential sins is long, and I'd rather not waste most of the night trying to figure it out. I'm sure they'll miss me in a few days."

"I wouldn't hold your breath about that," the Devil muttered. "Your fathers will corner your mother, I'm sure. And at that point, they won't care about you at all until your fathers are satisfied there is a little one on the way. They might not even notice you for an entire month or two, giving me plenty of time to work with you."

"I'm not seeing the problem with this. If you have any spare succubi willing to teach a young man how to properly care for a woman, I'm game. Let's just say I've gotten that drilled into me by all three of my parents, and I don't want to find out what sort of hell they'll toss my way should I cross them on that one."

I grinned at Darian's admission he had no idea what he was doing while seeking solutions to his ignorance. I didn't have to marry him—or have children—to rescue him from his virginity. Or mine, for that matter. Society was more likely to mock Darian for his virginity while valuing me for mine, something that never failed to annoy me. As hitting two birds with one stone appealed right along with meeting a man who actually cared about his partner's satisfaction, I'd have to discuss the situation with him in private, after buying birth control, making sure to use it sufficiently, and purchasing condoms.

"I was more thinking you could educate yourself with the woman you'll conveniently be spending several weeks with. Try asking her what she wants, and then use your ears to actually listen and try the things she says she wants. You'll be fine. And you won't learn any bad habits from a succubus that way. That said, it might be a good idea to recruit a few succubi for trainer programs for virgin men who actually give a shit about pleasing their woman. I'll have Darlene take care of that."

The Devil was a lot of things, but at least he was honest about his intentions. "You don't need a succubus to teach you anything, Darian. I mean, succubi love virgins, as do incubi, but you don't need some sex demon to teach you. Just find a consenting adult, use protection, and have a good time. Set your sex life on your terms, not theirs. And especially not on the Devil's terms."

"Hey," Lucifer protested. "My terms are amazing."

"Unless your terms involve temporary infertility and immunity from STDs, your terms are useless for this discussion."

Darian snickered. "I see you're not shy, Diana."

I snorted at the thought of being shy when my job involved browbeating a bunch of divines, demons, devils, and other species into doing what I wanted to make the CDC's life easier. The woman who'd been hired before me had been an introvert, and she'd lasted an entire month before having a mental breakdown. I gave her credit; she'd survived long enough to train me before enrolling in therapy, which the CDC provided to avoid a lawsuit. "I talk to the Devil at least two or three times a month. This is tame for him. And don't get me started about the number of times I've been forced to go to a brothel because I needed to talk to a succubus or incubus and couldn't get a hold of any of my contacts on the phone. I'm more concerned you, as the son of a triad finally allowed to leave home without supervision, might be overwhelmed by the vast quantity of sin now available for your enjoyment. Add in the fact the Devil is here, and that's a recipe for disaster."

A knock at my door brought the conversation to a halt, and I sighed. "Lucifer, I'll give you an extra twenty minutes to your hour of advice I'm forced to listen to if you deal with the police in a fashion that gets them out of my hair in a hurry while meeting all of the insurance requirements, especially if they aren't going to be useful for the investigation."

"They won't be useful for the investigation. Bargain made." The Devil strode to the door. "Learn from her, Darian. That was a slick deal. It's going to cost me an hour, during which she can pick through her belongings for the things of most importance to her, and all it's costing her is twenty minutes of listening to me prattle about whatever I want."

Darian waited for the Devil to step out of my home to speak to the police before asking, "I'm not sure how good I'd be at this, but would you like to be rescued, kidnapped, or otherwise taken away from this situation?"

"That must be your archangel of a father talking, as your devil of a father would have just gone straight to the kidnapping portion of the plan. I'm not sure what your mother would do, and honestly, I'm afraid to ask."

"She would accidentally participate in a kidnapping, especially if she's off her meds. She'd just grab you and go and then realize she'd kidnapped you several hours later."

That sounded rather entertaining. "I need to rescue my cat first, but honestly? If it gets me out of listening to the Devil for an hour and twenty minutes, it wouldn't be a kidnapping, as I would be a willing participant. Maybe it was a good bargain, but it's still going to be hellish to pay come time for my appointment for life advice from the Devil."

"Well, it seems like we have an hour. What can't you live without for the next few weeks?"

"My cat," I complained. "Beyond that, I'll just buy new clothes, because the fuckers opted to ruin just about everything I own." After a moment of thought, I said, "I guess I better find out if they fucked with my safe, my vital documentation, and the rest of my paperwork."

"That might be wise. How would you like me to help?"

I pointed at my bedroom. "See if any of my panties survived."

"My mother never warned me about the possibility of a woman telling me to go through her panties to find survivors."

"Bonus points if you find any salvage-able bras. Those things are not cheap."

"And you're really okay with me going through your clothes?"

"You're saving me from facing that dis-aster again. I cried once over torn lace, and I refuse to do so again today. I'll be in my of-fice if anyone needs me. The Devil will be doing everybody a favor if nobody needs me."

FOUR

"My manly status as the Devil certainly helps, though."

MY SAFE, one of the best five-thousand-dollar investments I'd ever made, had withstood the attention of the asshole cat thieves. Gouges marked the metal where somebody had tried to get in, but my practitioner tricks and the safe's good construction had barred them from entering. I touched the side where I'd set my magics and traced my fingers in a circle, which I sliced through to interrupt the protective spells I'd layered over the steel, iron, and other metals layered together to prevent unwanted parties from stealing my most precious property, including my cat's adoption papers.

I cracked open the safe, smiling my satisfaction over nothing having been disturbed. I unraveled several more protections before checking my closet for my empty folder totes meant for hauling important files around the office or to an unexpected meeting, which had been tossed around but remained undamaged. It would take all three of them to unload my safe, and to make sure nobody made a mess of it, I'd take everything to a security vault, one with a reputation of being tighter than Fort Knox.

Or I could give everything to Darlene. Was anyone stupid enough to try to steal from the Devil in his many hells? If I had to deal with an hour and twenty minutes of life advice from the Lord of Lies, I may as well make the most of it and make sure nobody got their hands on my papers.

I took the adoption forms and put them in the briefcase with my laptop, which I planned to haul around with me until I could secure the documents. The rest of my critical paperwork went into my folder totes, and I took some care to organize them by type. I closed the safe and restored my protections, muttering curses under my breath while I drew the invisible patterns on the metal.

In my living room, the Devil informed the police they would photograph everything, do their best to not bother me, and promised they would receive angelic verification I'd had nothing to do with the theft of my cat and destruction of my belongings, which would be delivered by archangel within forty-eight hours.

The cops kept quiet, and when I emerged from my office, I discovered them hard at work taking pictures of everything.

Had I been in charge, we'd likely still be in the doorway arguing over the necessity of doing any investigating at all.

"Things are simple when you give clear and concise instructions," Lucifer informed me. "My manly status as the Devil certainly helps, though."

It annoyed me the Devil openly acknowledged how gender often played a role in how victims were treated, and that a wise woman armed herself with a pushy, stubborn, and egotistical man when she wanted to get something done without having to wage war over it.

For the most part, I'd gotten used to that facet of life, although it never failed to annoy me.

With a low, rumbling chuckle, Lucifer patted my shoulder. "It'll be all right. Change happens slowly, but it does happen. Sometimes, it happens faster than you might like. After all, it only took my darling about five minutes to successfully conquer my many hells."

One day, I would have to ask Darlene how she managed to conquer the Devil within five minutes. "They tried to access my safe, but they failed. That was where I was keeping Mr. Flooferson's adoption records.

Would you please hold onto it so nothing happens to it? I figure you have some secure place in your hells you can stash it for a while. The rest of the papers I'll take to a vault for holding."

"I can hold onto all of your paperwork. I've plenty of space, and doing this helps me, as you'll remember I kept your paperwork secure when we make a future bargain."

Bastard. "But this is a freebie. For now."

"I will hope for beneficial terms during future bargains in exchange. And that's just hope. You can disappoint me at your leisure."

Despite everything, I smiled at the thought of disappointing the Devil. "All right. I'll bring everything out here, and you can handle their security. I suspect they were after his adoption papers. It lists the lab he came from."

"That would provide excellent motivation for them to want to break into your house and destroy your things. They were probably hoping the adoption forms were not kept in your safe."

"Well, they managed to scratch the safe, but they did not access the contents."

"Would you prefer if I stored your safe until this matter is completed?"

When the Devil made good offers with no strings attached, I accepted them. "Yes, please."

He snapped his fingers, and the stench of brimstone wafted into the living room from the direction of my office. The folder totes also disappeared. "I took the liberty of snatching the adoption forms from your briefcase as well, so do not panic when they are no longer where you expect them to be."

"All right. Once the police are done here, where are we headed?"

"I will be sending you to a hotel near the lab that originally had your cat. That way, you can start your investigation there. What they were researching is important to you and may help you learn more about who stole your cat and why. I will warn you, however, it will not be a pleasant experience for you."

I could make a few guesses as to why. "Because I like animals and won't like what the lab was doing?" I guessed.

"No, because you cannot adopt every feral feline that has taken over the building since it was raided and the other animals were taken to shelters and rehabilitated. If you wish to know why this happened, I will bargain with you for an additional twenty minutes of time giving you important life advice at our meeting."

I considered crying. An hour and twenty minutes with the Devil while he prattled on about what I should do with the rest of my life would test my patience, but an hour and forty minutes might drive me to madness. Damn it, I loved my cat enough I'd deal with far more than an extra twenty minutes to help him. "All right."

"You were likely told that the lab animals were from an official lab rehabilitation program, but your cat was taken from an illegal operation, which is why he had so many behavioral problems and was a candidate to be euthanized. It's your job to figure everything else out. The legal lab operators don't treat the animals in the same way, and they're closely monitored for abuse. Your cat was abused. That is the only clue you need to understand he did not come from a sanctioned lab. That should appropriately motivate you to handle this matter. But I'll give you a bonus piece of intel."

Bonus intel worried me, because it meant the Devil had a vested interest in my cat and the resolution of his disappearance. "What intel?"

"You are about to become a player in a very dangerous game. Your future is hazy, which indicates everything could change based on even a single decision. There are a million possible futures created from what you do now. Do try not to screw it up. I do not have any time penned in for an unexpected End of Days right now."

"Are you implying my cat might trigger an unexpected End of Days?" I blurted. The

End of Days came up often at the CDC, as the organization wanted to keep everything from being wiped out, but everyone came to the same general conclusion: the CDC couldn't do a lot to prevent it beyond confer with the Christian pantheon and hope for the best.

"No, I'm implying *you* might. That's the fun of mortals. You change everything, for better or for worse."

TRUE TO THE Devil's prediction, it took an hour for the cops to clear out, and Darian spent the entirety of the time in my bedroom sorting through my laundry. I had no idea which of his parents held responsibility for his inclinations, but he'd organized every piece of clothing I owned into piles. The largest of them contained the clothes he deemed unfit for salvaging.

A startling number of panties and bras had made it to the folded piles organized by color and type on the shredded ruins of my bed, which he'd put back where it belonged. Had I thought the cops cared about me or my cat, I might've been upset over the destruction of evidence, but they couldn't care less even if they tried.

They had more important and glamorous things to worry about in the city.

"Not all of the cops are like that around here," the Devil scolded.

"Those ones are, and those are the ones I got stuck with."

"All for the better, as if you'd gotten the more attentive ones, you'd be staying here far longer." Striding into my bedroom, Lucifer considered Darian's neat piles of laundry. "That must be your angelic side. I would never create a devil so fixated on generalized perfection."

"Have you met my father? The one that's one of your generals? You created him, and he's definitely fixated on general perfection." Darian snorted and shook his head, waving his hand at clothes. "This is, unfortunately, a triple dose of parental influence, unless my mother is off her meds, in which case she fully embraces chaos and sows it whenever possible. I don't have my mother's chaotic tendencies, and I take after my fathers a little more than I appreciate some days. As such, I tend to be thorough when I decide to do something. Once I got started, I saw no need to skimp on the whole task, and I had an hour to work with anyway. So, that's the junk pile. The tears are in places that just wouldn't be easily mended without a huge amount of effort, and it wouldn't look good once done, not without paying a professional an obscene amount of money. It'd be cheaper to buy new ones." He pointed at a second, smaller pile on the floor. "Those ones are questionable. Someone with skill with a sewing needle might be able to repair them to be serviceable, although I wouldn't wear any of it to important business meetings."

I took aim at the pile, wound up, and kicked, sending it scattering to the larger pile. A few kicks later worked out most of my nerves. I went to work nudging the scattered garments into the main pile. "My entire life is basically a string of important business meetings."

"I had noticed a startling lack of casual clothes."

"What are casual clothes?"

Both Darian and the Devil stared at me.

Great. I'd managed to confound the ruler of the many hells and the son of a triad. At the rate I was going, I'd flabbergast the entire Christian pantheon. "I just see no need to wear anything other than pajamas while in my home, and why go through the hassle of changing out of my work clothes to run my errands in the evenings?"

Darian scratched his head. "Have you ever gone bar diving?"

"No. I deal with enough men leering at me during work hours. I don't want to deal with it when said men are drunk."

"Hobbies?"

"I read books and pet my cat."

"Pajamas are good casual clothes for that," he conceded. "Traveling?"

"I just wear the clothes I have. I'm comfortable in them. They're what I'm used to."

"When was the last time you wore a bathing suit?" Darian prowled around me, and he looked me over. Having worked with every species under the sun, including lycanthropes, I recognized when he'd gone from generally harmless to a predator on the prowl. Considering I'd tormented the poor man with lingerie for an hour, I accepted my role in his current state, chuckling over the emergence of his more devilish side. "I couldn't find a single one in that mess."

"I can't swim, so never as far as I can recall. Maybe my parents tossed me into a bathing suit as a baby, but I developed a healthy fear of the water by age five. I have zero interest in drowning."

Darian straightened, and the predatory edge faded to surprise and a more general interest. "You need to learn how to swim."

"No, I don't."

"Yes, you do. You could trip and fall into a fountain or something."

"I have never, not once in my life, tripped and fallen into a fountain. Are fountains even deep enough to drown in? Is there a reason I can't just stand up if I fall into a fountain?"

"Fine. You could trip off a pier and land in the water."

"The chances of me going anywhere near a pier is zero." I generally refused to go within a quarter of a mile of the water when at all possible. "No."

"Someone could pick you up and throw you into a pool."

"I will struggle and scream, after which I'll probably drown unless someone rescues me. This is a fair point, but it doesn't mean you're getting me anywhere near a pool without the struggling and the screaming happening."

Darian smirked. "You can't go into a deep lounging tub unless you can swim."

I snorted my amusement that he thought I even owned a tub. I pointed in the general direction of my bathroom. "Go into my bathroom, Darian. Tell me what you see."

His eyes widened. "You're one of those?"

"Those?"

"Those people who only take showers."

"I frantically scrub and get as clean as possible as quickly as possible to reduce the risk of drowning. When a hurricane is scheduled to blow through, I am among the first to evacuate, because I do not wish to drown." I lifted my chin, as I refused to be ashamed of my fear of the water. "My cat does not like baths, either."

"Well, yes. He's a cat. They typically don't."

"Well, I'm a human, and I don't like baths."

"But they're *baths*, Diana. Baths!"

The Devil turned around and bowed his head, and his shaking shoulders exposed his silent laughter. Would Darlene miss him if I did my best to murder him? "You're an asshole, Lucifer."

"You're a delight." Turning to face me, the Devil cast a grin my way. "You're marvelously resilient to the divine. I wonder if you'll be one of those pesky mortals who learns to see through the shroud. Some do."

"And live to talk about it? I don't have any desire to be wiped out of existence, Lucy. That's what the CDC's files say on it. To pierce the shroud is to die."

"It depends," he admitted, and he gestured to Darian. "He would survive if I were to remove the shroud masking my true nature. Belial does not need a shroud because of his nature. Raguel does. This mixture of genetics has given Darian an advantage. But a lot of his more troublesome abilities come from his mother, who has divine ancestry from prior emergences. His fathers have woken those tendencies. Most children of triads are limited; they're as close to vanilla humans as humans get nowadays, although their children tend to come into their powers young. It's not the children of the triads that tend to change the world, but it's their children that take the reins and bring more power and magic to the mortal coil. Really, I should be praised for my hard work. Because I encourage triads, magic will last for a long time and blossom fully in this age. If I can get enough angels to tango with my demons and devils, this emergence might last for centuries. Most don't."

Sometimes, the Devil annoyed the hell right out of me, but others, he reminded me of the one thing I thirsted for above all else: knowledge. "What heinous things are you going to force me to do if I want you to elaborate on that?"

"You will allow Darian to purchase a swimsuit for you, and you will learn how to swim. I will give you a period of five years to learn how to swim, and I expect you to pursue making use of a bathtub for soaking purposes."

What a complete and total asshole. "I'm terrified of water, Lucifer. Do you know what happened the last time someone tried to make me go near a pond?"

"You fainted from fright."

I nodded, wondering if the Devil had learned that gem from rummaging in my thoughts or if he'd poked his nose in my business at some other time. "I had a panic attack, and I fainted. I think I'm lucky I didn't have a heart attack. And if I'd been near that pond, I would have drowned." I forced myself to take deep breaths. "I have a bad relationship with water."

"And you don't even know why. Perhaps that might help you overcome your phobia." The Devil patted my head. "Darian will take excellent care of you. And he won't mind catching you when you inevitably faint from getting too close to the water. I'm sure he'll be fine with teaching you to enjoy the wonders of a nice bathtub as part of your new therapy plan. It's a decent deal. You get what you want, and I prevent Darian from having a string of anxiety attacks when he worries about your inability to swim. The children of triads tend to be anxious little creatures. It's their conflicted natures. It's also part of what makes them so fun to have around. They're like overexcited little puppies who try so hard to please. When one parent is an angel, one parent is a demon or a devil, and the other parent is human, it's hard for the little puppy to please everybody."

Darian nodded. "It's absolutely true. If I tried to make my father happy, the archangel one that is, my dad, the devilish general, would just ooze disappointment. How can I possibly become a bringer of ruin if I am always trying to make the feathered menace happy with me?"

How had Darian survived to adulthood? Had I called an archangel a feathered menace, I'd be dead. Or at least scheduled to be sent to the Devil as a plaything in one of his many hells. "Did you just call an archangel a feathered menace?"

"Well, they really are. Once I was old enough to trip and fall without doing any real harm to myself, if my father caught me in the act, he'd just smack me with a wing. Those wings are no joke. Half the time, I never needed a spanking because my father would smack me with his wing, and that would put an end to whatever he disliked in a hurry."

"That sounds rather painful."

"Pain is an excellent teacher, and my father's general approach to raising a child involves making sure said child, me, survives to adulthood. After I survived to adulthood, his general plans involved me not being a useless layabout. He doesn't like useless layabouts. My dad doesn't either, as useless layabouts only ruin their general health, their finances, and little else. Just don't ask about my mother. We'd be here for years if I tried to explain that mess."

I bet. "Your mother seems like a very interesting woman."

"That's one way to put it. Hey, Lucifer?

My mother is going to change her mind within an hour if we aren't out of here. She will convince herself she is a terrible parent and start crying to my fathers, and I can't stand when my mother starts crying because I tried to skip town. And don't get me started on how far my fathers will go to get my mother to stop crying. The reason I visit most days of the week is *not* because I want to. It's because both of them will get pretty pissy with me if I make my mother cry because it doesn't look like I love her enough. Frankly, I'll bargain with you to make sure I have a brother or sister on the way soon solely so I can escape from their clutches."

While I sometimes thought my life growing up had been tough dealing with a pair of controlling but loving parents, I worried the taste of freedom might do Darian in.

Apparently, I wasn't the only one who needed a life outside of work—or in his case, his family *and* work. Maybe, assuming time allowed and I found my cat sooner rather than later, I'd take Darian home with me and expose him to normal parents. Well, as normal as my parents got, who leaned more towards embracing everything normal in a world of magic, which made them a little eccentric on a good day. They attended church, but they didn't believe in *magic*. They limited their faith to praying because it was part of their religion, but they couldn't quite fathom the reality of the divine and the magic surrounding them.

They would not approve if they learned the realities of being a secretary for the CDC.

I found it ironic they attended church loyally but struggled with the idea that religious figureheads weren't just figureheads, but actual beings with personalities, opinions, and a general lack of care for most mortals.

The Devil chuckled, and I couldn't tell if he laughed at me or Darian—or at both of us. I suspected both of us. "I'm sure your fathers will keep your mother appropriately distracted. I'll send somebody over to meddle with your mother when your fathers aren't looking to make sure you get the result you want, but you'll have to sit in on the life advice session with Diana. Also, you can thank your dad for your future brother or sister later, as he finds fatherhood much to his liking for some reason. Somehow, I got yet another damned defective devil running around my hells, as that's what he's become." The Devil sighed, held out his hand, and snapped his fingers. A leopard print suitcase appeared. "My wife enjoys reminding me she has spots, so she insists we should purchase spotted things. To torment me with constant reminders they aren't *her* spots. You are under no obligation to give this back. Darlene insists on buying a new one every time she goes out and one catches her eye. I've given up asking why."

I heaved a sigh and grabbed the handle of the suitcase. "Thank you." I dragged it to the pile of dead clothes, opened it up, and eyed the survivors. "Pick your favorite color, Darian."

"Blue."

Well, he was in luck. The thieves hadn't destroyed most of my blue lingerie, and I grabbed it off the bed and tossed it in the suitcase. As my work clothes tended to blend together, I went the route of efficiency, snatched enough for a few days, and chucked it in with the lingerie. After a desperate search through my closet for surviving shoes, I found an intact pair of black heels and a pair of flats to tide me over until I could get to a clothing store to purchase more. I tossed them into the suitcase. "All right. You can fill the rest of it with whatever you want. I'm ready to go."

Both the Devil and Darian stared at me as though I'd lost my mind. Then again, I probably had. Before someone had stolen Mr. Flooferson the Magnificent, I'd been fairly stable. Now, I counted as a crazy cat lady, and I'd tear apart the heavens and the Devil's many hells to get him back. "What?"

"Wouldn't you prefer if you picked your

own clothes?" Darian asked. "You're the one who has to wear them."

"No. If I preferred to, I would have. I had you pick a color so I wouldn't have to decide. The sooner this is done, the sooner we get to this hotel and start looking for information about my cat. Better yet, we'll be looking for my cat."

With a shrug, the tall, dark, and handsome son of a triad grabbed the remainder of my panties and bras and dumped them into the suitcase. "I regret to inform you that your pajamas were among the casualties, but hopefully these will suffice."

"I can go buy new pajamas."

"But why?"

I grinned at his tone, which strayed between disappointed and curious. "Well, you're the one who said you wanted to start your adventures with women using a succubus. As such, I need pajamas." And birth control, and however long it took for the birth control to start doing its job. After that, I'd need to actually get to know Darian, see if he was worth sleeping with, determine if I had time to actually sleep with him, and otherwise explore the uncharted waters of having a relationship with someone outside of work.

Damn. I needed more help than even the Devil could provide.

"Or a single trip to a brothel," Lucifer stated.

I aimed a kick at his shins, but the bastard dodged me while laughing. "You are pure evil."

"Thank you. I do appreciate when my work is noticed and appreciated. To address your other thoughts, that can be arranged for immediately, and yes, at some point in the future, you will have time, but you won't have time until you're satisfied on other fronts, which you've already considered, accepted, and plan to address."

Huh. "Since when are you actually useful without driving a bargain over it?"

"I already have you for an hour and forty minutes of life advice. At that stage, I figure I may as well balance things a little in your favor. You really are getting the short end of that stick. I know me. I'm an asshole. I'm just one of many assholes in my family, and I have dedicated thousands of years of my life to mastering my craft."

Arguing or questioning the Devil would only waste time. "Okay. Now that the cops are finished here, where are we going now?"

"We're going to California," the Devil announced.

"California? They shipped my cat from California to Florida before putting him up for adoption? Honestly, I skimmed the part about the lab where he came from. It didn't matter to me." I frowned. "That's a great deal of expense. Pet transport can't be cheap."

"The shelter you adopted him from volunteered as an overflow. The lab had so many animals they couldn't all be cared for in California, so they shipped cats and dogs wherever they had space. More information on this will cost you twenty minutes."

"Give it to me," I ordered.

"Bargain made. Have Darian use his magic to find the drug testing facility used on Mr. Flooferson the Magnificent, using fur from his brush as the focal point. Look for information on the animal shippers they used for the labs. That may also provide you with information. But the drug testing facility with your cat's fur as the focal point will get you to the right part of the lab. I recommend you do a cage count, and then look into similar pet thefts and determine why someone would want *your* cat. Darian can't direct you to your cat, but if you pretend you're a detective out to solve a crime, you'll learn important things. While the lab has been shut down, much of it is intact."

Finding tufts of my cat's fur took me all of ten seconds, as he tended to leave it everywhere. I set my briefcase on my bed and shoved the fur into one of the inner pockets. "I know nothing of being a detective, Lucifer. I'm a secretary."

The Devil smiled. "You don't right now, but your tall, dark, and handsome here does. Darian, is there anything you need from your home? I have a few succubi and incubi who must pay back some favors, so I will have them teleport in with what you need."

"Apparently, I'm going to need my good laptop, my briefcase, my notepads, my pens, and appropriate attire for this venture. Since I'm being signed up for putting up with you for at least two hours now, add anything to the list you'll think I need but I don't know I'll need."

"Clever boy." The Devil held out his hand with his palm turned up. "I am not as gentle with teleportation as my brothers. It would cost you more time and money than you like to get there in traditional fashions, so I'm sure you'll forgive me in a few hours. Darian, she will not handle teleportation well, so you can decide how to handle it. Me? I'd let her hit the floor, but the only women I tend to catch when they fall include my wife and daughter. The rest of them can learn not to fall the hard way."

"Darlene lets you do that?"

"Let is such a strong word. She struggles so delightfully, which is half the fun. And don't ask what my cupcake does. It's simply not suitable for polite company."

"You're polite company?"

"Not really. Just take my word on this

one. You don't want to know. And off we go. Darian, do try to keep her from hitting her head. Trying to find her cat with a concussion would make her even crankier than she already is. Take it from me. The last thing you want or need in your life is a woman you're living with being extra cranky because of a headache you can't cure with good sex."

FIVE

Somebody had dressed me in silky,
snow leopard print pajamas.

FOR SOMEONE DUBBED the Lord of Lies, the Devil liked telling the truth. Had he informed me teleportation would hit with the force of a semi at highway speed and give me a damned good idea of what it might feel like if someone were to spear a white-hot hook through my nose in an attempt to liberate my appendix, I would have walked to California.

While naked, barefoot, and armed with a sharpened stick.

As warned, I failed to retain consciousness. I appreciated waking up tucked in a warm, soft bed, although nearby voices did a good job of jolting me awake and back to awareness of the theft of my cat, the trashing of my home, and my odd bargain with the Devil. As Lucifer had a sense of humor, I peeked under the covers.

Somebody had dressed me in silky, snow leopard print pajamas. Upon wiggling my toes, I determined they weren't pajamas, but an adult-sized onesie. I patted my head to discover a little hood with rounded kitty ears. I could make a few guesses who was responsible for the snow leopard onesie, and the bitch would wait nearby to admire her handiwork.

"Darlene, you are such a cat!" I announced, flinging off the blankets and sliding out of bed. The memory of teleporting lingered, but a few stretches dispelled the worst of the phantom sensations. Rather than a traditional hotel room with the bed in the main room, I was in a proper bedroom with a small television and a dresser. The lack of a closed door reassured me I was in a hotel.

In the neighboring room, the Devil's wife cackled. "I really am. Lucifer didn't want to give you any reasons to take off his head or go for Darian's throat, so he asked me to make sure you got tucked in all right. Then he had one of his brothers stop in and check on your health. You're working too much, and you have an underlying medical issue. Come on out here so we can handle that problem. Then I'm taking my lout home and having words with him for not having checked sooner. He's supposed to check everyone we work with frequently."

I headed for the connecting room to discover a sitting room with a kitchenette and a pair of doors, one of which led to a bathroom. To my surprise, the Devil and his wife were perched on the opposite arms of the couch while Darian slept sprawled over the cushions, oblivious to their presence.

I'd have to inform him adults could share a bed without getting into any trouble or indulging in sexual activities.

First, I had to deal with the two guests imported straight from the darkest pit of some hell.

"There's something wrong with me beyond teleportation making it feel like somebody was driving a hot poker through my nose to rid me of my appendix?" I possessed unfortunate first-hand experience of what having a dud appendix could do to a woman, and I didn't miss mine in the slightest.

"The underlying medical issue is why that happened," Darlene replied, hopping off the couch to stride to me, indulging in a hug before grabbing both of my breasts. "These beauties need some work, babe."

I stared down at her hands, raising a brow at her rather intimate behavior, something I expected from a succubus. Having been grabbed by succubus before and well aware they either indulged in such behavior to attract a male or they were starved and hoped for any form of energy possible, I decided to ignore her posturing.

Knowing Lucifer, he likely hadn't been home for a day or two, resulting in a hungry Darlene who needed to rile him up before she could be fed properly. Hungry women, especially me, often made poor choices, so I went with her flow and opted to be amused by her behavior. Then, the reality of her choice to grab my breasts smacked me, as there were three options I could think of for what she meant. "Are my breasts too large, too small, or did I lose the roll of the dice and develop cancer? I'm not sure what other problems breasts can have beyond cancer and sizing. If you say they're mismatched, I will dunk your head in the toilet, Darlene. Honestly, while they're a bit of a bear to buy nice bras for, they're perfectly matched, and I think they're a good size. I'm just large enough to get decent variety and colors with lace, but I'm too large to get them for cheap."

Darlene gave a squeeze, adjusted her hold on my right breast, and jabbed me with her thumb.

The jolt of pain sent me jumping for the ceiling, and I slapped her hands away and cradled my abused breast. "No. Bad. You do not do that to somebody, Darlene! That is just absolutely rude and terrible, and I hope the Devil takes you for that one."

The Devil chuckled. "This is the most entertaining thing I've seen in at least a year. I had no idea you were so liberal about people touching your breasts, Diana. And yes, I will take her, but not in the way you mean. You're one of the few mortals who consider the comfort of demons when one unexpectedly decides to start touching. Most just get angry."

"I just don't mind when Darlene does it because Darlene is a cat, and cats like warm, soft things. While I'm intellectually aware she's also a succubus and likely hungry, it's just mean to deny a cat access to warm, soft things." I gestured to my chest. "These? These are warm and soft. I'm not going to hold that against her, especially not when she has to deal with an eternity of putting up with you. If anyone else tried that stunt, they would probably have received a knee to the groin in exchange. And yes, I would knee you if you tried that, so don't even think about it."

"Oh, I'm going to feel that one for a while. I might need to count some spots to get over this cruel treatment of my person, my darling. She didn't even bother to soften that blow. My ego might not survive."

The Devil always found some way to amuse me, even when he was annoying the hell right out of me. "Does anyone actually care if your ego survives? Really, Lucifer.

You're the Devil. If you're so weak you can't handle a little criticism, you need someone more mentally stable doing your job for a while. Anyway, I've been around Darlene often enough to know she doesn't just grab somebody's breasts without having a good reason to, so I waited to find out what the reason is. It could be she's just hungry and wants to rile you up, but I doubt that. Just because I'm not upset she decided to serve as breast support doesn't mean I want just anyone grabbing me."

"She likes me more than she likes you," Darlene taunted. "And yes, after a long day of being in a bra, it's a daydream to have someone just hold them up for a while. The straps dig in, the underwire pokes, and it's tiresome. There's a reason so many succubi refuse to wear clothes in our house. Bras *suck.*"

I smiled at the woman's bizarre way of flirting with her husband. As I doubted Darlene was the kind to poke fun at my breast size without provocation, that left one unwanted and unpleasant option. "What stage of cancer do I have?"

Darlene glanced at Lucifer, and I found it interesting her expression begged him to answer the question.

He sighed. "It's early enough you wouldn't locate the first lump for at least another three or four months," the Devil informed me. "You would catch it right away, because you are dedicated to checking at least once a month. At this stage, it's quite simple for myself or one of my brothers to put an end to that nonsense. A bargain can cover the treatment, and the bargain won't even cost you all that much."

"Cancer is hardly nonsense," I reminded him, wondering how I'd work at finding my cat while coping with my state as suffering from cancer—not that I'd started suffering yet. "Why are you being so liberal with your bargain offers, Lucifer?"

"I really want you to be my secretary. My current secretary is pregnant again and wants to spend more time with her family. Her husband and her wife are handling the rest of the finances, and I've been looking into a way to kick her out of the nest for a while. Her human is getting older, and she'll need time to grieve once he's gone."

Ah. Another triad. "How long does her human have?"

"He'll be paying the man upstairs a visit shortly after their next child turns eighteen. It'll work out for the child in many ways. I have meddled to make sure her husband lives that long barring unnatural causes. But his natural lifespan ends there—and it ends there only because I am meddling. Otherwise, it would be sooner. Phenexia isn't stupid, so she's aware time is short and getting ever shorter. Her wife won't peek because that's how angels operate when it comes to their human partner. I'm not above meddling or peeking. This is meddling I can do without violating any of the universal laws, and he makes both of his wives happy."

If the world found out the Devil had a rather compassionate side to him, his reputation would be irreparably damaged. Worse, people might look up to him as a somewhat evil role model. "Okay. So, you want me as a secretary, and my breasts rising up and killing me would put a damper on any plans to claim me as a secretary. As human lifespans, typically a period of sixty to a hundred years depending on gender and general health, would result in you needing to replace your secretary yet again in a somewhat short period of time, you have some method of extending my lifespan. Of course, removing the cancer would be required, as that would kill me much sooner than reaching the end of my natural lifespan. That means you also have other ideas in mind for me, possibly including a conversion, as a human's lifespan isn't really tolerable for someone acting as your secretary."

The Devil stared into his wife's eyes. "Now do you understand why I must have her?"

"I understood why you wanted her from the beginning. You've been gunning for her for years. I'm disgusted you're taking advantage of a catnapping to pursue your wicked plans. And cancer. You're taking advantage of cancer. Actually, that's a little evil, even for you."

"It's not *my* fault she's developing it. And it's not evil. It's just slightly underhanded. It's not like I'm going to make her bargain hard over it. Mostly, I'm going to bargain she go through the interview process and seriously consider my offer—"

"Bargain made," I announced. "If the cancer isn't going to be a menace, I would prefer to rescue my cat first, but I will pay up and listen to your pitch within a week of the recovery of my cat. I'm not even going to stipulate it's a safe recovery, as you are already bound to do what you can to safeguard my cat's life until I can find and rescue him myself."

The Devil grunted while his wife tossed her head back and cackled.

"What?" I asked.

"You just outplayed him at his own game. Because you're accepting that bargain, and because he really wants you for his secretary *and* you called him out on his little act of evil there, he's basically obligated to handle your healing for a pittance. That would have been his baseline offer, and he would have talked you up."

"His baseline offer is completely beneficial to me, and he does get serious consideration, which beats the resounding no I would otherwise give him if I have to stress about having cancer in the first place. Now, of course, I'm going to absolutely have a stress-induced meltdown regarding the current status of my breasts, but I suspect Lucifer is damned good at eradicating things like cancer."

"He's actually one of the best divines for treating cancer. It's the disease's general malevolence; he just has an affinity with it," Darlene explained. "But truth be told, none of us had any idea you had cancer until he teleported you. He expected you to react poorly because he peeked, but he hadn't peeked more than a little. The reality of your reaction clued him in there was something really the matter with you, so he asked one of his brothers to do the diagnosis work. They're better at things like that. But you don't have to wait for the treatment. It'll just take him a few minutes and some of his holy fire. It'll let him set in some protections for you, too. There, Lucy. Bargain with her over the protections."

The Devil scowled. "I don't want to."

"Don't be a mule. Just because she cornered you doesn't mean you need to sulk. You need your future secretary alive to do secretarial work, so you need to protect her. And because you need her alive for the rest of your nefarious plans, you can do the protections because you can. And if you won't, I'll just call one of your brothers and ask nicely. I'll use several dirty, filthy, and utterly rotten words on them."

The Devil made a warning gesture against evil, something I found to be so absurd I giggled. "I married a cruel feline!"

"You begged for it, too. On your knees."

"You're so ruthless."

If the pair got any sweeter with each other, I'd throw up on them—or at least gag. For the sake of my pride, I'd do my best to stick to gagging. "Should I leave the room? Just don't engage in your perversions on Darian. He's obviously wiped out if he's able to sleep through this nonsense."

Darlene turned and smiled at the man, who remained prone on the couch. "He wasn't feeling all that well, either. And since the last thing we need is his parents freaking out because he isn't in perfect health, he got a dose of holy fire. Unlike you, Lucifer blindsided him. Holy fire is rough on mortals, even the children of triads, so he'll sleep it off."

"What was wrong with him?"

The Devil chuckled. "High blood pressure, probably partly induced from stress and having three overbearing parents riding his ass all the time, and his liver was displeased with him due to some unhealthy eating habits. He also had a rather nasty ulcer in the works because of those unhealthy habits. While I'm usually all about people facing the consequences of their actions, these issues would have impaired his ability to help you find your cat. I don't think you'd appreciate him having a stroke or vomiting blood during one of the touchier phases of your mission."

"You would be correct. Why didn't you just punch me with the holy fire at the same time?"

"The work for you is a little touchier, and while I'm best at handling cancers, I'm going to ask one of my brothers to help. I also want to discuss the matter of your mortality. You have options."

Interesting. From what I understood, the converted didn't have an option in what they became; the Devil—or *Him*—decided. "I have options? Like what?"

"Your soul can be infused with divinity from a variety of pantheons, even beyond the limitations of Christianity. You could opt to take on the lycanthropy virus, which I can revive at my whim, essentially granting you a form of immortality. It wouldn't stop you from dying from injury, but you wouldn't die from old age, for example. There are a variety of species you could be converted to, including unicorns, although most unicorns will only convert their mates. However, I'm acquainted with a few mares who might be game to offering blood donations to an interested party for a shameful amount of money. As I need my secretary to be working for me and *not* resenting me for my influences on her lifespan, this decision must belong to you. Your soul will remain yours, but it would undergo some changes. There are also other species of demon you might find interesting."

"I was a mortal before the lout here got his filthy hands on me," Darlene said. "It's just something you need to be aware of and decide for yourself. Find your cat first, and then you can ask one of the archangels for full disclosure. Had I been smarter, I would have asked for better disclosure before he'd converted me into a succubus with a very restricted diet of Lucifer."

The Devil grunted.

"What? Somebody should have warned me how damned moody I'd get if I'm hungry. Take it from me, Diana. Being a succubus has its perks, but the hunger is no joke, especially when your man decides to go throw a party instead of staying in bed where he belongs. Or he decides to come to the mortal coil and stick around for a few days, leaving me to run the show at home while I'm hungry. I think the bastard knows when I'm getting peckish and decides he wants to be hunted, so he runs off so I'm forced to chase him. I do not recommend becoming a succubus unless you have a dedicated food source who isn't a jackass."

I could imagine the Devil forcing his wife to hunt him so he could enjoy her frustrations without any effort at all. "Lucifer, stop being a jackass to Darlene."

"But she's so delightful when she's hungry. Why do you want to rob me of joy?"

"You might be an asshole, but until I have my cat back, I eclipse you in my base capacity to be a complete and total asshole. I'm only accepting delaying my search until morning because if I had to come here myself, I wouldn't arrive until sometime in the afternoon, and that's unacceptable. Starting fresh is better, assuming you're keeping your word about Mr. Flooferson."

"I have taken steps to make certain your cat should survive, although there are limitations to what I can do in this matter."

"Good." I wrinkled my nose. "Can you tell how long I would have if I didn't get treated?"

"It would be a long, drawn-out battle."

"It's too bad you and your angelic siblings can't just wave your hand and rid the world of cancer."

"Like many things in life, cancer is a consequence. From the polluted air humans breathe to the foods eaten, all of these things contribute to the development of cancer.

Sometimes, the consequence is a matter of genetics. In your case, Miami's air and deodorant is the primary cause of your cancer. I recommend you throw out your current deodorant and use something a little less toxic."

My eyes widened. "My *deodorant*?"

"Location, location, location," the Devil informed me.

I lifted my arm, stared at my armpit, and realized he was right. I poked at my armpit, feeling at the connecting tissue linking my breast and my side. "I guess the chemicals get pretty close to my breasts, don't they?"

"That they do. You're a practitioner. Your magic would be far safer for you than the commercialized chemicals. For the record, it's more the antiperspirant that was causing the problem than the perfumes. Once you make that change and your current problems are fixed, you'll be fine."

"Fine is relative."

"The cancer won't return because you'll no longer be poisoning yourself with poorly chosen deodorant."

Huh. The Devil had it out for deodorant manufacturers. I sniffed my armpits. "I don't suppose you can help a woman out on that front, can you? If I let these pits go untended, they'll be classified as biological weapons."

Darlene laughed. "There are plenty of

good solutions for your problem. That's something you can deal with tomorrow. Tonight, you have a date with some holy fire, a little bit of pain, and that nice big bed in the other room. And, because it'll be glorious, I'll have that lout of mine move your man in there so you can witness his delightful reaction to realizing he woke up in bed with a woman without having any memory of how he got there."

"Has anyone ever told you that you're evil, Darlene?"

"From time to time."

"You're pretty damned evil, and as such, it comes as no surprise to me that you rule over your husband's many hells."

"See, my darling? See? This is why I must have her." Lucifer pointed at me. "Accept my job offer, you!"

"Wouldn't I have to hear what the job offer is first? Plus save my cat. There will be no consideration of job offers until my cat is safe and in my custody."

The Devil scowled. "If I can't have your soul, I will have you as an employee."

"I think your husband needs some time on a couch with a shrink, Darlene."

"Oh, I know he does."

"You are a most cruel wife. Why are wives such cruel creatures?"

"Just call your brother, use one of those filthy words you hate so much, and take care of Diana. You can work on putting a good job offer together while you wait for her to finish her work. You only have yourself to blame for this. If you were more willing to break the rules, you could just steal her cat back. But no, you don't like breaking the rules."

"You know I can't do that, and you know why."

"I know, but she doesn't, and it's important she understands your inaction now before she resents you, likely sometime tomorrow, when she realizes just how big of a mess she's landed in."

Great. Just what I needed. Even more of a mess to deal with. "And one of your rules doesn't allow you to interfere. What rule and why?"

"I can't answer that," Lucifer replied.

Interesting. "Will I find out why?"

"Possibly, but that depends on you and what you do in the coming days. You like learning forbidden things. Go learn them." The Devil sighed. "Starting tomorrow morning, after I deal with the matter of your cancer and layering on some protections. It would be really, truly annoying if the woman I want to be my secretary expires on me prematurely."

"It's like milk that should still be good for another week going sour. It's just *wrong*,"

Darlene muttered. "No premature expirations."

"You two are crazy," I informed them.

Darlene winked at me. "Give it a few months, and you'll be just as crazy as we are."

"Heaven help me."

The Devil grinned. "Watch what you wish for, Diana. You might get it."

SIX

The Lord of Lies often used honesty as his weapon of choice.

WHILE I POSSESSED vague memories of an archangel coming to the hotel room and conferring with the Devil and his wife, someone had pulled the plug before I reached the holy fire portion of my evening. My phone's alarm going off to warn me I needed to go to work clued me in I'd somehow gone to bed. A rather persistent and uncomfortable pressure and ache in my chest reinforced someone had done something to me. The Devil, assuming he'd spoken the truth.

The Lord of Lies often used honesty as his weapon of choice, but he spoke falsehoods when it served him. Without my memories of the night before, I'd have to trust in his word—or not—as I saw fit.

I grumbled curses, winced, and rolled for

my phone, colliding with a rather warm and male body.

Right. Darian.

Between my phone and being jostled, he woke up with a startled cry, launched out of bed, tripped over the bedding, and crashed to the floor. Grimacing, I sat up, stretched for the nightstand, and tapped the button to silence the damned thing. "It's only partially my fault you were moved from the couch to the bed, but really, Darian. Sleeping on the couch is bad for your back, and there's no reason to let half a good bed go to waste."

He groaned from the general vicinity of the floor. "Are you a demoness?"

"Not yet at any rate, but that's up for potential debate. I'm sore, that's what I am." Putting on a bra would test my patience, and upon peeking into my top, I discovered someone had performed an act of bondage on my poor breasts using self-adhesive bandages.

Interesting. I prodded at one of the more tender spots, which was located near my arm pit. The burst of pain indicated a wise woman did not poke, prod, or otherwise touch the tender bits until further notice.

"Ah. The Devil had started cursing and mentioned you had a health problem he wanted to address immediately. Then he laughed at me, told me the same, and I got my ass handed to me." Darian got to his knees and rested his elbows on the bed near my feet. "If you're sore, tell me what you need handled, what your limitations are as you figure them out, and I'll take care of what I can. Lucifer had mentioned early cancer, and that's nothing to joke about."

The Devil might be the death of me one day if I kept letting him interfere in my affairs. Worse, I needed to put up with it, as the mundane treatments for cancer would be far worse. I could handle showing gratitude to Lucifer. I'd promised to listen to his job offer. I'd give it serious consideration, too.

I nodded. "It's nothing some coffee can't conquer." Even if the coffee didn't conquer it, I would pretend, as I had no time to sit around and complain about being in pain. "How are you feeling? You had some troubles, too, or so I heard."

"I got a scolding to go along with a kick in the ass. Since I know what's good for me, I'm not going to complain over any lingering aches and pains, nor will I breathe a word of this to any of my parents, who will not take any form of ailment I might suffer from with even a scrap of dignity." Darian lurched to his feet. "I deserve a little pain and suffering for my idiocy, and we'll leave it at that. I consider myself to be educated on the error of my ways. What would you like for breakfast? I'll order something for us."

Someone knocked at the door, and Darian's eyes narrowed.

"Darlene was involved with this. There's probably enough breakfasts for five people at the door now, and she'll expect us to eat it all. Darlene gets upset when hungry—and she gets even more upset when she thinks others are hungry."

Darian grunted and headed into the other room. A moment later, he yelped. "Damn it, Lucifer!"

Some things couldn't be missed, and I ignored my aches and pains to get a good view of the show in the sitting room. Darian faced off against the Devil, his body tense, his back straight, and his arms crossed over his chest. Darlene waved from her spot by the door beside two carts loaded with plates.

"We brought you breakfast." Darlene grabbed one of the platters, took it to the coffee table, and pointed at me before pointing at the couch and snapping her fingers until I obeyed. "You need to eat, and you need to eat a lot. You need to eat a *lot*. You, stubborn thing you are, put up a fight. I swear, you're just a delight, and it disgusts me I have to side with my husband on this. You're almost as good at giving him a run for his money as I am. Also, don't panic that you can't remember it. His brother wanted to spare you the trauma, and when his brother gets fidgety about something like that, it's best to just give him what he wants. You are only missing a bunch of cursing, screaming, and threatening to rip my husband's dick off and feed it to him if he didn't stop trying to incinerate your breasts. I shouldn't have laughed at your suffering, but once you decided you'd had enough, your curses and threats got vicious."

Well, I didn't regret missing the screaming and cursing portion of my night, but as making such a statement fell outside of my normal behaviors, curiosity ate away at me. "Did I actually do that?"

"You actually did that," she confirmed. "Lucy even asked his brother to protect him out of fear for his life. Or his prowess. More for his prowess, really. He's a vain creature."

"I'm pretty sure any man would be concerned in that situation," I replied, grimacing at the thought of having been that vehement. "I apologize, Lucifer."

"No need to apologize. Sit down and have your breakfast. Anyway, I am who I am, and I find that thing to be quite attractive. I took my frustrations out on Darlene later, so don't you worry yourself any."

With a sly smile, the succubus ferried more platters to the coffee table. "Thank you, I had a wonderful time, in case you were wondering."

"Not particularly, but you're welcome. I'm glad one of us had a wonderful time." I pointed at my chest, which still hurt. "What's the deal with the bandages?"

"My wife demanded 'we keep them from bouncing' while healing, thus converting you into a mummy. Bouncing would not be good right now," the Devil replied, taking a seat on the arm of the couch near me. "Bouncing would really not be good right now, and not a single one of those lacy bras you brought will do a sufficient job of breast bondage, so you got bandages. You are to leave them on for three days. Shower or bathe without removing them. My brother is a far kinder being than I am, so they'll stay clean until it's time for them to come off."

I appreciated that. "Thank you. Please thank your brother for me, too. Just don't tell me which brother. It's bad enough I run a high risk of encountering Raguel. I've reached my limit of divines for the week. Introduce me to more divines next week."

"That's our cue, my darling," Lucifer said, helping Darlene to finish emptying the carts before shoving them out into the hallway. "Eat until you can't possibly eat another bite, and then go do the things pesky little mortals do when bored and left unattended. Do not get into more trouble than you can handle alone. Try not to have too much fun getting into trouble. I've learned once mortals discover the delights of creating trouble and mayhem, it becomes habitual. My secretary needs to balance the perfect amount of containing vs creating trouble and mayhem."

Without another word, the pair teleported away.

Darian sat down beside me, selected a platter, and took off the lid, revealing a breakfast of scrambled eggs, toast, bacon, sausage, pancakes, and fruit. Silver vessels tucked to the side contained maple syrup, jam, and butter. "There has to be magic at play here. There is no way I would normally finish *one* of these." Pointing at platters, he counted, where they were scattered everywhere, including taking over most of the kitchenette. "They expect us to eat ten plates each."

"Whoever can't eat another bite first loses. Whoever eats the most in the shortest amount of time without throwing up wins," I proposed, as only my competitive nature would get me through one plate let alone ten. Two would be pushing my luck, but for the sake of victory, I could cram enough into my stomach.

"What are the stakes?"

"Good question. Any reasonable favor? I'd say sex, except it seems I'm out of commission for a while." I glared down at my chest. "Society has convinced me sex should be sinfully pleasurable, and I do not want to be disappointed because of this mess."

"You really are not shy at all."

"Why should I be? I got the talk young, although it was presented in a way to keep me a pristine virgin for religious reasons. Really, the only reason I haven't dragged a man to bed involved paying off that wretched mortgage and time. I worked hard to get rid of that mortgage, but I did such a good job at it I just don't have time for a man. I really don't. At least right now. I mean, what am I supposed to do with a man? Hang him up when I'm done with him in bed and pull him out whenever I have an itch I want him to scratch?"

Darian laughed. "Your view of life is definitely refreshing. My mother is convinced I'm reckless and should not be trusted anywhere near a delicate flower of a woman. I keep trying to tell her women aren't fragile. She throws a temper tantrum about how she is the most delicate of women, pretends to faint against one of my fathers, and otherwise disgraces all women everywhere. Really, she thinks I'm excessively sensitive and will be a wilting lily if there's any pain or bloodshed."

I stared at him. "Please tell me your mother explained how women's bodies actually work."

"I am well educated about the blood tithes women pay every twenty-eight days. My mother claims she is sacrificing blood to some blood god once a month. And if chocolate is not sacrificed to her, everyone around her will pay. Also in blood. I'm also educated in how to identify lumps, as my mother is convinced that wise men should be intimately familiar with the texture of their wife's breasts."

"If you win, I will take you to a brothel, where you can get whatever education you desire about sex in application. And I'll pay the bill. Try not to bankrupt me. I feel you have been unfairly restrained and deserve to get lessons from a succubus if you want them."

With a grin, Darian replied, "Okay. If you win, I'll help you negotiate your job offer with the Devil, and I'll make sure you have the appropriate time off. I would offer to take you to a brothel, but you're pretty enough that you might be asked to stay as a worker, and my mother would really kill me dead if she found out I was leading delicate women into darkness. I will also offer to drive you to any clinics you need for cancer screening and health checks, as that shit is stressful and having someone to go along for the ride can be helpful."

"I can live with those terms. The way my chest hurts, I'm thinking somebody fucking lied to me about the severity, because it seriously feels like he flash fried my breasts before boiling them to mush. I touched. I am not making that mistake again, Darian. I am not touching them as much as possible. Frankly, I might ask you to help me in and out of my shirts, so I don't have to move my arms as much." I lifted my arm and pointed at the muscles connecting my breasts to the rest of my body. "Doing this is not comfortable. I'm getting painkillers before we go out today. And I'll try not to whine about it, because this beats cancer, but it is not comfortable."

"Well, I'll do what I can," he promised. "After we eat, we'll talk business. With a little luck, we'll be so busy searching for your cat you won't have time to remember it hurts. And even if we waste half of this, we'll be grateful for it later, because with my luck at wayfinding, we will have quite the hike ahead of us."

TO BOTH MY relief and disappointment, we tied at who could eat the most and how fast we could shovel food into our bottomless pits formerly known as stomachs. Magic played some role for certain; every now and then, flickers of blue-white flame danced over our skin and arms before soaking in and vanishing without a trace. Every plate I packed away helped to ease the soreness in my breasts, something I appreciated—and would appreciate later, once I had to move around and get work done on finding my cat.

"I hate when I owe people for anything," I complained, tossing down my napkin on top of the pile of dishes. As part of my feeding frenzy, I'd licked every plate to come my way clean, and I'd even scoured the little dishes for every drop of syrup and scrape of butter. I'd abandoned all dignity, and I suspected I had jam or syrup on my nose. "I'm essentially obligated to accept the Devil's job offer, and while I'm good at negotiating with others when my boss tells me to, I clam up when it's time for my yearly review. Every damned time. It was beaten into me as a kid to be grateful for what I had, and this makes it hard to do things like ask for a raise. But I'm supposed to be an adult. I should ask for raises. Or negotiate higher, because my work is worth more. Great. Now I'm whining."

"You've had a hard day yesterday *and* today. I think you've earned a chance to whine. I'd be whining, too, if someone stole my pet. Honestly, in your shoes, I would be tearing the planet apart stone by stone, and I don't even have a pet. But if I did, I would."

I straightened, pleased he directed our conversation to the matter of finding Mr. Flooferson the Magnificent. "Oh, good. Then you won't judge me too badly when I go to drastic measures." I could work with that. A willing accomplice made everything easier. With a little luck, easier would mean we could find and rescue my cat sooner.

"I admire that your first line of offense was to call the Devil. That takes serious courage. Or insanity. I'm not sure which, but I'm here to find out. That leads me to the problem of my wayfinding ability. While Lucifer told the truth about my general abilities and limitations, we still need to talk about it."

"He said you couldn't go to people or other living things, and that you had some restrictions."

"Correct. For example, I can take the fur you gathered and search for if the fur had been used in an experiment, and if so, where. The fur is not a living being, especially once taken from the cat. I'm not searching for the cat, I'm searching for the fur, a non-living entity."

"But the fur came from my cat."

"I could pluck a hair from your head and search for the brush that last touched your hair and create a path to the brush, but I couldn't search for *you*. The hair isn't you. It was, until plucked, a part of you, but it lacks the spark of life. That's typically where the line is. So, we will have to make certain we frame all of our searches with that. I can only establish one path a day. Once the path is set, we have six hours to get to where we're going before it disappears. Reestablishing the same path is feasible after I've gotten some rest. That's limited compared to some wayfinders, but my magic will usually take a good route to where I need to go. Most wayfinders take direct lines only. Mine at least *somewhat* understands roads exist. It will take the path of least resistance. Unfortunately, if there is a river, it might try to follow the river rather than a road, as it doesn't really distinguish the difference between water and asphalt." Darian shrugged. "If I'm in an area with a lot of water, I tend to make sure I have an ATV so I can follow along. I usually will get a truck rental, load an ATV into the back, and go for a look. I'll have to check out the terrain here to see if an ATV is a good option. I've been to California only once before, and I made a pretty direct trip to where I needed to go."

"I've been here a few times, but it really depends on what part of California you're in. Some areas are desert. Some? Forests with huge trees. Where *are* we?"

"Good question." Darian reached over the arm of the couch and grabbed the leather-bound hotel guide, flipping it open. "It seems we're in Redding, which is somewhat north of Sacramento. We're getting close to not being able to go much farther north before entering Oregon."

"What the hell could possibly be up here?"

"Drugs," he announced. He turned the guide my way, which showed a map of the state, and it included nearby counties. He tapped one of the counties along the coast. "This is Humboldt, and it's considered to be one of the drug capitols of the United States. Ironically, this is where I was during my only visit to California. From illegal variants of pixie dust, plant-derived drugs, and various illegal labs, if you're looking for some form of narcotic, chances are, you can get it here. The residents are pretty closed mouthed about it, too, so you have to be careful around these parts."

"How do you know that?"

"I busted down a business that was running illegal labs out of Humboldt. I got the run around on the operations, so my first wayfinding took me to a different lab, but what I found there led me to Humboldt. Since your cat is a rescue from a lab, I already have a feel for how the illegal operations work."

I frowned. "Which would be why the Devil pointed you my way. Not because you're a wayfinder, but because you've already been involved with labs. And not just any labs, labs in this area. This makes sense. And he would know, because he's the Devil *and* he can look into the future when it pleases him, so he is killing a bunch of birds with one stone, which is what he likes to do. And the more inevitable the future, the clearer and easier it is for him to see it."

"If he bothers to look. But yes, you're correct. According to both of my fathers, the Devil doesn't look all that often; he likes the surprise and uncertainty, but if it's an important matter to him, he'll definitely peek. Since he wants you to be one of his right-hand women, he would look to see what would offer him that specific future. He got caught with this when he met Darlene; he refused to look because the game is better with surprises, so he got hoodwinked by *Him*. Lucifer still throws temper tantrums about it sometimes, although honestly? I don't even see how the End of Days would work out right now. Lucifer loves Darlene, and the only reason he still has her is because of *Him*. That does not make him inclined to want to wage a war to the bitter end. And he's always operated his many hells in a balanced fashion. He's always been about the reformation of souls. Sure, he punishes them and beats morality back into them, but it's always about the balance. If there are too many good seeds in the world, he releases the dark ones to keep things nice and orderly and balanced. *He* does the same. It's something my parents were always telling me about growing up. Dad thinks the

Devil is going to be the reason we never truly reach the End of Days, although for the purpose of the universal laws, it must always remain a possibility, because in order for there to be life, there must be death. Father, on the other hand, just shrugs. I always wonder what my father's expressions are. While I would probably survive if he lowered the shroud, Mom wouldn't."

"Why would you survive? I certainly wouldn't." The research material I'd come across, from an old book written during the prior emergence and definitely classified as a forbidden text, had taken me several years to translate, requiring that I fumble through Hebrew, two different dialects of Arabic, Egyptian, and Hindi in order to understand its secrets. I'd returned the book to where I'd found it, but I'd made a copy with all of my notes, which I'd locked in one of the high-security vaults operated by the CDC, claiming it was heirloom family research I didn't want stolen.

In reality, I wondered what would happen if the knowledge of the shrouds and their purpose did make it out into the world.

I'd read between the lines of that old text, determining the End of Days was less about humanity dying because of *their* sins but more about humanity dying as a consequence of the complete removal of the shrouds and *His* presence during the war to end all wars. The title of the end book of the bible made a great deal more sense to me when I looked at it beneath that terrible, divine light.

Revelations, indeed.

Darian drummed his fingers on the map of California, and his display of impatience drew my attention back to him. "Genetics. As far as devils go, Dad is pretty high up there; he need not be shrouded, but he is only one step below and can withstand the visages. Father is an archangel. Put those genes together, and I can withstand it. Father is very cautious about even mentioning the shroud, but we're aware of it. It's par for the course of having an angel in the house. Well, an archangel."

"I'm guessing Lucifer will have to meddle with me quite a bit if he wants me as his secretary. His shroud is a world ender. So is *His*."

"Yes." He scowled. "You would no longer be human, that much is for certain. Your soul would be irrevocably changed. Well, partially. Darlene started as a human, too. She seems human enough, but she's not anymore."

"Well, she's a succubus now. She acts human except when she's hungry, has her wings out, and is hunting Lucifer because he finds being the prey of a cranky feline enjoyable," I muttered, shaking my head over the pair. "I have had plenty of practice dealing with that train wreck during business hours. He probably planned for her to start getting hungry right around when I needed to work with him to test my abilities to handle his bullshit." Taking a moment to think about my situation, I shrugged. "I'll worry about it after we find Mr. Flooferson. I mean, what are the odds we have to worry about shrouds while looking for my cat?"

"Well, considering you had the attention of several archangels and the Devil, and they're going out of their way to make sure you survive this through use of holy fire, I'd say whatever is going on with your cat is a game changer. Likely something along the lines of humanity discovering, testing, and experimenting with ambrosia. An illegal lab out of Humboldt makes a lot of sense, as it's easier to hide the operations in a place where the locals tend to look the other way as long as the trouble doesn't come knocking on their door. Some areas are worse than others, but there is a lot of untamed land around there. It's not like San Francisco or Los Angeles, which are packed tight with people."

"You officially know more than I do about California."

"Only because of my background with one busted lab out of Humboldt. But if the lab *is* in Humboldt, we'll be good with an SUV and some practitioner magic."

"What sort of practitioner magic?"

"The kind that prevents our SUV from getting shot full of holes if we happen to make a wrong turn into an area somebody doesn't want us to be in."

For fuck's sake. Making a trip to the worst of the Devil's many hells was starting to sound better than visiting Humboldt. "You have got to be kidding me."

"I'm really not, unfortunately." Darian turned and lifted the sleeve of his shirt to show me a pale scar. "I got this as a reminder of why to step lightly around illegal narcotics ops. Ironically, this scar helped me dismantle the company so I could buy it out; the guy who pulled the trigger was on the board. It turns out when members of the board start going down for attempted murder, the rest of the operation starts scrambling and is willing to sell out for a pittance to preserve their reputation."

Nice. I could appreciate that sort of ruthlessness—something I needed to use on a daily basis in my line of work, as for some reason, a lot of executives, divines, and everything in between seemed to believe the presence of breasts excluded the presence of brains. "You don't play nice ball, then."

"I definitely don't. The less ethical the business, the harder I play ball, too. That's my father's fault. Honestly, I like blaming my father for a lot of things. It makes my dad happy—and then he doesn't mention when I do things more his way, which will inevitably upset my mother and my father. Cultivating my dad into an ally was one of my smarter moves. Making sure my father has limited exposure to my other activities was my next smartest move. Making sure my mother wasn't inclined to help was my third smartest move. I want to say my smartest move was moving out of their house, but they make me visit often to prevent the crying. I really hope my father and dad can keep her busy for at least a week. They're needy, Diana. So damned needy."

Considering the CDC had records of an angel crashing an airplane to retrieve her child, it came to no surprise to me that an archangel would go overboard trying to protect his son. "Have you infiltrated a lab before?"

"I have."

"But not with cat fur, I take it?"

"Human hair. The lab was experimenting on people, so I stole a sample of a vic's hair. The path led me to somewhere in Missouri, which gave me the intel needed to bust the Humboldt lab. Finding the Humboldt lab took some work, since it was in one of the worst areas for the drug trade, which meant I had to bypass the involved locals.

When they figured out which lab was getting busted and why, they were more willing to leave me alone about it. They'll deal with drugs, they'll kill people to protect their trades, but they draw lines at human experimentation. Morality is a strange beast in the area." He glared at the map of Humboldt, tapping at a spot in the middle of the county. "It's probably somewhere around here. That's a lot of mountainous territory, difficult to generally access, and fairly established as a place where labs like to set up. There are plenty of legitimate labs in the area, too."

"Why are the labs in such an inaccessible location?"

"Privacy and secrecy, mostly. And it makes it easier for the operators to establish illegal labs with legal labs as fronts. The inspectors check out the legal labs, deem them to code, and either fail to notice or miss the signs of the illegal labs. Some of the labs are underground, with the entrances hidden within utility sheds. Since there are legal labs in operation, the transports of supplies looks legitimate on paper. They just smuggle anything illegal in and out of their locations, which is much easier when it's hidden among a lot of legal shipments. The government doesn't check the trucks going in and out of the legal labs. Why bother? The most they do is surprise inspections, and the operations are set up to be hidden within ten minutes of an alarm going off. They have at least an hour of warning from where the general watch posts for the area are."

The way Darian talked about the labs led me to believe I'd really landed in more of a mess than I had anticipated—and that my poor cat had been involved with quite the mess, too. "This doesn't sound good for Mr. Flooferson. What will they be doing with him?"

"If it's anything like the human labs, they'll start with a health check to see if he is showing any signs of whatever condition they wanted to create or cure. With the people, they would do basic tests for about a week. I'm no expert, but that's probably our time frame before they'd start doing more invasive tests. They wanted him alive, however, so it's probable they'll want to keep him alive. How was his health when you adopted him?"

"Good, but he was abused. He wasn't starving or anything, and he wasn't really in need of much actual care beyond needing a lot of work on his coat because he has long, thick fur. They didn't really brush him or anything. But magic fixed that. He was definitely traumatized. Or so the paperwork said. He has gained a little weight since coming home with me, but I spoil him."

"I'll do my best to help make sure we get

him back for you. When we go to do this, there are some rules we need to follow if we want to be able to use any evidence. Before we set the path, we're going to go buy some investigative equipment, protections, and so on."

"Protections?"

"A lot of gloves so we don't leave our fingerprints everywhere, coverings for our shoes so we don't track in anything new onto the site. We'll need cameras, bags to store any evidence we pick, and we'll have to take a lot of notes. The cops just won't really go up here, even during a lab bust; they're in and out, because they don't want to lose law enforcement personnel to cranky locals. It's a really dangerous area. I'd say we should go in vested, but it's a crime to commit a crime while wearing protective gear, so I'd like to limit the number of actual crimes we commit. There are ways to skirt the trespassing laws, so I'll deal with that." Darian dug into his wallet and pulled out a card, holding it out to me. "This card helps, too."

I took it, raising my brow at the CDC mandate stating Darian had applicable experience in the collection and handling of evidence to turn over to law enforcement personnel, and it was listed as valid for the entirety of the United States. "How did you get this?"

"My father asked the CDC very nicely,

as it helped me bring crooks to justice. They didn't want to upset the archangel who is essentially in charge of justice being served. Basically, he cheated a little on my behalf after some pressuring from my dad. Mom thought it was hilarious. I find it highly useful. So, this card lets me violate certain laws, but I have to be exceptionally careful about how I use it. After we gather evidence, we have to immediately take all of the documentation to the police and verify by angel. I always use an angel that is *not* my father because it annoys him. Really, he likes saying I ruin his peace of mind. I tend to tell him he doesn't have a head, so he doesn't have a peace of mind to ruin. That gets his feathers in a bunch."

"How are you even still alive? Do you know what would happen to most people if they angered an archangel?"

"My father informs me he questions why he hasn't blasted my scrawny, irreverent ass out of existence already. I just tell him he loves me almost as much as he loves my mother. Listening to a headless being scream from general frustration is amusing. Of all the children to get, he got me. I say he did something pretty terrible to deserve it, probably in the form of being in league with a devil or something like that."

"I bet your dad just loves that."

"He usually goes out of his way to get

pizza or something like that on those nights, just so we can eat it while my father is forced to go sulk since he can't drop his shroud to have any. He's terrified of slipping for even a moment, so he absolutely won't take any risks, not with me or my mother, and that's even being aware I'd survive." Darian frowned, and he got up, headed for the door, and rummaged through the pockets of a brown leather coat hanging in the closet. When he returned, he had his cell in hand. Sitting down, he dialed a number and held it to his ear. "Hey, old man. Got a question for you."

I debated scooting out of the way in case the old man decided he was done with having an independent son with an enjoyment of causing trouble.

"Yes, she's doing all right. Breakfast seemed to help, and she doesn't seem to be in much pain, but I'll keep an eye on her. Wait. Prescriptions? For what? Ah. Okay. Yes, I will take us to the pharmacy before we go on our outing. Anyway, my question. If I'm using my CDC card, and I have Diana with me, can we legally get away with using vests? It would absolutely not bother me to take advantage of my old man to get a permit to investigate in Humboldt, California for the next week or so. In fact, it would make my life easier, and I can then give the local law enforcement a lot of good intel on a busted lab operation they probably couldn't access before. Sure. Call me back. Tell Mom I love her once she's coherent. If you could work with Dad to keep her incoherent for another week or so, that would be great. I am expecting a healthy brother or sister in the appropriate amount of time, and I will be very disappointed in my parents if this is not given to me." With a laugh, Darian hung up. "The feathered menace is going to try to secure a permit for us. His willingness to do this tells me he's peeked, he didn't like what he saw, and he wants to make sure justice is served. Manipulating archangels is surprisingly easy when you work within the restraints of their portfolios. Michael and Gabriel are both inclined towards healing in some fashion, so when presented with someone sick and a good reason to heal them, they have a hard time saying no as long as *He* doesn't say no. The Devil likely manipulated both of his brothers on that front, especially Michael, who is very aware of the conditions for the End of Days and works to avoid it. Really, it's humanity that seems to delight in the End of Days far more than any of the divines do. The End of Days ends *them*, as well. And however much some of the more destructive divines enjoy their dark works, they don't want to be blasted out of existence, either."

"They need something to destroy," I

agreed. "Honestly, it worries me how much divine attention I'm getting." Pointing at my chest hurt, but I ignored the pain and said, "My current count of involved divines is at four. The Devil plus three archangels. What I do not understand is how either me *or* my cat could possibly be that important to any one of them. I can understand the Devil to some degree. I am a good secretary, and I can work with divines of most pantheons without it turning into a disaster. But the rest of them? The rest being involved tells me there is something far more than just a missing cat and some mortals at play here. Thoughts?"

"It probably involves the lab that had your cat. They could be trying to obtain immortality and using animals to test it. They could be trying to find a way to wipe out humanity and using animals to test it. There are a lot of potential options, and none of them are good. There are a lot of demented people in the world. Some want to kill all of the divines to free humanity from their evil influences. Some want to become divines to gain power and rule. Some just want to rule over all humanity, something that tends to annoy most divines. Generally, the divines enjoy their status as divines and do not wish to give up their portfolios to some uppity human. Even *He* has a portfolio and isn't truly immortal, not like the Devil is."

"How did that happen, anyway? It's in the Devil's file he's a true immortal and simply *cannot* be killed. But there are records of *His* portfolio being switched, often once or twice between emergences. Now, that would be quite the surprise, don't you think? One day, some poor guy is just minding his own business, and then *bam,* he becomes God, the head big guy of the Christian pantheon. And *He* has to use a full shroud, because *His* radiance is so severe it kills mortals if he shows even a hint of his form. Or so the CDC's notes say."

The book I'd translated had claimed similar, and it contained speculations ranging from an overabundance of magic to the Holy Light being too bright for mortality to withstand.

"Those notes have it pretty close to right. My father sometimes talks about *His* portfolio. Every version of *Him* is slightly different; it depends on the mortal who becomes *Him.* The current *Him* was a pretty compassionate being in life. It shows in his behavior. My father holds hope *He* will remain as *He* is; it's a good change, one befitting the original *Him.*"

"But what happened to the original *Him?*"

"What do you think?"

"I have no idea. I never really thought about it before," I admitted.

"*He* sacrificed *Himself* for the sake of mortals, much like *He* sacrificed the Devil to humanity through allowing him to have free will and fall. It just happens the universe cannot abide with the imbalance and moves the portfolio to a new host. There will always be someone with *His* portfolio. Beyond that, I don't know. Dad was actually the one who brought up *His* first sacrifice. But it's always a sacrifice of some sort. *He* can't just be killed—*He* has to choose to end *His* existence for the sake of others."

"Like the story of Christ."

"Sometimes, humanity gets it right, although Christ was real enough, just not in the way most believers think of him. But *He* was actually the first sacrificed in such a way by *His* own will. Then the Universe passed the portfolio onto the next poor bastard deemed willing and capable of holding the role. My parents were strangely vocal about this sort of thing. Probably because they think I would go digging on my own and find out more than they want me to. They're not wrong."

"As evidenced by your investigative tendencies, coupled with your drive to acquire justice while also pursuing wealth."

"See, the Devil is absolutely right to want you as one of his right-hand women. You're smart. He collects smart people, especially women. I mean, he's the Devil, and he absolutely relishes in sexist behavior and prefers to surround himself with pretty women because he can."

I shrugged. "I mean, if the option is to surround myself with asshole but pretty men or asshole but pretty women, I'm probably picking the asshole but pretty women. And if they're surrounding the Devil, they're probably assholes. I mean, I enjoy Darlene's company, but she can be a severe asshole when she wants to be, especially when hungry."

"My dad warned me to never stay in the same room with Darlene when she's really hungry. He was concerned I might not survive the experience. When my dad issues warnings like that, I believe him."

"Smart. So, back to finding my cat. We have to wear protective gear so we don't screw up any of the evidence. We also have to take pictures and notes. What else do we need to do?"

"Mostly poke our noses where they don't belong, don't contaminate any of the evidence while we're gathering it, and try to avoid being shot while we're investigating. Being shot complicates evidence gathering. And it hurts."

"Do you need some time with a therapist before we head to Humboldt? It sounds like you need some therapy, Darian."

"I just have a healthy dislike of pain, and

being shot hurts. Being shot especially hurts when you have three parents you *really* don't want finding out you were shot. They found out, but at least they found out well after the fact, thus sparing Humboldt from being razed by a cranky archangel. Dad, on the other hand, just gives me a severe case of the eye and suggests if I'd done my job properly, I wouldn't have been shot in the first place."

"Are you sure you don't need to be rescued from your family? It sounds like you need to be rescued."

"I'm fairly sure. And anyway, I'd rather not incite mass panic among the archangels. Archangels get ridiculous when one of their nieces or nephews gets into trouble. And when one of your grandparents is *Him*? Yeah. Let's just not go there. I'm hopeful my fathers will help with my escape plans by keeping my mother exceptionally busy. That, plus I want to try out being a doting big brother. I admit this with absolutely zero shame. I'm pretty sure it's a genetic defect, but I love children. I'm going to blame my father for this sometime later, after it's confirmed he's done his fatherly duties to me, his currently only son."

Well, Darian wouldn't have any problems on the jealousy front. "I'm an only child. I think I'm an only child because I was possibly possessed by the Devil when I was little." I glanced around the room in case

Lucifer decided to show up. All remained quiet, to my relief. "I wasn't even allowed to have a pet, not even as a teen, as my parents believed I would terrorize the poor thing."

"In reality, you are a doting cat parent who might set the entire world on fire to rescue Mr. Flooferson."

"Precisely. Can we get started on that?"

"As a matter of fact, yes. Get dressed. Wear comfortable clothes, bring extras. If things go sideways, we might not make it back to the hotel tonight. We won't know until we get there and see how the locals handle our presence—if they care we're there at all. It can go either way."

"Just what I wanted to hear."

SEVEN

"You're pure evil."

AT THE CAR rental place down the street from our hotel, we bickered over who would pay for the vehicle. As we were searching for *my* cat, I felt I should pay the bill. Darian, probably thanks to his archangel of a father, wanted to be a gentleman and cover the expenses.

I ultimately won, taking my credit card out and handing it to the man behind the counter, staring into Darian's eyes and hissing whispered threats of general dismemberment if he didn't cooperate.

I amused him.

I needed to work on my threats, but I paid for the rental, the replacement insurance, and every other protective policy I could get my hands on, just in case his prediction of gunfire and vehicular destruction proved to be true. While I filled out the paperwork, Darian scowled. I took the keys, and because I could, I pointed at the passenger side. "And just because you tried to be all manly, I get to drive first. You should be happy the rental allows me to allow you to drive."

"You do this to the Devil, too, don't you?"

Darian had a lot to learn about my life and the extreme measures I needed to take to maintain some semblance of control during a busy workday. "Absolutely, whenever possible. The trick to being an effective secretary is making sure I maintain as much of the power as absolutely possible. The meetings times, places, and dates? I typically control those. My bosses make recommendations on venues, but ultimately, I'm the one who makes everything happen. A good boss is backed by an even better secretary, and I can make or break meetings just from how I prepare for them. Since I'm an excellent secretary, I arrange things to best enable my bosses to do their jobs, even when they would prefer different arrangements. And since my arrangements work, they trust me to do my job. The Devil is a lot of things, but he's not stupid, and he recognizes when I can make *his* life a living hell through the power of clever scheduling. Or not, depending on my mood at the time. It's funny how my bosses can suddenly become so busy they just don't have the time to pen the Devil in."

"You're pure evil."

Grinning, I got behind the wheel of the SUV, and I waited for him to climb inside. I placed my purse on his lap. "Mr. Flooferson's fur is inside in a baggie. Do what you need to so I can get to driving. When I'm tired of driving, or we get close, you can take a turn. Honestly, when we get close, I'm probably going to be hiding somewhere hoping to limit my chances of getting shot. I have enough problems without adding being shot to them."

"Is secretary another word for control freak?"

"It can be," I admitted.

"I always wanted to see if I could tame a control freak. I appreciate a challenge. How do you rank yourself in terms of your control freak level? Are you a little minion, or are you an end-game boss? Am I going to have to get that special sword I found at level one and kept in my bank for the entire game *just in case* I needed it for the end boss?" According to his tone, I did far more than amuse him.

I challenged him.

I didn't need to be adept at taking men to bed to recognize I'd caught his attention, and all I had to do to hold his attention for a while was to just be myself. The next time I spoke to the Devil, I needed to tell him miracles could happen. "I'm definitely the end-game boss, and I shall maintain this status until I have my cat back. Then my cat and I will be the actual end-game boss you discover upon believing you vanquished your foe. The game designers care nothing for your first perception of victory and must make you pay for your hubris."

"I did not see video games in your home. I looked. Yet that remarkably sounds like I have gotten into the same vehicle with a gamer."

I pointed at my briefcase in the back with my laptop. "It runs games, and I play them there. Sometimes, I'm particularly naughty, and I play the games at work."

"I did not bring a gaming laptop with me." Darian got out his phone and tapped on the screen, then he reached over and tapped in an address in the SUV's navigation system. "I brought work and no play, so I'm going to go buy myself something to play on while getting the few things we'll need for proper investigations. Like a dedicated phone and camera for the purpose. It sucks when personal equipment is confiscated during an investigation."

"When I get Mr. Flooferson the Magnificent home, he is so getting scolded for how many bills he's currently incurring. He better pay me back in cuddles. I need my kitty's cuddles."

"You're going to insist on paying for everything, aren't you?"

Raising a brow, I glanced his way before forcing my attention back to the navigation panel. "What clued you in?"

"The entire rental process, really. My father would fully approve of your choices. Dad would be suggesting you need to partake of at least a little greed. Mom? Mom would just ask where her presents are. She really likes gifts, especially when the gifts are coming from my fathers. She views their gifts as compensation for putting up with them." Darian retrieved the baggie with my cat's fur and put my purse on the floor at his feet. "I hope you're not expecting a whole lot in terms of displays of magic. I'm not one of the more flamboyant wayfinders."

"As long as you know where we need to go, that's fine. Flamboyant doesn't mean better, anyway."

"I'll know where we need to go. You might not see anything, however. Most don't."

"Most implies some do. It's visual for some people?"

"For some, yes. I get a shimmer, much like a mirage, along with a sense of hot or cold. We're getting warmer applies with my magic, and the shimmer also becomes stronger the closer I am to the end of the path. You may or may not see it. It depends on how perceptive you are or if you have divine blood. Fortunately, I tend to be able to see the shimmer far enough away I can drive while following the path. Do you have divine blood?"

I shook my head. "Not that I'm aware of."

"That's pretty rare. The more the CDC studies humanity, the more it discovers that most humans are touched by the divine *somewhere* in their ancestry. What's your rating?"

"My license states I'm a practitioner." I eyed him, but I decided if I'd be living with him for an unknown period of time, he may as well have a better idea of what he's getting into. "The CDC doesn't believe it's possible for anyone to be purely human, so my files for genetics have been flagged as probably incorrect."

"You scan at a hundred percent human?"

"I don't even have any Neanderthal in me, apparently. They're not convinced it's possible, because the current belief is that *homo sapiens* evolved from Neanderthals. They originally believed Africans lacked Neanderthal DNA, but that was recently disproven. So, the current theory is, for me to exist, the foundation of both sides of my family had to sprout out of the ground, fully formed, after the Neanderthals no longer existed as a race. The CDC thinks it's possible. Djinn could wish humans into existence, so it's entirely possible others could, too. I mean *He* can also create humans at his whim."

"Darlene is one such creation. *He* cultivated her seed and picked a pair of humans, but her genetics are considered to be fresh; the genetic data from her seed completely overrode the contributions of her mortal parents. They're her parents, but genetically, she's the first of her line." Darian grinned. "Darlene was so mad about that. Apparently, she stormed *His* high heavens and scolded *Him* for several hours. Lucifer had to retrieve her because she was *so* mad she wasn't carrying any genetic material from her parents. My father was telling me about it. She's also upset it technically means she isn't genetically related to her brother, either. *He* foresaw her temper tantrum from ten miles away and distracted her with fostering a baby angel for a while. *He* had to go retrieve the baby several months later, which was apparently fun because Darlene didn't want to give the baby angel back. Father says *He* wanted the angel to be particularly nurturing, and there's no better way to foster a nurturing soul than to hand Darlene the baby and let her do her thing. Kanika appreciated the respite, because Lucifer is incapable of being anything other than doting when in the presence of babies. Unfortunately, now Lucifer *and* Darlene are giving Malcolm fits because they want grandchildren."

I laughed, as Malcolm had a rather lengthy file with the CDC due to his status as Kanika's husband. The CDC wrongly viewed him as the actual inheritor of the Devil's many hells. The kelpie, while a demon, had exactly two thoughts rattling around in his thick skull: protecting his wife and convincing her they should have many children.

He excelled at protecting his wife, but I wished him luck on his quest for children.

Kelpies required water to reproduce.

Like me, Kanika couldn't swim.

"I take it your work with the CDC has put you into contact with Malcolm?" Darian asked.

"Where Kanika goes, Malcolm tries his best to follow, unless he can't because of his work. The CDC doesn't want a cranky kelpie making a mess of negotiations, so part of my job is to make sure Malcolm is present whenever we need to have a meeting with Kanika. We try to keep the Devil and Kanika separated, as for some damned reason, if we put them both in the same room, there's at least one property damage charge leveled at them. Usually at her, as few are stupid enough to sue the Devil. Unfortunately, many are stupid enough to try to sue the Devil's daughter. A piece of life advice, Darian: never sue the Devil's daughter. That is how you earn Lucifer's ire."

"When I heard I'd be working with a secretary, I had something completely different in mind. Like working with someone who has a stable and safe desk job. Why am I starting to think your desk job is anything but safe?"

My job, which involved facing off against divines most days of the week, hardly classified as safe. Lucrative and fulfilling, yes. Safe, not precisely. "Frequent exposure to the Devil has something to do with that impression, I'm sure. Honestly? Lucifer is really pleasant to work with. He doesn't want to waste time, so he is efficient. He comes to the table well aware negotiations will become complicated, but he complicates them in ways that don't waste time. If a decision can't be made, he will schedule future negotiations to give people a chance to think."

"So, you're saying it's complicated."

"It's complicated. The Devil works best when people are comfortable with the decision they're making. He doesn't like when bargains create extra difficulties for him. My job is to set up the negotiations with the best CDC staffers to handle how the Devil likes to work. In terms of working with the CDC, he's usually trying to manipulate people or situations to fit his needs, so he brings a good deal to the table in the first place. We know he's doing something for his benefit, but he presents it in such a way the CDC has a difficult time refusing his requests. Take Kanika, for example. Darlene initially controlled Kanika's file with the CDC as her guardian, but once the Devil started getting involved, he cut a bunch of deals to make sure her paperwork issues didn't become issues. Whenever there was a snag in her paperwork due to her circumstances, either Darlene or Lucifer showed up to make sure it didn't stay snagged. Kanika has no real idea how much background work those two have been doing on her behalf. Lucifer also has an agreement with the IRS to make certain she never really understands the horrors of taxes, especially now that she's his heir. He works with Malcolm on that, too. And pays the bills when Kanika's efforts render more of a financial windfall than she—or Malcolm—expects. Lucifer absolutely adores her, and Darlene cannot handle the thought of Kanika's adulthood being as difficult as her childhood was. Honestly, they're disgustingly good parents. And since Kanika doesn't see the tax documents, she has no idea her husband is working with her father to make sure she gets to experience the calm peace she missed during her childhood. Usually, life works the other way around."

"I'd say I'm more like Kanika in that regard. My fathers did not want me to be a wide-eyed innocent entering the world completely unaware of life's dangers. I mean, don't get me wrong. I was loved and consider myself to be happy. My mother made sure I wasn't sheltered."

I bet. "And they molded you to do what you're doing now. Helping a crazy lady rescue her shelter cat from a lab. Because you know the world isn't all happiness and rainbows."

"Right. How about you?"

"Let's just say my parents will turn me over their knees and spank me if they find out I have gone on numerous dinner dates with the Devil and liked it. They have limits. That's one of their limits. If they find out I'm temporarily living with the son of a triad because I cut a deal with the Devil? Christmas dinner is going to be interesting."

"Especially if the Devil *and* several archangels show up and they learn there is little the Devil loves more than dinner with his family."

I grinned at the thought of the Devil showing up with his family at my parents' place. "Yeah. Honestly, I'd love to see that."

"That's probably fairly easy to accomplish. Make the Devil do it as part of your hiring agreement. He'll do a lot more than just visit some mortals on Christmas to win you as a secretary. Ask for presents, too. I *still* get presents from Lucifer. Apparently, until I'm at least a thousand years old, I will never be too old for presents."

"I'm going to drive us to the store now. I need more time than we have to wrap my head around Satan acting like he's Santa."

"Nobody's got time for that, Diana. Just remember something while we're doing this. The Devil bargained to secure your cat's life, but he is *not* giving us the solution to this puzzle. We need to take our time, and no matter how worried you get for your cat, we need to be meticulous. We'll lose a lot more time if we have to come back to California because we weren't thorough. I'd rather spare you that, because you'll be far more upset we lost twelve hours compared to one."

I got the SUV on the road, and it didn't take me long to come to the conclusion Darian spoke the truth. "I'll do my best. I know I was impatient yesterday. I'm just worried about Mr. Flooferson."

"It's okay to be impatient. It's not okay to rush our investigation. It'll just make our lives a lot easier if we do this right the first time."

"I'll do my best," I promised.

THE STORE DARIAN picked had two of the high-end laptops he liked, and in a moment of weakness—and a desire to interact with another human without it being on my work machine—I bought the second one for myself. Then I bought a new phone, the kind I liked rather than the CDC liked, put it on a good personal plan, and gave myself enough data I could play games on the road without worry. To meet the requirements for our investigative work, I got a burner phone with a decent camera and a memory card in case the cops confiscated it, three cameras with a collection of memory cards for the same purpose, and one high-end camera solely for my personal use.

I'd always wanted a nice camera.

As I'd already taken a dive into insanity and credit card debt, I picked a tablet with a pen so I could take notes without chopping down entire forests.

Darian followed me around with his selection of a single camera and his laptop, chuckling every time I added something to my cart, as I'd filled the basket within ten minutes of stepping foot into the store.

"You know, if you're out to improve your general life, they sell consoles and televisions here. There's no reason you can't go on a bender and get some controllers, games, and everything you might need to transform yourself into a true gamer."

My eyes widened. "But how would we carry the television around?"

"You don't need a huge one to play games, and we'd just put it back in the box and stash it in the SUV between stops. The Devil won't even blink twice about adding five minutes to his lecture to teleport everything to somewhere safe if needed, but I expect we'll be driving a lot."

I sighed and bowed my head. "I'm probably the only person in Miami who doesn't own a car. I just cab or take the bus because my work is at a stop, and it's only twenty minutes by bus. I picked my house because it was right near a bus stop and on the same line as my work."

Darian stared at me, and his mouth dropped open. "You picked your house because of the transit system? You don't even *have* a car?"

"I don't have a car."

"How can you do your job without a car?" he blurted.

"There are CDC vehicles at the office, and I use one of those if I have to be the driver. And I'll drive the limousines sometimes, depending on the importance of the meeting and the secrecy involved. Driving the limousines can be fun."

"Well, the more you talk about your work, the better I understand why the Devil is after you. He would definitely want a right-hand woman who could handle the touchy work—and doesn't feel herself to be so superior she won't handle driving. I'm just stunned you don't have a car."

"The grocery store is in easy walking distance. I haven't missed having a car."

"Add a personal vehicle to your hiring conditions. The Devil will enjoy the process, and he won't miss the money. He can just take a gemstone from his many hells and sell it to a collector. There's your new car, the taxes, your hiring bonus, and basically anything you want paid for right there. If he's feeling particularly nasty, he'll convince one of his brothers to sell the rock to a fanatic and offer a blessing. He gets double the price when he pulls that stunt, and he tends to share the profit with his brother. Angels tend to have a bunch of bills, and if some dumbass mortal wants to spend millions on a rock an angel or archangel said a few words over, that's their business. If the mortal wants an actual miracle, the going rate is closer to five times that price."

Ah-ha, mystery solved. "I've always wondered how angels made money. That is not in any of the files I have access to. I do have access to account information, but only the current balances. Some of the archangels? They're ridiculously rich."

"People will pay a lot when it comes to religion and superstition. Angels and archangels have no real concept of actual money. They understand the concept, but because they're seriously lacking in the greed department, it doesn't mean a whole lot to them. For example, my mother wanted a new car. It was not an expensive new car. Basically, she wanted something that would become a reliable junker in ten years and could fit a destructive child, me, in the back seat. My father opted to answer a request for a miracle to pay for it. The rich bastard was willing to pay millions for something he could have done at a hospital for much cheaper." Darian laughed and added his stuff to the cart and took over pushing it. "So, he brings home millions to Mom so she could buy a cheap car. He'd never done anything like that before because Dad is pretty good about being mortal and made sure Mom always had just enough to get the things she *really* wanted. My father? He had a lot of adapting to do. My mom does good with her career, especially now, but when I was little? That wasn't really the case. She *freaked* when my father came home with the money. And then she bought the best model of that same line for the car, because she didn't want some stupidly expensive car. The rest went into my college fund and everything I might possibly need for the rest of my life, basically. When I escaped home, I made it clear Mom deserved the money for putting up with my fathers. I opted to earn my own way. That was when she bought her first luxury car, although she keeps a lot of the money around for emergencies. The other archangels have their ways of earning money, too, but my father likes visiting Lucifer and going the gemstone and miracle route. He often uses it as a way of bringing justice to false believers. Now that he's discovered this trick, he pulls it often. He really likes securing justice through human greed, and my dad encourages him, because my dad loves nothing more than shepherding in some good old ruin on the deserving."

Interesting. "Is that a warning not to accept blessed gemstones from archangels?"

"As a matter of fact, yes."

"Noted." I pointed at my new laptop. "This will run just about any game I want, correct?"

"Correct. That is why I selected mine. I brought a work laptop that can be confiscated without issue, and that is the one we'll review data on as we investigate. The memory chips should generally suffice for keeping the other systems in our hands, and if they want to confiscate them, I have an archangel for a father, and I'm not against making use of my various aunts and uncles. It's much easier to control what law enforcement is going to try to confiscate if a headless, winged menace is hovering and asking questions. Once an angel asks if something is *really* necessary, law enforcement tends to back off."

"Okay. Anything else I'm missing for this?"

"We could use a scouting drone and a small camera if we think we're about to go into a bad area." Darian pointed across the store. "As you're in the Devil's sights, I'd rather not upset him taking unnecessary chances."

"I'm just saying, there is no better loved cat on Earth than my Mr. Flooferson." As he'd taken the cart, I aimed for the next section of the store destined to lighten my bank account. "I don't suppose your dad or your father takes requests, do they?"

"You would be surprised what devils and archangels will do when asked. The thing is, most humans just won't ask. They'll pray for deliverance, but the angels and archangels aren't the ones who typically answer *those* prayers, and *He* won't do things *He* feels can be accomplished through other means unless *He* is feeling charitable. That is not often. A clever human might direct a prayer to a specific angel or archangel, however. And those sometimes *do* get answered—if the human walked the straight and narrow. Most don't. Prayer is a lot like the concept of karma. You're going to get back what you put in. Someone who spends all of their life helping others is more likely to find themselves the beneficiary of an unexpectedly answered prayer versus a churchgoer who prays daily for everything and everyone. Sincerity and frequency matter."

I frowned, considering Darian and what I knew about my parents, who did hold a lot of faith in their religion and the general power of prayer without truly believing in *His* existence. "The churchgoers, as you call them, aren't going to like that. But then again, the church my parents attend believes in the bible and its concepts but doesn't hold much faith that *He* actually exists. Divines and magic are not real to them. They consider magic to be sacrilege."

Darian stared at me as though I'd grown a second head. "Wait. Your parents go to church but don't believe in the divine and magic?"

"Correct."

"Are you sure you don't need to be rescued from your family? I may not have a house yet, but I'm willing to revamp my entire apartment until I can buy a house if necessary to rescue you from that. That's just crazy."

"Says the man with two fathers."

"That is crazy, but not as crazy as your parents wearing blinders, believing in a religion but refusing to believe that *He* actually exists."

"There is a reason I tend to only visit for the holidays and haven't disclosed the specifics of my job. They are happy thinking I'm just a low-level secretary in the CDC." I grimaced. "I love my parents and don't want to be disowned, so I'll go to their church with them when they ask, I participate in their religious holidays, but I otherwise keep my head down."

"You? Low level?"

"That is what they think."

"You go to dinner with Lucifer fairly often. How are you a low-level anything?"

"It's easier than trying to challenge their beliefs. I'm also a practitioner. They believe all practitioners are going to hell." I shrugged. "At the rate I'm going, I will be. I'm not going there to be punished, but I'll help run the place."

"There's something to be said for making challenging goals."

I laughed. "Are you sure all this stuff will help us find my cat?"

"I'm a hundred percent certain the television and gaming console stuff won't help you find your cat, but it will help you lower stress levels while searching for your cat, which makes it a sound investment."

"Think I can teach my cat to play games with me?"

"Well, you definitely won't know until you try, but I suspect your cat will be happy to sit on your couch with you while you play. That said, why have a couch at all if you don't have a television or console?"

"Reading books," I answered with a delicate sniff. "I don't have time for television."

"I'm starting to think I was recruited to be a therapy plan to normalize you for life outside of work. I'm okay with this. But as I'm taking a role as your personal therapist, you have to let me buy the console, the starter games, and the travel television. As I'm a spoiled personal therapist, you'll also have to consent to me purchasing the actual television, too. I have needs, Diana, and they must be met."

"Frankly, if you help me find my cat, you can basically do whatever you want, and I'll probably be all right with it."

"I'll keep that in mind."

ONE SMALL FORTUNE LATER, we escaped the store and loaded the SUV. I expected some form of ritual for Darian to find a path to where my cat had been experimented on, but he rubbed Mr. Flooferson's fur between his fingers, frowned, and waited. Within a minute, he nodded and pointed to the west. "My guess about Humboldt county is looking pretty good. The path is stronger than usual, so I've got a general fix on direction *and* a path for us to go. It's not usually that clear. It happens sometimes, but I try not to question my good fortune when it does."

"Got a town I can plug into the navigation system to get us close?"

"Alderpoint. Once we start getting close to there, we'll go based off the path. I'm hoping the lab is closer to Bridgeville. Alderpoint tends to be basic narcotics operations, but they've got a reputation I'd rather avoid. There are some spots around Bridgeville with known labs, and it's a bit safer. It's along a more major route."

"And anywhere tourists might go tends to be better monitored by law enforcement?" I guessed.

"Precisely. Law enforcement doesn't like when the tourists go missing because of illegal activities. They're less inclined to care what happens to the illegal drug runners and lab operators." Darian tapped in the town, selected the general store, and started the navigation system. "If it does take us to Alderpoint, don't be too alarmed by the town's sign. Folks find it amusing to shoot the sign. People don't actually open fire on each other on the streets." After a moment of hesitation, he added, "Usually."

"The usually part of your statement is a little worrisome."

"In good news, if it is towards Bridgeville, we won't be taking the route that heads to Alderpoint. To get to Alderpoint, you turn off to a different road before reaching Bridgeville. In bad news, we'll be getting well into Humboldt county before we know for certain."

"That's something." Aware his magic had a timer and we had almost a four hour trip ahead of us, I got on the road, focusing most of my attention on driving while Darian rummaged through the bags of loot we'd purchased at the store. "You're not paying me back for that laptop."

"And you're not paying me back for the ninety-inch television I will be purchasing for our gaming adventures. Or the other consoles. Or the rest of the games I fully intend on ordering and having shipped to my parents to hold while you handle the driving. I'm also going to send Lucifer a text informing him you do not own a vehicle."

"That's rather ruthless. What did I do to deserve that?"

"I figured you would neglect to mention your lack of a vehicle, which would result in it not being added to your hiring terms, thus you'd short yourself on your hiring bonus. My mother warned me about the complications women usually face when being hired, and I'm going to make certain the Devil pays his dues for a change rather than the other way around. Mostly, I get to help Lucy spend his money, and this is highly appealing to me. I'm blaming Dad for this."

"The freedom must be getting to your head."

"Possibly a little. To be fair, I set my parents loose to buy a house, so I'm going to have space for my new television, and considering the terms of the agreement, Lucifer is going to take his time deciding justice has been served. I have plans on sending my house wishlist to my parents while we're on the road. Lucifer will let you work wherever you want, although I expect he'll want you in an area with an easy portal so you can head to hell whenever you want, unless you pick a species that allows teleportation."

"Well, I won't be picking succubus, that's for sure. Half the reason I haven't engaged with men is because I'm a little more loyal than most of the men to catch my eye, but I'm smart and realized this before I even tried to date them."

"Smart. With my genetics, monogamy is basically inevitable. Sure, Dad's a devil, but he's hardwired to be loyal; it's part of how Lucifer created him. Lucifer needed an ally he wouldn't have to worry about all that much. My dad is quite good at his ruinations, but he does it on Lucifer's behalf. He has no tolerance for even suggesting he betray Lucifer. Add in my father's tendencies, and I won't even be a candidate for a triad myself. I'm a little *too* greedy and selfish when it comes to any potential partners. And jealous. Mom thinks I'm hopeless."

"My parents are actually pleased I do not live in a state of general sin. I'm sure the instant they find out I'm running around with a single man roughly my age, I will be deemed a sinner."

"Showing up with a bunch of archangels and the Devil on Christmas is going to test them, won't it?"

"I will be very disappointed if it doesn't. Don't get me wrong. I love my parents, but they're a little prejudiced, and it'd be nice to see them change their tune. They probably will once unassailable evidence is presented to them. They've seen me do magic tricks before, but they view it as sleight of hand, not actual magic. I decided against rocking the boat more than I already had. They insisted I go to church and repent multiple times. They even made me get baptized to soothe their souls. My soul, by the way, was absolutely not soothed." I shuddered at the memory of being utterly convinced the pastor would drown me, but I'd been taught if I *didn't* get baptized, I would go directly to the Devil's many hells for punishment. Later in life, I'd learned that their way wasn't necessarily the right way. "I was in my teens for that dunking."

"Did that scare you?"

"It scared the hell right out of me, frankly. I didn't even curse for a few weeks after that. They might've made me do it again. Unfortunately, that incident did nothing to discourage my interest in magic and lore. I find magic and the divine to be absolutely fascinating."

"Your job would definitely allow you to pursue those interests."

I nodded. "Exactly so. Planning research trips is tough with my work schedule, though. I usually wait for the CDC to ship me abroad and extend the trip a day or two. They usually let me do that, as I rarely take other days off." I grinned at the thought of how many times I'd done some rather naughty things while traveling under the CDC's banner—and since the CDC got protective about its executive secretaries, as often as not, I caught chartered flights across the pond, which made smuggling illegal texts back to the United States rather simple. "There are a lot of people who do private flights overseas who want the CDC to treat them kindly, so they offer to let people like me ride along if they're going back home anyway, and then I catch a flight or drive a rental back home."

"How often are you abroad?"

"It depends on what's going on. Last year, I spent three full months abroad, jumping from country to country. I had another two week trip, too. Mr. Flooferson actually came with me both times. He got pixie dust for the flights, and he rode in the cabin. Did you know pixie dust works on cats? It's like catnip but better for him, so he had a great time. Half the time, he just chilled on my lap. One of my bosses was doing a tour of Europe and wanted me with him, and I refused to board him because he was abused. The CDC talked to my vet, decided it would be best for him to come with me, and they accommodated him. If I'm only gone two or three days, he stays home alone and someone checks on him." I frowned, drumming my nails on the steering wheel. "I don't know I'll want to leave him home alone now."

"That's something you'll want to talk with Lucifer about. He tends to take his pets everywhere, and he's got two cats. Well, Darlene has two cats. I'm sure he can work something out. Just make sure he knows that's not something you're willing to negotiate about."

"You are just a fount of good advice. Anything else I should do?"

"Pick a species, or it'll be picked for you, and Lucifer has a sense of humor and a fondness for unicorns, kelpies, and really, anything equine. He also has a fetish for felines, but Darlene gets jealous, so if he gets a choice, he's going the equine route with you. And since you're afraid of water, there are high odds of you being converted into a kelpie, as that would nullify that problem. You'd be able to breathe water. Kelpies can live for thousands of years. Old age takes a long time to catch up with them. I wouldn't be surprised if he is hoping for a kelpie for you. That way, Malcolm will have company of the same species. Kelpies don't enjoy solitude, and he doesn't really have a clan now. He could form a clan with you. That would make Lucifer happy, as kelpies are on the same vein as his unicorns, and he's obsessed with his unicorns. Converting humans into kelpies is probably child's play for him, assuming *He* appropriately counters with the creation of an angel. I don't know what the current balance is. The Devil may be owed a seed or two for all I know. Lucifer would get you two seeds, as he'd match you with someone of the same lifespan. Date with caution, because Lucifer takes the 'until death do you part' portion of marriage vows seriously."

"You're well educated about Lucifer and what he's likely to do."

"Dad wanted to make sure I was aware of my uncle's tendencies. He can't properly ruin his enemies if he doesn't take care to be as thorough as possible, so he tries to learn everything he can about everyone who is around him. He thinks I'm a troublemaker, so he wanted to make sure I didn't cause the wrong sort of trouble with my uncle."

"Are you a troublemaker?"

"Definitely."

I grinned at that. "I recommend you run as soon as you can. The Devil doesn't just have his eyes on me. You're in this game, too."

"I have no problems with conversion. There's something to be said for long years with the right person along for the ride. Conversion would also make it more likely that my dad and father will stick together after my mother passes, and they're generally a good team. They enjoy spending time with each other. Their natures are complementary. So, the way I see it? I'm being an extra good son playing along with the Devil's plans."

"But your mother won't be converted?"

"The human part of a triad rarely is. There's only one long-lived human member of a triad right now, and he's a lycanthrope."

"Ah. Yes. The swan. Paperwork about him has floated through my boss's office before. His daughter caught an FBI agent for herself, and my one boss needed to review, as the FBI wanted her for their operations. She's an agent now, too, although they're not in the field right now because he's infected, and his virus opted to rapidly accelerate development. They're undergoing tests before going out in the field." I considered the pair and chuckled at the mayhem a pair of birds might bring to an investigation. "Swans have tempers, so the CDC is monitoring them."

"Lycanthropy is an interesting option," Darian admitted. "But I'd rather be an equine."

Ah-ha. "You just like horses."

"I do. I'd make a fantastic stallion. And I'd be able to run really fast, and that appeals to me. And I'd have hooves, which are excellent for kicking people I don't like. Horse lycanthropes are ridiculously rare, too, so we'd get extra protections from the CDC. The CDC does like to protect the uncommon variants."

"Like the swans. I'll admit, I've never considered lycanthropy to be a bad infection, and it wouldn't bar me from doing my work, so I'm often exposed to them during work. The other secretaries are afraid of being infected, where I'm not."

"You do seem rather fearless in general. Honestly, that is a little disturbing. Fear is a good way of preventing you from doing something I'll regret."

"Not that I'll regret?"

He chuckled. "I'm more likely to regret it than you, I suspect. That's a lesson I've learned from both of my fathers. When my mother decides she's fearless, she makes them regret it every damned time. Also, my father when concerned that my mother has gotten into serious trouble? Absolutely hilarious. His feathers stick up on end. It's remarkably cat-like. It also takes *hours* for his feathers to settle after an incident. And since I'm pretty sure I heard Lucifer mention you delve into forbidden lore, I'm confident you'll do something I'll regret."

"How about you? You're the one who gets shot while taking down corporations."

"I will definitely do things you'll regret, although I'm not accepting any responsibility for your decision to buy us high-end laptops for our gaming pleasures after we're done work."

"Obviously, the loss of my cat has killed my common sense. I really hope this helps us find my cat."

"Me, too. But when the Devil gives his word, he means it. Even if we botch this, he's got something up his sleeve in terms of protecting your cat. It might mean he works with the assholes we're taking down, but if it protects your cat, I don't really care if he jumps teams."

"I have no problems with him jumping

teams if it means my cat gets out of this unscathed. However, I will make his entire existence miserable for a while if he makes it harder for me to rescue him."

"As he's smart, I doubt that. He'll just secure his safety, I think. The Devil's end goal is to get you to work for him, and making it harder to retrieve your cat won't help him reach his goal. Really, you have the advantage, so take him for all he's worth. If you need help, we'll ask my dad for advice. He's good at that sort of thing."

I bet Belial could give me some damned good advice if I asked for it. "Think he'd help with the game plan to totally destroy this outfit behind the theft of my cat?"

"I think we'd be opening Pandora's box if we did that. If my father joins in? We might end the world. Literally. It's safer for the world if we handle this ourselves."

"They can't be that bad, Darian."

"I love both of my fathers, but they can absolutely be that bad. Let's not end the world unless it's absolutely necessary."

I drove for a while, considering his words. "Do you think it'll be absolutely necessary?"

"Considering these assholes weren't bright enough to look into who they were stealing a cat from first, I'm not sure, and honestly? That concerns me. If they were after you, they would have left a note, called you, or otherwise found some way to contact you to ransom your cat. They also would have ambushed you and taken you along with your cat."

"CDC employees are sometimes kidnapping targets," I admitted. "Especially people like the executive secretaries. We know a lot, our bosses tend to value us, and we're easier to grab than the executives. They tend to have high magic ratings to go with their job positions."

"I'll admit, I was surprised how far up the chain you are considering your lack of a known high magic rating."

"I'm decent at my practitioner tricks. I'm not sure if I outclass your mother, but it's entirely possible."

"You'd have to be able to summon Lucifer to outclass my mother, Diana."

I smirked.

"You think you can summon Lucifer?"

"No, Darian. I know I can. I am just smart enough not to. And really? Summoning Lucifer is easy. Just spell his name wrong in some glitter and do a little dance while singing from a musical. That gets his attention every damned time, and he likes me too much to kill me."

"I will pay just about anything to watch you do that," he admitted.

"Don't tempt me. I just might."

EIGHT

I opted against heaving my most dramatic sigh.

FOUR HOURS after leaving Redding and taking a twisting, narrow road north of Dinsmore, we arrived at the ghost of a nameless town, hidden off a dirt road the rental could barely traverse. Time, fortunately, hadn't had much way with the path yet, although I spotted signs of nature reclaiming the place. "This wasn't what I had in mind," I confessed.

Somebody had hauled in a bunch of trailers and mobile homes, creating a little community. The overgrown brush implied at least several years had gone by. I'd had Mr. Flooferson for almost two years, and the decay matched roughly when he'd been sent to the shelter. Some cars remained, and I parked, got out of the SUV, and armed myself with one of the cheaper cameras, taking pictures of everything. Darian joined me, and he carried my purse along with my new tablet, which he'd set up while I'd been driving.

We hadn't switched drivers, as he'd expected a farther drive, and I'd enjoyed navigating the scenic and somehow desolate route.

"This wasn't quite what I had in mind, either. That said, I'm not all that surprised. The place was probably a lab town; everyone here was part of the lab ops, and when it got busted, those who could ran—the rest would have been arrested. And since this town isn't on the map, I'm betting they didn't own the land."

"Which makes us trespassers."

"Crap. The permits." Darian checked his phone and chuckled. "By some miracle I refuse to question, I have a single bar. Let me get our permits." He dialed a number and held it to his ear. "Hello, my most wonderful father. Do you have good news for me on the permit front? I'd really like good news on the permit front. I have been driven to a secondary location, and I don't want my kidnapper to get ideas because I failed to present a permit to her promptly."

Unable to help myself, I grinned. Before I had a chance to do more than raise a brow at the tall, dark, and handsome I'd be tempted to kidnap under other circumstances, his archangel of a father popped into existence in a flash of golden light. Raguel hung up his cell phone, and it vanished in a second flash of golden light. "You're going to have to try harder than that if you want to tempt her into kidnapping you, and should you tempt her into kidnapping you, you will find yourself the captive of a very methodical being. The kidnapping would be quite orderly, you would be tricked in such a way you would not realize you were being kidnapped until it was too late, and I do not believe she will be at all inclined to return you. I recommend you leave a schedule out, so she can appropriately plan your kidnapping, as doing anything unscheduled, frankly, is rather against her nature."

Laughter bubbled out of me before I could stop it. "It's true. This is about as far outside of my comfort zone as I go. Even when one of my bosses needs me for an unexpected business trip, I usually have a day of warning and time to schedule it. Then, as my job involves sticking to schedule, I work hard to make sure everything gets done in a timely fashion. I'm not sure where I'd fit a kidnapping into my current schedule, really."

"You might want to take on the role of the kidnapper," the archangel advised his son. "As I'm a loving father, I'll even help you plan it so you don't completely ruin her schedule. Ruining her schedule would create certain pitfalls you would not enjoy."

"Why are we discussing kidnappings, anyway?" I asked.

"Some seeds require careful planting in order to grow, and neither one of you would come up with the idea on your own. As such, I'm planting the seed. I do enjoy some harmless chaos at times. It gives me something to gossip about with my brothers." Raguel held out his hand, and a manilla envelope appeared, which he handed to me. "Here is the paperwork you need to be able to legally poke your nose, with some limitations, in places you otherwise should not be. As this is state-owned land and should not have been occupied in the first place, these papers give you basic rights to be here. I am not feeling any obligation to inform you of what you will find. I do hope my son takes more care this time, as I do not like when foolish mortals shoot him. And yes, your other father is definitely aware of that incident, and he has been doing what he does best. Your mother is also aware, but we have taken steps to keep her thoroughly distracted, as we do love our son and do not wish him to perish at his mother's hands."

I opened the envelope and looked inside, discovering several different permits giving us permission to operate as private investigators in the states of California and Florida.

"I don't feel I'm qualified to be a private investigator," I admitted.

"Private investigation requirements are fairly lax for a temporary permit," Raguel replied. "You simply need to have a clean record, which you have. Of course, Darian has more robust qualifications, and you are recorded as being in partnership with him, which helped pave the way for you to have your own permit. If you wish to pursue private investigation in the future, I am sure my son can assist you. How are you feeling?"

I stared down at my chest, which ached, although I had ignored the discomfort throughout the drive. "I hardly noticed when I was driving, but it does ache a little. I'm still a little baffled over all this."

"My brother does not appreciate when mortality comes for mortals he particularly likes, and he likes you—as does his wife and daughter. He is a sentimental enough of a creature, burdened with unbecoming emotions he prefers to ignore or bury. We are onto our brother, no matter how much he tries to hide it. Your nature would make you a very good companion for him and his family. It would also grant him more time to be with his family while costing you less time than your current employment. With all that in mind, healing your body is a small price to be paid. The value of a soul is judged by the deeds of one's hands, and your hands are hands of compassion. You give far more than you receive, as it has been since you were a child who discovered the joy of giving. You just give in different ways. Your curiosity is a troublesome thing, however."

I opted against heaving my most dramatic sigh. "Translate one forbidden text, and I get labeled as troublesome. It was one forbidden text. And it wasn't like I was all *that* aware it was forbidden. I mean, sure, it was buried in a vault in the middle of a desert to prevent people from just wandering to it and finding it, but if they *really* hadn't wanted me to find it, someone wouldn't have left directions to get there in a library. Or ten."

"Closer to twenty," the archangel chided.

"So maybe it was a little bit hidden, but I found it with no real problems. I even avoided all of the traps, and I put it back when I was done with it."

"Except you created a copy for yourself."

"I put the copy in a safe place."

Somehow, despite the shroud cloaking his head and preventing him from wiping me out of existence, the archangel managed quite the stare. "To translate it, you needed to read several dead languages, several old dialects of current languages, and decipher an ancient cypher."

"Is it a sin to be prideful of that accomplishment?"

"No. But I did wish to speak with you regarding your copy of that text."

"You can go steal it out of the vault and make it disappear if you would like." I tapped my temple. "Sometimes, I wish I could forget what I read, but I understand why it was buried. It does explain a little too much on the nature of the shroud and what really happens during the End of Days. I can understand why that knowledge was buried. While the End of Days will have a war between a father and his son, the end of all life on this Earth is but a consequence. Everything has a consequence. It's just that when *He* finally loses *His* temper with *His* son, all life being lost on this Earth is the consequence of that moment. Or any moment that upsets *Him* so much *He* loses *His* shroud while on the mortal coil. *His* presence is omnipresent. Only those of divine blood might withstand *Him*, and only if their bloodline is pure enough. But then the war will happen, and with so many divine entities abandoning their shrouds, the surviving life will inevitably end, leaving the Earth as a husk by the time the war is finished." I considered the whole situation, which left only one ending I could fathom. "*He* would be so distraught I can only imagine *He* would sacrifice *His* life for but one more chance for a better future, thus renewing the cycle. That's just my guess."

With his mouth hanging open, Darian stared at me as though truly seeing me for the first time.

"What a clever little human. Little humans like you may be what prevents that foretold fate from coming to pass. But it must always linger on the horizon. Mostly, as a reminder to *Him* of the consequences should *He* lose his patience. And make no mistake, Lucifer is very good at making our father lose *His* patience."

"May I ask a question?"

"You may always ask, but I cannot promise I can answer."

"Am I a creation like Darlene? Is that why I register as a pure human with nothing divine? Or even other?"

The weight of the archangel's regard fell on me. "My brother likes to believe he is a master at playing games, cultivating seeds over many generations to create a perfectly flawed, beautiful being. Many of his nephews and nieces are such beings. Even you, Darian, are such a being, cultivated as a consequence of Lucifer's desire to gift Belial with something meaningful. Your mother is as much a gift to Belial as he is a gift to her. My brother dragged me into this because he fails to understand how to be a good brother without being awkward about it. But yes, you are a creation much like Darlene, but you have been one in the works for many generations. *He* created every seed needed for you to be as you are now. *He* did so well aware you would fall into my brother's sights and become a prized treasure. *He* did so making your seed one Lucifer could shape however he sees fit. You, like Darlene, are a gift. Unlike Darlene, however, you are a gift who is also a sword."

"And to think the CDC thinks archangels are contumacious and unwilling to share knowledge."

"The CDC does not ask the right questions, nor do they deserve the answers to those questions. With you, the scales are unbalanced, for you have given much with little being given back. The high heavens and my brother's many hells exist for one reason: to maintain the balance. Angels, demons, and devils all work for the same cause in different ways. Your nature will do much to maintain the balance in my brother's domicile, although you may find having to beat the resident demons and devils tiresome at times. Belial can offer assistance with that. He is excellent at his craft."

"I bet he is. When do you want your son back?"

"Keep him. He is troublesome and costs a great deal to feed. He can come visit when it's time to babysit."

"Thanks," Darian muttered.

"Fly from the nest, annoying child. Try

to land appropriately, for it would be annoying to have to rescue you from excessive amounts of trouble. Fly. Be gone with you. We will contact you when we are feeling in need of your affections. This may take a while. I am sure you can handle this burden."

"Dad paid you to say that, didn't he?"

"I was offered certain incentives to do my best to offend you and keep you away from home for a little longer," the archangel replied.

"Let me take a guess what actually happened. My mother, because she tries to be the perfect parent, convinced herself she's the world's worst mother, and she went to Dad for attention. Dad brought you into it, because Dad does not like when my mother is upset for any reason and is a fixer even worse than you are. As such, there was a three-way pity party. Dad, being among the most sensible of the threesome that is my parents, told you to check on me because Dad tends to make a mess of things when he's fretting and tries to be a parent rather than the devilish general he is. As such, he offered you something to do his dirty work, probably resulting in you spending a few days up visiting *your* old man, but you had to deal with me and my paperwork issues first. After you're back, because you can't stand the idea of being able to recharge while he's stuck on Earth, you will keep my mother amused for a few days while Dad goes hunting some gemstones so you two can pull stunts on some humans with morality issues. Somewhere in here, you two will scheme for a second child, as I am really old enough to take care of myself. Frankly, I feel like I'm the mature adult in our family, Father."

"You are not wrong."

Darian sighed. "How do you deal with triads, Diana? Do you have some secretarial magic trick that makes them be somewhat saner?"

"You have two divine beings who are fretting over the short lifespan of their wife and child. There is no magic trick to make them saner," I informed him. "This is just a guess from what I've read in the CDC's files on triads, but shower all three of your parents with affection. That should calm them down for short periods of time. The devilish parent likely needs more attention because the angelic parent should be unashamed of requiring affection from his offspring and wife. So, you should probably corner Belial at some point and do a father-son evening where he gets a chance to just have some time with you. That will rile your other father, as he will want a father-son evening. Then your mother will want a mother-son evening, and once everyone has an evening with you, they'll probably be good for another month or so with minimal care. Once you have a brother or sister, you will find your parents to be easier to care for."

Raguel's laughter chimed. "Her suggestion has merit, Darian."

"Noted. Thank you for bringing the paperwork, Father. Do try to take advantage of my extended trip away from home to get my mother pregnant. Try for twins or something. With three parents, twins should be doable. You could probably handle triplets with minor difficulties."

"Did we not give you enough presents for Christmas and your birthday, that you would wish twins or triplets upon us?"

"Daily home visitations to care for the special needs of my parents is more the reason why I'm wishing twins on you. Then the next set can share duties. This is my bid for freedom, old man."

"That is wishful thinking. We would only seek additional attention from all of our children. Take care with your investigations, and do avoid lifting anything heavy, Diana. You do need to heal, and doing so would hurt."

"I'll keep that in mind. Thank you, Raguel."

The archangel disappeared.

I raised a brow and engaged in a staring contest with Darian. "What, precisely, was that all about?"

"Mom probably freaked out I was not

readily accessible, Father probably told Mom about my paperwork request, so Mom made Father handle the paperwork and check on us. Dad is probably making use of his devilish powers to help my plan of having a sibling along, which is why Father left without making even more of a fuss. He likely cheated a little, determined this abandoned lab is safe enough, and wanted to get to the portion of his night where he gets to do unspeakable things to my mother with his devil of an accomplice. If I do get into trouble, he will simply shrug, as he did his best, but I am a troublesome son. Then he'll suggest to Dad they should have a daughter, because daughters can't be as much trouble as sons."

"Maybe he was onto something about you being the target of a kidnapping. But it wouldn't be a kidnapping, would it? You'd be a willing participant. It's not a kidnapping if you're willing. This is something that we go through yearly during training. We're taught to identify if someone is being trafficked. There are a lot of cases where parents will level a kidnapping accusation against a boyfriend or a girlfriend because they don't like them. But if the couple is willingly together, it's not a kidnapping. You're old enough where your parents can't stop you from running away with someone."

"I'm at the stage where I believe they wouldn't press charges or try to stop me.

They might offer you monetary incentives for you to take me off their hands."

"How much is the son of a triad worth?"

"Good question. We'll ask Lucifer after we investigate this place. I foresee a lot of time paying back bargains by listening to him spout damned advice before we get to the bottom of this."

"I just want to know why they couldn't just rescue my cat for me."

"Oh, I already figured that out," Darian replied. "Or I'm pretty sure I have."

"Tell me."

"It's simple. The lab operators are playing at being some god, and the divines are not allowed to interfere when mortals try to break the universal laws. They need mortals to do their dirty work, so they sent us."

"I don't like that theory," I muttered.

"Good. I don't, either. But it's the only one that's making any sense to me, because the fastest way for Lucifer to gain your favor right now is to bring your cat home to you safe and sound—which means he *can't*. If he could, he would. But he can't, so that tells me someone is breaking a universal law, and the only ones allowed to interfere with that are mortals—or beings born naturally with free will. Lucifer was given free will, but he was not born with it, so he cannot act. If anything, Lucifer is the least likely divine of them all to break a universal law, which may very well be why *He* cast him out of the heavens—not because of Lucifer's nature, but because *He* foresaw what *His* fallen son's role would truly be."

"Remind me to bust Lucy's kneecaps for this later," I grumbled, getting my camera ready to take hundreds or thousands of pictures. "And if this nonsense gets my cat hurt, I'm going to line up every fucking demon and devil and give them a piece of my mind, and the angels are next!"

"I'm so not warning either of my fathers about this. Just invite me to come along for the ride. Some things can't be missed."

WEARING all of our protective gear, including face masks, hair nets, shoe covers, and gloves, we documented every trailer and mobile home in the abandoned community, picking through discarded, rotting property in search of any clues that might help us learn who had stolen my cat and why. Most of the papers had been chewed on by animals, rendering them useless, but a few drawers in decaying desks offered a single name: Kingston Miller. The name meant nothing to me, but Darian grunted every time we stumbled across a receipt or note mentioning him.

"You obviously know something, Darian. I wouldn't have noticed anything if you'd limited your sounds of disapproval to the first time, but every time a new paper shows up, you get progressively crankier. What's the deal with this Kingston Miller?"

"Kingston Miller is a lycanthrope who has been attempting to cure the virus. However, since experimenting on lycanthropes is even more illegal than experimenting on cats and dogs, it doesn't surprise me if he's trying to figure out a way to treat the lycanthropy virus using pets."

"But regular animals can't contract the virus."

"Well, obviously, the first step would be to make the virus spreadable to cats and dogs then, if that's his goal."

My eyes widened. "But wouldn't that make lycanthropy even *more* contagious?"

With a worrying shrug, Darian poked through the trailer, which had been ransacked for valuables long before our arrival. He kicked aside rotting clothes in a tiny closet to reveal a cardboard box in decent condition, which he opened with a pocket knife. A metal case caught his attention, and he lifted it out. "Hello. What do we have here?"

"How did that get missed?" I crouched and examined the box, discovering some charcoal marks, which had worn away over time and from exposure to the elements. "Oh. Practitioner wards. They've finally worn off enough that they're no longer effective."

"Are you good enough at practitioner magic to check this over before I open it?"

"I can literally summon the Devil if I really want, Darian. I think I can handle checking over a box." I examined the cardboard, finding six distinct protective wards, all of which had been smudged in some fashion or another. "Whoever was protecting this box didn't want anyone to find it. Every side had a different ward on it. They're too destroyed to see what they were intended to do, but the base outline makes me think they are protective and to prevent people from noticing it."

"Is it common for somebody to put a ward on every side of the box?"

I shrugged. "Would I do it? No. I'd put it on the top of the box, and if I wanted it to stick, I would have put tape over it to make sure nothing happened to the ward. The person who made the ward is probably a hack."

Hacks annoyed me. Hacks gave all practitioners a bad name, as the hacks tried to make use of cheap tricks rather than practicing refined control over magic. Runes, symbols, circles, or whatever form of expression the practitioner chose to use could do almost anything, including transform iron into gold.

I'd done the iron into gold experiment a few times, although I'd always reverted the gold back into iron when finished.

Magic had a way of exacting prices for its use, and while I'd successfully performed the transmutation, I didn't want to find out what the other prices might be involved beyond requiring a ridiculous amount of iron to create even an ounce of gold.

"I take it you dislike hacks."

I pointed at myself. "Hacks give people like me a bad reputation."

"Diana, you claim you can summon the Devil. You're exactly why people are wary around practitioners. They aren't scared of the hacks. They're scared of people like you."

"Just because I can doesn't mean I will! When I want to summon the Devil, I call him like a sensible being. Now, if he ignores my calls, well, he deserves to be summoned for daring to ignore me."

"That is not helping your case."

"Why not? It's rude to just randomly summon somebody. Call first."

"That does not change the fact you're capable of summoning him—and if you can summon him, you can probably summon any divine you want. Sensible people fear someone with that sort of power running around. My mother can't summon Lucifer. She doesn't have the skills or aptitude, and frankly, I feel my dad only showed up because he found the situation interesting. Don't tell my mother that. She's convinced she forced him to show up."

"Raguel showed up because he wanted to, didn't he?"

"That may have happened. Mom is convinced she could force either to stay at her whim. My fathers do not correct her about her misconceptions, although they have warned me against following in her footsteps. They think I'd just chain summon succubi for my depraved enjoyment. I keep reminding them I'm not like them and have zero desire to have multiple partners. Anyway, we keep from correcting my mother because it might encourage her to try harder to summon other devils and angels. Mom *can* summon lesser demons and devils against their will and cage them, however."

"That's still a major accomplishment." I pointed at the metal box he held. "Do you want me to check that or not?"

He handed the box over, and I ran my finger in some of the dust covering everything and drew a circle on the top of the box, which I sliced in half with a single swipe, concentrating on purifying the exterior of the container and erasing any runes that might be etched inside. Dark shadows engulfed the metal, and when it dissipated, the box shined as though freshly cleaned and left out in the sun. "This should be safe, but I make no promises about the interior."

"If I drew a circle and then disrupted it, what would happen?"

"Nothing, probably. When I first started, that was a complicated circle I often spent an hour or two drawing and perfecting before I'd disrupt it. Time and practice means I can use simpler runes to accomplish difficult jobs. Summoning circles always remain complicated, as you have to capture the essence of the specific entity you wish to draw into the circle. Lucifer's summoning circle would take me about eight hours to draw properly, and don't get me started about the literal headache involved with summoning a higher power like that."

"That implies you have," Darian stated, and he took the box to the nearby table, set it down, and flipped it open. "What do we have here? Somebody has been naughty."

I got to my feet and joined him at the table, wrinkling my nose at the presence of a gun and ammunition in the box, along with several vials containing orange fluid. "The gun doesn't surprise me all that much, but what's that stuff?"

"I have no idea, and I'm not brave enough to open it to find out. This will go to the police, although I may get a sample to have tested. I bet my dad could do a damned good job figuring out what it does."

"And prevent any contagion if it's a virus sample." I frowned. "But what does that have to do with my cat? The CDC has extensively tested lycanthropy infections in animals. It just doesn't happen. A lot of lycanthropes have pets and do shelter work now because the animals can't contract lycanthropy."

"Well, it would take a lot of experimentation and observation to see if a strain can take root in an animal. That *could* explain why the Devil was so confident that Mr. Flooferson would be kept safe. They can't monitor if he's been infected or if the infection is taking root if they harm him. And if he *is* infected, then he would be in a good position to survive testing."

"But what would he transform into?"

"A human?" Darian shrugged. "It'd be very strange if a cat suddenly started transforming into a wolf. But if the adapted virus could turn animals into humans, then that would definitely be something the divines couldn't work directly to stop. That's humanity trying to play at being gods for certain."

My eyes widened at the thought of my cat, who could be a troublesome little demon on a bad day, having access to hands. "They might end the world, if cats could become human. The entire world would end. There wouldn't be a need for the End of Days. Cats would take over the world, and they'd have the hands needed to do it. The only reason cats *haven't* already taken over the world is due to their lack of opposable thumbs."

"Take a few deep breaths, Diana."

I gulped a lungful of air.

"Try taking a few deep breaths without hyperventilating. I'm sure if your cat develops a severe case of humanity, you're fully capable of handling him and the consequences. You've worked with plenty of lycanthropes before. For all we know, it could be something as simple as trying to make cats and dogs asymptomatic spreaders. If this Kingston fellow has been able to develop a vaccine or cure for lycanthropy, he'd become one of the richest men alive overnight. The CDC would pay high amounts to be able to treat those who do not want the virus."

I considered the number of lycanthropes who didn't want the infection versus those who had successfully adapted to the virus. It came out fairly close to equal, leaving a lot of people unhappy with their longevity and new circumstances and restrictions. Following his instructions, I drew in a deep breath. "I can respect those who don't want the virus, but to experiment on innocent cats and dogs searching for a cure—and potentially infecting others—really trips my trigger."

"It would also trip Lucifer's trigger. Forcing the virus on somebody is no different to him than other forms of assault. It's a major violation, and he enjoys punishing the sinners who are guilty of such crimes. And while Lucifer enjoys tricking people into bargaining away their souls, he almost never goes after those who have earned their way to whatever paradise their heaven is. A bargain simply secures the final placement of those with souls burdened with guilt."

"It's a test," I guessed.

"It absolutely is." Darian picked up one of the vials, lifted it up, and turned it every which way, testing the seal. I tensed, but none of the fluid escaped. "Whatever this is, it's not blood."

"The color tipped me off it's probably not blood."

"Some beings have odd colored blood, but this is way too thin of a liquid to be blood."

"I'm going to take your word on that, as I try to avoid situations where I can watch other beings bleed."

"That's generally a wise course of action."

I considered the metal box with a frown. "What should we do with this?"

"We'll put it in the rental. I have a feeling nobody is going to be bothering us today."

"Because your father left without bringing you some form of weapon?"

"He left, period. No matter what impression you got, he is definitely the doting father type, and he would not abandon ship if he thought I was at any actual risk. It's one thing to let me go off and find trouble, but it's another for him to leave me alone if he thinks trouble is about to happen. It should be safe enough."

"So we don't have to play secret agents in here?"

"Oh, we don't *have* to, but I want to," he replied with a boyish grin. "And being dour won't rescue your cat any faster, so let's try to keep stress down while we investigate. Your cat won't get upset with you if you relax."

"He'll get upset with me because I'm not giving him his meals at the appropriate times."

"I recommend bribes in copious quantities until forgiven in that case. It'll be all right. Let's finish documenting this and find out if there are any more of these boxes now that we know what we're looking for. If one like this was missed, maybe we'll find something else. We've played enough. It's time to get to serious work."

NINE

We didn't live in a perfect world.

DARIAN UNDERWENT a transformation from laid back and casual to a dictator, possibly one of the Devil's minions straight from hell, demanding perfection so the investigation would not be compromised. As the possibility existed we had missed other boxes thanks to the practitioner runes obscuring their presence, he demanded we go over every trailer again, but more thoroughly—and using my practitioner skills to flush out any secrets we may have missed on our first pass.

The effort, which involved drawing runes in the filth caked onto the trailer floors, sapped me of energy and dished out a serving of pain. The pain didn't surprise me.

Magic had a way of amplifying things, and my entire chest offered it an easy outlet.

Usually, it just charged in energy and general exhaustion.

I could tolerate some extra pain, especially if it meant we found more information on what had happened to Mr. Flooferson.

Of the trailers we had searched, two held secrets obscured with magic, and my magic tore through the protections with fire-red tendrils. Sparks of blue illuminated the interior before encasing the revealed boxes in a pulsating aura.

On the second box, Darian waited for the lights to fade before revealing the contents, which included more of the silvery cases filled with vials. Unlike the first we'd found, they lacked weapons or ammunitions.

The gun scared me a whole lot less than the vials and their contents.

"The blue is holy fire," Darian announced. "That's probably a consequence of the healing you underwent. Does your magic usually manifest as red?"

"No. It's usually invisible, although there is often a flash of light when I disrupt some form of obscuring magic like this. It's not usually red."

"Likely hellfire, then. You've had a lot of exposure to Lucifer lately, and he has a vested interest in you. Did you know Lucifer still uses holy fire? More often than his hellfire, really. But he has access to both. Now

I'm really curious what he's up to; they're not conflicting. They usually do. I'm really annoyed we're not getting more of a paper trail, but these vials are going to be a goldmine of information for us. The first step is to get our hands on a scanner and get what information we can before we turn them over to the police. Think you can hook us up?"

"Sure. There's a scanner in my safe. I'm sure Lucifer would be happy to talk my ear off for five extra minutes to retrieve it. That's really his plan. To nickel and dime us into eternal servitude through listening to him giving us advice. If we rack up enough minutes, we'll be doomed."

He chuckled. "You're probably right, but this will be worth the five minutes, especially if you have a good scanner."

"It's a good scanner." My bosses hated inefficiency almost as much as I did, and a good scanner made a difference, especially when I needed to work with a cranky lycanthrope who disliked being monitored. I understood the lycanthropes; being tested for virus levels served as a frequent reminder they were no longer fully human. I also understood the CDC's stance on it, too.

In a perfect world, only those who wanted the infection would contract it.

We didn't live in a perfect world.

"Good. We might get some answers about what's in these vials and what they're used for. More importantly, if someone is after your cat, why haven't they come back for these vials?"

"They might not have known they were here because of the obscuration runes. They were pretty potent to have lasted this long in these conditions. All the windows had been left open, same with the doors. Animals have been in here." I wrinkled my nose at that reality, as I didn't want to think about the nasty things I'd stepped in since starting the search, even when wearing protective covers over my shoes. "You didn't warn me how gross this would be."

"It's not usually this disgusting. But I'm also not usually looking through things abandoned for at least a year. Let's get these vials into the SUV so we can move on with our search. The next step is locating the actual lab itself. That might be interesting."

"Because your path is gone?"

"Yes. The lab is close, and I know the general direction. It's better if we have to search around for it. We might find clues."

"Do you think these vials are what they were cooking up in that lab?"

"I don't know, but it was important enough they used high-grade magic on it, so we're going to look into that mess, even if it isn't related to Mr. Flooferson's catnapping."

Fucking catnappers. "And even if it isn't directly related, it is—those vials are part of the operations as a whole. And if they're targeting one lab animal from one part of the operations, they might be looking for others, too."

"Has anyone told you that you're disturbingly compassionate?"

"What? No."

"You're disturbingly compassionate, and I'm pleased to be the first to tell you so."

I frowned and regarded Darian through narrowed eyes. "Explain, please. I'm not feeling compassionate right now. Really, I'm feeling a little murderous. I'd be tempted to take one of those vials and ram it through these assholes' skulls, using the blunter end of it." I pointed at the stoppers. "That end, to make it hurt more before the glass finally shattered."

"It's safer for you if you use the other end on them."

"That is not as satisfying."

Darian laughed. "While it's not as satisfying, murdering them with some vials is probably unwise. You'd be exposed to whatever fluid is in these things."

"There is that. So, why do you feel I'm compassionate? We'll ignore the disturbingly part for now."

"You're concerned other pet rescuers might have their animals targeted during a high-stress situation. Most people become rather selfish in times of duress. You're actually considering the consequences to others in a situation where most are focused solely on the goal. It's something I've noticed about people since starting this line of work. Compassion is far easier in low-stress situations. Let's say you're just walking down the street, and you're in a good mood. You're more likely to show compassion to someone you meet solely because *you're* doing okay. It's much harder to be compassionate when you're not okay." He pointed at my chest. "The bandages and wincing you're doing says you're not okay right now, and you're still concerned about others. That level of compassion is way above average. And that's not a bad thing, but it's a little disturbing in some ways. It's also concerning. That sort of compassion means I'm going to have to keep a close eye on you. Someone could put a puppy in a cardboard box and use it to lure you into a dark alley so they can kidnap you."

"You jump to strange conclusions."

"It's my mother's fault. She does strange things, which means I have to jump to strange conclusions. That said, keeping compassionate people from being kidnapped can be a problem. They'll go help stranded puppies in alleys, resulting in them being an easy mark for nefarious kidnappers."

I believed his mother had warped him, and if anything, he needed to be plucked free of his trio of parents and set loose in the world without one of them popping up and influencing him. Maybe Raguel had been onto something regarding the necessity of someone indulging in a good-natured kidnapping. "You only have your father to blame when you're kidnapped, Darian."

"Why am *I* being kidnapped?"

"I'm a compassionate being, apparently. And that is too crazy." I checked the box for any stragglers, and I discovered a folder with another rune at the bottom, which I erased. "What do we have here?"

"Papers!" Darian set the box with vials down and crouched with me. "I love when people leave me papers. Papers are the lifeblood of a good investigation. Do you know what we can do with paper?"

"Dust it for prints?"

"Dust it for prints," he confirmed. "Do not touch that any more than you have. As it happens, I do know a practitioner trick, and I'm quite good at it, but I need to get my supplies out of the SUV."

I could make a guess at what he meant to do. "You're going to expose the fingerprints?"

"I am. Then we'll photograph them, seal the papers, and make sure the fingerprints remain intact so law enforcement can properly register them. With some careful planning, asking really nicely, and some money, I will get the fingerprints run before the cops get the fingerprints, thus helping me to identify who was handling the paperwork. This is what I then use to help narrow down my search—and get the right information for the job I'm doing. These cases are designed to be difficult to get fingerprints off of; between the texture and the material, the prints are hard to remove. It can be done, but it is a tricky job—and it doesn't last as long. If the surface has been treated to prevent fingerprints from sticking, that's another issue, too. But, with the right magic, if there are prints on these, we'll find them. Getting them off and in a useable format is another matter entirely."

"Can I help?"

"You can help by not touching anything, and if you wouldn't mind breathing in a distance of, say, at least ten feet, that would be great."

I raised a brow, but as he wanted space, I left the trailer to wait outside while he worked his magic and acquired fingerprints for us. "I will get that method out of your hands one way or another," I informed him. "Your magic will soon be mine."

"We shall see about that."

DARIAN SPENT over three hours hunting for fingerprints in the trailer community. Some he lifted using white paper and some gel, and he meticulously labeled where it had come from, took pictures, and stored them in a special case he'd brought with him, one I hadn't noticed him having when we'd packed the rental for our trip. I blamed my chest; the discomfort had done a damned good job of distracting me.

"I thought the police were going to properly register these," I stated, once it appeared he'd completed his work.

"They will. My license and training will allow this to be admissible evidence, and doing it this way means I can run the prints on my own. With a few phone calls, we can have some results in two or three days."

"That long?"

"There are billions of fingerprints in the world, and each one of these will often pull up at least twenty possibilities, which someone has to manually go over or use magic to match. Usually, I get someone to manually do it, but I'll go the magical route this time. It takes a few days to get the right person to handle it. Those folks have to verify prints for the police, international law enforcement, and governments, so there's always a bit of a line. Some of these prints are in really good condition, so we'll be able to get some good computerized matching, which just require verification." Darian hauled the precious box containing the fingerprints to the SUV, along with the vials and the weapon we'd found. "Can you obscure all of this, so no one pokes their nose into our business?"

"Of course." Grateful to have been given a task I could do, I went to work setting up a set of runes, going the excessive route and warding every side of the containers to prevent others from noticing it.

Darian frowned. "I thought I wouldn't be able to see it once obscured. Are you done yet?"

"You can see it because you know it's there. This type of protection doesn't usually work on those who are already aware of what is being hidden and where. So, because you watched me place the magic, there's no chance your attention will be diverted. There are other magics I could use, but we're getting into forbidden territory."

While I'd learned how to shroud people, places, and things, I'd left that to simply being knowledge of the lore, without crossing the line into using powers better off left in the hands of the divine.

"You can place a shroud?" Darian whispered.

"I know the theory on how to do it," I replied, frowning at the realization I'd said enough to land me in a lot of hot water. "I've never actually tried it."

"That's power on the level of the divine, Diana."

"So is summoning the Devil at my whim rather than his."

A pop and hint of brimstone behind me warned me I'd summoned trouble. "Yes, summoning me at your whim rather than mine *is* rather forbidden—and fringing on powerful enough to compete with the divine. It was so nice of you to call, Diana."

Somehow, I kept from shrieking at Lucifer's manifestation. "You, sir, are a complete and total asshole. But thank you for helping with the cancer problem. I do really appreciate that. However, I seem to have contracted a case of hellfire to go with some holy fire?" I breathed until my heart rate lowered to something closer to sane before turning to face the fallen angel. He wore a suit and had opted for a tanned beach boy visage, although his horns peeked out of his dark hair. "Darian, if you ever need the Devil in a hurry, clicking your heels together three times and saying his name might actually work. There's always a chance you can capture the attention of a divine when you invoke their name. That's the core principle of summoning a divine successfully. The circles use that connection forged during a name invocation. If your circle is strong enough and you bring potent enough magic to the table, you might get the divine you invoked."

"Look at you, sharing forbidden lore with a susceptible little human. How naughty of you," the Devil purred.

"I see Darlene has been teaching you certain habits. You're not a cat."

"I got to enjoy my kitty last night. She was frisky for some reason."

"Well, when was the last time you fed her?"

"I may not have fed her as well as I could have. I enjoy when she gets clingy and demands attention aggressively."

The Devil would drive me to the end of my patience, and knowing him, he would shove me right over into the realm of the insane while laughing about it. "How can we help you?"

"I couldn't help but notice you two were gossiping about me."

"You're a hover uncle, aren't you?" I accused.

The Devil regarded his oxfords, which were polished to a high shine. "I do not seem to be hovering at this point in time."

"I'm pretty sure *somebody* would pay me a fortune to strangle you," I muttered.

With a laugh, Lucifer patted my shoulder. "My darling has been trying since the day she married me. Attempting the impossible amuses her. For some reason, her attempts at strangulation never get far. She has a short attention span, especially when she realizes her hands are close to my chest."

"I'm going to have to remind Darlene strangulations only work if she focuses her attention on the task rather than turning an attempted murder into a sexual assault." I loved the woman, but she might drive me almost as crazy as her husband.

"It's not assault if I like it, Diana."

"I'm going to need to be bribed to put up with you, Lucifer. Why are you interrupting our investigations?"

"I wouldn't call it interrupting."

"What would you call it, then?"

"Assisting." He pointed at the general direction of the obscured boxes. "You're about one step off from a shroud on that rune combination, by the way. I can take that off your hands and get the fingerprints checked. I have a few forensics investigators in need of some rehabilitation in residence, and I'm sure they'd love to dodge some torture in exchange for working diligently at identifying those fingerprints and doing lab work on your samples."

I narrowed my eyes. "Darian?"

"It's allowed, especially when he bargains with you for the work. He can't tell us directly, but he can provide a service. He'd trim the time down to a day rather than several days when using the sinners to get the intel we need. Then he can hand the mess over to an angel, which would then be admitted to the police. Obviously, whatever they're up to has the divines in an uproar, so they're doing what they can without violating the universal laws."

I expected my future would be filled with moments where I contemplated strangling the Devil because of the convoluted nature of the universal laws. "That definitely adds some weight to your theory, Darian. I'm not sure I like that."

"I definitely don't like it." Darian considered the Devil, his frown a match for mine. "Uncle, we aren't facing an End of Days scenario, are we?"

According to Lucifer's expression, Darian had hit the target dead center. "Right this moment, we are not."

"That sounds less than good. I don't want to end up like Kanika," I complained. "You gave her a complex."

"I didn't give her any complexes. She already had them. If anything, I've helped her get over some of her complexes. She no longer lives life looking over her shoulder afraid some assholes will try to sell her off into a marriage she doesn't want. If I'm not keeping the idiots at bay, Malcolm is—and Malcolm is very good at his job. It's not *my* fault she's a sphinx, and she's one of those annoying guardian ones. Now she views the entire planet as hers to protect. I'm constantly having to rein her in. I'm hoping you can help me rein her in, honestly. She will *not* be happy unless there's a permanent stay on the End of Days, and that's not how this works."

"How did I get brought into this?" I sighed. "Why did I accept that damned job promotion?"

"It doubled your salary, which meant you could move out of your tiny studio apartment into a house," the Devil reminded me. "You just didn't read the fine print or ask if you'd have excessive exposure to my majestic self."

Heaving another sigh, I gave in to the inevitable and said, "Okay. What do we need to bargain to get you to handle this matter?"

"Darlene thinks Kanika needs a sister, and your application has been approved. You can either choose adoption into the family or marriage into the family. I have plenty of single nephews, Darian here included."

I bowed my head, lifted a hand, and rubbed my temple in the futile hope of preventing the headache about to spring up and stab through my skull. "I'm supposed to be your secretary."

"You can still be my secretary, and frankly, I'd be forced to pay you even more as a result."

"I have two parents. Both of which are still alive and will remain alive. That means you can't go give them heart attacks. Despite our disagreements on certain elements of life, I do love them. They just make me want to indulge in an act of defenestration is all."

"Diana, they're assholes. Coming from me, that's saying a lot. Now, they do also love you, but this does not change their asshole tendencies. They're at least half the reason you're terrified of the water. Anyway, I'm a far better parent than them. I've decided I will collect children with asshole parents and prove I can be a far better asshole parent. It's my latest hobby. For once, my darling actually likes one of my hobbies. She just makes me get approval of the adoptee rather than tricking them. My little cupcake really doesn't mind having been tricked. She knows she's a wanted child. You, on the other hand, will be a trickier acquisition. You need special cultivation to fall in line with my plans."

"You are in dire need of a therapist." I sighed, took hold of the first box, and handed it off to the Devil. One by one, I stacked them on top until he couldn't cause me extra trouble without damaging anything. "In exchange for you handling this matter properly, I will consider your proposal in one way or another. I do not mind entering the dating pool, but having four parents would likely result in the compl—" I blinked. "Does that mean you'd come to the family dinners?"

"I fucking love family dinners," the Devil announced. "Especially when the other part of the family can't decide if they love or hate me."

What a demented, twisted being. "How about this as a bargain instead: you can come to Christmas dinner with three of your brothers, Kanika, Malcolm, and one guest of your choice and their family. The guest of your choice, assuming I am not in a relationship with someone, can be a gentleman you want me to try dating. Note, this person must be a *gentleman*."

"Incubi can be gentlemen, especially during religious holidays when they're given away as a gift to some deserving woman."

I narrowed my eyes. "I'm understanding the lure of your succubi scheme a little better than I did this morning, Darian."

Darian snickered. "It's a situation you both lose and win, right? But all you have to do is bring a date if you don't want some incubus being a gentleman with you after dinner. He might also find you a kelpie or a unicorn. They have a reputation, too."

"For some reason, I cultivated a lot of sex demons of various types. The unicorns are the most nurturing of them, though I have a few incubi who enjoy nothing more than pampering the women they're feeding from. They're lucky women, really. I really need to do something about my darling's brother. I did too good of a job adjusting his general temperament. If he gets much more nurturing, he'll cry if he can't be in a stable relationship. Why can't I kill him?"

"Darlene would cry," Darian replied. "Why not just partner him with a unicorn mare? That should keep him busy for a thousand years or so."

"I don't *have* any available unicorn mares that would partner well with him."

Darian huffed. "So make a new species the next time you have a chance to create a new seed. This should not be difficult. Why not an ice one? You have fire. Ice would be fun. Can we get back on subject now? Just accept her offer so we can get back to work. She's going to snap if we waste too much extra time before checking out the lab itself."

"Ah, yes. That reminds me." The Devil snapped his fingers and several cat carriers manifested and dropped to the ground. "You will need these."

Uh oh. "There are cats here?"

"There is a litter of kittens you can rescue. Their mother is in need of some tender loving care, and she could use help nursing them. You will find milk for their care in the carriers. That should keep you amused until you can take them to a shelter or decide to keep them."

I did not need an entire litter of kittens, but there was no way I was going to leave them or their mother to starve to death. "Let's find the kittens first, then we can go check out the lab, Darian."

The Devil pointed into the forest. "There is a utility shed that way. You will find the kittens and their mother inside."

"Was the mother part of the lab operations?" I asked.

"Yes."

That poor cat. "She's hurt enough she won't fight, isn't she?"

"It's nothing you can't handle. But I can tell you this much: if the assholes knew about her, she'd be as much of a target as your Mr. Flooferson."

I sucked in a breath. "You think we can figure out what's going on with her?"

"And you can do so with one additional present from me, but it will cost you."

Fuck. Yet another bargain. "How many times will I have to bargain with you?"

"As many times as needed for me to get what I want."

What an asshole. "I am not going to experiment on that poor cat!"

"You don't have to experiment on her. You have to love her, and then you have to run a touchless scanner over her and read the results. If the scanner requires blood, you need to just prick her shoulder long enough to get the sample. Then you can shower her with affection and rehabilitate her to your heart's content before finding her and her kittens an appropriate home."

I frowned, wondering if I'd be able to send off the poor cat to another home. "What breed is she?"

"She's a ragamuffin. The kittens are purebred, as her boyfriend was also a ragamuffin escapee. They opted for that breed in the lab due to their dispositions."

Fuck. There was a boy cat. "Where is her boyfriend?"

The Devil grimaced. "He had an unfortunate encounter with a mountain lion."

Oh. I joined him in grimacing. "Poor little guy. Okay. Momma cat and her kittens in the utility shed. What are you going to ask of me for the appropriate scanner?"

"Your soul would be nice, but I'll accept your agreement to listen to a proposal that should take approximately thirty minutes of your time."

At the rate the Devil usurped my time, I'd end up his minion through owed minutes. "I get to permanently keep the scanner."

"If you want to own the scanner, you must be able to provide ten good reasons, verifiable through a third-party arbitrator, to refuse my proposal. Otherwise, you must agree to it."

I foresaw coercion into marriage or adoption in my future. "The third-party arbitrator must be one of your archangel brothers, and it can't be Darian's father."

"Bargain made."

"You're going to get yourself into more trouble than you can get out of, Diana," Darian muttered.

"I'm a sucker for cats in need, and Mr. Flooferson needs a girlfriend. Except like Mr. Flooferson, she will no longer be able to produce little kittens after her litter is grown up and she can be spayed. Responsible cat ownership is important. I have no idea what I'm going to do with a litter of kittens, though."

"Beyond keep them and be overrun with cats?" Darian shrugged. "There are worse fates."

"Being overrun with cats is a concern," I confessed. "My house is not big enough for an entire murder of kittens."

"I don't think a group of cats is called a murder."

The Devil laughed. "No, it's not, but

frankly, if you're late with their supper, there *will* be a murder, so it's the most accurate statement regarding cats I've heard in a long time. Have fun, children. Go off and rescue your new family of cats before you go lab diving. I'll leave the scanner in your vehicle, and I'll even be a generous being and prepare their milk and use some magic to keep it the right temperature until needed. That's on the house, mainly because I don't want to hear any damned crying over your murder of kittens today, and if you have to figure out how to warm their milk while off in the middle of nowhere, there will be crying. It'll be the frustrated sort of crying, but I've had enough weeping for one week."

I could make a guess what had gotten the Devil riled up. "Darlene got upset about the cancer and cried, didn't she?"

"It's like you've met my wife before. There is very little in the universe I cannot handle with grace. My wife crying is one of those things. My daughter crying is another one of those things. Fortunately, my wife and daughter usually cry from frustration, but I've learned my lesson: my wife will not learn about the kittens until they're happily in *your* custody, so they don't end up in *my* custody."

I grinned. "She'd make you rescue and keep them, wouldn't she?"

"And a lot of the pets we have in our

house are immortal pets who will not die of natural causes until my darling breathes her last. It amuses me that my darling has not quite realized the extent of her lifespan at this point in time. When she figures it out, I am sure she will be extra vicious when she gets her hands on me. I'm looking forward to it."

Of course. The Devil was an eternal pervert. That much I'd figured out on my own. "You owe me for taking the cats so you don't have to. Make it something good, and since Darian has to help care for these cats, he is owed as well."

"Clever girl." The Devil vanished, leaving me with a mess of cat carriers.

I checked inside each one until I found a frightening number of nursing bottles and enough formula to sink a battleship. "How many kittens are in this litter?"

Darian counted bottles. "I'm guessing thirteen."

"That poor momma. So many mouths to feed!" I grabbed two of the carriers and left the formula out where the Devil could make use of it. "Move it, Darian. We have kittens to rescue."

THE BROKEN RUINS of a greenhouse drew me to a halt, and Darian locked onto the utility shed nearby. "Hey, Darian? Do you think that greenhouse was for drug operations?"

"Definitely, and it was probably built to grow marijuana. It loves the mountains up here, so they'd be able to set up a good operation around here. It would make for a decent cover story if nobody looked too carefully at the place." He opened the door, and something inside hissed. "Goodness, she's fluffy. And matted. And angry."

"Well, you're near her kittens." I hurried over and peeked into the shed while Darian checked the place over with a flashlight. The cat, a pale-coated fluffy, matted mess, cowered in a corner with a bunch of furry wiggly bodies surrounding her.

Bye-bye, heart. Hello, vet bill for fourteen or so felines.

"I'm going to need a really big raise to take care of these cats," I muttered, grimacing at the filth covering the floor. "And a new pair of shoes. I don't even want to think about what I'm stepping in. I'm going to end up bargaining away my soul for clean clothes. And that's with these stupid booties on. Obviously, whatever is on this floor is going to eat through the booties."

"I'm more concerned with how to catch

the cat without the cat tearing us a new one," he replied.

I handed my extra carrier over to Darian and stepped deeper into the shed. "Close the door behind me so she can't escape. This looks intact enough it shouldn't be easy for her to get out, right?"

"Here's hoping."

The cat carriers would need to be purified, preferably with fire, after touching the shed's floor, but I'd cross that bridge later, after I caught the cat and herded her kittens. With luck, I could fit everyone inside one carrier temporarily, separating them only as needed while driving.

"Poor sweetheart," I cooed to the animal, opening the door and pointing the interior in her general direction. "Darian, arm yourself with a carrier or two and basically stand behind me, so she hopefully won't go past us. I'd like to get her into the carrier first, then we'll move the kittens in."

"She looks exhausted and thin. I doubt she's going to put up much of a fight."

Beneath her matted fur, I suspected he was right. Careful to keep my movements slow and smooth, I approached, set the carrier on the ground, and waited to see what she would do.

The cat limited her protests to hisses and trying her best to keep between us and her kittens. While shoveling the cat and kittens into the carrier bothered me, the tactic worked. I risked life and limb to scoop the extra kittens into their containment vessel, earning several scratches and a bite for my efforts. Everybody fit into one carrier, and I worried at how little the momma cat seemed to weigh.

"I hope Lucifer is bringing food for her," I muttered, grimacing at the filth on my gloved hands and my arms. "And possibly antibiotics to keep me from catching my death. I don't want to catch my death."

"I'm sure Lucifer will take care of your health once you're done contracting various diseases rescuing these cats." Darian took the carrier from me and hauled the hissing momma and her mewling babies out of the shed. "It seems he really wants us to find this lab, as I couldn't help but notice there's a suspicious square in the floor that you uncovered shuffling around to get to the kittens. By directing you to the cats, he probably made it so we could find that rather suspicious square."

I checked, and sure enough, I spotted an indentation in the floor in the shape of a trap door. "That is going to be so gross lifting that up."

Grunting, he shouldered through the door and waited for me to follow. "There's a crowbar near the door, so it should be all right. I'm going to bathe in sanitizer later, though."

"Me, too. I can help carry them."

"You could, but you won't. You might injure your chest. You can do the thinking, I'll handle the manual labor. However, as I'm not an idiot, I won't try to bar you from feeding the hungry kittens. It'll be tough enough making sure everybody is fed as it is."

"I can accept that."

The Devil waited at our rental, and he had set up a black plastic and mesh pen, which had a covered top to prevent any furry escapees. When I approached, he handed me a pad of paper and several permanent markers in various colors. Aware the Devil didn't do anything without a good reason, I put his gifts in my pocket.

He announced, "You'll need these. I have put puppy training pads in your vehicle along with food and water for your queen, and I've also provided everything else these feline entities will require while you're adventuring. My wife has taken the liberty of providing a list of emergency vet clinics in the area so you might choose one."

I read between the lines: if I knew what was good for me, I would be taking my new murder of kittens to a vet as soon as we finished at the lab. "What will I have to bargain for a full cleaning after we're done in the lab?"

The Devil gave a sniff. "That will be a gift, for my delicate sensibilities would be sorely offended should you catch some illness from your adventures. As such, I will check in with you when you're done with your base explorations and abuse my holy fire in amusing fashions. I'll even make one of my brothers watch, as you should be checked for any complications."

"I'll put in a good word with your wife, which should be approximately equal."

"If you do that, I'll owe you," Lucifer complained. "She likes you more than she likes me right now."

Darlene never failed to amuse me, especially when it came to her hot and cold treatment of her husband, who adored her no matter what her mood happened to be. However, she tried to be reasonable—usually. "You told her she couldn't have any of the kittens, didn't you?"

"I did. It's her fault she's going to be hungry and cranky in a few days, as I have been banished to the couch. Really, I like you a lot right now, as my cranky and hungry wife shows off her wings *and* her spots when she goes on a hunt. If I talk about how wretchedly adorable the kittens are where she can hear me, she'll likely hold out for a week or two, which means she won't be hiding even a single spot from me."

"You have a serious obsession with her spots. I'm sure there is a therapist somewhere who can help you with that problem. You could take two and have more immortal kittens running around your house. It's not like I won't have extras."

"Wicked woman, suggesting I should bring two more terrors into my home! I already have two furry terrors, and they always side with my wife. Sometimes, they pretend to like me. But that is only sometimes."

I crouched and peeked into the carrier, where the momma cat cowered in the back while the kittens, old enough to have their eyes open, rolled over each other in the tight space. Most were pale with colored points, although there were two orange tabbies and one calico. "You can't have the calico. She's mine. You can't have the momma cat, either. She's also mine." I considered the wretchedly cute and filthy animals in the carrier. "Can you abuse your holy fire to clean their fur? That would be worth me putting in an almost good word for you while I gush about my new kittens."

"I appreciate your ruthlessness in negotiations. Yes, this is an acceptable bargain. Do go about your investigative work, children. I will handle caring for your new friends in the meantime. Go ahead and take your time. Go on. Shoo, shoo."

Darian regarded the Devil with a raised brow before he sighed, set the rest of the carriers down, and headed off in the direction of the shed and greenhouse. "Come on, Diana. It's going to be a long night unless the first batch of investigators did a better job of cleaning up after themselves."

The Devil waved as we left. "Have fun storming the castle, kids!"

TEN

"Your mother is a marvel."

DARIAN HAULED up the trap door, revealing a wide staircase descending deep beneath the ground. His flashlight revealed a landing some thirty feet down, which turned and disappeared into the darkness. "Well, whoever built this meant business. How the hell did they do such a massive concrete pour with nobody catching on?"

"I'm going to bet it has something to do with the several miles of road through the forest we needed to navigate to get here." I tested the first step, which held up as I expected from concrete. "Despite being aware of the reality of things like this happening from working in the CDC, the reality is not what I was expecting."

"What were you expecting?"

"Something more along the lines of a warehouse hidden in a busy port, where nobody would notice anything weird coming from the place. That has been the kind of stuff to cross my desk on the way to my bosses. Not a hidden lab deep in the woods hidden beneath some damned garden shed." I scowled. "And now I'm extra mad at them because of the cats."

"Mr. Flooferson's situation angered you, but seeing more than one cat caught up in this mess made it real, which in turn has angered you even more?" Darian guessed.

Damn. Darian must have done some psychology studying—or I had zero ability to hide my state of mind from him. "Something like that. I might also be cranky because my chest aches somewhat."

"And you probably underwent hormonal adjustments while they were at it, so you're primed to be cranky. Dad is constantly monitoring Mom, and he warns me when she's getting an adjustment, so I don't get into more trouble than I usually do. Apparently, women are gloriously complicated, and I should be aware that this complexity could result in the loss of my fragile life, should I anger the wrong woman at the wrong time."

I laughed at the thought of one of the Devil's generals warning his son about the perils of his hormonal mother and other women. To spare him from the details of how my hormones could transform me into an ice-cream binging monster several days of every month, I asked, "Keeping the limitations of your magic in mind, what do we need to find here to get us to our next location?"

"The paperwork and vials we found here will help. For example, I can make a trail that will lead us to other chemicals made in the same batch. Fluids like that don't tend to count as living beings, much like your cat's fur. If I can get a list of locations to exclude, my trail would only take us to samples that *aren't* in the CDC's hands. That would stand a good chance of getting us to where we need to go."

"Could you find someone based on their blood?" I asked. "Like, let's say I cut myself and left some blood on the ground. Could you use that to find me?"

"I could use it to find another source of the same blood, so if you were having your period and I used your blood to track you, I could find you that way, yes. Or if you cut yourself and left blood somewhere."

I went down a few steps, turned, and raised a brow. "How do you know that?"

"Those are the only ways I can find a missing person. As for figuring that out, you can thank my mother. She was curious and had me do the experiment. I'm sometimes called in if they expect a body or violence. If I have a blood sample of the missing person, I *can* go to another blood sample. I've found murder sites that way before. The blood doesn't count as the person if it's not still in the person. Once it's been spilled, it's just another lifeless liquid. Once my mother clued into that, I did some experimentation, and that seems to be my limit. As far as wayfinders go, I'm not all that impressive, but I'm good if you're trying to solve a murder mystery and there's a blood sample. I've found corpses by their hair before. After a while, the hair on the corpse no longer classifies as a person, but that's usually a day or two following brain death. Hair doesn't really keep growing for long after death. People just think it does because the other cells are retracting as part of the putrefaction process."

"I guess I won't be growing epically long hair after death, then?"

"You would not be growing a mane, I'm afraid. That's just a myth. My mother was really disappointed to hear that. She tried to convince my father to perform a miracle so she could have her hair continue to grow after death. He refuses."

"Your mother is a marvel." I resumed descending, taking my time so I wouldn't trip, fall, and bash my brains out on the landing below. "I find the lack of railing in here to be disturbing."

"Railings would make it harder to move equipment in and out. I bet there's a larger trap door around the one we used to give space for equipment. The steps would make it tricky but doable, unless they have some massive pieces in here. Who knows? The equipment is probably long gone, claimed as a part of evidence. I'm not expecting to find much, and I'll be looking for fingerprints to help give us more information on who might have been involved with the operation. If we're lucky, we'll find some paperwork that was obscured. That'll be your job once we locate the lab."

We turned the landing, which continued deep into the ground. "I feel like I should have asked if they were doing contagious disease experimentation on my cat now. Or if we're likely to be targeted with a bunch of bombs. This deep, do you think we'd survive through a bombing?"

"That's a really good question. Also, I agree. You should have asked. But if it was some form of contagious disease, wouldn't there have been warning signs outside warning of plague or contagion? They have plague markers up in the mountains because of the rodent populations, so it would make sense they'd warn people if there was plague here."

I contemplated bolting for the safety of the SUV and taking a turn caring for the kittens and momma cat. "It's dark, and this is not the kind of scary story I want to hear in the dark, Darian."

"I'd claim to protect you, but honestly, I'm kicking myself for only having brought one flashlight." He directed the beam onto the ground. "In good news, this section seems clean of animals. It's pretty tidy for something that's been covered up for at least a year."

I halted, crouched, and touched the concrete. Dust clung to my fingers. "There's some dust."

Darian pointed the light at the ceiling, which proved to be of more concrete. "Maybe some leftover bugs from when the lab was in use? Or the concrete has broken some during earthquakes?"

As I could buy into the earthquake theory, I decided to do my best to keep from thinking about what might have produced the dust on the steps. Rising to my feet, I resumed heading deeper. "If I see any centipedes, I'm out of here, Darian. You will have to battle it on your own. And if I faint because of some damned centipede, just let me crack my head open or something. I'll deserve my fate."

"I hope you can settle with me trying to catch you before battling the centipede. I might not battle it, though. I might just leave. I could be talked into taking you with me when I leave."

I grinned. "If I faint and you have to rescue me from a centipede, it seems reasonable you can make demands. Otherwise, my gravestone will inform the world I was killed by a bug."

"But it's a bug with way too many legs. It also is out to kill anything in its path, and they are the definition of terror. If I see a centipede, I'm leaving. I'll be valiant and take you with me, however."

"I also dislike scorpions."

"I am sensing a trend," Darian stated, and he pointed his flashlight at his chin in an attempt to make himself appear spooky. For the most part, it worked. "Creepy crawlies that are venomous scare you because you're a sensible human being."

"And I refuse to test if they're poisonous. I absolutely refuse. I don't care if you dunk them in chocolate and wrap that mess up in bacon. I will not eat venomous bugs in an attempt to determine if they're also poisonous."

"As I said. You're a sensible human being. However, why would you put bacon and chocolate together?"

"Because it's good?"

Darian gasped. "But why would you do that to *bacon*?"

"Have you never had chocolate and bacon together?"

"Never."

"It's good." I grinned and continued down the steps. "So is candied bacon, and so is regular bacon. Chocolate is good in most of its forms as well."

"I like bacon, and I like chocolate, but I am not sure if I want to try bacon and chocolate together. That said, I am far more willing to try bacon and chocolate together than I am to eat a centipede or a scorpion."

"I am not ready to start eating bugs."

"But what about shrimp or lobster?" Darian narrowed his eyes. "I really like shrimp and lobster. Technically, they're bugs."

"Why won't you try other bugs if you like some bugs, then?" I smirked, well aware I could do hefty damage to a cocktail ring given half a chance. "Are you a selective bug hunter?"

"Yes, I am. I like when my bugs come from the ocean. It makes them special bugs and defy the rules of all other bugs. It could be I just really like salt, and they're properly brined for my enjoyment. Watch your step. It looks like somebody dropped something heavy and broke the concrete ahead of you."

Sure enough, one of the steps had seen better days, and I crouched on the step above it to get a better view. Whatever had hit the step had done a good job of exposing the steel support wires in the concrete. I pointed at the bent metal. "Maybe the dust is just from whatever did this. That took a lot of force. It bent the metal, too."

Darian joined me, and he touched the ground before rubbing the dust between his fingers. "I don't suppose any of your practitioner tricks can capture reflections from the past? I'm now really curious what caused this."

"Unfortunately not. You could probably ask your father, though."

"I could, but the chances he'd answer me are pretty slim."

"Nothing ventured, nothing gained." I hopped over the damaged stair and resumed my journey to the next landing. "What the hell? It's going down even farther. What *is* this place?"

"A very deep lab, apparently. We must be at least fifty feet down by now. There's actually a logical explanation for doing that," Darian announced, joining me. "After about forty feet, the temperature becomes consistent underground. Oxygen, however, becomes an issue. Can you use practitioner magic to make sure we get fresh air down here?"

"Actually, yes. That I can do." Chuckling over how easy the Devil made it for me to use my magic for that purpose, I took one of the sheets of paper from the pad and drew a rune representing air and a second one representing a light wind before binding the two together with a drawing of a chain. I concentrated and waved the paper back and forth until it began to produce a gentle breeze. I offered the sheet to Darian. "You can just put it in your pocket or something. No need for it to be out. It'll last until you break the chain."

"How do those runes produce fresh air?" He took the paper from me, examining the drawings. "Actually, what are these runes? I don't recognize either of them."

"Wind and air. They're an older form of practitioner magic—think Biblical times older. I had to learn older rune sets, and the older they get, the closer to the elemental sources they go. I'm tapping the elements themselves with those runes, which is why the air will be fresh." I pointed at one of the exterior circles I'd drawn around the rune for air. "This is a symbol for renewal, which I combined with air, which translates to fresh air we can breathe. Intent matters as much as the runes or symbols drawn."

"These runes don't use squared edges," he noted.

"That's because they aren't that sort of rune. Squared edges were easier to chisel into stone or wood. These were originally drawn into sand or mud. It's also a lot faster to draw in a hurry. Straight lines aren't as friendly when you're trying to work magic;

going off kilter can create problems, where curved lines are friendlier when you toss magic into the fray. I *do* know some workings that require straight lines, but I get out the tools when I need to work on those. That's how you summon demons like your dad without having a way to contain them, Darian."

"Do you think my mother really drew a squiggle when she meant a straight line and summoned Dad?"

"I think she had no idea what she was actually doing and played with magic she should not have been playing with. It could have gone very differently for your mother if she'd summoned another demon or devil. There are plenty in the many hells that would have eaten her, spit out the bones, and destroyed the circle to make certain nobody repeated that trick. The only smart thing she did was summon your father to help contain your dad, really. But I do admire the amount of power and skill required to make that sort of mistake."

"I'm telling Mom she's never allowed to be left alone in a dark room with chalk and candles ever again. I like my mother and do not want her to be eaten by some demon that's not my dad."

I laughed at the innuendo. "She reeks of devil and archangel; the worst that would happen to her is a kidnapping, and Belial wouldn't let that stand for long. Demons and devils generally aren't *stupid*, and they won't hurt the mortal member of a triad. That's how you trigger an unauthorized End of Days. That's also how to lose favor with the Devil, and he takes his triads seriously. I think, in some ways, the triads are how the Devil fulfills his basic needs to be a family man," I admitted. "I don't recommend following in your mother's footsteps as a general rule."

"Oh, trust me. If I'm going to summon somebody, I'll be doing it very deliberately, I will have the appropriate bribes, and I'll be prepared to make the most of my summoning. I mean, it worked pretty well for my mother."

"You're going to bite off more than you can chew," I warned.

"Should I take that route, I will do so with the utmost care."

Of course he would. I shook my head, made a mental note to talk to the Devil about his nephew's desire to create a disaster, and continued into the depths. Two more landings and at least a hundred feet later, we came to a set of steel double doors which were cracked open. Thanks to my rune, the air remained fresh, but thick layers of dust coated the floor beyond.

Cages, some of them occupied with skeletal remains, lined the walls, reminding me of a sterile shelter. The animal shelter cages, however, offered the animals far more space. The ones containing cats included a small litter box.

I clenched my teeth, and my cheek twitched.

"I wish I could say I'm surprised. I'm really not. I don't even want to know if they were already dead or dying when this place was busted." Darian cringed. "My bet is on dying and couldn't be saved, so euthanized and left in the cages where they died."

"That's horrible."

"And the theory plays very well to the concern of some contagion; I can't imagine why the animals would have been left like that unless there was some concern of a contagion that could spread to people, so they likely just gassed them and left the bodies to rot. They may have cracked open the door later to confirm the animals had died."

"Wouldn't that make this dangerous to go into?"

"They would have neutralized the toxins after making sure the animals were dead."

"That's even worse."

"They were probably beyond saving, and it was less traumatizing for them to just kill them in the cages without rounding them up and traumatizing them even further. I don't like it, but I can understand it. Cats like your Mr. Flooferson would have been taken for medical care and put in a shelter's care while the others were left to die."

"Wouldn't that shoot down the contagion concern, though? If the animals were contagious, why would they rescue some and not others?"

Darian shrugged. "It's just a possibility. With the mix of science and magic available, it's not exactly hard to treat sick animals. If there was a contagion, they would care for the ones they thought they could save and leave the rest. It's a lot harder to make sure contagion stays with the corpses than it is to dump a bunch of angry cats and dogs into some neutralizer and force feed them the treatments. Leaving them to stay down here, sealed, would solve a lot of problems. The contagion would die out on its own over time. And that's *if* that's the case."

"I find the possibility disturbing at best, but that I find it plausible is giving me a serious case of the creeps."

"I feel the same way. Until we can evaluate what's in those vials, pretending a contagion took out the animals is the safest. Or some form of poison."

"Well, there was that case of somebody developing aerial rabies," I muttered, shaking my head over the audacity that someone would try to weaponize rabies, something easily treated with neutralizer. "Outside of having to hire a lot of pixies to cover the unexpected demands for pixie dust, a mass outbreak of rabies would not have been all that bad after it had been diagnosed. The human race would be pink and sparkly for a while, but the contagious could have been contained and cured, although there would have been major changes to how neutralizer was manufactured to make up for the increased supply and demand. There would have been a problem for two or three months, but that strain of rabies had a long onset time. Once diagnosed? It would have been eradicated quickly. The CDC is taking steps to make sure it's possible to respond to a large-scale incident of that nature without any disruptions. That's a major project one of my bosses has been working on lately. If the contagion is treatable with neutralizer, it won't be much of a problem."

"Well, at least *something* is going right in the world."

I shrugged. "Unless your theory on lycanthropy is correct, as that's one of the few things neutralizer *can't* stop."

"Maybe they're trying to end the world through overpopulation? Lycanthropy heavily extends someone's lifespan. The planet can't sustain the entire human race should they become lycanthropes. There would be mass food shortages."

That was something I could readily believe. "What does it say about me that I'm scared to go into this lab?"

"Well, in good news, lycanthropy doesn't survive all *that* long on surfaces. A week or two at most unless it's in a special solution."

I considered Darian with interest. "How did you learn that?"

"My parents suggested I should educate myself on the various ways I could be rid of my base humanity. My dad likes the idea of me undergoing a conversion to become some form of demon. My father just shrugs and tells me I'm an adult, and if I want to contract a contagious disease, that's my business and not his. My mother just likes the idea of me living forever and taking over the world. I have not told her I'm not really interested in living forever *or* taking over the world. I wouldn't mind an extended lifespan, though. I enjoy living."

"I enjoy living, too. Some days, I feel like I'm an exception to the rule on this one. However, I've noticed I work too much and don't do much actual living, so I feel like I'm not living my best life or living life for somebody else." I frowned. "Which doesn't help me resist the Devil's various temptations. Or other certain temptations, like brutally slaughtering the assholes who did this to these poor animals."

"Yeah. I'm not usually the kind to want to kill people, but I am having some rather nasty urges right now. Unless we're dealing with something like gorgon dust, we should be safe enough from whatever was in here. It's been well over a year."

"And if it was gorgon dust, there wouldn't be any skeletons; everything would be stone." As I was a brave, confident woman who could handle anything life threw my way, I shoved the door open. I winced at the grind of metal on concrete. The dust swirled around my feet. Darian swept his flashlight over the room, which had hundreds of cages lining the walls and a few examination tables waited. Like everything else, those were covered in dust, and one of them held the bones of an animal. "Why would they just leave that poor thing like that?"

"If I had to make a guess, it died while they were trying to save it, or they put it out of its misery while setting up to euthanize the other animals. If they opted to leave the bodies, that's a sound enough theory. It could have already been dead when they arrived, too."

"Think if I summon your father and use my magic to bind him to seeking out justice for these poor animals, he would one day forgive me and *not* kill me for having done it?"

Darian pointed the flashlight in my general direction, although he was careful to keep the beam out of my eyes. "Diana, if you do that and get away with it, I'd be forced to propose to you in increasingly embarrassing fashions until you agreed. First, that sort of power is ridiculous. Mom was able to summon my dad, but she had no ability to actually *control* him—or make any demands of him. That's why she panicked and summoned my father. Who she couldn't actually control, either. The two of them just found her hilarious to the point they fell for her charms. I'm very grateful she summoned them rather than the other options. There are some archangels who would have taken her straight to the Devil for some scolding. She may have still been alive when they took her down to his many hells. Or not. Depends on which one she'd snagged. Some days, when my fathers annoy her, she bitches she hadn't snagged an incubus instead; at least if the incubus had broken out of the circle, she would have been guaranteed a great time before coming to a swift demise."

"Would an incubus actually kill her?"

"No, but she'd have a lot more than one kid by the time he finished with her. It's a vicious circle that tends to backfire." Darian snickered. "When she pulls that stunt, Dad just asks how many more kids she wants. But, yeah. Dad would definitely play ball with you if you summoned him for that purpose, but you'd have to do an exceptional job on the seal to actually avoid him breaking out of it. He's one step below Lucifer."

"I feel like Lucifer deserves to be summoned and bound, and once I had him where I wanted him, I'd call Darlene and demand a vacation for his safe return, but I would invite her to do what she wanted with him while I had him down."

"And that's how you become Darlene's friend for life."

The problem with magic was the temptation of its use. "I wouldn't, though. I could, but I won't."

"With great power comes great responsibility?"

"Not even. With great power comes greater consequence, and every action has a consequence. It is human nature to attempt to surpass one's limits. Right now, I'm confident I *could* do that—but I won't. I would look to see who—or what—I could summon next. Some things are best left buried—which was why I had no problems telling your father to make that book disappear."

"Because they taught you how?"

"In part. I think that book is how power stays balanced—the buck *doesn't* stop with the divines. People like me exist. And that scares me on a good day."

"And on a bad one?"

I glared at the skeletal remains in the

cages filling the room. "On a bad day, I consider doing it for the sake of long-dead cats and dogs who will never witness justice."

"I think you will find *Him* a compassionate being. The universe has a way of repaying those who have suffered in the next life. Just think about the better futures they'll likely get. In the meantime, let's see what we can find in this mausoleum."

CAGES AND CORPSES filled most of the lab with several rooms we determined to be for operations and experimentations on the unfortunate animals in residence. Unlike the trailers, the lab had been completely cleaned out and swept of fingerprints. Even with his magic, Darian couldn't find a single one to lift with his kit.

"Damn it," he growled.

"We'll have to hope we find something in the papers we found in the trailers. I'll check the place for anything hidden. There might be stuff in the cabinets." Every cabinet we'd checked had been opened and empty, but we hadn't pawed through them or done more than a visual inspection or checked for fingerprints using Darian's magic.

My magic might tell a different tale, and I took one of the scraps of paper, grabbed a pale marker, and debated how best to draw the symbol to sweep through the whole place and reveal its secrets—if there were any secrets to reveal. The runes obscuring the boxes in the trailers had been potent enough, so I went for intricate, complicated, and thorough, playing off what I'd drawn to bring fresh air into the lab and casting a wide net. In the two symbols, which I drew on top of each other, I added one more, the simplest of the runes at my disposal.

An incomplete circle could be used for many things, but it worked best for me when I used it to break bindings—or to lure unsuspecting entities into a trap.

I drew a single, red line diagonally across the gap in the circle so it couldn't be closed and would reveal dark secrets, inhaled, and gave the paper a shake before releasing it.

A gust of wind burst from the sheet, and it spun in the air, as though it'd been caught up in some twister. I expected the dust to swirl, but my magic flattened it to the floor. Blue flame engulfed my hands before sweeping out to the paper and devouring it. Light spilled throughout the lab, a gentle radiance imbuing everything. Most of it faded, leaving a few glimmers in a cabinet and within one of the cages.

The cage lacked a skeleton, to my relief, and I investigated to discover some intact, dust-covered fur from the previous resident.

Darian followed me, and he gathered the sample in a bag.

"Can you use that fur to find similar fur, like you can with blood?"

"As a matter of fact, yes. It can get complicated, and the fur can't still be attached to the animal it belongs to, but we might find somewhere else to go after we're finished here from this sample."

While he labeled the bag with the fur sample, I checked the glowing cabinet. The light enveloped a box-shaped object affixed to the bottom of a shelf. I touched, discovered something hard and metallic, and gave a brisk rub to wipe away any obscuring runes on the surface. The ploy worked, and a shimmering shroud flashed before revealing the case beneath, some twenty inches long, a foot wide, and four or so inches thick. It rested in a bracketed shelf, and I slid it out. Dust shed from its surface, revealing several other runes, which I wiped away. "They had a decent practitioner, but their practitioner was either overconfident, or this was their best trick."

"Why do you say that?"

"No traps." The magic I'd worked would have turned anything malicious red to match the color marker I'd used. "They either trusted their obscuration—to the point of being a low-grade shroud—to protect their secrets, or they pushed the extent of their abilities. This level of obscuration working is no joke. It's not the same level as what the divines use, but it's no surprise to me this stayed a secret." I placed the box on one of the examination tables, drawing a second working to make certain I'd run into no surprises. Like the first paper, it burst into blue fire. The metal remained unchanged, and I eased the lid up.

A haphazard mess of documents greeted me, and beneath them, I located another collection of liquid-filled vials of varying colors. "Well, I'm going to have to go make sure the Devil gets me a real damned good meter. We're going to need it. And a way to get samples out of this without unleashing whatever the hell this substance is. I don't suppose you have any contacts who run labs? The CDC won't give us the results, neither will the police. They'll lock it down for certain."

"Yes, I have a contact, but she's not cheap. Worse, she's an elf. Well, half-elf. That's just as bad, really."

I raised a brow at that. "You know Missy?" Everyone who was anybody in the CDC knew about Missy. Nobody dared to piss off the lycanthrope, who acted far more like an elf than any wolf. Where Missy went, her mother wasn't far behind, and nobody screwed around with a lonely full-blooded elf. When the two paired up, trouble happened—and the other elves came out to play.

When the other elves came out to play, somehow, I got roped into self-defense courses. The last time I'd been tossed to an elf, I'd drawn the short lot and gotten Samantha. In exchange for practitioner magic lessons, I'd gotten off lightly.

I'd learned to dance rather than fight, but the elf promised all I would need to become a tolerable fighter would be a few weeks and a weapon.

"I know Missy. Wait. You know Missy?"

"Worse, I know Samantha."

Darian made a gesture to ward against evil. "I, too, know Samantha. Dad worried I wouldn't be able to take care of myself. As such, Father asked Samantha for a favor. Samantha thought it was adorable there was an archangel bold enough to ask *her* for a favor. She had me for two weeks. I almost died."

I laughed. "She had me for a month spread out over the course of a year, and she taught me how to dance. She was supposed to teach me how to defend myself, but I'm either hopeless or she just was tired of teaching fighting. I actually really like Samantha. Missy is a piece of work, though. I actually really like her, but she's psychotic. If you can talk with Missy, just tell her you're working with me. She'll probably give you a break on the bill. We just have to hope she doesn't call her mother. If she calls her mother, she might call Samantha, too. If she calls Samantha, we might have to run away. Quickly. With Samantha, the longer we evade her, the happier she is. We need that head start, Darian."

"Yes, we do. And if you agree to undergo a conversion, Samantha would be a good teacher for you. I approve."

Interesting. "Why?"

"Well, you won't be a wilting lily if Samantha is teaching you."

That was true. "Once we're upstairs, I'll give her a call."

"Okay, there's crazy, and then there's flat-out insanity. Calling Samantha is insane. It's the definition of insane. Calling her means she might show up."

"That is the idea." I gestured to the cages, which easily numbered in the thousands once I added all the research rooms in the labyrinth of a lab. "I'm going to tell her about this, and I'm going to tell her I wish to make even elves proud of me when I'm finished with these bastards."

"That's how you sign yourself up for weapons training."

"Yes, and?"

"That's how you sign *me* up for weapons training, Diana."

I shrugged. "Some prices are worth paying."

"That is absolutely ruthless. No wonder the Devil wants you as his secretary. I don't want to be tenderized before being eaten by an elf. I barely survived my first round with her."

"But did you die?"

"Not quite, but it was close."

"Don't be such a baby about this." I closed the box, secured it, and did a walk-through of the rest of the lab. My magic revealed nothing else. "Let's get back to the surface before the Devil convinces himself he needs to steal my kittens. I'm only keeping the momma cat and the calico, as three cats seems like a reasonable number of cats. And the calico is really cute."

"All kittens are really cute."

Smiling, I nodded. "Mr. Flooferson is especially cute, and I will always love him the best. As such, I must prove my love and devotion by making elves proud of my brutality when I bring this operation to its knees."

"Please don't end the world acquiring justice for your cat. I like living."

"So do I, so I will do my best to avoid such a thing. That said, I might take a page out of Darlene's book and take over the Devil's many hells for a while if I need to. I bet Darlene would cooperate, and she could lure the Devil off to *His* place for a while. I can take over while they're out. Hey, think your dad would help out? If I have a general backing me, I might actually get away with it."

"I'm fairly sure Dad will only help if I'm joining in. He's been trying to corrupt me for a while."

"Sure, you can help. I'm not above manipulating you to get access to your dad. I'll ask your father to help keep them upstairs for a little while longer so I have time to finish my plans. He'll be into that, right? By doing so, he helps secure justice for the helpless, and that seems like his sort of thing."

"It really is."

"Good. We have kittens to take to the vet, a meter to coerce out of the Devil, and work to do. Let's get this show on the road."

ELEVEN

"Only little demonesses or devils may take over my hells for any period of time."

THE DEVIL HANDED me one of the CDC's best scanners before I had a chance to ask for it. "You may not take over my many hells, but you may have this meter instead. It is yours to keep. But you may not evict me from my home."

Damn. He must have been snooping. "I'd only need five or six hours to lay down the foundations for my plan."

"Only little demonesses or devils may take over my hells for any period of time."

I considered. "You have me for a set period of time to job pitch and give me life advice. You can try your best to convince me then. I'm not sure I'd make a good unicorn, though. I know that will disappoint you."

"You'd make a terrible unicorn, but I have a few ideas of the equine bent you'd enjoy. Demonic in nature, with an even longer lifespan than my unicorns. Well, demonic with a twist."

Raising a brow, I considered the Devil before putting the metal box we'd found in the back of the SUV and checking on the kittens and momma cat, which were locked in the play pen. "What do you mean by demonic with a twist?"

"That's for me to know and you to find out."

"I'll keep that in mind." I eyed the meter, sighing as I'd already accepted the damned thing, thus rendering me technically unable to take over the Devil's house per my original plan. "We can talk about a temporary takeover later. More accurately, I'll talk to Darlene about a temporary takeover."

"You are so going to hell," Lucifer informed me.

"Surprisingly, I had figured that out at this stage. I may as well earn it. Can we do the health checkup so we can get the cats to the vet?"

The Devil reached into his pocket, sent a text, and a few moments later, Gabriel manifested nearby. I appreciated the efficiency of the divine, although I suspected it would take at least ten minutes for my heart rate to come back down to something sane.

Then, because Lucifer could be the crowned ruler over all assholes when he wanted, he opted to remove the evidence of having gotten into a fight with a murder of filthy kittens through unexpected exposure to flame. The heat stung enough I yelped, although the blue fire didn't burn me.

Rather than curse or indulge in my desire to participate in some wholesome violence, I turned to the archangel. "Hello, Gabriel," I greeted. "How did you get suckered into doing the Devil's dirty work tonight?"

"I have a soft spot for kittens."

Of course he did. "I'm planning on keeping the calico and the momma cat, but the other kittens will be in need of a good home once they're old enough to be separated from their mother safely. If an archangel can't help find good homes for these kittens, can any being possibly do it better?"

Lucifer cleared his throat.

Ignoring the Devil—and resisting the urge to roll my eyes—tested me, but I kept my attention focused on the archangel. My awareness of the nature of his shroud created a unique problem with him, one I hadn't suffered through with Raguel.

I could see the shimmering barrier safeguarding me from the reality of his visage.

As I didn't wish for my life to end prematurely, I focused my gaze on his chest. "Why don't archangels have nipples, anyway?"

Lucifer crowed his laughter, and to my amusement, Gabriel also chuckled.

"I don't see what's so funny," I admitted.

"My brother's wife is very serious about her enjoyment of male nipples, and she is forever complaining I do not have appropriate nipples for her voyeuristic enjoyment. If you would like me to make arrangements for the kittens to find good homes when the time comes, I would be pleased to help you with this endeavor." The archangel pointed at two of the paler animals. "Lucifer, these two beasts would fit well in your home. Their natures are troublesome, and your wife will believe you are not bringing home kittens, for you have already told her no, and she does not believe you are capable of lying to her."

The Devil snickered. "What does *He* want?"

"The usual."

"We just visited two weeks ago," Lucifer complained.

Gabriel shrugged. "You know how *He* gets. *He* has noticed your interest in the mortals."

"Mortals is plural."

Both Lucifer and Gabriel pointed at Darian, who heaved a sigh and bowed his head. "My fathers are sentimental, which means it's going to be bad enough once my mother passes on that the rest of the divine family is likely eyeballing ways to make me live a horrendously long time. I'm sorry, Diana."

"Why are you sorry? The last I checked, they were trying to imply we should team up, and I'm supposed to take over the role of a succubus." I gestured to my chest, which ached. "I'm not going to be very good at this role, in case you were wondering."

"Well, honestly, I assumed you were lacking the demonic genes required to take up that role. And the only reason I was considering a succubus is due to my fathers' insistence I be a good and considerate lover. And when my mother supported their fatherly advice, I thought it was a good idea."

Gabriel patted my shoulder. "Do not fret over Darian's circumstances. He will be happier to deal with a being he can dedicate himself to, and there are many varieties of demonesses and devils who are as good—or better—than succubi at her art of seducing and caring for men. If you do not pick, it will be picked for you, and my brother is quite good at matching nature with species. Darian, on the other hand, would be saddled with your species, as he is smitten and would whine. Truly, we cannot abide by the whining. His entire family? Masterful whiners."

"It would serve you all right if we picked different permanent partners," I muttered.

The archangel's amusement manifested as a sound suspiciously similar to a giggle. "You could try that, but there would be significant whining."

"Why are divines so very much like children?" I scowled, careful to keep my gaze fixed on the archangel's chest. "Is your shroud weak, or did I really fuck myself over this time?"

"As you say, you have really fucked yourself over this time. That is why it is a forbidden lore. Awareness of the shroud's nature often results in the weakening of the shroud—and it is why it has remained secret. Those who have discovered its truths find themselves viewing what they should not. Your strengthening vision is part of why my brother monitors you as closely as he does. He uses healing the illness of your body as an excuse to make certain what happened to his darling does not happen to you. There is no intervention in your future, although there is salvation from your circumstances, should you opt to play the game. Otherwise, your eyes will kill you long before the cancer could have, had it been allowed to take root. It is one of many consequences you face. Darian's fathers are sentimental beings, and they would try to find a way to recapture your seed and bring it back to life for their son to pursue in many years. Darian is a creature prone to fixation, much like you are. Becoming a new species would not change much for you, beyond offering a resilience and ability to withstand the shrouds you will one day pierce with ease. Normally, we make a point of showing up once a mortal has dabbled in powers they cannot control or understand, but you are a useful mortal. You will pay other prices for your meddling ways."

I turned to Darian. "I'd like to mention I've reduced an archangel to cursing, and he's basically told me I'm screwed. Should I be grateful they're working with my base desire to rescue my cat *and* get justice for those poor animals before finishing me off?"

"It does not seem they have interest in finishing you off, but I can understand why deer freeze in headlights a little better now. No matter which way I turn, there's a divine out to get me."

"We are more after your virginity and mortality rather than you," Gabriel replied. "More specifically, we are doing our best to rid you of both of those things, which do not serve you well at this point in time."

"One of those things is easier to address than the other." Darian sighed. "I'm not sure what I did to deserve this, however."

"You were born."

Despite everything, I laughed. "This is why I like the divine so much. They're so disgustingly honest most of the time, and they really don't care if they hurt your feelings. If you can't handle the truth, you shouldn't give them any openings to tell it to you. In the hands of a divine, the truth is a truly dangerous weapon."

The archangel shrugged, and I got the feeling he smiled. "Most humans are inclined to become offended when the truth is presented to them. You are exceptional in your drive to acquire the truth. But you have toyed with things beyond your control. As such, you must take great care with yourself before you see something that has irrevocable consequences. My nephew, lacking clothes, for example, would have irrevocable consequences."

I raised a hand and rubbed at my temple. "Anything else you'd like to get off your chest, Gabriel?"

"I can recommend two humans who would be happy to pretend they are dating you both for a chance to watch my brother and his partners have a rather delightful meltdown as they try to make certain you date each other rather than the humans I would invite to play the game. Of course, Belial would catch on quickly, but my brother is sometimes more dense than the average rock."

"Are we discussing pumice or granite? There's a pretty significant difference in the average density of rocks, Gabriel."

The archangel sighed. "Closer to granite. I forgot pumice existed, as most rocks are rather dense."

"How dare those volcanoes ruin your metaphor," I replied, careful to keep my expression and tone neutral.

"Please take her off and charm her ruthlessly, Darian. This would simplify matters and force my brother's hand into motion faster."

Darian snorted. "I see. As I'm your nephew, and you can't meddle as much as you would like, you're assisting Lucifer, who *can* meddle. And since I'm your relative, Diana got dragged into this because you think, probably due to her overwhelming competence, she's worthy of being part of the family."

"You would be correct."

"Don't we get a say?"

"I am a telepath," Gabriel reminded his nephew.

Darian sighed. "I'm just going to apologize now, Diana. I'm sorry."

While I remained inexperienced due to personal choice, having a busy life, and otherwise spending my time creating trouble for myself, I did not need any guidance to figure out Darian had been enjoying some impure thoughts aimed in my general direction. "You should have heard when I was trying to mentally scold Lucifer for daring to bring a tall, dark, and handsome to *my* house after my cat went missing. That's just rude. If you can accept that I'm going to be staring at your physical attributes when I don't think you're looking, I think it's fair for me to accept that you might be staring at my physical attributes." I pointed at my chest. "Just wait a week or two before you admire these. Right now, they just hurt, the bandage look isn't a good one on me, and I would prefer to wait for encouraged judgment until I'm able to wear a good bra. If you're lucky, I might even allow you to admire said bra. It seems a decent selection of them were rescued from my house. I wonder why that might be?"

"I couldn't possibly tell you that," Darian lied, and the corners of his mouth twitched.

Gabriel sighed. "I thought you would like to know she speaks the truth."

Darian gave up trying to hide his grin. "Do you ever give Lucifer a break?"

"No. Why should I?"

Darian stared at the archangel rather intently, and I wondered what he was trying to communicate with his uncle.

A moment later, Gabriel laughed. "While I can understand the general attractiveness of such a thing, a permanent relationship should be founded on more than a woman's willingness to tell my brother no."

"But *why*?" Darian asked.

"Goodness. It amazes me I have so many brothers and sisters who deliberately seek out a human *and* some demon or devil so they can have children. Then, for reasons I cannot understand, they insist on teaching them that word and how to use it in question format."

"You have to admit my mother is pretty amazing."

"You are a biased child."

"Well, yes. If my mother finds out I didn't say good things about her to the in-laws, she'd find some way to make me pay for it later. I'm already guilty of being independent. I don't want to be guilty of hurting her feelings on top of my daring to be more independent than she would prefer. She does not like when the nest is empty. How about this as a thought. I will bargain with you to ask Diana on a single date *after* we have recovered her cat and have handled this matter. It's not my problem if she says no, but you meddlers, in exchange, have to not bother us about it until *after* her cat is home with her. The faster we recover her cat, the sooner you'll be able to start meddling again. Remember: it's not my problem if she says no."

The archangel took his time thinking it over. "Very well. I will inform my family of my bargain with you, but I cannot control their actions, nor will I bargain on their behalf. I, however, will not meddle with you, and I will recommend they delay their meddling until after Diana's cat has been recovered."

"That's fair. Bargain made. Now, we need to go take these kittens to a vet."

"I could handle that matter for you. It would speed your efforts on recovering Diana's cat, and this is a small matter. I will make sure they have excellent care, and I will begin the work on finding all but the mother cat and the young calico permanent homes suiting their natures. Then you would not worry. More accurately, she would not worry. She has transformed worrying into an art, although it would be prudent of her to learn to worry a little more about herself rather than the fate of others."

"The cats didn't ask to be experimented on in a lab. Somebody has to make up for what horrible people did to them," I muttered.

"My brother will learn to rue and lament he is inviting you into his many hells for a permanent stay. You will not change your colors, not even with power available to you. Oh, no. I expect you will corrupt my brother's residence with your philanthropic ways. This is not a bad thing, as it will help streamline the reform of the…"

I grinned at the archangel's hesitance to

call the sinners by Darlene's preferred moniker. "Fucking assholes," I supplied.

"Yes. Them."

"If they had done a little better at being decent beings in life, they wouldn't be in residence. They only have themselves to blame for their fate. Admittance into Lucifer's care has nothing to do with belief. That's just something the so-called believers concocted to make themselves sleep better at night. No matter what faith or lack thereof, souls have three destinations."

Darian went to work checking over the SUV and making sure everything was packed away. "Only three?"

"Heaven, Lucifer's dungeons, or in limbo waiting for a chance to go back to Earth as a new soul. Purgatory. The listless beyond—whatever you want to call it when the soul sleeps. Those who don't believe in any form of heaven but have not earned their way into Lucifer's care just rest." I glanced in Gabriel's direction before helping Darian with his task, setting out everything for the cats so they could be cared for properly until I could claim them. "That's mostly right, isn't it?"

"For your purposes, you are correct. We do not intentionally bring harm to souls who have done good but have no belief in any religion's heaven. But the lack of belief does not spare the sinners from meeting my brother in his full glory. The balance must be kept."

"I always wondered about the souls who sleep," I admitted.

"They are neither here nor there, and their existence as seeds is enough to maintain the balance. I am sure my brother negotiates with *Him* for the seed that will become your future. He would want a pristine one for you. That means there'll be yet another baby angel running around the heavens creating trouble, a situation *He* enjoys, for Darlene inevitably comes to visit—and steal—the little one for a while. The balance is best served this way, and no matter what humanity believes, neither *He* nor my brother wish for life to end."

The book I'd recovered had reinforced that ideal enough times I believed it. "It must remain an ever-present risk, as the universe did not intend anything to be eternal, not even *Him*."

"Yes. Even *He* was born from a seed."

"Is it bad of me I'm picking the calico because she's cute?"

"No. You meant to take home but one cat, your own, but you are opening your home to two others, knowing you cannot take them all for the sake of your sanity. And yes, you would struggle to take care of so many cats. Three cats will be a challenge for you, but one that will make you happy. With no other criteria for you to choose from, selecting the feline that you feel is cute is perfectly acceptable. You would love any of these kittens equally. The kitten you have chosen will love you without condition, and she will be friendly company with her mother and your cat. Of course, we will help with that. You will find transitioning your new pets into your home a simple matter."

After working with the Devil for so long, I recognized when a divine wished to strike a bargain with me. "What is that going to cost me?"

"It would be a safe assumption I would request you accept going on a date with my nephew."

Tricky archangel. "You are so lucky I love my cat, Darian."

"How is this my fault?"

"You're the one who suggested we go on a date to placate the nosy archangel."

"That's a good point. Gabriel, thank you, but please go before I get into even more trouble."

"I will come pay a visit to check on Diana's health when you sleep tonight. Should I have to do anything other than check, I shall wake you—or not, depending on how stealthily I can do my work." The archangel laughed, bowed, and disappeared. A moment later, the cats vanished as well, and all of their supplies went with them.

"The 'vet' will be in the heavens, those animals will be spoiled rotten within ten minutes, and *He* is going to be overwhelmed with angels wanting cats," Darian predicted. "Then the kittens will find their way into homes of those who need them the most on the mortal coil. As for you, he'll sneak in while shrouded, he likely already had a look at you, and wants to do some minor workings without worrying you about it. Cancer can be tricky even for the divines, or so I've been told. I don't think it's anything serious, as he would tell you. Mostly, I bet he wants to go play with the kittens in the high heavens for a while, and *He* will enjoy that."

"Why would you come to that conclusion?"

"So many reasons, so little time. Mostly, *He* hates when *He* can't do anything to ease the suffering of mortals who deserve better than what life has given them. Or so says my father. It doesn't hurt *He* loves cats. *He* loves most animals, but there is a reason Darlene was not a canine of some sort."

Huh. Darian was a veritable fountain of wisdom when it came to the divine, something I would need to pursue later to augment my future role as Lucifer's secretary—assuming he talked me into doing the work. "I thought that was because the Devil needs someone who'll tell him no rather than tell him yes all of the time. Dogs tend to have a reputation of being obedient."

"That, too, but canines aren't relentlessly obedient. Well, they can be." Darian grimaced. "Okay, they definitely can be, at least domesticated ones. Even in the wild, most canines follow a set pack structure. *He* wouldn't have wanted Darlene to fall prey to that. So, she's a cat."

"How do you even know that?"

"Dad. He was around when Darlene charmed Lucifer, so he tells stories about them all the time. *He* created her specifically for Lucifer, and Dad never fails to be amused about how *He* totally goosed everyone. Darlene had charmed Gabriel and Michael from first blasphemy, too." Darian closed the doors of the SUV after one final check to make sure we'd gathered everything. "Personally, I think *He* is still up to something."

"Why?"

"Lucifer? Get married?" Scoffing, he got behind the wheel of the SUV, holding his hands out for the keys, which I gave him. "Those two are going to have a flock of children, because *He* is a family man… except Lucifer is infertile as a consequence of his fall. But he now has Kanika, and I do not see their family stopping with just her. What I don't know is how *He* is going to fling additional children their way. Darlene loves children almost as much as Lucifer does. I remember him being around when I was little. Dad would have him babysit when Mom and Father weren't paying attention."

I'd pegged the Devil as a family man within sixty seconds of seeing him with Kanika. The only being he loved more was his wife. If I hadn't known better, I would've assumed Lucifer was a being of love rather than the ruler of the universe's many hells and reformer of damned souls. "I'm placing bets on abandoned children finding their way to Lucifer's house and becoming spoiled." I circled around the SUV and claimed the passenger seat, pushing the seat back so I could fully stretch my legs. "You're taller than me. Why didn't you fix this while I was driving?"

Darian laughed. "I would've taken a nap if I got too comfortable, and that probably would have cut off my trail, and then I would've gotten into a great deal more trouble than I'm already in."

"Didn't your fathers teach you that you shouldn't bargain with divine entities, especially when it involves your love life?"

"If they had, I forgot."

I buckled my seatbelt. "I am becoming increasingly more concerned over their interest in us teaming up."

"If it makes you feel better, it's probably not because of *us*, but because of any children we'd probably have. The divines play the long game. But, in your case, having an efficient secretary would free Lucifer up for a lot of other things—like reforming souls. Time is not infinite, and it's fairly difficult to maintain the balance. He's probably stretched thin. If they saw a future where I make you happy, and you work better when happy, they'd pursue that future. But probably, we'd have kids, and those kids could be useful for some plan or another. That's doubly the case if you like children."

"I have no idea if I like children. I *hate* when people ask me when I'm having children, though. It's so damned rude. How is it any of their business if I reproduce or not?"

"I tried telling that to my parents once. Mom faked a tear, and both of my fathers gave me a dose of the eye. Getting the eye from an archangel is pretty disconcerting, Diana. I had to swear I'd consider, if I found the right woman, that I might have children."

"The last time my parents asked, I inquired if they wanted me to have one out of wedlock, if I could pick up some prostitute to handle the deed, and if they'd like to reevaluate their stance," I admitted. "This is part of why I don't have a great relationship with my parents."

"You don't have a great relationship with your parents because they tried to drown you as a child."

"I'm not sure I'd count an unwanted baptism as an attempted drowning."

"I do. But then again, my fathers and my mother made sure to teach me that I was under no obligation to participate in any religion unless I genuinely wanted to, and they made sure to go over most major religious celebrations each year. I was not required to participate in any of them unless I wanted to. Honestly, I've tried telling them it's pretty hard to deny the existence of things like devils, demons, and angels when I happen to live in the same house with them. I'm not even sure how your parents can deny like they do when the evidence is right there in front of them."

"Except it isn't right there in front of them. Neither have seen an angel. They have convinced themselves that the demons running around are people corrupted by the limited magic there is. Lycanthropes they have an easy time with. They're diseased, and they understand diseases."

"Except it's a magical, incurable disease."

"I tried to lick a lycanthrope once. I was pretty young, she was a tiger, and I would've given just about anything to be a tiger, too."

"How did you get close enough to a tiger to lick her?"

"My parents took their eyes off me for like half a second." I giggled at the memory.

"Maybe that's why I rescued a cat instead of a dog. That tiger was absolutely magnificent. Mr. Flooferson is obviously an oddly colored miniature tiger."

"Can I revise my opinion about wanting children? I'm now utterly terrified and no longer convinced I can keep a child alive." He hesitated. "Or free of disease or injury."

"I would not have minded becoming a tiger, Darian. I don't know if she had the hybrid form or not, but she was magnificent. If my mother hadn't sworn I'd earn a quick trip to hell, I probably would have started licking lycanthropes with frightening frequency."

"I'm trying to figure out why you thought licking lycanthropes would give you the virus. Also, I'm highly disturbed that your mother used a blatant fear tactic on you as a child."

"Honestly, the threat didn't scare me, but it was pretty effective on other kids in the church. I was too fascinated with magic and everything it represented. As for licking lycanthropes, that's simple. I was homeschooled. My parents opted against education of magical species using a religious exception. Let's just say high school, where they sent me to public school, was quite the eye opener."

"How did you rate going into public school?"

"My math was ahead of the curve. My science was so far behind the curve it was laughable at best. I scored well in English. I took foreign languages because they interested me. My history was so-so, but it turns out my parents tried to erase some important facts from my education. Honestly, they're probably the reason I started researching forbidden lore. Once I learned how much they'd skipped out on because of their religious beliefs, I began doing my best to educate myself. It took me two years to get caught up, but I emerged triumphant by the end. I had a perfect GPA in my senior year."

"Maybe my uncles are trying to marry me off to you because you're smart, beautiful, and single. That's a rare combination, Diana."

"They're trying to marry you off to me because triads tend to refuse to have another child until the first one is safely in the custody of some other being. I think it's something to do with the angels. I mean, triads have zero failure rates for pregnancies and deliveries. The angel takes care of that. So, it could be that your uncles just like you a lot —or hate you with every fiber of their being. That part is rather unclear to me."

"It's unclear to me, too."

"Marriage does include good tax benefits," I commented, narrowing my eyes and considering the pros and cons of going along with the scheme. "We haven't tried to kill each other yet, and apparently, we need to go on a date. A divorce is also very easy to acquire, and we could easily sign a document that states that anything we had prior to our marriage remains ours, and anything earned during the marriage is split equally. We could scandalize every single member of our families *and* make the heavens and hells have a conniption all at once if we don't like the realities of marriage. I work a lot. You seem to work a lot, too. So, we'd be basically bed buddies who see each other infrequently with tax breaks. And three cats."

Darian leaned back in his seat and fiddled with the keys before putting them into the ignition and starting the SUV. "I'd still have to ask you on a date after this mess is finished."

"Do married people not go on dates?"

"I have no idea, honestly."

"I'd think married people should go on dates, because how else would you go have fun wining and dining? Or going bowling or anything like that? Does signing marriage documents somehow suck out the enjoyment of doing something with their partner? That seems wrong somehow."

"I never put any thought into this. I've always heard dating was for looking for someone to marry."

"I'm of the opinion that if you aren't interested in continuing to date the person after marriage, perhaps marriage is not a good idea. The whole point is to find a partner to live with permanently. If you can't stand doing stuff with the person you're married to, why get married?"

"I'd say because of the societal expectations on sex," he admitted. "Out-of-wedlock sex is a big deal to a lot of people."

"It's none of their business who I sleep with, unless I'm sleeping with someone in *their* bedroom," I countered.

"I feel like I'm in shark-infested waters, and that I happened to have cut my foot open on something. Will the shark toy with me before my inevitable demise?"

Laughing, I shook my head. "It just seems stupid to me. Why do people insist on pushing their personal morality on others? How is it any of *their* business who I decide to take to bed with me?"

"I don't have a good answer to that."

"Damn. I was hoping you did, because I certainly don't. Oh, well. The only reason I'm a virgin is because I haven't felt I have time to dedicate to the person I'd be sleeping with. I want a relationship to go with the sex. If I really wanted to ditch my virginity, I'd just walk to a brothel and cut a check for an incubus for a few hours."

"And with an incubus, you'd be guaranteed to have a good time."

"I might be a virgin, Darian, but I'm not a prude. I'm perfectly capable of taking care of myself as needed."

Darian opened his mouth, made a thoughtful noise, and closed it.

"Go ahead and say it. As I said, I'm not a prude."

"There are so many ways in which I can get myself into trouble. I would like a few minutes, possibly a few hours, to decide which approach I take. If I'm going to get into trouble, I wish to do so in a spectacular fashion. That way, when you kill me, my parents can write something interesting on my gravestone."

I laughed. "Sure, Darian. That sounds like a plan. Take your time. Just announce you're committing yourself into getting into trouble so I'm prepared. Where are we going for the night? I'm assuming we're not headed back to our old hotel, as you checked us out of there despite the Devil footing the bill."

"We're heading for Red Bluff. If you want to call around and bag us a reservation, go for it. It'll take us about two to two and a half hours to get there. While I'm not committing to getting myself into trouble capable of landing me in the grave, I will take you out for something to eat unless you would prefer bad room service."

"It has been a long time since I've indulged in junk food."

"Well, you're going to be easy to please, then." Darian shook his head, put the SUV into gear, and headed out of the tight confines of the trailer community to the overgrown path that would take us back to the main road. "Maybe I'll get out of this alive."

I went to work booking us a reservation for the night. "You better. You owe me a date."

TWELVE

"You aren't seriously pissed already?"

PER DARIAN'S INSTRUCTIONS, I reserved a room for us for two nights in Red Bluff. As we would need the space, I got the biggest one available, which had a king-sized bed and a sitting area with a couch, coffee table, television, and a tiny desk. When we arrived, we unloaded the SUV, transforming the room into a makeshift lab. The all-important scanner, brand new and ready to be calibrated, would drive me insane.

As part of my work with the CDC, I'd been taught how to calibrate the damned things in case of an emergency. To my disgust, the Devil and his wicked family of archangels had made a point of including every diagnostic doohickey required to successfully tame the machine.

"I am convinced the whole lot of them truly hates me," I announced, taking over the coffee table so I could work some technological magic. "Do you know why my bosses had me trained on this shit?"

"In case you were with them during an emergency, and they didn't have any lab techs around?"

"Disasters are generally more likely to happen when my bosses go to investigate something. They're not sent out unless it's really important, and they got tired of trying to find someone to calibrate a tool if it went haywire while out. So, I was trained on all the good scanners. The cheap ones? Wouldn't know what to do with them if you beat me with it. But this model? I can make this model sing for you. Assuming Lucifer paid for it, it cost him at least a million, and once I'm done calibrating it, it'll be able to tell us about just about any known substance. It takes a long time to run the tests, but if these samples are something the CDC has seen before, we'll know about it within a few hours." I glared at the metal cases containing the vials. "If we get infected with some sort of plague, I'm going to be seriously pissed."

"You aren't seriously pissed already?"

"Apparently not. I should be."

"I'm very curious to see what you'll do once you reach the seriously pissed stage." Darian sat on the couch, making sure to give me enough space to work, and watched with interest. "Once you're set up, I'll guide you through how I like to record evidence, especially when dealing with samples. Once that's set up, I'll work on the fingerprint angle. With luck, the computers will be able to narrow the fingerprints down to a decent number that need manual confirmation. Reading fingerprints is a pretty tricky art."

"Unless you happen to know an archangel and can ask."

"I might know an archangel or two, but I've determined they're assholes out for my virginity and marital status. If I ask, they'll tell me they'll do it if I do something to resolve my statuses. Does this mean I'm a pure maiden?"

Snickering, I began the tedious process of calibration, using the various tools to test the system, confirm the readings, install updated firmware as needed, and otherwise enslave myself to a ridiculously expensive portable computer with an attitude problem. "It's sweet they think you're such a prize. If you decide to play at being a damsel in distress, I'd consider rescuing you. But I'm not sure if being a sweet, pure maiden means you're marriage material."

"Hey! I am a prize. You should be honored to have been selected. Don't you know what marriage to me wins you?"

"Beyond becoming an in-law of the Devil and sucked into the insanity of the high heavens and the many hells? Do you know what that lot causes? Trouble. Do you know what the children of that lot causes? Even more trouble. You, sir, are nothing but trouble."

"I cannot deny this accusation." Then, to make it clear he found nothing at all wrong with my opinion, he smirked at me. "I'd even consider wearing a gown for your amusement and swooning, but you'd have to play the part and dress up like a gentleman in exchange. Honestly, I find women in suits to be rather attractive. Skirts are lovely, but a confident woman in a good suit definitely catches my attention."

Someone needed to inform Darian his smirk classified as a dangerous weapon. Afterwards, someone needed to take me in for some serious talks with a shrink to discuss how much I liked the smug look on tall, dark, and handsome men.

Yep, he was trouble. If he kept checking off my various boxes for what I liked in a man, I would be in trouble.

"I feel the Christian pantheon is unfairly using my interest in tall, dark, and handsome men against me." I wrinkled my nose and glared at the meter, which would be put to serious work helping us figure out what the lab had been researching. "While I do this, why don't you work with the paperwork? I'm hoping you can manifest the address of where they have taken my cat, honestly."

"I doubt it will be that simple, but considering how much work they put into hiding the papers, it *is* possible. I suspect it'll give us the names of the main operators. Using the various law enforcement databases, we might be able to locate someone willing to talk. I have my doubts, though."

"Why?"

"Operations like that tend to shut betrayers up in a rather permanent fashion. That's how I ultimately got shot. They failed to shut me up."

"Now that I've met your parents, how did any of them actually survive?"

"I have made a point of not checking into their fates, as it's not my parents I'm worried about. Lucifer, however, has no scruples about telling some mortal somebody annoyed him. People will do a lot to earn the Devil's favor, as though that will somehow prevent them from going to his many hells for reformation." Darian stretched out his legs and made himself comfortable. "Also, I wouldn't trust any member of my family. They do precisely what they feel will get them the result they want. Unless you explicitly tell them you don't want to become, say, a succubus, if they think you'll be best off as a succubus, that's what you'll become. Personally, I wouldn't complain, but it's a lot of work keeping a succubus monogamous, and it involves a great deal of attention from her partner. I'm not sure I'm up for taming a succubus."

Well, I could think of one good reason why Lucifer wouldn't work that angle. "Darlene would likely attempt to assassinate me within a week if I became a succubus. She is the true definition of jealous."

"This is true. How disappointing for me. I won't get to have my very own succubus to wrangle and tame. I'm heartbroken from disappointment."

"I'm not kissing anything to make it better right now. I'm busy."

"'Right now' implies you might later, and I view this as a promising and encouraging development. When would be an appropriate time to inquire about such a thing?"

While awkward, Darian also counted as wretchedly adorable in his tentative explorations of flirtation. After excessive exposure to the Devil and Darlene, I'd become a master at identifying such hints, although Darian was a step below using a bat to get his point across compared to Lucifer's sly seductions of his wife. As consent topped the sexy charts, he'd already done a lot to earn a later invitation. "We can talk after the bandages are gone."

"Ah, right. Those. Does it hurt? I usually

keep some ibuprofen in my briefcase. Idiots give me headaches. I keep acetaminophen, too. If you want anything stronger than that, I'm going to need to call in a few favors from some doctors I know, but I'm sure I can get you something to take the edge off."

"It's not bad enough to take anything, really. It just aches when I forget and move more than I should."

"Pain can hamper recovery."

I kept myself from rolling my eyes through focusing on the temperamental equipment I needed to calibrate to make sense of the vials we'd pilfered from the site. "Okay, hit me up with a pair of each and some water, and if there's chocolate anywhere in this joint, I could use a hit."

While Darian handled that, I resumed work, starting with the easier calibrations, which involved testing the samples included with the scanner. Either I'd gotten lucky or someone, likely the Devil, had already played with it, as I had a perfect score on the common live samples. The trickier work, which included a through-plastic scan of a sample of gorgon dust, always put me on edge. The device did as it was supposed to, much to my relief.

I returned the samples to their carry case in case I needed to recalibrate the device, and I waited for Darian to bring me my requested water, medications, and chocolate. I popped the pills, guzzled the water, and attacked the foil wrapper of my favorite treat.

"My mother always told me to come prepared with chocolate. Until this moment, I had no idea how right she was."

"It has been a long week." I bit off another chunk of chocolate and pointed at his hand. "Hold that out. It's time to test this on a live sample."

"Is that all I am now? A live sample?"

"Yes." I grinned at him and set up the device to do a complete diagnostic scan. "If you were in a hospital setting, the tests I'm about to run would cost fifty thousand. I'm going to know *everything* about you within the next hour."

"Everything?"

"Everything, including your sperm count. At least you shouldn't be getting any surprises about your parentage, so that's something."

He sighed. "I now have performance anxiety, and I don't even have to perform. I like children and eventually want to have them."

"If you can't, your uncle is the Devil. I'm sure he'd bargain with you for a trip to the angelic body shop. I will say, the angelic body shop? Might be worth the price paid in various bargains. Had I gone to a clinic, it probably would have taken six months just to get a diagnosis, and then treatments can take months to complete—if they work. A week of some aching is not a big deal." I frowned. "Plus, that weird blue flame whenever I use magic. I wonder if I should be concerned about that."

"Holy fire," Darian replied. "I'm guessing they gave you a fairly hefty dose of it to get rid of the cancer. That you're going to have an archangel sneaking in after you're asleep tells me you're going to be getting another dose of that, too. It wouldn't surprise me if Lucifer joins in with demonic or devilish energy. Either will make you easier to convert, too. Conversions infused with holy fire tend to have ridiculously good natures."

"How do you know that?"

"Dad and Father like telling me about this, because they're determined to have me extend my lifespan. In a way, I feel guilty because I'm really aware of how much all of my parents love me and how often other parents just don't. Like yours."

I sighed, grabbed Darian's hand, and jabbed him with the scanner's needle. It beeped to confirm it had detected blood, and after several beeps, which I translated as a successful sample acquisition, it went to work figuring out what made Darian tick. I set the scanner on the table. "It'll take a while for that to work, and when it's done, I'll hook it to my laptop and get the full diagnostic reading. Once I confirm everything is working as intended, we'll begin with a proximity scan of the vials. In the meantime, show me how these papers are to be handled. We may as well make the most of our time."

"I think you should run a scan on yourself, too."

"I'm scanned every year as part of working with the CDC."

"You should run a scan on yourself, too," he repeated.

I chuckled. Shrugging hurt, and I muttered a few curses for having forgotten. "Sure. I'll run my scan. So, while this handles the heavy work, is there anything I should know? Any infections, diseases, or whatever, so I won't panic when I spot them on the diagnostic? If you have cancer with a tumor size of larger than a centimeter, the scanner might even pick it up."

"Through a blood sample?"

"It's not just reading your blood. The instant that needle enters your flesh, it pulsed with magic, which 'echoes' through your entire body. The scanner then reads the echoes and translates the echoes into data using even more magic. Honestly, what amazes me is how accurate these things can be. The DNA tests can be really wonky, though. It turns out there are very minor differences between what makes someone a human versus elf or pixie, satyr, or centaur. Once you get into the lycanthropy virus, things get exceptionally strange."

"This was a far geekier conversation than I was expecting to have. Are you going to start talking to me in genome next?"

"I could," I confessed. "We sometimes need to break into the relationship between cellular interactions during an emergency, and it makes a great deal of sense for me to have some idea what the scientists are talking about when there is a genome architectural disorder, their class, and if the disorder could result in something like heightened infection risk of a generalized plague. For example, take the rabies outbreak recently. Somebody hacked the virus to give it heightened infectivity through aerial transmission. The CDC discovered that people with certain common numerical chromosomal faults were more likely to contract the disease. Interestingly, that fault made those people more likely to be asymptomatic carriers. We think the initial modification of the rabies virus was to take advantage of the fault to help spread rabies through humanoid populations. Until recently, it was believed mice share eighty-five percent of their DNA with humans, which is what the culprits initially used to create and spread the modified virus. In reality, the differential between mouse and human DNA is less than three percent, which made this even more effective. The culprits then worked with gorgons, isolating the numerical chromosomal fault found in roughly forty percent of gorgons that is shared with humans. The fault is present in roughly twenty percent of people."

"Is it a fault if it's that prevalent? I'm not sure I understand. What is this fault?"

"The CDC classifies it as a fault because it results in an immune system a little less inclined to respond to certain types of illnesses, including rabies. This allows the virus to replicate without the immune system reacting. In this specific case, the uninterrupted replication of the virus results in the victims being asymptomatic for longer." I wrinkled my nose at the clever exploitation of a human oddity. "It's a fault because the lack of immune system response is a result of this specific element of the human genome; it's considered harmful."

"I think I'm having an unreasonable and unfair reaction to you talking science to me."

I laughed. "Fortunately for you, the scanner does not typically register sexual interest as a condition unless you're under the influence of a demon or devil. If you want to learn more than the basics of that, go ask a scientist. The last time I tried to wrap my head around numeric chromosomal faults, I gave myself a migraine and cried for several hours."

"That you're specifying numeric means there are other kinds of chromosomal faults."

"Don't ask questions you will regret hearing the answers to, Darian."

"Okay. Can you explain a numeric chromosomal fault in a way that won't make me feel utterly inferior, thus making me even more attracted to you and your discussion of science than I already am?"

Men. As far as human males suffering from lust went, Darian did a good job of controlling his urges and impulses, although I wondered how the hell I was supposed to explain such a thing *without* adding to his attraction problems. "Down syndrome is a numeric chromosomal fault, where a person has forty-seven chromosomes instead of the standard forty-six. That's one of the more obvious numeric faults. Any time cells have an abnormal number of chromosomes, whether they have more or less than what is anticipated, it's an abnormality or aberration or anomaly. I haven't quite figured out what the nuanced differences between those terms are, honestly. I had a hard enough time figuring out how cell division or multiplication failures during stages of conception and fetal development create numeric chromosomal faults. Basically, these problems typically happen sometime after or during fertilization of the egg. When, how, or why remains a mystery I might understand better if my mother cared more about science than trying to convince me I had to be properly subservient or go to hell. I can't say she's wrong, since I *am* going to hell, but I'm not going for the reasons she believes. Anyway, the CDC uses the term fault because calling someone's chromosomal situation an aberration didn't sit well with anybody, so we changed the language. People understand there's something wrong with the patient with that word, and the last thing we need is telling someone suffering from a genetic disorder they're an aberration! Most of us can stomach abnormality, but even that one is sketchy."

"Nobody warned me to be aware of the education levels of secretaries. You say your education is lacking, but then you start talking about cellular structure, and I'm thinking I need to go dig out some science books to keep up, and I *wasn't* home schooled."

I laughed. "I have a high school diploma, Darian. I never went to college. I started in the CDC as entry level because that is what I could do, there was an opening, and I was honest on my resume about my situation. My education was too haphazard to qualify for the kind of colleges I wanted to attend, and I couldn't afford the colleges I *could* attend without scholarships, so I decided to educate myself. Just because my GPA was good my senior year didn't mean the rest of my education didn't count as a black mark against me. I sucked at the tests for college entry, too. And don't get me wrong. Not all home schooled kids have my problems. It was the excessive influence of religion at the cost of science and history that screwed me over. A lot of parents do a great job home schooling; the CDC often checks for that because the home schoolers are often more self-driven than the publicly educated. Having a mix results in a more robust employee base."

"Is your problem due to the fact you missed foundational education?"

"Yep. It's fine. It worked out. I mean, it worked out until I educated myself into accidentally being able to see through divine shrouds. That's a problem. I like living. But first, I have to find my cat. To find my cat, I have to make sure the scanner is working properly. That means waiting for your test to come through and evaluating if it's taking readings accurately. Humans make the best fodder for that. After it looks like the scanner is working, then I can evaluate the samples. Unfortunately, this model can't do dual readings. It's good at what it does, but it's inflexible in that regard."

"Relax, Diana. We should get a lot of good information out of the paperwork, and waiting for a few hours to start working on the samples shouldn't be an issue. Considering how my family operates, your cat is probably as safe as a bunch of nosy archangels on a mission can make him, the Devil probably has the culprits pissing their pants—or he has sent a minion or ten to steal your cat from the lab operators. Now, that said, it's entirely possible Lucifer's keeping an eye on the situation explicitly to get you to go in and raise hell. Some things he really can't meddle with or he could break everything. But he really wants you on his team, and that means making sure your cat emerges from this unscathed." Darian snapped on a pair of gloves and grabbed the first stack of papers we'd located in the trailers. "We'll start with the exterior paperwork, as I expect that will be the quickest to sort through. Mostly, you need to write down anything I tell you to while I shuffle through these. We'll bag them after we've looked through and photographed copies for ourselves. We rinse and repeat until we've handled every sheet of paper we grabbed. By the time we're done, your scanner should have my results finished. At that point, it'll be late, we'll need some sleep, and we'll start again tomorrow with the vials. Ready to show me just how good of a secretary you are?"

I got up and put the scanner on the bed

so it could do its work without us banging into it and potentially scrambling the results. "As a matter of fact, yes."

"Good. Hold onto your britches, because this is going to be a rough ride."

DARIAN UNDERESTIMATED my tolerance for mundane paperwork along with my base ability to transform chaos into order. After five minutes of twitching through his haphazard attempts to organize the mess of documentation, I slapped his hands and took over, shuffling through the sheets to figure out what they were, who they were intended for, what purpose they served in the general scheme of lab operations, and otherwise determining a coherent method for filing and registering every paper.

Within an hour, I had everything separated into piles by type and age, and a sea of note stickers flagged the important sheets.

Darian stared at me the entire time I worked, his mouth hanging open.

"I'm a secretary," I reminded him. "You should see what my one boss gives me. His office is the equivalent of a disaster zone. He walks in, and paperwork disasters happen. It's my job to organize his disasters. This is barely a blip compared to him. He's a brilliant man, but he views tossing the used sheets across his desk to deal with later as a viable way of storing important papers. We're not here to glean every single sentence from every single sheet. We need the important information, such as addresses, names, phone numbers, and subjects." I pointed at the largest pile. "Those are the invoices for various animal care products. No services. The veterinarian supply store they were using might be a place to check into, as they're probably involved. Some of the drugs are restricted, and this lab likely doesn't have the right licenses to order the classes of drugs they were receiving. So, the supply center is a good place to investigate."

"Drug licensing is something I can access with my various permits." Darian grabbed the stack and shuffled through until he found the sheets dedicated to the supplier. He went to his laptop, typed in the names provided on the receipts as the recipient, and shook his head. "There's no valid drug licenses under these names in the state of California *or* in the state of Utah, where the supplier is located. The invoices imply the orders were picked up in person. No shipping addresses listed on the forms, no shipping fees."

I nodded, and I gestured to the next stack in line. "Those are their tax documentation; it looks like the company was about to file various documentation with the government to cover up their activities, but the bust happened before the filings could happen. At first glance, I suspect a lot of it is generally falsified. There's no evidence of any actual incoming monies from the other documents I looked over, so someone was funding it out of pocket and pretending to have expenses and earnings." I pointed at the next stack. "That's definitely falsified payment information on them receiving money. The CDC doesn't issue payments out of the office they picked for their cover up. It would have triggered a flag, leading to their downfall if they *had* submitted it. It's a trap the CDC likes to use; they have an office that looks like it *should* be responsible for issuing payments, but that building *never* issues payments, so it's used as a trap."

"That is disgustingly clever of the CDC."

"Fraud is common, and it's an easy way to catch people in the act. The CDC issues a lot of payments, so making claims of receiving a payout is often done. But the CDC is meticulous about tracking payouts, so it rarely works out for the crook."

"Yet you're telling me about this."

"I would hope you're not stupid enough to claim the CDC paid you when it did not."

"Surprisingly, I am not that stupid," he replied. "I'm just surprised the CDC actively pursued something like that."

"It's necessary. The CDC is a pretty common target of fraud, and the company moves a significant amount of money. These papers will bring the CDC into the investigation, which is a good thing for us—mostly. It's *mostly* a good thing for us."

"They have the resources needed to deal with it, and there's evidence they targeted a CDC employee, which will escalate it in the firm. Since you're a person-of-interest to Lucifer, that will send it even higher up the chain. Correct?"

"Correct, and if it is decided that I am being targeted to cripple the CDC, it will create issues." I narrowed my eyes. "I could see Lucifer taking advantage of this to transition me to his employment. He doesn't really care what happens to the CDC. It's a tool to him, although it's often a convenient tool."

"Won't poaching you earn the CDC's ire?"

"That depends. There are a ton of people who would make a great replacement for me. If me working for him makes it easier to deal with the demons and devils, the CDC will embrace him poaching me." I shrugged. "I'm going to make the Devil pay me extra if he wants me, especially if there's any evidence he planned it to work out this way."

"We're talking about the Devil here. The

only time he's really surprised is when Darlene is involved. He loves when she surprises him, so he absolutely will *not* peek into the future. Unless he's really bored, he peeks enough to make sure things will work out in the way he wants. It's just easier to accept we're being played."

"That was my general impression of the situation," I admitted. "All right. Do we pursue the tax documentation angle?"

"No, but we'll take pictures of everything if we think it will be useful later. It *might* have the identifications of those not already in custody, though. Actually, I've changed my mind. Yes, we'll pursue the tax documentation, but only for addresses that aren't near the lab. We want to catch those who *weren't* busted in the operation." Narrowing his eyes, he checked something on his laptop. "The trailer park *was* registered as a communal living center, but they were using PO boxes located in Dinsmore. And yes, there is a small post office in Dinsmore. So, if we eliminate all PO boxes in Dinsmore, that should save us some time."

"Unless we can gain access to those boxes."

"That's probably no good. PO boxes are cleared out shortly after a failed payment and transferred to someone else or are no longer receiving mail. The boxes would have been cleared out by now. We can call them in the morning, but the likelihood someone has been paying for those boxes after the bust is slim." Darian frowned. "But if someone has been paying the renewal bills, that could work. I'd have to use a contact in law enforcement to get access to the post office systems, though. That's not something I have access to."

I shuffled through the tax documents, pulling out the few sheets that didn't have a Dinsmore address and handed them over to Darian. "Next up are standard IOs."

"IOs?"

"Insertion orders for products and services. Some is for lab equipment from websites, things like that. It looks like they spread this stuff around to a lot of places to hide their activities. It looks like they tried to spread out where they purchased their equipment as much as possible, limiting the bulk orders for places that are specialized. They were definitely doing some form of medical research—and your concern about contagious diseases may have been accurate. They ordered several scanners meant to detect common infections in animals, including rabies, distemper, anthrax, bird flu, and so on."

"Anthrax?"

"Bacterial infection. It's a nasty one because it can live on surfaces for a while, so it's a common terrorism target. It spreads through spores rather than person-to-person transmissions."

"How do you know all of this?" he blurted.

I pointed in the direction of the bed and the scanner. "I have to be familiar with a lot of contagions, and terrorists like trying to spread anthrax through the spores. It's something we check for at sites when there's an unknown illness. There are a lot of really contagious animal diseases found across multiple species. The scanners they ordered are specialized and meant to be used with animals and humans to detect diseases. That they ordered more than one of these implies they were definitely working with some sort of common contagion. Unless I'm mistaken, these models *can't* have new diseases loaded into their software or firmware, which means they were working with a well-documented contagion. It's possible someone could hack them, but it would be difficult—unless they stole the software for the devices from the manufacturer."

"Always a possibility, especially with an operation of this scale. How much did they spend on the equipment?"

I leaned over to check Darian's IOs, grabbed my phone, and tallied the entirety of the expenditures. "Just over two million dollars."

"And they're all paid in full?"

"Upfront payments on all of them," I confirmed. "That Kingston guy. Could he afford this sort of payout?"

"I don't know. Do I think he could get the funding? Yes, with time. He's pretty charismatic, and there are enough people who are unhappy they're infected with lycanthropy that they would contribute to such a thing. However, I'm of the opinion Kingston is crazy enough that he'd infect *everybody* with lycanthropy if it means he gets treated like everybody else."

"The law isn't always kind to lycanthropes," I reminded him.

"And the lycanthropes who pay any sort of attention or take care with their behavior can get by without any problems. It's the ones who think they're entitled to do whatever they want that are the problem for the rest of the lycanthropes."

Ah. I'd found one of Darian's flaws.

He let his personal opinions and beliefs color his view of the world. On that, I couldn't really blame him, but it would prevent him from looking at the whole picture. I'd learned early on I needed to leave my personal feelings on work alone, as I might miss something if I allowed such things to get in the way of trying to look at a problem from all angles. "Darian, maybe you should reevaluate your stance on Kingston and start over, this time, without your opinions about lycanthropes judging what he may or may not have done. You probably have opinions about Kingston himself, but you need to forget those when you're contemplating the options. You can't figure out as many of the possibilities as possible when you've already established someone's behaviors, patterns, and beliefs. The first step is to figure out all of the possibilities, then you start evaluating which of those possibilities is closer to reality. That's what we have to do in the CDC when we have a hot case that needs to be solved before people get killed. It's too easy to let assumptions control our choices."

"Are you sure you've never done any investigating before?"

"I've watched people investigate before, but my bosses tend to get upset if I'm anywhere near the front lines for some reason."

"Well, losing their secretary to something avoidable would be a problem for them. Honestly, if you were my secretary, I'd have a hard time letting you leave my office."

I raised a brow. "Or your bedroom?"

"Definitely. You keep saying sexy things to me. I'm only a man. I'm a sorely tested man, and I'm going to have to patiently wait, bide my time, and plan the best way to ask you on a date now. While hoping for mercy."

"Considering I've basically promised to go on a date with you as it is through a bargain, I think you're safe from the dark throes of disappointment. But I will remember all I need to do to flirt with you is talk about something technical or scientific. Damn. If I'd known men were this easy to flirt with, I would have done this a *lot* sooner."

"A lot of men don't like feeling like they're inferior to women, so I'm pretty sure you'd have a bunch of offended, grouchy assholes with that approach. But then you'd get lucky with me, because your first scientific pickup line would have had me eating out of your hand. I'm blaming all three of my parents for this tendency." Darian flopped back against the couch and shuffled through the papers I'd given him before setting them aside and reaching for the stack of tax documents. "Men like Kingston piss me off."

"Why?"

"He doesn't care who he hurts in order to make his life better for him and only him. One of his previous attempts at curing the lycanthropy virus killed ten people through generalized human experimentation. If he's not afraid of killing people, he's definitely not afraid to kill a bunch of animals. This *is* something he would do. Or so I think. The references to his name in these papers definitely implies he's involved."

Interesting. "You hadn't mentioned that earlier."

"I try not to think about his lack of regard for life in general. It just makes me angrier than I like." Darian waved one of the tax papers in my direction. "At least he's, on paper, paying his accomplices fairly well. It doesn't look like anybody made below a hundred thousand a year in this operation. That's a damned good motivation to live in the woods in a trailer."

As I didn't make quite a hundred thousand a year before benefits and bonuses, I could easily see somebody deciding to live in a half-decent trailer doing sketchy things for a good paycheck. "Crime pays better than secretarial work, apparently."

Darian shot me a look. "You're paid less than these clowns?"

I shrugged. "I do get bonuses, but my base pay isn't that high, no. The bonuses make it go higher, but they can be a bitch to earn."

"You keep the higher-level bosses functional in the CDC for less than a hundred thousand a year?"

"Considering I don't have a college degree and learned everything on the job, I think I'm doing pretty well for myself, thank you very much." I shot a glare at him, huffed, and went to check on the meter, which churned through Darian's blood sample and magical pulse with impressive speed. "Huh. I must have gotten one of the upgraded models. This is almost done. Maybe ten more minutes."

"Upgraded model? I thought you knew the scanner?"

"There are different models of the same scanner. The only real difference is what is under the hood. I didn't check the memory in it. I just assumed it was the base model. Apparently, I should not make assumptions when it comes to Lucifer." I picked up the scanner and flipped it over to check the information on its back. Sure enough, he'd gotten me the top-of-the-line model. "Yeah. I made a mistake there. I made a stupid assumption. This is not the base model. This is the best model sold."

"When you negotiate with Lucifer, it doesn't matter you don't have a degree, and you're worth at least three times what the CDC is paying you. As you will have to deal with him most days of the week, go for a baseline of half a million a year plus bonuses and whatever other concessions you can think of. Take him for an apartment or condo in every major city he expects you to work at often, for example, unless you like hotel life. I mean, he might give you the ability to teleport, which would simplify things for you, but you might not want to live in his domain all of the time. Even Lucifer has properties on Earth to get away from work."

I considered, and while pride demanded I stand up for myself a little better, I checked my knee-jerk reaction and forced myself to nod. "I've always thought I needed to be grateful I've done so well without a degree."

"You're skilled, you're smart, and you do a good job. A degree can open doors, yes, but you're the reason you're being poached by the Devil. Lucifer doesn't care about degrees. My mom? *She* cares about degrees, but my fathers? They couldn't care less. They just paid for my education to keep my mother happy, and they suggested I continue educating myself so I don't look stupid in front of women. I'm starting to think at least *one* of my fathers has been investigating my future in some fashion or another. Worse, I've already made myself look stupid in front of you several times."

"I am of the opinion stupidity can be cured."

"There is hope for me after all. I'll try to keep from making you hate me by the time I can ask for a date."

I grinned at that comment. "All right. I need to be less crabby, because right now, I *should* be cuddled in bed with my cat. It took months to get him to come join me in bed, and I resent some asshole has probably undone all the hard work I've put in convincing Mr. Flooferson to trust me."

"Obviously, I should be sneaking out and

trying to locate your cat, so when I bring him back to you, I can successfully inquire about a date after you have him settled."

The scanner beeped in my hand, informing me it was done churning through Darian's biologics and was ready for me to evaluate his DNA, his general health, and even his sperm count if I really wanted. "I'll admit, that ploy would stand a good chance of working."

"I might be an idiot at times, but you've made it clear you really love your cat. I'd end up feeling guilty if I tried that, so I'd try to slink away without asking. Just being honest. I'm pretty sure I'm the reason I haven't had any luck with women."

"Yet you're being particularly bold and forthcoming with me?"

"Well, it helps my uncles are encouraging it. I mean, they can be complete assholes, but they generally don't set us poor children up for complete failure without a good reason. I'm probably too trusting for my good on that one, though. So, am I dying of some undiagnosed disease?"

I took the scanner to my new laptop, plugged it in, and went to work setting up the diagnostics software and importing Darian's health and DNA record so I could make sense of the results. Within three minutes, the first red flag popped up, involving a positive lycanthropy result.

I clicked into the software to begin diagnostics on the virus strain to encounter the second red flag: no matching species listing.

Great. New species of lycanthropes popped up yearly, but the last thing I needed was having to explain to a triad their son was the latest person-of-interest to the research and development department of the CDC. After a few more minutes of checking, the virus count in his blood stream put him at the earliest stages of infection detectible. "Remember what we were discussing about lycanthropy? This states you are positive, earliest stage of detectible virus levels in the blood—or in the magic pulse. I haven't confirmed which. In good or bad news for you, there's no matching strain in the system."

Darian's brows shot up. "I mean, I work with lycanthropes often enough, but I take the base precautions. They're all wolves, though."

"You do not match any known wolf strains. It's just a blank on species type." I tapped on the species result, went into the diagnostics software, and tapped in the request for a classification of species rather than a specific species. Narrowing it down to mammal or avian would help, and if I got lucky, I'd be able to narrow it down to a family. "I'm trying to get a family classification out of the system, but we'll see."

A minute later, the system pinged, informing me it was unable to detect a base class of virus strain.

How odd. I frowned, pulled out the test samples, including the wolf strain of the lycanthropy virus, and set up a new test. Within thirty seconds, the scanner did its job, reporting everything I might ever want to know about the wolf virus. Puzzled over the complete lack of data on the strain, I went back into Darian's DNA results and tapped in a request for the system to check for known shapeshifter DNA combinations.

It, too, returned back negative.

Interesting.

"According to your expression, you either hate or love me right now, and I'm not sure which. Should I be worried?"

"Normally, when these things register a lycanthropy infection, it's able to judge the base classification of the virus, which is typically mammal or avian. It has no idea what kind of virus you've been infected with. You also are negative for any of the known shapeshifter DNA combinations, which can flag people as infected with lycanthropy without actually having lycanthropy. But this is reporting you are infected with the virus."

Darian shrugged. "That would explain some of my uncle's behavior."

"Which one?"

"All of them."

I nodded. "With how many cases of

early onset lycanthropy have been cropping up lately, to the point doctors are pursuing it as viable treatments for terminal patients, it's entirely possible you haven't been infected long. You'll want to monitor the virus levels for progression, but beyond that, you shouldn't be contagious unless you go really wild."

"Can you be a little more specific about that? How wild is wild here?"

"That depends. How's your dad compared to an incubus?" With a wicked grin, I began tapping through Darian's DNA to see if he might pose an infection risk should he unleash his inner beast—or his devilish side. "Is your daddy just a big, nasty devilish general, or is he secretly some sort of sex god on top of it?"

"This is not a question I have ever wanted to ask my mother, truth be told—or either of my fathers. Some things a son just doesn't want to know. That's one of them."

"I regret to inform you that we're about to find out." Giggling over having turned the tables on him, I delved into the dark depths of his genetics, clicking through the DNA trees to the section dedicated to reproduction. "Congratulations! You're eighty-nine percent male."

"Pardon?"

"Humans don't express gender as pure male or female. It's a range. In this software, we use a range of zero to a hundred, one side of the chart leaning towards male, the other side of the chart leaning towards female. A zero sometimes presents as a hermaphrodite, although that's not always the case. A better example of someone who is near zero on this chart would be someone with asexual tendencies, neither presenting as male or female. Eighty-nine percent male is pretty up there in terms of pure masculinity."

"And what percentage are you?"

"I'm an example of extreme femininity; I have less than a percent of male traits in my genetics. This is pretty rare. Honestly, I'd consider you to be at a healthier percentage than I am—as evidenced by my development of cancer. Too much of a good thing can easily become a bad thing, and it wouldn't surprise me if my high percentage on this specific chart led to the cancer problem." After a moment, I shrugged. "It could also be the deodorant. I'll switch to something with fewer harsh chemicals, but you know how something can be too little, too late."

"This conversation may have just changed my relationship with my deodorant," he admitted.

"And with your non-existent sex life. So, your manliness levels are pretty healthy, but you're not registering on the incubus charts.

However, your daddy is packing goods in some departments, as your sperm count is high, and you're registering as highly fertile. That is not an angelic trait. That said, the pulse came back with a high percentage of female sperm, so if you're wanting sons, you're definitely going to be a source of frustration for your wife unless she wants a lot of kids hoping for a boy. Frankly, I recommend you hire an incubus if you want a son."

"Alas, I am not a king of any country, so I am not terribly concerned with what gender my children are, should I have any. What else can you tell me, Dr. Diana?"

"If I'm your doctor, you're probably going to die, but I'll recommend you go ask a real doctor—or your smug uncles. I bet they were aware of your current situation."

"For the record, I really do not see this as at all a disadvantage. As I said earlier, I quite like living. Since I work with lycanthropes as part of my investigative work, I already know the rules for the newly infected. I just need to report to the CDC and register, which doesn't bother me."

I eyed his records. "I could probably figure out how to register you, although you'd be better off having your father go with you for the registration. The CDC doesn't tend to give the children of triads who somehow contract lycanthropy much of a hard time about it. They *will* want to do a contact tracing to see where you got the infection."

"Are *you* infected with lycanthropy? I mean, we've been sharing a room."

"Sharing a room isn't sufficient to pass on lycanthropy, and I'm tested every year. That said, I am *not* tested with the high sensitivity scanners. The scanners I'm tested with could have a ten year or longer incubation without the virus being picked up. It catches the virus a stage before becoming infectious, typically." As I already had his data, I went to work preparing the scanner for a new reading. "I'd like to test the vials first, but then I can run mine through to see if I have picked it up. Like you, I do have a lot of contact with lycanthropes, so honesty? It's viable."

"The Devil is underhanded enough he'd help the virus along, too."

Lucifer would. I frowned. "But who would he have taken the virus *from*?"

"You, because he knows full well I'd consent to contracting the lycanthropy virus. Can your machine tell us how long I've been infected?"

I shook my head. "The virus is pretty individualistic, and replication times have been changing a lot lately. Some people are still taking forty years or longer to incubate their viruses, but a lot of younger people are shifting far younger. Early onset is becoming rather common. It's on the CDC's radar, because with transmission and maturation rates, it's actually possible for lycanthropes to outnumber humans, and it won't take nearly as long as people think. It becomes even more complicated when the virus mutates, although it mutates at a fairly slow rate. Then there's the issue of species. For a long time, people believed only mammals could be lycanthropes. The avians kept to themselves and either played wolf or just refused to admit their species. The percentage of avians is also really low, with some species only having one to three members. Because of the nature of the lycanthropy virus, the species usually ends up with two members, but some of the avians simply don't pass their virus on to their children, and the virus itself is less likely to infect somebody else. The CDC expects most avian species will only last one or two generations."

"And reptiles?"

"We haven't seen any known reptile species, but I've come to the conclusion maybe we shouldn't assume it's an impossibility." I checked the scanner, went through the settings, and adjusted the device so it would read through glass, plastics, and even clear metals. "Lucifer really spent too much money on this thing, and I refuse to give it back. I will fight him for it. I'll bite his bloody kneecaps off if he tries to take it from me."

Darian snickered and dug out one of the cases and began to check over the vials, making notations on a sheet of paper before tying a tag to the handle with a few notes. "In bad news, I can't actually mark the vials, so once we hand this over to the CDC, we won't have access to them again. Please tell me we don't have to open these vials."

"We don't have to open the vials. Lucifer gave me a scanner that can penetrate through just about anything. We'll have to rely on the magical pulse readings, but it's sensitive enough we'll be able to get a reading on common toxins, viruses, bacteria, and so on. The bacterium readings can get sketchy, although things like anthrax are typically easy enough to identify. It's a matter of numbers, as there are a ridiculous number of bacteria in the world. Hell, our guts have a huge number of bacteria."

"Surprisingly, I did know that. Will the scans take as long as my DNA?"

"No. It'll take me probably half an hour to get through the whole lot of them. Just set out the cases, and I'll hold the scanner's probe to the vial. It'll register the results, beep to let me know it's done, and I'll move onto the next one. If we get any bacteria, it'll add twenty minutes to test the sample, but it's not bad. I have it set up to save the data to be more efficient. If you get bored watching, feel free to crash out. I'll wake you if I find anything interesting."

"I'll watch, if you don't mind. If I can con Lucifer out of one of these, too, I want to see how this is done. I'm not above begging to be able to give using it a try."

"Well, you're easy to please. I might be going to hell, but it's not because I don't know how to share. Just don't you break my scanner, because I really will cry if you do."

"I'll be careful," he promised.

THIRTEEN

"All miracles come with a price."

SIXTY-FOUR DIFFERENT VIALS, sixty-four different diseases, viruses, and bacteria, all of which were used in some fashion or another in biological warfare. Most importantly, one of the vials contained Darian's strain of the lycanthropy virus.

I had questions, but the scanner provided me with zero answers. Darian, who'd realized I hadn't been joking about it taking at least twenty minutes to check over each bacterium, hadn't made it to bed before passing out. Initially, he'd been seated upright, but an accidental bump while reaching for one of the metal containers had startled him enough he'd fallen over directly onto my lap although he hadn't woken.

Either that, or he did a damned fine job of playing possum, and I figured he'd earned using me as a pillow for tricking me.

Lucifer manifested in the room along with Gabriel, and the Devil opted for his inhuman form, his tail lashing side to side. Like his brother, a shroud engulfed him, shimmering whenever he moved. "You're *supposed* to be sleeping. How can we commit nefarious acts when you're awake when we're supposed to be tending to you?"

"I'm trying to figure out how Darian got infected with a lycanthropy virus strain the CDC doesn't know about but this lab does. There's no evidence of his animal strain."

"That is because there is no animal strain," Gabriel informed me. "He caught the virus from your new cat. She and her kittens are all doing well. Two would have died, but *He* opted they would become eternal kittens, gave them to Darlene to be trained as guardians, and live in my brother's many hells when she ultimately gives them to you, although they will no longer be in kitten format. *He* has a sense of humor, although *He* often pretends he does not. *He* also felt if the kittens died, you would feel nothing but guilt for many years, so you have two extra kittens to contend with, although they have been blessed with heightened intellect and will require little of your care beyond companionship. Consider them to be the first of your minions in my brother's domain. One has an angelic nature and one has a demonic nature to maintain the balance."

I froze. "Does that mean Darian's theory of this lab trying to spread lycanthropy is accurate?"

"To a certain degree. As you would find out yourself soon enough, you are infected with the same strain, although you were exposed through a different avenue."

"Mr. Flooferson."

"Correct. Mr. Flooferson, as you have named him, has not infected any other humans, but that is in part due to your care for him and his nature. He's also less contagious than the momma cat and her kittens. The entry to the lab has a great deal of the virus, and Darian contracted the virus there. The interior of the lab has had nothing for the virus to thrive on, so it had died out." The archangel shrugged. "He would have contracted the virus from you given time. This just speeds it along. I highly recommend that you take that vial to the CDC for use in the medical field. It will allow for the lycanthropy virus to incubate without symptoms or harm to the host, and when exposed to a live virus with a strain, the original virus will pick up the strain and establish itself quickly and without many of the unfortunate side-effects early onset lycanthropy typically causes. With the right patient, you might be able to perform miracles."

"All miracles come with a price." I

frowned. "What price would this miracle have?"

"Nothing particularly nefarious, I assure you. *He* does not view the strain you are infected with as an aberration. *He* recognizes much good can come from their experimentation, and that they will pay the price for their transgressions through you. You are simply the weapon *He* has chosen for their punishment, my brother is the tool you will use to aid your cause, and one might say Darian is the reward you will reap for doing good in the world. Much like my brother's Darlene, you will become a tool of balance meant to keep the End of Days at bay."

"No pressure there," I muttered, shaking my head. I pointed at Darian. "Are you sure he's a reward? I mean, he's a bit rowdy and a lot lusty for a reward."

Lucifer laughed. "He's only rowdy and lusty because you keep proving to him you're his ultimate woman. He's cut from his parents' cloth, so he'll be a patient hunter. You'll enjoy when he realizes he'll have to work to tame you. Now that you've ruined our fun by exposing the infection, we have come as bearers of gifts."

"Please tell me the gift is a confirmation the fur we got out of that one cage will help lead us to Mr. Flooferson."

"No," the pair replied.

Well, shit. "But that was our best bet!"

Lucifer snickered. "As you are a bleeding heart who might destroy this whole world should any additional animals be injured as a result of this, the feline who shed that fur is safely in custody and being pampered at a CDC lab. I, being a benevolent and kind being, insisted they have feline lycanthropes handle the animal."

My eyes widened. "But doesn't that mean the cat's virus might pick up the feline lycanthropy strain? If it's a blank virus?"

"As a matter of fact, yes." The way Lucifer grinned promised trouble. "With a twist."

"As in the strain will have human DNA and be a reversed version of the lycanthropy virus?"

"It's like you work for the CDC and have been taught to look for the worst-case scenario," the Devil teased. "From that cat, the virus will mutate several times, making the lycanthropy virus friendlier to humans—as in the people infected with that specific strain of the virus will lead fairly normal lives with minimal awareness of their virus or the animal they could shift into with work. The strain will also be significantly less infectious. Extreme cases will be able to shift into their animals, but a lot of the prejudices lycanthropes currently face will be restricted to a flag on a driver's license and only a concern in major bleeding events and reoccurring sex. A single evening with a lycanthrope should not result in a mating bond or disease transference."

Huh. "And this Kingston fellow is behind all this? What about Mr. Flooferson and his virus?"

Gabriel chuckled, and while I usually found angelic laughter soothing, his had a sharp edge to it, and I tensed. "He is but one. This was not the result he desired. He will get the result he desires in another way, but that is not your problem. *He* has already made plans regarding that situation. *He* sends his regrets. You will not get the pleasure of killing Kingston. You will get to take your temper out on somebody else, so don't you worry about that. As for Mr. Flooferson, his virus will be of no consequence. My brother would not handle your grief over your lost cat very well, so he will be gifted with a more angelic nature while your new queen will get a more demonic nature. The calico will be gifted with an angelic nature, and the kitten *He* has selected for *Himself* is demonic in nature. *He* felt there needed to be a minor amount of naughtiness in the high heavens to counter all of the disgusting goodness and order that keeps finding its way into the many hells."

I would never understand the Christian pantheon. "Lucifer, you're an idiot."

The Devil shrugged. "I don't like when

my women cry, and Darlene has given me permission to classify you as one of my women. I'm even allowed to admire the scenery as long as I take my frustrations out on her."

Darlene would drive me insane, and the Devil would absolutely test his luck in the hopes of earning a punishment from his wife. "You're paying me extra to put up with that crap."

"I will make certain that your initial offer is itemized by inconvenience to prove I am a somewhat tolerable employer—or that I'm at least paying you well enough to put up with me." The Devil prowled across the room, bent over the vials, and picked up the one I'd marked as a sample of *ebolavirus Zaire.* "He almost made a very lethal mistake with this one."

I'd almost fled the room upon realizing what the vial contained, although Darian's position on my lap had done a good job of keeping me in place. "Only an idiot fucks around with ebola. How long have I been infected?"

"Mr. Flooferson infected you shortly after he discovered he could sit on your lap and be brushed without fear of retaliation. It was his tendency to lick your fingers that got you. He'd scraped his gums with his teeth and licked you, and that was after he'd gotten a few swats in on you earlier that day," Lucifer explained. "Since you hadn't gotten upset he'd swatted you out of fear, he'd tested his luck. You did a very good job convincing him to enjoy affection."

Go figure. My poor cat had been transformed into a lycanthropy virus carrier, and I'd contracted it trying to convince him life could be good.

No good deed went unpunished, although I didn't consider contracting the lycanthropy virus to be much of a punishment. "And his current status?"

"The catnappers have gotten what they wanted from him, so their current plan is to dump him in the woods and let him fend for himself. They have no interest in taking the next step of the research using him, but the general compulsions I've put in place make them hesitant to hurt or kill your cat, so they're improvising. This is where things become complicated."

As one of the few subjects my parents had actually bothered teaching me without modification, math had become something of a safe haven for me. Some formulas were easier to solve than others.

Mr. Flooferson's catnappers would have wanted to see if their little test worked, which meant they'd be after me next. I straightened. "They're going to come for me?"

"As a matter of fact, yes," the Devil replied, and he flashed a toothy grin my way. "As such, my brother here and I are going to get to you first, take you to a location of our choosing, do nefarious and awful things to you, and sit back, relax, and have a beer while you stretch your legs. Once you're done with that, you'll get to do more investigation work, although you'll find it's more along the lines of rescuing more animals. You like that sort of work. Your new lap ornament is not going to be happy with us, as he won't be invited for the first stage of this adventure."

I hated being played, and I hated being played by someone who knew exactly what was going on, made me do the work anyway, and then decided for me what I needed to do next. However, as my end goal involved rescuing my cat, I would dance to Lucifer's tune. I needed him to make some key adjustments to my soul if I wanted to avoid an accidental departure from life. "This is supposed to be more complicated. We're supposed to be going to a bunch of dead ends, gathering more evidence, and struggling to figure this out."

"Not interested," Gabriel and the Devil announced.

Divines. Give an inch, and they'd take over the entire universe if permitted. "What about that whole bargain to stay with

Darian each day? Isn't this going to blow that out of the water?"

The Devil smirked. "I'll leave him a set of clues, and I plan on teaching him some interesting tricks during another bargain I strike with him. He'll get delightfully cranky with me over it, but he'll cooperate, as I've accomplished my original goals with the first bargain. He's seen you for how you are, and he likes what he sees. As he's just like his father, he'll pursue you to the ends of the Earth if needed."

"Which father?"

"Both, really, although I meant Belial. Now, we do have a few things to discuss. Darian won't awaken, so you can escape his clutches if you'd like. I expect your incubating lycanthropy virus is already attuning to him because he's carrying the same strain. I expect you'll put up a fight about leaving him now that you've had a chance to be around him for a while."

"That's not how the virus works."

"It is with your strain. It's more empathic in nature compared to the standard virus. This is in part due to the lack of animalistic genes guiding the virus's behavior, so it's relying on your perceptions of the world. It recognizes you enjoy spending time with Darian even when he annoys you. In turn, it recognizes Darian has a matching virus. The virus has always been linked with strains of the same type despite being individual to the host. As such, your viruses are perceiving safety in numbers and a general compatibility. They did some unusual alterations clearing out the animalistic DNA. A little magic, a little science—a lot of progress, truthfully. I'm quite impressed with the work they've done." The Devil returned the *ebolavirus Zaire* sample and picked up a different one, a fungus I hadn't recognized the name of and couldn't spell let alone pronounce. "If they'd started with this instead of the lycanthropy virus, they would have changed—or destroyed—the world. Well, change is inevitable. The Earth would have balanced on a coin's edge if they'd brought this one out."

"What is that one? Beyond being a fungus."

"*Ophiocordyceps unilateralis*," the Devil announced. "It's thc ant zombie fungus. Essentially, the fungus infects ants with spores and gradually takes over the ant. Near the end stage of infection, the ant leaves the safety of its nest, goes somewhere favorable for the fungus, and is latched into place while the fungus eats its host before dispersing to take over new ants and continue spreading the infection. With some modifications, it's possible for humans to become infected with this fungus. With the right scientists working for the wrong cause, it would be possible to control the fungus's purpose and hijack the hijacker. I suspect this wasn't chosen because nobody has found a preventative or cure for it yet. It doesn't do much good if the controllers end up infected, right? With the blank lycanthropy virus, that's not an issue. Lycanthropes make excellent fighters, so if the goal is to start a war, well, it would allow them to make an army rather quickly."

Crap. The war angle made a lot of sense, especially since the planet couldn't sustain billions of hungry lycanthropes. The planet *could* sustain a bunch of lycanthropes for a short period of time. Dooming them to be killed in some battle or another made a great deal of sense.

Each and every year, the CDC became entangled in some form of uprising or another as those seeking power concocted new ways to achieve their goals. Some went the biological warfare route. Others pursued kidnapping or coercion. Others bribed their way to the top, corrupting leaders into doing what they wanted. Terrorists were an entirely different breed of cat, using the same tools the greedy and corrupt did but with the goal of targeting and horrifying the populace before making their demands—if they made any demands at all.

Sometimes, I hated people. "Dare I ask what else these assholes were trying to cook up?"

Lucifer returned the zombie sample to the tray and lifted up the one containing the black death. "Humans are such interesting creatures. Do you know what they believed when this was killing over a third of their population?"

"I'd guess they believed you were behind it."

"Surprisingly, no. They believed it was *His* will, and that those who survived were favored by *Him*—and that many who suffered and died harbored secret sin in their hearts. For the non-believers and other religions, they blamed *Him*, too—but as a punishment for humanity as a whole. It spread so badly because they were at the end of an emergence, and the magic was dying away. The magic they once used to heal such plagues no longer worked, and because they'd relied so heavily on magic to heal the body, their bodies no longer had any defenses against things like the black death. By the time the black death died out, their bodies remembered how to work without magic helping it along." Placing the vial in its appropriate slot, he picked up another sample, which my scanner had identified as smallpox. "*He* made this one when humans began making earnest efforts to obtain immortality, a reminder they were anything but immortal. For the most part, *He* failed to do anything other than motivate humans to try harder. Someone must have bargained to get this, as humanity had successfully eradicated smallpox, and the last of the virus had died during this emergence. The CDC had samples in the lab, but after some thought, they were destroyed. Russia had a sample, but after learning the CDC destroyed theirs, they followed the example and destroyed theirs as well. The last act the CDC did with their smallpox sample was to save a copy of the registration so scanners like yours could detect it. *He* is quite pleased humanity was able to use their powers for something good for a change. I will be taking this sample—and you will delete your scanner's results and pretend you did not see this. And you will bargain with me to make certain any other samples of smallpox that might exist become deceased."

I raised a brow at the order. "What am I bargaining away to do what you want?"

Lucifer sighed. "My wife wants a hug. But she doesn't want a hug from me. She wants one from you."

If hugging Darlene would make sure the smallpox virus stayed dead, I'd give her two hugs and tolerate her the next time she needed to cuddle with someone who wasn't her husband. "Bargain made."

The vial vanished. "You're protective of your soul, but you really don't have any scruples about other types of bargains, do you?"

"Maybe if you cut better bargains, I'd be more hesitant about accepting them. Oh, no. I have to hug someone I like. Whatever will I do?"

Gabriel erupted into chiming laughter. "Just be careful about any paperwork you sign, or you might find yourself coping with life as Kanika's sister, especially as my brother is offended over how your mortal parents have treated you over the years. He's been investigating, and he does not appreciate what he has learned."

"Don't you go spilling my secrets, Gabriel!" Lucifer snorted and stomped a hoof. "I wanted to see if the same trick would work twice. Now you've gone and ruined it."

The Devil would drive me crazy, but at least the ride would be entertaining. "Does Kanika *want* a sister?"

"Desperately. Or a brother. Honestly, she'll take anything that makes me stop gracing her with so much attention. My little cupcake has about had it with my affections. If she didn't make giving her affection so delightful, I'd probably be a little less annoying, but she bristles so nicely. I *love* cats, and she's just so catty."

Right. Darlene took her cattish nature to extremes, and Kanika ran hot at her mother's heels. Add in the menagerie of pets, which included at least two other cats, and I should've guessed. "That doesn't explain your interest in me."

"You love cats, therefore you're equipped to tolerate the attention of two large felines who will give you attention when you don't want it. I've learned. My kitties love attention and require it in copious quantities, but they do not want to admit they need the attention. Especially Darlene."

"Well, you made her a succubus with a restricted diet of you and only you, and she does need your energy. As for Kanika, you're just trying to convince her that she can be loved just as she is, bristly temper and all. She's not easy to convince, so you have to go to extremes to get the point across." I rolled my eyes at their weird family dynamic. "If your wife and daughter need an emotional support whatever-I'll-be, that's fine. Just tack on the appropriate compensation to my job offer if it means I won't be able to run away after work is over to do what I want."

"You should have limits," Lucifer complained. "And a *little* regard for my wallet."

I shrugged. "I do have a little regard for your wallet. I have faith it can pay out, even when your mouth gets you in trouble and results in you having to use your wallet a little more than you would have if you had just kept your mouth shut."

"She has you there," Gabriel stated.

True to the Devil's word, Darian slept

through the ruckus, and I eased out from underneath him. Retrieving the blanket from the bed along with a pillow, I covered him and made him as comfortable as I could. "Are there any other samples I shouldn't turn over to the CDC?"

"No. The rest are acquirable through other methods."

"Have you already decided what you're going to convert me to?"

"As a matter of fact, yes."

"What will I be?"

"The worst nightmare of anyone who crosses you. I promise you'll have a great time."

Why had I thought the Devil might give me a straight answer? I gestured to my chest, which ached less than it had earlier. "And this mess?"

"You still get the bandages for a week when you're in your human form. The conversion won't help too much with that. The holy fire and devilish energy will take that long to fade out, and their presence is what's making it ache. You'll be fine. Those energies will make your conversion easier on you, and you'll appreciate that tomorrow. Of course, tomorrow, you're going to be a little psychotic. I'll enjoy it immensely."

"Psychotic?" I narrowed my eyes and considered Gabriel, the most likely of the brothers to give me an almost straight answer. "Mind illuminating me?"

"He's going to try you as a hybrid, converted with equal parts devilish and demonic energy. These forces will take some time to settle, and you'll be the rope they're playing tug-of-war with. You'll be fine. You'll just be a little crazy for a few days. Considering his plan is to drop you in the middle of a bunch of hostiles and let you work out your temper on them for a while, it will work out for the best. Add in the holy fire, and you'll be an indestructible ball of fury. You'll calm down eventually. More importantly, you'll force the playing of several important cards, and once they're played, the forces of heaven and hell combined will need an indestructible ball of fury. We won't be able to directly act, but there's nothing in the rules stating that a psychotic devil-demoness hybrid hopped up on holy fire can't make a mess of things."

"Wait. Why are the forces of heaven and hell combining? What the hell memo did I miss?"

"We strongly oppose an unscheduled End of Days," Gabriel announced. "We're using you to prevent it. They prepare for war. Right now, it's a war we cannot wage. But there's nothing in the rules stating we can't send in a provoked agent who neither truly allies with the heavens or the many hells to do our dirty work for us. And by stealing your cat, they provoked you. Those conditions are met. Darian is considered to be an ally of both the heavens and the many hells due to his heritage. You have no such restrictions. You would deny *Him* and my brother your soul, and as such, you fall outside of our rules. In this war, you are a free agent—and us giving you the tools and the ability to handle the problem doesn't break those rules."

"That seems questionable at best."

Both the archangel and the Devil shrugged.

"What rule are these people breaking?"

Gabriel picked up the vial containing the lycanthropy virus, turning it. Through the ever-weakening shroud, I could make out the shape of his head tilting. "They wish to become God and control mankind—and *He* revoked *His* ability to control mankind through gifting them with free will. Should they succeed, the End of Days will begin, for the universe itself opposes such things, especially now that most beings are free willed."

I averted my eyes and realized why they'd moved their plans forward. Given a little more, and the shroud would hide no secrets at all. "Lucifer isn't changing his form much, is he?"

"I'm not," the Devil confirmed. "This is my devilish form, shrouded enough you won't see what you're not ready to handle.

My angelic form is that of a dark-winged angel. And we aren't headless beings at all."

"You just sacrifice what you are for the sake of the mortals you encounter. You're not all the same, are you?"

"We have slight variations, but we are what humans could only be if it were not for their sin—which is what makes them human and made them human from the very beginning. My angelic form is a little more complete compared to my brothers."

I could make a guess. "You have a dick to go along with your nipples."

The Devil snickered. "How crude, but yes. Among other things. Angels do not need reproductive organs to reproduce. When they join a triad, their unconditional love for human and devil or demon is what transfers the angel's life force into the triad's coupling. It's complicated. But the triad cannot have children unless all three of them are in sync in that regard. Amusingly, Raguel believed Belial would be the problematic part of their triad. It did not take long for Darian's mother to become pregnant with him. Belial is among my favorite of my devils. But it takes a keen understanding of love and everything it entails to thoroughly bring about ruin. I tempered Belial, and I have been waiting a long time for him to become entrapped by a mortal. Darian's mother complements him perfectly. Raguel is one of my more annoying brothers, but he fits well with them, too. They'll be delighted when they hear I've entrapped their little innocent boy." Still snickering, Lucifer took the vial from Gabriel and began the tedious process of packing everything away. "I think I'll handle taking this to the CDC. I will also make certain they understand you will be tendering a resignation due to circumstances, mostly involving your new status as a hybrid devil-demoness with a hefty adaptation period ahead of you. I'll even be considerate and permit them to observe you from a distance while you play warrior queen."

Me? A warrior queen? "Have you been taking drugs, Lucifer?"

Gabriel snickered. "He is not partaking of any drugs. He just knows precisely what he will make you, and there is only one thing for you to become, and that is a queen over your domain. As you will be put in a position where you will want to fight, you will be a warrior queen. Now, I recommend you leave everything you don't want to be destroyed here in Darian's care. Write him a note asking to tend to everything. That will drive him a little crazier than he will already become when he gets Lucifer's note, which claims you are being held hostage."

"Why are you telling Darian you're holding me hostage, Lucifer?"

"Simple. I want him to show you how far

he'll go to be able to stake some claims. That boy loves his family, make no mistake about that, but he has never truly committed to someone outside of his family unit as anything beyond passing friendships, and it's time he learned how to do so. I'm just using you to give him a slight attitude adjustment. Don't forget, Diana. I am an asshole. I'm the king over all other assholes, although I am second only to my heavenly asshole of a father."

I'd been exposed to Lucifer and his family enough to recognize the only reason *He* and the Devil didn't fawn all over each other was because of circumstance and general stupidity. And possibly their gender. "You two are so disgustingly male," I complained. "Just invite *Him* to a private family dinner and get your hugs so you stop annoying everybody else. Please."

Gabriel giggled, and he turned away, the shroud flickering and thinning.

I focused my gaze on the floor. "I think I'm just either going to keep my eyes closed or not look at anyone for a while."

"That would be wise. I turned for that reason. Lucifer, you will want to tread with care, caution, and haste. The combination of holy fire, devilish energy, and the blank virus are strengthening her other natural abilities."

"We'll go the blindfold route so there are

no accidents. Close your eyes, Diana. Your time to shine has come, and I will give you sufficient prey to hunt. And while you hunt, I will retrieve your cat and prepare him for the reality of living with you. It would not do for your beloved pet to fear you."

I closed my eyes. "How long would it have taken for me to break through the shroud if it hadn't been for the cancer?"

Gabriel chuckled, and his voice drew close. A moment later, a soft cloth touched my face and wrapped around my head. "The next time you had attempted a summoning of any sort, you would have pierced the shroud. Before your cat was stolen, you were already progressing to pierce through the shrouds. You would have been eradicated during a meeting with my brother in the other futures. It would have been unexpected. My brother noticed your problems with the shrouds because your cat was stolen. As such, in a way, these thieves saved your life. You should repay them with a merciful death."

"That's one hell of a repayment. Why is giving them a merciful death a repayment?" I blurted.

"Because if they so much as scratch you, my brother will turn their deaths into a masterpiece, one that will strike fear into humanity for years."

According to Lucifer's grunt, Gabriel

had spoken nothing but the truth. "So, you're saying I've really made a mess of things. I mean, I'd figured that out. But it was even worse than I thought. Also, me falling over dead would have been a spectacular interruption to a business meeting."

"And my brother would have been distraught, and *He* would have been brought into it, as my brother would want to recapture your seed and bring you back into the world immediately to begin cultivating you again. I've been told finding a pair of adults who would raise you in a similar way would be difficult at best."

"Well, I'd certainly hope so. I do the bare minimum requirements when it comes to being grateful to my parents for getting me to adulthood somewhat intact. I will even protest somewhat so you can act like you actually participated in a kidnapping, Gabriel. I'm already blindfolded, so it's not a stretch. You seem like you could use some fun."

"Why are you worried about us having fun when we are worried about accidentally erasing you from existence?"

"I'm not worried about being erased from existence," I replied. "I'm more worried about being 'accidentally' adopted, as Kanika gets very upset with her father over many things for some reason. Lucifer, you are that reason, as I have heard from

Kanika, repeatedly, how much she adores her mother. It's her father driving her insane."

Lucifer chuckled. "I adore my little cupcake. And you're going to be my little cookie. I haven't decided what I'm calling Darian yet. Malcolm is a little shy still, so I'm going to have to ease him into it, but he's my little saltwater toffee."

The Devil needed some time with a good therapist, and *He* needed to be sat down and scolded for having evicted a ridiculous sweet yet naughty being to rule over the hells. "Can we negotiate? I'd rather be a candy cane. I will join forces with Darlene if you try to call me a tart."

"My little candy cane is a little weird, but I'm open to negotiations on this matter. Honestly, little has the same ring as cupcake, but I'll cope. Somehow." Lucifer took hold of my elbow. "I will write your note for Darian on your behalf, and I'll be a gentleman and explain the shrouds were dropping. The goal is to get him to chase you, not to make him completely panic. He needs to progress more before I test how well he panics when you get into trouble. Also, I will permit you to attempt to summon me once and only once. The second time you try it, you'll be put in time out for a while to think about what you've done—and yes, you will be summoning me without my consent, as I strongly dislike doing things other people tell me. Just ask Darlene."

"I don't have to ask Darlene, Lucy. I already know. Anyone who knows Darlene already knows."

"Every time I think I couldn't possibly love my wife any more than I do, Diana opens her mouth and proves me wrong. I have the *best* wife, Gabriel. You need to find yourself a best wife, too. They're so much fun."

"I have seen your wife, Lucifer. She is nothing but trouble. I love her, but she was born trouble, and she will remain trouble until the End of Days. I do not need relentless trouble until the End of Days," the archangel replied.

"He probably needs a calming wife who has a high tolerance for bullshit, Lucifer. If you want Gabriel to have a wife or a husband, you need to think about it from his perspective. His partner needs to be someone who has an unfathomable amount of patience and a high tolerance for idiocy without scruples regarding devils or demons to go along with a tolerance for headless beings." I reached over and patted Lucifer's hand, which kept a firm grip on my elbow. "We can discuss matchmaking for your brother at a later time. I'll even test out a summoning circle for him and see if the trick Darian's mother used will work on him."

Lucifer laughed. "Don't stress yourself over it, Diana. Gabriel loves being an uncle, although he finds his uncle duties a little more stressful than he likes right now."

"He speaks the truth," Gabriel informed me in a solemn tone. "Try not to destroy the entire world during your upcoming rampage, Diana. But do feel free to destroy the spot we leave you at. It is contaminated, and we do not appreciate its existence."

FOURTEEN

Angelic blood tasted oddly sweet.

THE NEXT TIME the Devil offered to teleport me somewhere, I'd decline. After suffering through the equivalent of a punch to the gut, something I didn't remember from our first trip to the hotel, Lucifer dropped me to the ground, pinned me, and shoved a bloody finger into my mouth. I could only hope it was his finger. Having someone else's finger, likely severed, shoved into my mouth would cap an already bad week.

"While effective, that is a pretty rude way to go about it," Gabriel commented, his tone implying the struggle interested him. "I find it interesting she is not putting up more of a fight. You should fight him more, Diana. Make him earn his latest conquest. I fail to see why you are shoving your finger halfway down her throat, however."

Well, if the archangel thought I should

put up a fight, I'd make Lucifer regret putting his fingers anywhere near my mouth. I bit as hard as I could, as I doubted I could do more than wiggle in the Devil's hold.

"Thank you for encouraging her to bite," Lucifer replied in a strained voice. "I'm doing it this way because it's faster, and when the conversion takes hold, she'll be equally devilish in nature. This isn't exactly a precise art, and corrupting a seed is not as easy as it looks. You could help, instead of standing there grinning at me like an idiot. And don't forget the goal is to make her a hybrid. That works best for what I have in mind for her. Give me a break. I'm creating a species *and* a new seed type here."

"*He* finds you amusing, in case you were not aware." A strong hand seized the back of my neck, and Gabriel chuckled. "As *He* has as much of an interest in this plan of yours as you do, I would be glad to offer assistance. What do you think about an infusion of angelic blood to smooth the process?"

"What's *soothing* about your blood?"

"I said smooth, not soothe. It will streamline your efforts. She will not appreciate the infusion."

Damn, and I'd thought the Devil ruled over all other assholes, but Gabriel was nipping right at his heels. I struggled to spit Lucifer's finger out of my mouth, but he refused to budge. I opened my mouth to bite, and the bastard freed himself. I snapped my teeth in frustration and got a hold of the archangel's finger instead, biting hard enough to draw blood.

Angelic blood tasted oddly sweet to go along with somewhat metallic.

"I do love when the victims of our games play along. Also, she has quite the temper."

"It's my blood," Lucifer announced with pride in his voice. "It brings out all those little gems she's kept buried in a futile attempt to please everyone around her. She'll still want to please everyone around her when I'm done, as I can't remove that part of her personality without destroying everything that makes her who she is, but she *will* be more inclined to do things solely for herself moving forward."

"I am thinking I will owe her many presents for Christmas this year after the next few hours we will put her through."

"We will stop in on her family for their Christmas celebration, and I am thinking I will bring my nephew and his charming wife along with my little cupcake and her little saltwater toffee. A sphinx, two cranky unicorns, my little candy cane here, and her beau will be quite the disruption. Perhaps you should bring Michael along."

"It would be rude to exclude Raguel and his husband and wife."

"If we can lure the wife off, I will ask Belial to make use of his original form. I would rather not scar his wife for life."

"She summoned him in his original form. She knows about the crushed tentacled tomato with a face."

Crushed tentacled tomato with a face? "Say what?" I asked around Gabriel's finger.

"I was still learning how to create devils when I cultivated Belial. His original form is quite horrific. But he is among the best of my shapeshifters as a result. Honestly, he's so bad I think about throwing up when he shows up. My darling is *not* happy with me that my best and most loyal general can give her nightmares on a bad day." The Devil grabbed hold of my head and made sure I couldn't escape. "Make sure she swallows more than she spits. She's stubborn, so she'll probably need more than we appreciate. While you're trying to stick your finger down her throat, check on the cancer."

"It has not revitalized itself, and she has been assimilating the holy fire better than expected. I believe she was utilizing it when she was in the lab, as there is evidence of diminishment beyond expectation. Will you want another infusion for this?"

"I don't have any other devils capable of generating holy fire. Think she's viable?"

"I know she is. If you cultivate the hellfire, I will work the holy fire, and we should be done with that portion within a few minutes. I believe she has incubated the holy fire sufficiently. I suspect *He* has meddled with her to be so receptive."

"*He* would."

"I really would," a still and quiet voice murmured. Both Lucifer and Gabriel yelped.

Huh. *He* really did show up at times. I'd believed that to be some myth, although I'd been aware of the Devil's enjoyment of startling people who talked about him openly.

"Father," Gabriel greeted.

Lucifer huffed. "Old man."

"My beloved sons," He replied with amusement. *"Are you enjoying yourselves?"*

"I'm having a great time," Lucifer admitted. "She's mine. I've claimed her, so you can't take her away from me."

"Why would I take away a seed I carefully tended so you might have? You are a silly son. I have waited a long time for this moment, so I thought I would come pay personal attention. Much like your darling, I have played my part in young Diana's life."

"You are such an asshole," the Devil blurted, and the respect in his tone amused me.

"I do try. I find your method of handling the essence transfer to be amusing. I have never permitted a mortal to bite me before, but if you want her holy fire to be of appropriate potency, it will take more

than Gabriel's contribution. You would have been wise to involve Michael, as you wish for her to be your harbinger. I will ensure that her hellfire is balanced. It is no good if she is not balanced by the end. Lucifer, now would be the time for you to wake the violence you wish to cultivate. I will handle the matter of her compassion."

"Why are you helping?" the Devil asked.

"These mortals have offended the divines of many pantheons, not just ours. But as this falls into my domain—and yours—the other pantheons petitioned to me. I have opted to listen to their petition. These beings do not wish to start a war just against us, but against the others as well. Even the universe has taken note. If we were to become involved beyond this, the End would begin, and there would be no stopping it. This battle must be hers alone. But there are no rules stating we cannot shower her with our favor."

"Humans are insufferably *stupid*," Lucifer complained. "They would wipe themselves out for what? A little power? Some misguided and foolish belief?"

"Do not forget greed," He said. *"Please accept my apologies for my part in your discomfort, young Diana. I strongly oppose the End of Days, and I will not allow for it to happen because I would not act. This Earth and its many children are all my children, even those who do not believe, and I do not wish for them to die out. Not over something like this."*

It took several tries, but I managed to

evict Gabriel's finger from my mouth. "You're welcome to come to Christmas dinner to help join the party of those out to convince my parents they got it wrong."

"How amusing. Yes, that would be an appropriate gift to begin healing those old wounds the misguided inflicted upon you. It has been a while since I have crashed one of those parties. I believe I will start with the service. Consider attending the midnight service with these sinners. I shall bring along a few friends."

"Friends?"

"Ra, who is part of my family now through marriage. He will enjoy helping restore some of the light to the lost. And while they may never become good humans, they will at least be more tolerant of what they do not understand. I do not care if they choose to believe in me or not. That is not my role in this life. Now, as I am far more civilized than these sons I have produced, I will not require you to bite me, although you will drink. This will have consequence, of course. All things have consequence. But my son amuses me, and his goal for you is one of his better ideas. Sometimes, I question why I permitted these children of mine to have independent thought. But then every rare now and again, they come up with a good idea and do their best to implement it. Next time, those naughty sons of mine should ask for help. It will make things easier."

"You are such an asshole," Lucifer announced.

The idea of Lucifer, the crowned asshole

over all assholes, calling his father an asshole, made me laugh so hard I cried.

Gabriel massaged the back of my neck. "I will bring you extra presents each year for my part in this, as you will have to deal with this often. It is the least I can do to make up for your suffering."

"Brace yourself, Diana. This will hurt, but not for long."

The warning would have done me a lot more good if *He* had bothered to give me any time to prepare. The instant *His* blood touched my tongue, the world vanished in an eruption of blue and black flame.

MORE OFTEN THAN NOT, demons and devils possessed multiple forms. Their primary form, associated with their demonic or devilish nature, served as a warning for the wary.

With a little help from the Almighty, Lucifer and Gabriel had transformed me into something rather tall with four legs, a bulky body, and hooves. Upon closer examination, I determined there'd been some accuracy to Darian's speculations about transforming me into an equine, although I'd seen Malcolm's form enough times to recognize I hadn't been made into a kelpie. I snorted, and a mixture of blue and black flame blasted from my nose.

With no fear of my fire, Lucifer came up to me, took hold of my head, and dropped a kiss onto my nose. "You're lovely, and my darling is going to be so pleased when she sees you."

I had mobile ears, and I turned both of them back, stomping a hoof.

"You should be able to talk in that form, although you may find it a little tricky at first. Some catch on right away. The black is your hellfire, and the blue is your holy flame. You will have phases, unlike other demons or devils. When you're aligned more with the powers of good or order, foul things those are, your flame will burn a brighter blue. When you're balanced, such as you are now, you will blow blue and black flame. When you are more aligned with the powers of evil, your fire will be black. This will let you balance the situation however you see fit. If a bunch of archangels are running amok and doing excessive good, you can show up snorting hellfire until they behave. If the devils are being excessively naughty, you can correct them with holy fire."

I tested moving my mouth, and after some experimentation, I said, "I'm not a kelpie, right?"

"You're not a kelpie," Lucifer confirmed. "But don't you worry about that. You'll fit right in with my little saltwater toffee's herd, and your mate, who'll be your species, will fit in as well, so never you fear. Darian won't get the special treatment, but you share quite a few similarities with my unicorns. You'll have no trouble converting him to be the appropriate species. You, however, don't come with a horn."

A pity. "Why no horn?"

"You would stab everything you can because you can, because I make you cranky, and the last thing I need is a bunch of new holes because I made you cranky yet again. It'll be bad enough when you snort fire at me after I've annoyed you." Lucifer gave my nose a brisk rub. "Gabriel, why is she calmer than I expected her to be? She should be biting and finding the taste of blood to her liking."

"*He* fiddled, as is *His* way. She'll go completely psychotic after you set her loose on the party of evil catnappers. *He* also added a few extras to make sure her rampage doesn't hurt any of the animals. *He* said *He* would make certain the ones that could be saved would be saved, and that *He* has seen to the rest, so they do not suffer. *He* will handle their seeds personally. You were too busy cooing to your little Diana during her shift to notice or care what *He* was up to."

"It's true. Cooing to the new converts helps them get through it, even if they aren't aware I'm doing it. I always coo to the ones I really like. Shut up, Gabriel. You're annoying. Don't you go be bothering my little candy cane with your nonsense."

The archangel laughed. "She's not bothered. She's confused. Once you flip the violence switch, you will have problems calming her."

"Who said I would be calming her?"

"You're just going to let her rampage?"

"The nearest town is forty miles away in any direction, and they made a shit dirt road to set up their latest lab. I'll make her Darian's problem."

"Darian will have trouble getting here," Gabriel stated. "Why did we not bring him if your plan is to have him deal with her?"

"Who said he was going to deal with her here? I'm going to teach him how to summon her, but taming her is his problem. I figure it will take her at least a few days to wage her little war here. She'll be against a bunch of pre-shift lycanthropes and one lycanthrope too stupid to know when to quit. Diana won't have many problems with them. There's just a lot of them. I don't want to deal with an unscheduled End of Days, and if stupid humans would stop trying to make themselves go extinct from greed and ambition, that would be nice."

"It might help if you adjust your expectations," Gabriel chided. "You are upset because this incident will change how we operate again. I believe *His* help made that clear enough even for you. We are not supposed to be working together, yet here we are. Working together. You are surly because this is not how things normally go."

"Since when do we cooperate on *anything*? And Diana? Inviting *Him* to go to the family dinner was just ruthless and evil, and I'm so proud of you. That was so ruthless and evil that I'm planning on wearing my Sunday best, and I'll even give my old man a hug just to fuck with the prejudiced mortals. Assuming, of course, *He* opts to come out shrouded."

"I believe that is *His* plan. *He* is going to take the form of the Christ, as *He* has a rather twisted sense of humor. And not the whitewashed, offensive version. *His* son was not a white man, and *He* is very offended every time the humans opt to change *His* son's appearance to appease their personal prejudices. Honestly, it surprises me *He* has not triggered the End of Days over that issue. *He* regrets swearing *He* would not spank humanity and make them start over from scratch again."

I turned my head to face Gabriel, and the tattered ruins of his shroud fell away, revealing the archangel's face, a chiseled beauty of a man. I eyed the Devil, who shared features with his brother to a startling degree. "You could be twins, almost. Lucifer, you look more tired and worn."

"Yes," the Devil agreed. "We are what humans could be if not for sin. And as for being more tired or worn, *someone* had to play with the shrouds, and arranging the appropriate conversion is absolutely exhausting. After I set you loose, I'm going to go home, and my wife is going to hunt me. I'm going to be a worn out shell when she's done with me. She's going to have to pamper me back into good health."

Darlene would love every minute of it. I flicked an ear and began the important work of testing how I moved in my new form. "Darian thought you'd make me a kelpie to keep Malcolm company."

"A kelpie would make him mourn for his family. They're angels now, but it doesn't change much for him. He still misses them. His father is the only other member of the original Stewart clan still alive, and while most of his family hated him, Malcolm is a sentimental being. Everything they were is gone now. Bringing you in as a kelpie would have hurt him more than it helped. He'll just have to breed a herd of little kelpies with my daughter, as soon as he conquers her problem with water. And having two daughters with problems with water? Ridiculous. Absolutely ridiculous. I'm going to notify Darian he must cure you of your fear of the water. Anyway, your species is better for your temperament and personality. It will cater to your inclination to remain balanced, but it will allow you to stray without issue. You can be whatever you need or want to be. And if you *really* want a horn, it's within your power to manifest one. You can also manifest wings. You have a *base* form, which is that of an equine."

My eyes widened, and I snorted. "I can have *wings*?"

"Good luck, Lucifer. You are going to have to tether her to the ground now." Gabriel laughed and patted my shoulder. "Let us start with the horn first. I will help my brother teach you how to fly after you handle this matter. We cannot eradicate this group of humans while you can."

"Why can I while you can't? It doesn't make sense to me." I flicked my tail, turning my head to get a better look at my rump. I appreciated the full horse's tail, which swished at my command. "I seem to be gray."

"Mouse gray," the Devil informed me with pride. "You have dark socks and tips on your ears. When you are being your more angelic self, you'll be pristine white, and when you're being delightfully naughty, you'll be the darkest black. You can even play pretend at being a regular horse if you want to go investigating the mortal coil at your whim. Of course, this could create some fun if you decide to run off on me after you've finished handling your work here. So, we have some rules you need to follow."

I flattened my ears and snorted black and blue flame at the Devil. "Rules?"

"Yes, I know. Rules are so inconvenient. This facility was built to create an army of lycanthropes meant to unseat various important figureheads in government and religious positions and infect the remaining human populace with the virus. They experimented on people to trigger early onset, although their tests did not go as well as they would like. As far as lycanthropes go, they're fairly weak. Your job is to destroy their lab and eliminate the major players at this complex. We don't need any for questioning. If it makes you feel better, these beings are without remorse, and they would have killed your Mr. Flooferson if I had not instilled a rather strong compulsion to keep your cat happy and well. I couldn't erase their greed or need to test if he had done his work. While you handle that, I will pick your cat up, handle his care, and give him to Darian to watch while you finish your work. I will also teach him to know your forms, so he is not afraid of you. Your scent has changed substantially since he last saw you, but it is a small matter for me to address."

"I fail to see how these are rules."

"Destroy only what's here. Keep your rampage limited to this lab. You're not here to take over the world, and you can't hunt down the rest of the operation. Your job is to wipe out this portion of the operation. And yes, that means you'll have to let Kingston go for now. He's elsewhere. The better a job you do of wiping out this facility, the harder it will be for him to make progress later. You wanted to save your cat and get revenge on those who took your cat, and this is how you can."

I flattened my ears, stomped my hooves, and bucked. "Can I help eliminate Kingston later?"

"If you do a good enough job of razing this lab to the ground, I'll think about how you can help take out Kingston later. Don't forget, you owe me time giving you life advice, Diana. I expect you in good health following your adventure here."

The Devil annoyed me, and I snapped my teeth at him. He dodged my bite with a chuckle.

"That would be our cue to leave, Lucifer. Let us retrieve the feline and get out of her way. I will even be a good brother and help you with Darian. That one is simply no good at summoning circles and will need all the help he can get. Frankly, you might have to send him here with a golden bridle and hope he can tame her that way."

"As if I'd make it that easy. A golden bridle? What nonsense is that. If he wants to bridle her, he'll have to weave a rope made of Russian sage, unicorn tail hair, an angel's feather, snow leopard fur, sphinx fur, and strands of a kelpie's mane, all freely given. Unfortunately for her, there are plenty of beings who'll hand over the various bits needed to make the rope. Oh, and the bridle itself would need to be handwoven of silver, copper, and aluminum wire. There shouldn't be a bit used, as she'd melt it and it would hurt her delicate mouth."

"I am going to be a generous being and assist him with the bridle," Gabriel muttered. "Else we will be waiting most of his lifetime to figure out what needs to be done. Must you always be so difficult, Lucifer?"

"Yes."

Gabriel heaved a sigh. "Good hunting, Diana. I will try to keep my brother from turning this into a disaster, but I make no promises."

Lucifer pointed into the woods surrounding us. "The lab is that way. You can't miss it. While I expect this won't help much, do try to remember that there is nothing you could do to save some of those animals, which is why *He* had mercy on them. You can rescue and baby the rest, but don't wallow in your guilt too much. I'll permit a little wallowing, but not too much wallowing."

Without another word, the Devil and his brother vanished, and with nothing else to do—and annoyed neither had explained how to manifest a horn—I went in search of the assholes responsible for Mr. Flooferson's disappearance.

FIFTEEN

Asking for forgiveness only went so far.

A TRAILER COMMUNITY, much like the one we'd found at the lab in California, littered the forest, and the stench of male wolves permeated the air. How I identified the scent as male wolf baffled me, but it reeked, annoying the hell right out of me to the point my fur bleached to white. When I breathed, blue fire trailed from my nostrils, and the smoke emerged as shimmering white clouds.

Lucifer needed to pay for the various adjustments he'd made to me, including the repulsive stench of male wolf. Why did male wolves stink? How did I know the smell? The repulsiveness of the stench tested my already flagging patience.

I bet the damned Devil had made male wolves stink so I'd be tempted to kill them all without bothering to question them—or look closer at their activities. As defying the Devil and his plans appealed, I cooled my temper, gave myself a few minutes to become better acquainted with my new form, and practiced walking, trotting, galloping, and cantering around the forest.

I could only assume the Devil had imparted some base instincts on how to function as some hellish equine, as I didn't trip over my own hooves. Tripping while trying to stomp the life out of a bunch of assholes who thought illegal testing of animals was a good idea would not improve my day, although I looked forward to finding out how well hooves could crush through skulls.

With me, they would get some form of mercy in the form of a short death rather than whatever hell Lucifer would give the bastards. What the Devil did with them after they went to one of the many hells wasn't my problem, but I severely doubted anyone who worked with the operation met the minimum requirements for a trip to heaven.

He didn't seem like the kind to cater to users or abusers. Or so I hoped.

Asking for forgiveness only went so far, and humanity couldn't get away with false promises of redemption.

That was what the many hells was for, so those who crossed the lines got a taste of what they'd sown before being given another chance to get it right. The next time some idiot claimed God wasn't a benevolent being, I would remind them *He* could have made a soul's stay in the Devil's many hells a permanent affair rather than a temporary rehabilitation for those who strayed.

I pricked my ears forward at the thought of being stage one of an intensive rehabilitation for the misguided.

The first thing I needed to do to begin an intensive rehabilitation campaign was to create a multi-step program. Unlike other programs, meant to work with the victims of drug abuse or other serious problems, mine would make sure *I* walked the straight and narrow while enabling me to send the jackass animal abusers straight to some dark pit in hell where they belonged. Turning my ears back and snorting, I considered the best steps for a successful rehabilitation program.

Step one: check the trailers for evidence of children.

Step two: reevaluate plan if evidence of children located.

Step three: rescue animals.

Step four: kill bad people hurting animals.

Step five: burn it all down.

After the burning, I would need to figure out what weird demoness-devil horses ate, as my stomach informed me it would like a snack. As I was doing a damned good job of earning my place in hell, I added a final step to my program.

Step six: find a snack and eat it.

Pleased with my plan, I approached the trailers, peeking into windows for any sign they had little ones underfoot. I discovered the sort of slobbery a hoarding television host would flinch at, ranging from garbage left out to rotting food. The cleaner trailers opted to store their trash outside, where the local wildlife feasted. A few warning snorts drove the wild animals off, as I didn't want to hurt them when I started my rampage.

The deeper I went into the trailer community, the more I realized the Devil hadn't been kidding about an army. After sixty trailers, all of which showed signs of housing anywhere between two and five lycanthropes of the male wolf variety, I came to the conclusion the Devil and his brother had been onto something. Hundreds of lycanthropes made a legitimate army, and judging from the strength of the stench, they were all contagious. Given an hour and a city, they could spread enough contagion to begin an epidemic, one that could take decades to mature but begin inflicting consequences upon the victim within a few months, depending on exposure levels.

If the group had figured out how to accelerate the virus's replication, I could understand how they could trigger an End of Days playing God.

Idiots, all of them.

In the depths of the community, some two-hundred trailers in, I located the entrance to the lab, a concrete pad with a staircase leading deep into the ground, large enough for me to enter if I wanted. I decided to get a full headcount of trailers first, and I resumed my work, peeking into each trailer.

No evidence of children spotted, check.

I skipped step two, as I would not waste time with no evidence of children detected.

To rescue the animals, I likely needed to descend into the dark depths of the ground. I considered my options, eyed the trailers, and brushed my nose against the ground. The damp soil offered some reassurance I wouldn't trigger a massive forest fire with the next item on my agenda: burning the whole damned place to the ground.

I just needed to make sure none of the trailers contained animals first. I could handle that while lighting them on fire, right? With a little luck and *His* benevolent influence, perhaps the holy fire would only torch the trailers and everything inside rather than turn the entire place into an epic conflagration.

After some deliberation, I decided a forest fire beat an unscheduled End of Days, so I began my new plan of burning everything before killing a bunch of idiot lycanthropes out to end the world. While I'd already opted to sacrifice my humanity for the sake of survival, I refused to play a part in destroying mortal life for everybody else.

Fortunately, nobody seemed to have any pets, and I discovered if I snorted on the largest piles of garbage, they burned with little other encouragement, allowing me to blitz from trailer to trailer. As the lycanthropes either had no sense of self-preservation or simply didn't care, none of them had installed smoke alarms in their temporary homes.

What a pity. Not.

For the trailers with cleaner occupants, I torched their propane tanks, which did an excellent job of triggering miniature infernos. Rather than obey the natural laws of flame on the mortal coil, the holy fire remained a brilliant, pure blue—and stuck to my intended targets rather than jump to the nearby trees or foliage. To my endless amusement, the fire jumped to the garbage left around, as though it were also offended by the debris left to pollute the environment.

In the time it took me to light the trailers on fire along with the few unoccupied auxiliary buildings, nobody from the lab below came to investigate.

I figured they assumed their distance

from civilization and the thick canopy overhead protected them. I wondered if the pale smoke would alert somebody something was going on, but I refused to worry about it.

My job involved eradicating the lab. Even a week ago, I would have hesitated to bring violence to anyone.

But then someone had screwed with *my* cat.

I could understand why the divines would make use of me. When I boiled it down, I couldn't care less if the Universe Itself tried to bar me from my mission. I would take the war to them anyway.

Nobody screwed with my cat and got away with it.

I made sure the last of the trailers burned before descending down the staircase to bring ruin to the lab operators and salvation to the innocent animals they abused for the sake of their ambition.

LIKE THE LAB IN CALIFORNIA, the concrete stairwell descended at least a hundred feet into the ground. The steps showed signs of abuse and impatience, as they had been used more than a few times before they'd had a chance to fully cure. I stepped with care. The echoing click of hooves on the floor surrounded me, but nobody came to investigate.

Either they heard odd noises all of the time or nobody stood guard. It didn't matter which.

I would use their laze and lack of diligence against them.

Blue flame burst out of my nose with every breath, and my coat steamed.

At the bottom of the stairwell, a set of double steel doors waited, and their closed state likely explained why they hadn't investigated the destruction above. I snorted over their general idiocy, eyeing the panel barring access into the lab beyond. Could hellish demoness-devil equines still work practitioner magic? I lifted a hoof, blew flame on the curved edge in hopes of marring the concrete, and tapped the wall. To my delight, my hoof sliced easily into the material. With a careful application of fire, I drew a rune to expose the code to get in, and I gave the lightest snort of my flame over the design to activate it.

The circular pattern with a seeking spiral in its heart flared white, and the keypad began to glow. A series of ten numbers began to radiate a blue radiance, flickering in a pattern with a brief pause to indicate the end of the sequence. After a minute, I memorized the fifteen digits. Tapping them in with a hoof took some work, but I managed.

The door popped open, swinging into the lab.

Showtime.

To keep anyone from closing the door, I shouldered through it to discover the entry devoid of lycanthropes but filled with cages. The occupants whined or woofed, and the canines fit into the puppy category. More kittens than I could count were crammed together, and their litter boxes were in dire need of a good cleaning.

Fury swept through me, and I stomped a hoof. Holy fire sparked around my leg and rippled over the concrete floor, strengthening the farther it ventured from my body until a curtain of shimmering flame stretched from the floor to the ceiling and cascaded into the cages.

The filth vanished from the animals, revitalizing their coats to a silky shine. The whining cries quieted, and the kittens purred their contentment.

Rather than vanish, the holy fire curtained over the cage doors, creating a barrier barring anyone from reaching the animals trapped inside.

I would hold faith *He* would keep *His* word and protect the animals that could be saved, and I moved on, snorting at the various pieces of equipment and the surgical tables. While holy fire protected the living, black hellfire devoured the tools of research and torture, reducing them to a greasy smear and little else.

While I could have drawn another rune to reveal the code to access the next section of the lab, the asshole male wolves couldn't close a door reduced to a melted puddle, and I breathed hellfire onto the steel. The black flame clung to the metal, flared, and reduced it to a fine, powdery ash.

Unlike the first room, men worked, and they studied the bodies of numerous animals on the metal examination tables.

Understanding struck me hard.

He had not only put the animals that couldn't be saved out of their misery and reclaimed their seeds, *He* had created a distraction, one that brought the researchers into the lab so I could systematically judge them and send them to the afterlife.

The enormity of *His* scheming, and the sheer ruthlessness of *His* choice, would haunt me for a while. It would also make me far more respectful of *His* power.

When *He* moved, it was with a still and quiet hand—and *He* lacked any hesitation when it came to securing justice for the smallest of creatures.

It reminded me of a hymn from church, one that I had learned before I'd come to the realization the church had gotten so much of *His* truths wrong: *All things bright and beautiful, all creatures great and small, all things wise and wonderful, The Lord God made them all.*

And *He* loved all of his creations, as did the Devil.

The church would have a problem with that if they learned that truth.

The men, wearing the protective equipment I expected from those working with a highly contagious disease, gaped at me. I took the moment to regard the fallen animals, a mixture of cats, dogs, and even birds, grateful *He* had compassion for them in their final breaths.

The black hellfire winked out, and I stomped my hoof. Another rippling pulse of holy fire spread across the floor, attaching to a few of the cages. The rest were empty or their occupants had gone on to find shelter and comfort in *His* embrace.

The nearest lycanthrope, one of the male wolves according to his reek, gaped at me. If *He* had wanted some benevolent spirit handling the matter, *He* would have sent an angel—or something or someone other than me. While I had hooves for stomping and crushing, I rather enjoyed billowing a mixture of blue and black flame into his face, tearing through the protective gear surrounding his head. The holy fire winked out upon touching the lycanthrope, as though refusing to be tainted by coming into contact with him. The hellfire clung, as though I'd sneezed tar all over the lycanthrope's body.

He screamed once before the flames consumed him, leaving an empty pair of shoes and his untouched clothing in his wake.

How interesting. I remembered some about the bible's prophecies of the rapture. Their end would not result in a trip to heaven, but rather an extended stay in the Devil's many hells. Too bad, so sad.

One down, many to go, and my schedule did not allow for negotiations, excessive screaming, or anything that prevented me from moving onto the rescue portion of my plan. Had the lycanthropes been better people who'd left my cat alone, I might've harbored remorse about killing them.

Alas, they had opted to screw with my cat. The only mercy they'd be getting from me would be my haste in making waste, as I had better things to be doing with my time.

I BURNED the lab down to piles of smoldering ash and empty clothes, and when I ran out of lycanthropes to torch, I cursed my lack of fingers, which made opening the cages difficult. As I had no idea what had been done to the poor beasts, I opted to leave the cages. The holy fire helped, as it kept the animals quiet and content while I took my temper out on the ruins of the examination tables. Once my temper cooled enough I could think beyond trying to destroy or eat the evidence, I drew a searching rune with a hoof, revealing several more of the closed, metal cases hidden in the various cabinets of the lab. I trotted the first of them up to the surface to discover company waiting for me.

Lucifer wore a suit, and one of my bosses, Mr. Thernin, who oversaw international incidents with the divine within the CDC, was with him. I flattened my ears, shook out my mane, and thrust the case to the Devil, who would survive whatever was within. He accepted it, and he placed it on the ground beside him with a show of care and caution. As I had a bunch of extra cases to haul up, I headed downstairs, grumbling curses over my new role as delivery mule.

Eleven cases later, and I considered falling over to take a nap. Not even a strong snort manifested either sort of flame, and I glared at Lucifer in reproach.

"I don't know why you're looking at me like that. *I* wasn't the one who decided to abuse my hellfire and holy fire privileges.

Have you finished having your temper tantrum yet?"

I snapped my teeth at him, and the bastard dodged with a low chuckle.

"I see you are up to your old tricks, Lucifer," my boss stated. "What manner of being is this?"

"She's a nightmare. I'm quite proud of her. As I said, I've taken your secretary. She'd developed a rather unusual cancer, and she managed to wake a latent talent, which would have killed her. As I'm quite fond of her, I gave her a suitable form so she would continue to annoy me for many more years. Isn't she magnificent?"

"That's Diana?"

"She's Diana, yes. She's newly converted, so she's a bit short on temper, and I set her loose here to take care of more than a few problems. You know how the newly converted can get. I'm sure there are a bunch of infected animals below needing to be put in the care of more reputable lycanthropes. I have already reclaimed her cat and put him in the care of a mutual friend." Lucifer dared to rub my nose, and I tolerated his attention with a sigh. "You're just annoyed because I solved a lot of problems for you, but I'm requiring Diana be transferred fully into my custody. She's mine now. Of course, a corpse would do you no good, which is what you would have had if I hadn't taken her.

Such is the way life goes. Isn't she magnificent?"

"That depends on what a nightmare is," my boss replied with a shrug. "I'm glad she's alive, I'm annoyed you took away one of my best employees, but I'm more concerned about this mess, really. And the samples you turned in, along with the readings from that scanner you got your hands on. Are you even qualified to operate it?"

"I don't lower myself to such mundane things, Mr. Thernin, you know this. Diana operated the scanner. I merely gave you the results and the samples. However annoying it is to justify the activities of one of my rampaging minions to the CDC, I think we can agree it was better than the alternative. A slightly mad, newly converted beats the forces of my many hells and the heavens staging a more complete war on this outfit. She has removed the need. For now."

"You told me you would explain more once you had the evidence you needed. I assume those cases contain the evidence?"

"In part. This group is not finished their work yet. This lab merely worked on the more dangerous samples."

"Elaborate, Lucifer."

"Smallpox." Lucifer rested his hand on my brow between my eyes. "What she didn't destroy, I have. A bargain was made to bring the virus back to the dead, but the time was not right for us to act. Diana could because she bends the rules. Observe."

Warmth spread from Lucifer's hand into me, and when I snorted, holy fire blossomed from my nostrils, and what I could see of my forelock paled to a shimmering white. "This is one of her forms. Rather like a daydream, isn't she? A pure, pristine being. Yes, that's holy fire. Yes, *He* granted *His* blessing on her, for all she's one of mine. Her nightmare form is pitch black, and she wields hellfire instead, and a rather nasty version of it, truth be told. As the conflicting energies are part of what triggered her little rampage, I'll forgo the demonstration of her hellfire. She has a balanced form, which is a lovely gray, and she has access to both hellfire and holy fire while in it. As such, she could act where we, who are skewed to one extreme or another, could not. It's not yet time, and the consequences would have been dire."

"Why?" my boss demanded.

It amazed me that Mr. Thernin dared to question Lucifer in such a tone. Our previous business meetings had been far more cordial.

Flattening my ears, I eyed my boss—no, my former boss—and debated how to deal with him before the Devil took offense and did something I would regret.

Lucifer clucked his tongue and pulled my head to his chest, stroking his hand along my brow to my nose. "Easy does it, my little candy cane. You need to cool your temper. I know, I know, you ran out of mean doggies to correct. You can have a turn with them in the dungeons when you're ready to play nice with others. I brought the CDC here so your animals could get proper care. Wasn't I generous?"

Generous? Lucifer? When the Devil did favors, he expected paybacks later. "Maybe."

He chuckled and wrapped his arm around my neck to keep me in place. "Diana's nature makes her very protective of the helpless. After her adaptation period, you'll see her in a similar role, working for me rather than the CDC. You will find negotiations will continue as smoothly as always—perhaps better, as my little candy cane truly abhors inefficiency. Do mind your step when you're in the lab. Holy fire and hellfire make quite the mess of wayward mortals who play with powers they shouldn't. If they hadn't stolen her cat—and planned to perform tests on her, who had been exposed to her cat post testing—she wouldn't have had a reason to go stomping through their operations, now would she?"

"Becoming the subject of human experimentation does tend to offer a certain amount of leniency when it comes to self-defense," Mr. Thernin agreed, and he heaved a sigh. "And you are certain about her lycanthropy infection status prior to this conversion? And that it was a result of this group that intended to experiment on her?"

"You can have the word of an archangel about that truth," Lucifer stated. "Some things we cannot meddle with, but know this much: we step away from the End of Days because of what did not leave this lab. This is not their only lab. It was just the most dangerous of their labs currently in operation. For now. But know this. My many hells and the heavens will rise up against what these humans attempt to create. Consider yourselves warned. If the CDC is wise, it will handle this matter before we must prove how our alliance on the mortal coil works. And make no mistake: we have forged an alliance as we oppose an unscheduled End of Days. The time is not now, and we wish to keep it that way. We really don't care about eliminating wayward humans who try to make the end come."

"Next you'll tell me that the Christ is coming again."

Lucifer chuckled. "Soon," he promised. "Sooner than you would like, I imagine."

"Well, as a mortal, I also tend to oppose the End of Days, and you know what the Bible says about that."

"Haven't you figured out you've gotten

that wrong yet? Diana, say it. I simply cannot bear to."

I took a moment to consider what he meant, and then I sighed, as Darlene loved yanking her husband's chain whenever possible. "Well, Jesus Christ on a cracker," I dutifully announced, and I even packed my tone with the proper disgust over the situation.

"Do I want to ask?"

"It's best you don't," I replied, questioning every choice I'd ever made in my life leading up to the moment I'd left myself up a shit creek without a paddle or a boat. "It's just best you don't."

SIXTEEN

"I may have gotten slightly cranky."

THE DEVIL, asshole that he was, refused to tell me how to transform back into a human. Biting him appeased me a little, but he refused to spill his secrets. While the CDC worked at rescuing the animals, I stalked Lucifer through the charred husks of the trailers, snorting a mixture of holy fire and hellfire at him.

He dodged, which annoyed me into trying harder to bite him. When the CDC began the tedious process of bringing the animals up from the lab, wearing contamination containment suits to mitigate the risk of any contagions spreading, I abandoned my hunt to observe them, my ears twisted back.

Each cat and dog got a carrier by themselves, except for the kittens, which were grouped in small clusters. One such pair of orange kittens, which a lycanthrope without a containment suit carried by hand, caught my attention. I approached, sniffing at the small, still bodies.

"We're not sure if these ones will make it," the lycanthrope admitted, and he sighed. "It's warmer for them in my hand, and we aren't sure they'll make it for the drive."

Lucifer patted my shoulder. "Holy fire is useful for this, and I encourage you to abuse your holy fire privileges as often as you'd like. Once *He* gives such gifts, it's difficult to take back. You've experimented plenty with the more dangerous side of holy fire, so why don't you learn the gentler properties?" The Devil crouched for a closer look at the kittens, and he checked their ears before staring into their eyes with a thoughtful expression. "Malnourished and neglected for certain. They're developmentally stunted. They're infected with lycanthropy for certain, which is why they're alive at all. I'd bet on a starvation test to see how the virus would work to preserve the host."

I resented I couldn't kill the asshole lab operators again. "How do I use the holy fire to help them? I can help them, right?"

"You can. Focus on your intent. You want to protect, safeguard, and heal the kittens. Consider holy fire to be somewhat sentient. The gentler the soul using it, the more potent it is. You're a disgustingly gentle soul unless provoked, which is why you'll do well with both holy fire *and* hellfire. When you're provoked, it's for a cause, and that strengthens hellfire more than most would think. What's your name, boy?"

"Kris," the lycanthrope replied. "The boss told me to bring the kittens your way, sir."

"It's not every day divine intervention can be had for a pittance," Lucifer replied with a chuckle. "That, plus the boss knows how unreasonable Diana can get about cats and kittens. Her cat completed her transformation into a crazy cat lady."

Mr. Flooferson truly had. I stretched out my nose and nudged the tiny bodies, exhaling enough a small trail of holy fire escaped my nose. It coiled around both of the kittens and settled into the scruffy fur.

Lucifer scratched my brow. "Normally, you'd wait, but I'll have a small chat with *Him* about these two. Even with holy fire, they'll remain stunted and be in poor health. What's two more little demonic beasties running around my house?" With enough care for me to believe the kittens were in poorer health than I'd believed, the Devil cradled both animals in his hand. "I will return shortly, so try not to wander too far. Go breathe holy fire on some cats if you need to feel useful. You could use the practice, and really, it's fun encouraging you to abuse a higher power. Best of all, *He* can't even get mad at you for doing it. Have fun!"

Once certain the Devil was gone, I bowed my head and sighed. "Are there any other sick kittens or puppies?"

"Nothing to that scale," Kris replied, gesturing to one of the waiting CDC vans. "We brought a mobile clinic with us if needed, and we dragged a crew of ten veterinarians and their techs along for the ride, too. They'll be kept busy doing the initial intakes, but we're equipped to handle a busted lab, especially since we know we're working with a contagious disease. He's not usually that forthcoming in requirements for these sorts of ventures. Typically, when he shows up, he just tells us to get our asses in gear before he has to handle the work himself and make it an even bigger mess."

I regarded the destruction of the trailers with one ear twisted back. "I may have gotten slightly cranky."

"Slightly? If that's your slightly cranky, I don't want to see you angry, that's for sure. But being serious, it's for the best you beat us here. The instant we put them into the prison system, they would have been treated to the beating of their lives before turning up dead in their cells. I can't promise they would have had a good time before being tossed into prison, either. I'm a wolf, and my virus gets riled around a dog in distress.

Right now? Bloodshed wouldn't calm my virus. That's part of why I'm handling the kittens and cats. My virus is too sensitive to canines."

Interesting. I eyed the lycanthrope. "Are the rest of the team not lycanthropes?"

"I'm the only lycanthrope. They wanted my nose to confirm what Lucifer told us. It's well enough, since I can handle the animals without needing gear, and the rest can haul the carriers up top. We're about done, though. We were saving those kittens for last. They would have gotten better attention that way, with no other animals in line after them."

The poor babies. "Do *you* know how I might transform back to human?"

"I focus on what makes me human. That's what most lycanthropes do. It takes practice to get good at doing it. When I first shifted, I needed help transforming for the first four to six months, unless my virus took over. That can still happen, but it's less common now that I've been shifting for a few years. You'll probably have to get Lucifer to help you with it the first time or two."

Uh oh. I could see Lucifer abandoning me to my fate and requiring me to figure out how to shift back to human on my own. Rather than complain, I bobbed my head. "I'm sure he'll get around to it."

Eventually.

Probably.

Maybe.

If it benefited him at the time, he might help.

The Devil reappeared without the kittens. I snorted holy fire at him, my ears locked back and snapping my teeth. "Don't you worry about the kittens. They'll be tended to properly. Let's leave the CDC to their work, Diana. You have to get accustomed to your form and explore your new home. I have picked a lovely parcel of land not far from my home for you to call your own, and I have plenty of artisans in residence who would *love* to dodge a more hellish punishment to build you a little manor to call your own. You can even pick the style."

Before I could protest, Lucifer patted my shoulder, and the unsettling yank of teleportation ended with a thump and splash into thick lava. The molten rock oozed around me, did a good job of warming my coat, and left me standing belly deep. My new arch nemesis stood on a nearby rock and laughed at me.

I could understand why he laughed. Unlike me, he enjoyed his day.

Mine could use some work.

I sighed and trudged to where the ground solidified, scrambling up to escape the lava. It dripped from my coat. "Was there any half-decent reason you decided to do that?"

"I find it's best to teach the newest residents about their various immunities to lava through exposure. The reactions are usually delightful, but I see your general resilience to the absurd is still intact." Lucifer sighed. "Couldn't you have at least squealed once?"

"No." I shook the cooling lava off my coat. "How do I become human again?"

"This is a lesson you must learn on your own, Diana. You'll never be a human again—but you can appear to look as you did with some work. If you're clever enough. Don't worry. I want you for your brains right now, anyway. If I really need you for your hands, I'll force you to another form as I see fit—perhaps a spotted snow leopardess to keep my darling company?"

"You absolutely will not!" Darlene hissed from behind me. "Why must you do this every time? I saw what you did to poor little Samuel. You are not going to lock Diana outside and toss her into lava pools for fun." The Devil's wife patted my shoulder. "If you can't be nice to Diana, I will steal her."

"You will steal her anyway. You get to make use of her, too. She's *our* secretary. I stole her from the CDC fair and square, and as I'd like to be invited back to bed sometime this week, I am making use of a filthy word to please you. It doesn't get much worse than agreeing to share." Lucifer faked gagging. "Disgusting, filthy word."

Darlene hissed at her husband, wrapped her arms around my neck, and headed for her home. As resisting her might stir Lucifer's ire, I went along with her.

"You are an excessively cruel wife, stealing my horse!"

"Well, you're the one who gave the other horses to Anwen and Eoghan. I can't tell if you're trying to unleash the apocalypse or stop it most days. Really, letting those four just prance around the mortal coil?"

"It's not like their powers activate at random. It just means if someone *does* trigger the End of Days, I don't have to work all that hard to get them mobilized. I don't even care about the riders at that point."

"As though anyone other than Eoghan would ride the pale horse. He's the only one of that trio who would see the necessity of it."

I flattened my ears. "You unbridled the four horses of the apocalypse?"

"Oh, they're bridled and haltered daily. They are spoiled pleasure horses right now. Eoghan is still teaching Anwen how to ride. But yes. They're out in the world now. They were bored out of their minds here. There's just nothing for them to do. On the mortal coil, they're useful. They don't just *cause* famine, war, or death with a healthy splash of conquering mixed in for good measure. They control those things—and mitigate humanity's greed as needed. They don't want the End of Days, either. It's just work for us, and it's unpleasant work at that." Lucifer took long strides to catch up, and he smirked at his wife while draping his arm across my back. "You're not allowed to try to break her to saddle. I'm giving that nephew of mine first crack to see if he can tame her."

"You'd be on the couch for a month if you even thought about it," Darlene replied.

"I'm having a hard time deciding if I want to be on the couch because I know exactly what will happen to me if I'm stuck on the couch for a month. That is worth waiting for rather patiently."

"You will allow Darian his chance."

I flicked an ear back at that. "I'm a devil-demon-horse thing now. Do you think he'll actually *want* to have a chance? I could snort on him and light him on fire."

"Well, that's half the fun," the Devil's wife informed me. "Wondering if your future lover is going to light you on fire or toss you in some dungeon definitely enhances the experience. It amazed me Lucifer didn't do that to me. He even let me chain him to his desk and smack him."

"You're hot when you're bossing me around, and honestly, I was too stunned you were bossing me around to even think about killing you and tossing you in the dungeon. And at that point, the only place I wanted to drag you was to bed, but you kept saying no. Chained to my desk is almost as good as a bed. Well, not really, but I was hopeful you'd change your mind."

"No is a very powerful word, and I like using it."

"I know," Lucifer complained.

I ambled along at Darlene's pace, snapping my teeth at the Devil to make it clear I'd put one of my new natural weapons to good use if he stepped out of line. Darlene placed her hand on my nose, and I suspected the sneaky snow leopard wanted her dinner intact.

"Don't you mind him, Diana. He's just hoping for spots, and as I control the spots, he has to behave. I made up a room for you in the house, perfect for you to get used to your new form. Darian is methodical, so he'll need some time to get his act together. But don't you worry. If he can't figure out how to get your attention, I'll just start mailing your panties to his mother. Maybe *he* is denser than a rock, but his mother is smart—when she can actually focus. I'll send a note to take her medications and teach her son some of the more important tricks in life, like how to draw a proper summoning circle. I expect by the time he figures it out, you're going to be very hungry. I'm sure he'll enjoy himself thoroughly."

I flicked one ear forward while twisting the other back. "I'm not a succubus, Darlene. That's you. You're hungry, and you want to eat Lucifer for dinner. Don't turn me into a man-hunting succubus like you."

"Oh, you're not a succubus, but I know my husband and his unicorns. Darian will end up being your ultimate dessert, and I'd bet away all of my spots he wired you to convert through seduction of your man. There are worse ways to go, really."

I glared at Lucifer. "You are very bad. Doesn't Darian get a say in this?"

"Well, I'd say he forfeits his say in how you drag him off to be your dessert the instant he starts drawing a summoning circle to catch you. He knows you've been converted, and he knows he has a pervert for an uncle. If he isn't able to figure this out on his own, he deserves all of the trouble you bring his way. Just try not to destroy my house in the time it takes him to figure out how he's going to approach being your conquest. But if you get tired of waiting, you can go claim what you want. And if you don't want him, you can start pursuin—"

Darlene vaulted over my back, manifested her wings, and attacked her husband, claws out, and her mouth opened, revealing pronounced canines, ready to tear into the Devil's flesh.

He caught her, tossing her over his shoulder. "She acts like she can banish me to the couch when she's already been protesting my cruel mistreatments of everyone in the universe. Isn't she a funny kitty, Diana?"

"Maybe you should go feed her before she razes every last one of your hells."

Darlene growled and bit at Lucifer's back, and her tail lashed back and forth.

"You might be right. Make yourself at home. If you see any devils or demons misbehaving, feel free to kick the sin right out of them. Just try not to kick Belial should he show up. He tends to take excessive measures when seeking revenge for some reason." Lucifer bounced Darlene on his shoulder while she hissed and snarled curses at him. "My wife's right, though. I am truly an asshole. In good news, you won't starve to death. You're just going to be really, really grouchy until you get a good meal and start converting your chosen male. You could go a thousand years before choosing a male. Please don't do that. There's little grouchier than a hungry succubus, and that's a hungry nightmare. I really did a good job with you."

"Lucifer, you are a wretch!" Darlene complained, and she pounded on her husband's back. "Put me down."

"And delay counting your spots? Nonsense. You're showing all of them off *and* your wings. If you're not fed soon, you really will trash my many hells, and I'm too busy right now to rebuild everything after you've vented your temper. I have better ways to deal with you, my little kitty. Don't worry, though. You'll enjoy it."

I followed Lucifer and his wife into their home, and as I wanted nothing to do with their bedroom activities, I explored in the opposite direction, wondering what I would find.

DEEP in the heart of Lucifer's home, I discovered a wing of the building dedicated to all things fish, and in the entry, a betta ruled over all in a glass bowl palace, showing off his red fins while some spotted fish hung out on the sandy bottom.

"His name is Ruby, and Lucifer selected him for Darlene when preparing the prison for the future inmates," Belial informed me from where he stood behind me. "The other fish are leopard cory cats. Before Ruby's conversion to an immortal devilish fish, he was the first fish Lucifer could approach without terrifying it. It amuses me that the Lord of Hell is fast friends with a rather small fish."

Rather than laugh, I whinnied, something that would take some getting used to. "It's not a problem that I'm in here, is it? Darlene went after Lucifer like she meant it, and she had her wings out."

"She's been fussy lately, and add in how she's been worried about you, and she hasn't been eating well. Now that you're mostly sorted, she's hungry enough she's manifesting. Try to relax. You're fine. At least now. I had not realized you were so advanced as to see through the shrouds."

"Well, I can summon Lucifer if I really want. Apparently, I'm allowed to once and only once, and I'll probably regret it should I do it."

"He wants to know if you actually can. He prefers not to peek at those futures, because being surprised is a rare state for him. The cancer was not something he expected. That was enough to rile him up, and with the cancer being an immediate concern, he opted to address the problem of your ability to see through the shrouds. He picked an interesting form for you. I should say I'm surprised, but I am really not. It was only a matter of time before he branched from unicorns to other equines. What has he dubbed your species?"

"A nightmare," I replied. "I think. Sometimes a daydream?" I concentrated on the darker, hellfire portion of my new life, and all it took to turn my coat jet back was thinking about the abused animals being rescued by the CDC. I snorted hellfire in Belial's direction, although I took care not to hit him with it. "The third form is between the two, and I can breathe hellfire and holy fire at the same time. I think he turned me into an even bigger mess than I already am."

The devilish general chuckled. "My son is having a conniption fit. I left the house because I couldn't keep a straight face. He has the general capacity of a half-dead newt at even the most basic of summoning circles, and his mother won't stop laughing at him."

I struggled to imagine competent, intellectual, and dangerously handsome Darian struggling with a basic summoning circle. "Are you saying summoning is out, then?"

"He can't even summon an earthworm from a jar right in front of him," Belial replied, his tone a blend of disgusted and amused. "I'm questioning how it's possible for someone of his superior genetics to be so useless at summoning magic. He even brought every scrap of your clothing and hair he could get his hands on. His mother is highly amused by the amount of lingerie he has brought over in an effort to give him some ability to draw a proper summoning circle."

It amused me someone who could, with the right tools, locate something, couldn't handle a summoning circle. Then it clicked.

He couldn't find people when wayfinding, either.

"His magic is the wrong type," I announced. "Consider his wayfinding. He finds *places*, not people. He finds *things*, not people. He has to make use of trickery to be able to use an object to find where a person might be. Summoning is all about people. His magic is attuned to *things*. It's like telling a fish he should grow wings and fly, Belial. There are some things I'm just better at when working practitioner magic, and summoning happens to be my expertise."

"I don't mind if you decide to summon my boy to the depths of hell and have your way with him. I can pilfer his favorite tie when you're ready to lure him to your lair."

"I don't have a lair."

"Yet. Once Lucifer finishes feeding his wife, I'm sure he'll be working on that project. Lucifer is not a reasonable being."

No, he wasn't. "Were you expecting Darian to be better at summoning rings?"

Belial heaved a sigh. "I even got him everything he needed to snare a nightmare. His other father did the crafting work, too. You even have a saddle. Lucifer provided the appropriate measurements."

"Doesn't it take more than a few hours to make a saddle?"

"You assume we started making your bridle and saddle upon your conversion. Lucifer gave us the measurements shortly after you called him about the theft of your cat. A little magic, and it's possible to make a saddle and bridle in such a short period of time. And they'd need a great deal of magic to survive, anyway. So, my horrified son is trying to convince us he couldn't *possibly* ride you."

I whinnied a laugh. "I'm definitely saddling and riding him."

"I had the foresight to warn him he'd be ridden in more ways than one, and that he'd have matching tack. That gave him pause. I feel I have failed my son in so many ways." Belial strolled to the other fish tanks and gestured to one of the occupants, a brightly colored fish swimming among some coral. "This is Alloces. He goaded Lucifer into revealing his true form to kill Darlene. He serves as an example for those who would try to hurt her. He's now one of Darlene's trophies. He was supposed to go to the dungeons to be used as a training tool, but Darlene becomes quite possessive over her fish, and she likes his colors. She invites devils and demons who have earned her favor to feed him. Let's just say she didn't need a whole lot of training in the dungeon." Belial gestured to the fish decorating one wall. "Those are the mortal fish, and Darlene has come to terms they'll live out their regular lifespans, and Lucifer does his best to ignore when she cries when one of her fish dies."

Darlene amazed me. "I thought they had a bunch of immortal fish."

"They do." Belial pointed across the room to another set of aquariums stacked from floor to ceiling. "Lucifer monitors the fish she loves above all others, and they are converted and moved to this side of the room. Deeper inside are their conservation efforts."

"Conservation efforts?"

"Darlene hates when humans make animals go extinct. We'll be descending into a different layer, as some of the animals needed a great deal more space than the house and this layer can provide. Come along." Belial strode across the room, and I followed him. The next rooms contained more fish, and some were devils or demons who needed an attitude adjustment. A staircase led down. "If the species is in true danger of going extinct, you'll find at least two of them here. Lucifer has his demons and devils go on hunts for poachers, so they kill the poacher and claim the animal that would have otherwise died. If a female and with young, the young come as well, as they are assumed to be in a situation where they would perish. That way, humanity doesn't realize where the animals are going—and there are better places for them."

"Like here? But we're in hell, Belial."

"And for beings like us, hell is our paradise. It just worked out where Lucifer has dedicated this layer—a sublayer, really—to animal preservation. It makes an excellent punishment tool for abusers. They're forced to properly care for and be subservient to the animals—and their every action is monitored. Lucifer makes a point of issuing a rather brutal punishment and warning the assholes in residence the next punishment will be far worse. It works rather well. The souls aren't really capable of defying Lucifer in his domain anyway, but it helps with the rehabilitation."

We descended, and after at least several hundred feet, the stairwell opened to a bright blue sky with clouds, with the steps curving to form a spiral staircase until we reached the bottom.

Navigating a spiral staircase with hooves took work, but it was spacious enough I managed with minimal worry, although it amused me Belial stayed close and in front of me, likely to stop me from breaking my neck if I fell.

"It should come as no surprise Darlene spends a lot of time down here. There's an entire section dedicated to prey animals she can hunt as a snow leopard. Common species or transformed devils and demons, of course. She usually preys on naughty devils and demons, as they're more of a challenge for her than mundane animals. She'll catch one of the mundanes to eat if she's of a mind. She has not yet figured out that Lucifer imbues them with his energy so she can feed if he's unavailable."

Ah-ha, mystery solved. "I was wondering how she could go for so long without feeding. She's told me there are times she's gone a month or two without feeding. But if she's hunting down here, he *is* feeding her."

"Lucifer is sly. Darlene forgets how far her husband will go to protect her and make her happy. Don't remind her, please. She gets upset, and when she gets upset, exactly nobody is happy. You'll get used to that. Part of your job will involve managing Darlene as much as you'll manage Lucifer. You're one of the few beings Darlene doesn't mind being near Lucifer. For whatever reason, she never perceived you as a threat. That's quite rare when it comes to other females."

"It probably has to do with my utter lack of interest in Lucifer as a partner. I mean, he's the Devil. I'm sure he's great in bed, but he's not my type."

"Darian is."

Right. I talked to one of Darian's fathers, a devil who supported the campaign for me to drag Darian off into some lair. "That is a rather accurate statement, yes. You produced a very fine son. What sort of lair would be appropriate to drag him off to? Darlene probably doesn't view me as a threat to Lucifer because I'm that useless around men."

"You're not useless. You're focused, and until my son caught your eye, you did not feel you were in a position to invest your precious time in a man who may or may not stick around. My son is flexible enough to handle the inflexibility of your critical work—and he will teach you how to be more flexible about the work you *can* be flexible about. You'll be equals on the financial front as well. My son cannot tolerate becoming bored, so he'll pursue his leads when you can't be stolen away from Lucifer. And don't get me wrong, he will steal you away whenever possible. That will be good for you. If you overly resist being stolen, I will help my son acquire you for his nefarious purposes. As you've made a point of informing everyone you're helpless, you will be helped."

As I had no eyebrows to raise at Belial, I stared at him.

"I'm a devil, not a monster. I mean, I can be a monster as needed, but in this instance, I'm a twisted angel on mission of mercy. It's painful watching you and my son flail. You both want the same thing, and I seem to have failed in my parental duties to help him be able to acquire a meaningful relationship with a woman. We won't discuss your parents."

All I would have to do to earn a disowning was show up, something that would happen at Christmas, along with a congregation of angels, devils, the Devil, a snow leopard, and whomever else happened to swing by to witness at catastrophe of a dinner. "We just need to stop dancing around, and I'm bad at this. Lucifer won't show me how to become human again."

"There is a good reason for that. You're still burning through a lot of devilish, demonic, and holy energy. Your human form wouldn't tolerate it well. You should stay as you are for at least a few days. Transforming will be a matter of envisioning the form you wish to take. You'll be able to take on almost any form you wish. Just visualize what you want to be. Your natural human form will be the easiest for you to shift through. I suspect Lucifer is blocking you from transforming to preserve your health. He likes to think he's clever."

"Yes, he does." I turned my ears back at being tricked by Lucifer yet again. "He was implying Darian would be required to transform back."

"I'm okay with this general development. I can go fetch the bridle, add some ribbons, and show you off to make it clear how spectacular you are."

"Darlene has gotten to you, hasn't she?" I accused, well aware the wily snow leopard would do far more than coerce a devilish general to get what she wanted.

"I value my life and wish to see the birth of my next child," he informed me in a solemn tone. "That I get to match my son with a good woman only makes me more inclined to cater to Darlene's wishes on this matter."

"I can't blame you for doing what Darlene wants. She can be vicious when she decides to be." As I didn't want to dwell on what Darlene would do if she didn't get her way, I turned my focus on the next important thing on my list. "How is Mr. Flooferson the Magnificent getting on with Darian?"

"Your feline keeps looking for you, as your scent is everywhere due to the rather shameful number of panties my son has gotten his hands on. I tried to tell him the panties worked better when the woman is wearing them, but now my son is even more annoyed with me than he usually is. When I left, he was talking to your cat, trying to convince the furry beast they'd have to share you. That was going about as well as you might expect."

"Obviously, I must go rescue my cat. Lead the way, Belial. Lucifer will be busy, and it's not like you can't sneak me out of this place if you really want to."

"Did you not want to see the conservatory?"

"I want my cat, Belial. And I'll do you a favor and steal your son while I'm reclaiming what is rightfully mine. He'll just have to take a raincheck on being dragged to a lair."

SEVENTEEN

"My work ethic is lethal?"

BELIAL GUIDED me across the wastelands of the Devil's chosen layer of his many hells, and he taught me the more permanent landmarks.

The places where crystals grew served as guideposts for travelers, and the colors of the gemstone spears mattered. Red led to Lucifer's sanctuary. Clear stones pointed towards the nearest nexus, which we would use to return to the mortal coil until I could be taught how to safely teleport.

I discovered one of the advantages of my new form along the way. Whenever the footing seemed uncertain or the ground shifted beneath my hooves, my body adapted to the terrain. Claws formed when I required them for traction. In the case of fast-flowing lava, my hooves developed cushions of air, which allowed me to trot over the pools without getting wet. The air amused me, and once on solid ground, I lifted a leg trying to figure out how my hooves could generate enough wind to hold up my body. "Lucifer may be a jerk sometimes, but he uses his powers of evil in interesting ways."

"He made you rather durable, as he would not be able to readily replace you. You're a favorite person of his, and he takes that seriously. The environment here can be brutal, and he made you to best adapt to it. You'll be able to handle the icy layers just as easily. He made you a lethal beauty, which is reflection of your work ethic."

"My work ethic is lethal?"

"For your emotional health, yes."

Damn. Darian's father didn't hold back when he went after somebody. "I would think my tendency to pursue forbidden lore and magic would be more lethal than my work ethic."

"The difference is simple. Lucifer wanted you meddling in such magics so he could make you his. Your work ethic will be refined so that you maintain your current standards while on the job, but that you have a life outside of work."

"I'm sensing a pot meeting kettle situation I will have to discuss with Lucifer."

"Darlene is very good at making sure he plays as much as he works, so don't you worry about that. *He* created her for that purpose, after all. Cats are as cats are, and all work and no play makes for a very cranky kitty."

That I could believe. "I will make sure to negotiate an appropriate amount of time off when I get around to the job interview. It helps knowing I already have the job and can just take the Devil for all he's worth."

"I expect that will happen as soon as Lucifer realizes you've given him the slip, which will be shortly after I take you to my boy. Just bite his hair and drag him off. You can pick just about anywhere here for your lair, although I recommend you take the crystal lake. It's an excellent place for one such as yourself, and it's a short trot over to the manor. It's one of the permanent landmarks, and it's seawater, so Malcolm is close to his element, so you'll see him and Kanika often, as she drags him over to recharge. And having other equines nearby will be good for him."

"I feel like this was an elaborate ruse to make Malcolm more comfortable."

"Lucifer does enjoy when he can accomplish many things with a singular act of evil." Belial pointed at a dark hole in the ground. "The nexus is in there. Now that you've seen the entry, it'll be easier for you to find. I'm not patient enough to wait the hours for you to figure out how to use the crystals within to teleport to where you want to go, so I'm going to teleport you to my home, where my son attempts to learn how to summon you. Badly. So badly. So very badly. He'll discover he's excellent at summoning your lingerie, but summoning you is far outside of his reach. Once he figures out the knack of it, I fear he'll summon your lingerie right off of you, because he is my son and he enjoys pulling tricks when he can. I recommend you ward your undergarments on the days you don't want him summoning them right off you."

Life had new perils, ones I appreciated. Did they count as perils if I looked forward to discovering how far Darian would go to get me out of my panties? I needed to dedicate some serious time thinking about the various ways I could encourage him on his quest to master panty summoning. "Is there a reason I can't just summon him here and drag him off?"

"Beyond upsetting his mother, who is trying very hard to teach him the arts of summoning, no. There's no reason you can't summon him here and drag him off. He might have enough hair for you to bite. You could also nab him by his collar, I suppose. Lucifer sometimes drags Darlene off by her hair when he's in a mood. The struggle is entertaining. I'm sure you'll embrace your darker nature in time. He is my son, so I'm sure he will enjoy whatever you decide to do to him."

"The archangel might be an issue."

"The archangel is trying to help his mother teach him how to summon you. He is holding your new halter. It's rather lovely. He decided to add a halter to your equine apparel. You also have full parade gear now, and if you have to venture into one of the levels with a lot of pests, he made an ear bonnet and face mask for you. Really, he went overboard with his efforts to dress you up. The last time I bothered checking, he had fashioned three saddles of different colors. He has one specifically for Lucifer's use, as I expect you'll be requested as a mount every rare now and again."

I considered that, pricking my ears forward. "He does not usually indulge in theatrics like that. Why me and not Malcolm?"

"Your holy fire and hellfire have something to do with that. That, plus Lucifer expects Kanika to ride Malcolm. That plan isn't going over all that well right now. Kanika gets flustered trying to saddle him, even when he's standing there waiting patiently for her to get a move on already. Life in the manor can become very entertaining when his heir is in residence. Perhaps if you saddle him and learn to ride using him, you'll help Lucifer accomplish his goals."

"If Lucifer will be riding me, who will Darlene ride?"

"Likely Darian, once you finish converting him. My son is a lot of things, but he'll do well as a guardian. You'll learn this on your own soon enough, but Lucifer always plays the long game, and I'm willing to bet he is after Darian as much as he's after you. Bundling you together just means he gets what he wants more efficiently, and you'll have a good working relationship. Of course, it'll backfire because he will have to compete with your amorous stallion, and he'll lose more often than he wins, but some sacrifices he's willing to make for the main goal."

I snorted. "Lucifer is a pain in my ass!"

"He'll be more of a pain on your back, but you'll get over it, I'm sure. If you're with Lucifer, my son will stick close to you, which means Darlene won't stray. Really, Lucifer's whole ploy is to make certain that Darlene stays close in less-than-ideal circumstances. And as holy fire can heal, he knows you or Darian can take care of her."

The Devil would drive me insane sooner than later, and I suspected the sooner would be within a few days at most. "Please just take me to your son, Belial."

The devilish general laughed, placed his hand on my shoulder, and the world dissolved into darkness.

BEFORE I HAD a chance to do more than blink and shake my head to clear it, Mr. Flooferson the Magnificent plowed into my legs and purred. He marked his territory with his face, and I lowered my head to nuzzle my cat. His time in captivity hadn't done him any harm, with his coat as soft and plush as I remembered. Belial crouched beside me and gave my cat a scratch behind his ears, which was accepted with more purring.

"This is my home, and my wife has dragged our son to the basement to use her lab. I believe she hopes that a more elaborate workspace will help. She is wrong. I love my wife dearly, but she is sometimes blind and delusional when it comes to our child. He's hopeless, but I love him anyway."

Raguel appeared, earning a hiss from Mr. Flooferson, who crowded closer to my legs. "I would say welcome to hell, but you were just there, and I am not sure which is worse right now," the archangel complained. "Thank you for coming. My wife's limited patience has completely frayed, and our son grows ever more frustrated. It was amusing for the first few hours, but the longer this goes on, the more absurd your fate becomes. He's convinced himself you are a man-hunting succubus at this point, and he wants to be the man you hunt. He has already begun strategizing how to keep a succubus loyal. I am not certain what he will concoct next, but I wish to avoid such things."

I kept nuzzling my cat, who pawed at my mane. "He recognizes me."

"You smell almost the same, and we helped him understand you would have new forms. He was well cared for while you searched for him, and beyond being upset about having his temperature taken and a single blood sample, he was not treated poorly. The blood sample was what they truly needed, which they acquired. Had they just taken the blood sample, they would have not brought ruin upon themselves. The compulsion Lucifer placed helped with that. He was given a large pen to play in, toys, and attention, and while he was frightened of some portions of his captivity, Lucifer helped make certain he understood his confinement would be temporary. The worst part for him was being abandoned outdoors. He is not fond of large, open spaces, but Lucifer recovered him quickly and put him in an environment he preferred. My son dotes heavily on your feline, so it is a good thing you are taking both home with you. Take my child. I no longer want him except for major holidays and occasional visits."

My poor cat. Another day, I might have felt a little sorry for Darian, who faced parental abandonment in a loving fashion. "You're the best kitty," I cooed to him. "And you're going to have a girlfriend and a little daughter to dote on soon, too. I hope you like other cats."

"He will appreciate companionship, especially when you must work," Raguel assured me. "Now, as for the matter of my son."

"If I had a lair, I'd drag him to it, but I haven't gotten to having a lair yet. Where is he? I'll bite his clothes and drag him off, but somebody needs to bring my cat. I'll need someone with hands to direct me to a good location to hold him hostage until I have hands. Also, I'm not leaving without my cat. Or your son. I have hellfire, and I'm not afraid to use it. I have holy fire, too, and I'm also not afraid to use it. I can even use them at the same time."

"I am aware." Raguel pointed at an open door behind him. "That leads to the basement. I ask your forgiveness for the theft of your lingerie, which is currently scattered all over the floor. I'm concerned some articles were damaged, but I will see they are replaced as needed. As I am a most loving father, I made a note of which pieces caught my son's attention the most, and I will share his secrets with you. I have come to understand women enjoy picking the best lingerie as a reward for herself and her partner—

and rewarding her partner results in rewards for herself."

For a being who was supposed to be a shining example of purity, Raguel understood more about having a love life than I did. "Thank you. I am not asking for forgiveness for the theft of your son."

The archangel laughed. "No forgiveness for that is necessary. In fact, you will be given gifts for taking him. Belial, we should come up with a suitable dowry for him. She's going to have her hands full with him, and we are the culprits responsible for her current situation."

"Belial said Lucifer was barring me from shapeshifting because I am a bundle of conflicting energy right now. Is that true?"

"It is true. My son will be very annoyed with this development, as he has a keen interest in pursuing you in your human form, but I intend on giving him some brushes and suggesting he pamper you until it is safe for you to shift back in a day or two. You can take him for rides around Lucifer's home in the meantime. It will be good for you to learn how to tolerate a rider, and generally, there are only three people you will typically tolerate riding you."

"Darian, Lucifer, and Darlene?" I guessed. After a moment of thought, I said, "I'd probably tolerate Kanika if Malcolm broke a leg or something."

"Yes, precisely so. And if Malcolm broke a leg, there is no chance Kanika would leave him behind, so that is not a future I have foreseen. That could change, depending on your actions."

Whatever. I'd deal with Lucifer, Darlene, and their daughter later. "I don't have a lair. That will make dragging Darian off difficult. I don't have a plan, Raguel. I like having a plan, and this is completely unplanned."

The archangel stroked my nose and gave my brow a brisk rub. "Don't worry about that. Just take over part of Lucifer's manor. He won't mind, and Darlene made him open guest bedrooms. Claim whichever spot you like best. If Darlene hadn't been attempting to put Lucifer on the couch for a while, she would have showed you where to go. She probably became hungry enough Lucifer needed to feed her."

"She attacked him. I left him to his fate. He didn't need any help from me. He seemed quite happy to be attacked."

"If she showed her wings and spots, my brother will be most pleased."

"She had her wings out, yes."

"It is for the best you left my brother to his fate. He will enjoy it fiercely. Belial, do you want to teleport her while I handle the annoying child?"

"That might be wise. I'd be tempted to dump him in one of the springs to teach him to be less obnoxious—and cool his temper a little."

"Just use the pool in the one guest bedroom. While he dries off, we will get her saddled so she can work off some of that energy on a good run. After she has run around, he can brush out her coat and shower her with affection, and our plan to rid ourselves of our child and put him in the care of a suitable being will be well underway."

Belial nodded. "Off you go, Diana. Be careful on the steps. Token drag him, and us mean fathers will take care of the heavy work. You're making a point, not applying for excessive exercise. You'll get to begin your conversion conquests soon enough."

"I don't even know how to convert him," I complained.

"Just keep him in your bed. It'll just happen. The only way you can screw this up is by putting him on the couch. The more fun you have, the faster you'll convert him."

Well, that simplified matters. "Can you do the incubus trick?"

"Incubus trick?" Belial asked with a raised brow.

"Birth control," I informed the devilish general in a solemn tone. "Children happen when both parents want children without reservation, not before."

"Ah. Yes. I've been meddling with that brat since he was old enough to realize women were interesting—at his request. You can thank his mother for that, as she is convinced Raguel and I cruelly tricked her into having him in the first place. For the record, we had not tricked her. She is the one who opted to throw out her birth control because of the side effects. That's not *my* fault." Belial smirked. "She's since learned she needs to ask if she wants me to function as her no-side effects birth control."

"He hadn't told me that." How interesting. "I should undergo something similar. Otherwise, it's not really fair if he's doing all of the preventative work."

"I'll inquire with Darlene, and she'll take care of it. She's better at working with women, and she's protective of you. For now, don't worry your pretty little head about it. Consider it an early dowry for tolerating the brat." Belial slapped my rump. "Get a move on, Diana. I want a house without any whining children in it. I have plans for tonight, and they do not include interruptions from whining children."

I caught myself before I whinnied a laugh, as whinnying would notify Darian he had an equine visitor. "I'm surprised he hasn't come up here to find out what the ruckus is about."

"There's a door into the summoning room. It's soundproofed, as our wife has the attention span of a gnat when something distracting happens, like unidentified noises. It's unlocked, so you can just push it open."

Most believed trusting a devil led to doom, destruction, or a quick trip to hell. I'd learned early on that religion tended to get the agenda of devils and demons wrong. They served a specific role in the Devil's many hells, and that purpose was to get rid of the souls they had. The End of Days would change that. The devils and demons I knew focused more on eating, making more demons and devils, and achieving their personal goals, which often had nothing to do with the Devil *or* his many hells.

Belial wanted another child, but his nature—and Raguel's nature—barred them from acting until certain their offspring would be cared for once outside of the nest.

Devils and demons often made good parents, and I figured the rarity of opportunities to procreate factored into that.

I hesitated before descending the stairs, considering Belial with interest. "What *did* you do to earn Darian's seed, anyway?"

"Oh, I expect I was played by Lucifer. He's been watching over you for a long time, and you're enough older than Darian to lead me to believe that Lucifer planned him just for you. I just happened to be in the right place at the right time, and Lucifer does like me most of the time, so I got lucky."

"And the second seed?"

"Lucifer has a shameful amount of remorse when he uses his favored people in his schemes, so he tries to make up for his various sins through good deeds. Or Darlene found out and made him pay penance. You can never be sure with those two."

Raguel laughed. "Do not worry yourself about this, Diana. All that matters is we have a seed for our next child, and we would really appreciate if you could drag our first child off. Keep him busy for at least a few months. Preferably ten to twelve, as I would grieve if our first child came to an unfortunate end taunting his pregnant mother."

"You both owe me an extra gift at Christmas for this," I informed them, before heading down the steps to stake a claim and run away to the Devil's home with my prize and my cat.

I CRACKED open the door with my nose and turned my head so I could peek inside. Darian sat in the center of a sea of panties, all mine as far as I could tell, while his mother sat in a corner, staring at the wall.

Darian's mother sighed. "Maybe we should try the bras, too. They're sets. Diana meticulously keeps her lingerie in sets. She's just so… so…"

"Perfect," Darian supplied.

Okay. The whole panty thing gave me pause, especially as he'd salvaged the busted sets from my home when Mr. Flooferson had been stolen. I spotted more than a few half-destroyed scraps of lace scattered on the floor, which meant he must have left no part of my bedroom unturned in his quest to branch into summoning magic.

"Your summoning abilities are shameful. How could I, a supreme summoner, have created such an inept child? How? Belial! Raguel! This is your fault."

Both devil and archangel popped into being in the center of the summoning circle, and the tenderness of Belial's smile caught me off guard. Crouching beside his son, the devil chuckled. "Darian, you're not your mother, and you don't have to worry about your magic not working on living beings. Your wayfinding doesn't, either. That said, I would like to remind you that you're working to summon a rather hungry predator, and you'll deserve exactly what you get. Eventually. You'll have to wait for any indulgences until later."

"If I can summon her," Darian grumbled, and he sighed, reaching out and swiping up panties and setting them aside to expose the floor and clean the chalk he'd been using to make his symbols. "I don't understand what I'm doing wrong."

Hooves on stone should have made noise, but something about the rock absorbed the sound. I eyed the material with interest, scratching at it to discover not even my claws could damage it. As far as summoning circle surfaces went, I appreciated the floor.

I bet I could summon the Devil in the room with little difficulty—and I wouldn't even need a pair of his panties to pull the trick off.

As he didn't understand what he did wrong, and his mother mourned that her genetics hadn't been able to overcome Darian's special blend of magic, I canted my head to the side so I could regard the circle he'd been attempting to draw. Drawing a clean circle took work, and he'd created more of an oval with a few squiggles here and there from his unsteady, uncertain hand.

Apparently, he lacked in any form of artistic ability.

Belial and Raguel joined me in regarding the remnants of Darian's work.

His devilish father heaved a sigh and said, "It seems we must give our next child more ready access to crayons and stencils. Artistic ability must be nurtured, and summoning circles are as much an art as a skill."

"There will be no stencils used in *my* summoning room, you fiends!" Darian's mother growled from the corner.

Raguel's snicker, rather dark for coming from an archangel, warned me there'd be a battle between the threesome within a few minutes, one I did not wish to witness. As grabbing Darian and leaving seemed better than getting involved with those three, I snagged my tall, dark, and handsome by his collar, grunted, and backed to the door.

Darian's startled squawk amused me so much I let go of his shirt and whinnied.

"You are really not good at this," Belial complained. "You have to finish dragging him off before you start laughing at him."

My coat paled to as white as snow, and I snorted holy fire at him.

Belial sidestepped with a grin. "Not very effective, but I appreciate your willingness to give me a few burns I won't forget for at least a week."

Darian stared at me with his mouth hanging open. "Diana?"

To make it clear I wasn't afraid of either one of his fathers, I went the nightmare route and snorted some hellfire at Raguel, who made a point of stepping out of the way to avoid being burned.

"I am not quite sure what I have done to be targeted, but I am a wise enough being to admit I do not want to deal with being burned. Is this, perhaps, a demonstration you can protect your territory?"

I considered the archangel's words, and

after taking the time to think about it, I bobbed my head. "That's close enough."

Mostly, I was hungry, didn't even know what I wanted or needed to eat, and longed for a nap. On second thought, a nap would go over well. How did nightmares sleep? I eyed my lingerie with interest. If I piled them up, would they make a suitable nest?

Darian's mother turned from the corner and looked me over. "Well, she's not a succubus, so your worries about having to launch a major seduction strategy no longer seem required."

I flattened my ears and showed the woman my teeth. "You're not helping."

Claudine cackled and bounced over, and with no fear of my teeth or my various flames, she looked me over and stroked my nose. "Don't you worry yourself at all. He can still make use of his major seduction strategy if you wish. You're absolutely gorgeous. What is she, Belial?"

"A nightmare or a daydream, depending on her mood at the time. *He* gifted her with holy fire, and Lucifer made certain she has a balanced access to hellfire. Darlene became rather hungry, so Lucifer is tending to her. As a result, I opted to retrieve Diana to put an end to this nonsense."

I eyed Darian's pitiful attempt at a summoning circle. "You should stick to wayfinding objects. You're good at that. And you will limit any summoning of my panties off me for after hours activities."

My tall, dark, and handsome considered my lingerie with interest. "I can do that with a summoning circle?"

"Well, you're certainly not going to be summoning me with those circles, but you're good with objects. Stick to your strengths." I grabbed his collar and resumed dragging him towards the door.

"I already told you I'd teleport you," Belial said with an exasperated sigh. "You don't have to make your point beyond what you've already done. We understand you're leaving with him."

I released Darian's shirt again and snorted some hellfire to make it clear the devilish general needed to watch his step. "And my cat."

"And your cat," he conceded. "And yes, Darian, that really *is* Diana. Yes, she fully intends on stealing you, and yes, you may begin your so-called major seduction plan in a few days, once she's able to return to a human form. Lucifer is blocking her shapeshifting abilities until she's physically adapted sufficiently. She's got a lot of conflicting energy pouring through her right now, so she needs to stay in her new form until that settles. Her human shape wouldn't handle it well. Instead of pursuing your seduction plans, you can help her adapt by going on rides and letting her burn her energy off while getting her used to a rider. You'll have your turn being the one ridden soon enough."

Darian got to his feet before I had a chance to grab him again, and he faced me, lifting his hand to touch my nose. I bumped him, and when he didn't start giving me strokes, I pushed harder.

"She wants you to pet her," Raguel stated. "She enjoys the attention."

Traitorous yet useful archangel. "We're going to conquer Lucifer's house and make him serve my bidding until he builds me a lair. Once I have a lair, I am dragging you to it. It will be near a lake, because your father said it's a prime spot."

"What happened to going to a bunch of hotels on Lucifer's dime?" Darian asked in an amused tone.

"He is now the hotel manager, and I will demand room service often. I will tell him it is to earn his way into my good graces when he tries to hire me. Now that I have my cat back, I can focus on the important things."

"Like what?" my tall, dark, and handsome asked.

"Conquering you and dragging you to my lair, of course. I heard there's a major seduction strategy in the works, and I wish to evaluate the plan and offer improvements. I'm good at improving major plans."

"Sorry, Mom. I'm going to have to skip out on the rest of my summoning circle lessons. I have a major seduction strategy to refine and implement."

If Claudine rolled her eyes any harder, she'd lose them in the back of her skull. "Begone, child. I don't want to see you until Christmas. I'd say try not to embarrass yourself, but you've done that plenty without help."

He sure had, although I found his efforts to summon me through the collecting of my lingerie to be amusing. To make it clear Darian hadn't embarrassed himself all that much, I picked through my panties until I found a particularly lacy pair and its matching bra. I dumped both on his head. "Is this a strong enough hint?"

Darian removed my lingerie from his head and took the time to fold both pieces neatly. "As a matter of fact, yes. It is. I'll see you at Christmas, Mom. I'll be occupied until then."

"I love you, but get out of my house."

I whinnied my laughter.

Epilogue: Fate had, for a rare change, smiled upon me.

WHEN I OFFERED to host Christmas dinner, a first in my entire life, I should have warned my parents that they would be making a visit to the Devil's many hells. A nicer woman would have warned her parents.

Over the months after recovering Mr. Flooferson the Magnificent and taking Darian home with me, I'd undergone more changes than becoming a living nightmare. I worked less and played more, I went out places I wanted rather than because work demanded it of me—and I planned to openly summon the Devil to Christmas dinner, as *He* thought it would be a good idea.

It would take getting used to *Him* showing up for a visit at *His* leisure, but as the Devil's personal secretary and general busybody, I got to entertain the bigwigs. I also got to plan the more unusual meetings between the world's varying pantheons. That would always disconcert me.

Nothing worried me quite as much as working to make sure the Egyptians didn't get into a fight with the Greeks, the Indians, or the Chinese. The Egyptians, I'd learned, enjoyed stirring trouble just about everywhere, and they were not afraid of using every tool at their disposal, including Lucifer's daughter.

Add in that one of Lucifer's nephews was a direct descendant of *the* Sphinx, who in turn was married to the sole daughter of Ra, and things became interesting. Interesting often meant destructive. I suspected the Devil had turned me into a nightmare to up my chances of surviving his extended family, especially his beloved cindercorn.

Fate had, for a rare change, smiled upon me.

The beloved cindercorn, her husband, and their entire herd of children had opted to come to dinner, although the young gorgons were having dinner at the main house and being entertained by a slew of demons and devils seeking Lucifer's favor, as several of the fosters were too young to have any control over their abilities to petrify people. To complicate matters—or add to my general entertainment—their two non-gorgon children came as cindercorn foals rather than human infants, which meant all of the equines of the many hells had made an appearance to play and care for them.

Two cindercorns, their foals, the Four Horses of the Apocalypse, Epona, and several other equines, including several standard unicorns, and Malcolm, in his kelpie form, romped around in my backyard, which had undergone a rather unusual transformation since the prior day.

Snowballs had a really good chance of surviving in hell, at least until dinner ended.

Kanika served as the group's referee, and she even had a whistle if somebody got too rough with one of the foals.

Darian would, according to Lucifer, require another year of tender loving care from me before he would sport hooves, so I was the only equine holdout, staying in my human form rather than joining the activities out in the snow.

I needed hands to help in the kitchen of my lair. To my delight, I'd discovered while Darian couldn't draw a decent summoning circle to save his life, he loved to cook, had a talent for it, and enjoyed when I sat on a stool nearby and did what I did best, which involved being pretty for his enjoyment and cutting the vegetables he didn't want to handle.

I'd finished my vegetable slaying duties early, so I'd become the nice view while he made dinner. As he served as a mighty fine view, I enjoyed ruling over the kitchen as a pampered queen with a tall, dark, and handsome servant.

Still, guilt nibbled at me for making him do the work for an entire herd of demons, devils, and my family, who likely counted as demons or devils by their deeds rather than species designation. "Are five turkeys going to be enough?"

Darian's dark chuckle made me wish I could get to my evening plans, which involved him and our big bed. "And three hams, plus the roasted pig Darlene is making. Just be glad she didn't talk Lucy into an entire calf. I'm pretty sure my fathers are bringing a whole deer, and we have the unexpected tuna, as an old one in the conservatory was dying. Its meat is still good, so why waste it?"

Crap. "What tuna? When did an entire tuna become involved in this?"

"You know how Darlene gets. Darlene's taking care of preparing the tuna. We won't be eating it for dinner, but everyone is getting a gift of fish for the road. And onto the next surprise of the day."

Uh oh. Surprises could be good or bad when Darian was involved with them. "What have you done now? Isn't it bad enough my parents are coming *here*? Worse,

Ra is fetching them. Why had I thought having dinner *here* was a good idea?"

"It's the only place any of us has that would fit everyone, and Lucifer really wanted Christmas with the foals. Ra's excellent at teleportation, so your parents won't get teleportation sickness. We've been over that before. Ra likes being useful, and he also enjoys getting stabs in at idiot parents who need an attitude adjustment. Unlike the Gardeners, *your* parents are redeemable, although it'll take some work. So, Ra is handling stage one of their redemption. Also, we're all onto you. If your parents earned a stay here, you wouldn't be a nightmare. You'd be a depressed mare. As such, steps are being taken to make sure that doesn't come to pass. What they do in their next life will no longer be your problem, but we've decided we're campaigning to prevent a severe bout of depression. In exchange, you'll have to take part in punishing the Gardeners."

I wrinkled my nose at mention of the Gardeners, who languished in a prison in New York for attempting to torch their daughter's house. "I still don't get why *I* have to be the case worker for that travesty. The last thing I want is to organize their community service and relocate them somewhere far away from New York. I'm in on rehabilitating them once they're here, though."

"You volunteered because you are well aware of what hell waits for them once they leave the mortal coil. You figured they might as well earn their stay, so you arranged for them to cause trouble and sin somewhere they *wouldn't* bother Bailey or Sam."

Right, right. "What's the next surprise?"

"I have been informed that Ruby's babies are old enough to need new homes, and as *you* can handle mortal fish having mortal lifespans, we are becoming the new caretakers for the babies she isn't keeping. Baby. She's allowed to keep one. Lucifer put his foot down, and she's only keeping one of the spawn. That means we're getting a ridiculous number of fish for Christmas, and if we know what's good for us, we'll let Darlene visit her fishy children. We will not let her know when one passes unless she asks, and should she ask, we'll tell her he or she died of old age, a happy fish."

I bowed my head and sighed. "She's looking for more excuses to come over, isn't she?"

"Yep."

Our lair, which was more of a nice, sprawling manor house rather than what most thought of as a lair, had plenty of space for a bunch of bettas, and it also had a connection to the conservatory, entering where Lucifer kept his beloved wild horses. As Belial promised, the shoreline of the crystal lake, which had actual water and crystals everywhere, made an excellent spot for my home. The lake even had fish in it—real ones, consisting mostly of endangered species we weren't allowed to catch. Given a few years, I suspected we'd end up helping to manage the conservatory. Darlene loved her conservation projects, and Lucifer refused to expand his home beyond working on the conservatory sub-level, as she'd take over the entirety of his many hells and leave no room to work with the fucking assholes in residence.

We already had a breeding pair of endangered parrots, one of the thirty pairs left, who might one day allow Lucifer to release some back into the wilds of Earth and create an unexpected miracle.

I'd named the talkative bastards Snack and Attack. Snack would snack her way to ruling our home, and Attack guarded his precious Snack most viciously. Conversion made healing from his bites a trivial matter, and Attack gradually learned we would pet him if he didn't try to remove our flesh from our bones.

Attack enjoyed being petted almost as much as he liked rock music, which we played for him when he behaved.

I sighed again. "Ten bucks and a glorious night for me, where you treat me like the goddess you claim I am, says that Lucifer is going to make us pay out our owed lecture over Christmas dinner."

"I hate losing a bet, because that's probably exactly what he's going to do, but I'm going to go along with this because I have ten dollars and want to spend a glorious night treating you like a goddess. If Lucifer was not planning on lecturing us over Christmas dinner, I'll yell at him in private until he does. And if he doesn't give us the lecture he's owed, I'm still paying out because I'm selfish and greedy."

I grinned at the thought of Darian going toe-to-toe with Lucifer. Again. The conversion process had done wonders for Darian's willingness to face off against the Devil, and I was the true winner of their disputes, most of which were playful in nature.

Fortunately for my sanity, I'd converted Darian enough he could withstand a dunking or two in lava, as Lucifer rather enjoyed punting my husband-to-be into one of the pools whenever he became annoying.

"I'm expecting it because we keep refusing to set a wedding date, and he loves weddings," I reminded him. "Just tell him we enjoy living in sin too much to ruin it with marriage plans yet."

"Well, if you hadn't informed him we wouldn't have any foals romping around until after marriage, we wouldn't be getting nagged right now."

I shrugged. "I'm sure we'll just hit up Vegas or something—"

"You absolutely will not," Lucifer announced, and the bastard revealed himself on the counter beside me, opting to show up as a Caucasian gentleman with horns and wearing a designer suit.

Uh oh. The Devil wasn't playing to my parents' expectations, which would inevitably lead to chaos.

"Merry Christmas, and you're an asshole," I told my boss.

"Merry Christmas. I thought you'd like to know Ra has met your parents, and they're now in a delightful state of shock, especially as Ra is almost as overprotective as I am, so he is laying out how they will behave at dinner. As Ra can be vindictive, he has not notified your parents of the rest of the guest list. *He* is already here, and *He* has opted to take a mortal form for the venture."

I considered the many ways *He* might offend my parents. "*He* went with dark skin?"

"Absolutely. Mankind didn't start as pasty pale beings, anyway. That happened due to migration and opting to live in colder climates with fewer days of sunshine. Humans always find a way to complicate things. It's so easy to play to prejudices, and *He* has almost as wicked a sense of humor as I do. *He's* wearing a suit, too. A rather nice one, actually. It's nice because I helped *Him* with it."

"It's one of your suits because *He* generally has no use for clothes," I guessed. "But *He* has a point to prove, so *He* is playing to humanity's conception of propriety."

"You're absolutely correct. It's been a while since *He* has manifested any form, so *He* would like you to add a shroud over his shroud. Just to be extra cautious. You need the practice anyway. Normally, *He* manifests as a presence."

Conversion had come with prices, but it had also come with gifts, and the magic that would have killed me had ultimately become one of my strengths. I could shroud just about anything or anyone, and my shrouds made most divines work to break through them.

He wouldn't be a risk to anyone, not with my shroud in place.

With me around, the End of Days might not wipe everybody out, forever changing the future. The more I thought about it, the more I realized the Devil had played an even longer game than I'd believed. Lucifer had wanted me for secretarial work, but he needed me to keep a dark future from coming to pass—or one that would end everything he held dear.

If I could shroud *Him*, the End of Days might not come to pass at all, not for Earth.

Instead, the battlefield would change to a new location. Perhaps the heavens, perhaps the many hells—but not Earth.

"You're tricky," I complained. "You better have brought me really nice presents to put up with this."

Lucifer laughed. "We have presents for you, never fear. Your living room is buried in presents, and Sam's going to play at being Santa. *He* thinks it's hilarious. What's really hilarious is that you told your mother how many people were coming so she could get a token gift for everybody. *He* is going to thoroughly enjoy her expression when she realizes she's giving me a Christmas present."

"I've become a pretty evil woman in the past few months."

"No, you've simply become a confident woman who isn't afraid of stepping out of line. You talk back to your boss now instead of doing what you're told with minimal questioning. That's me. You talk back to me. Often. You even like it. Anyway, all of this is necessary. They'll come away from today far better people *and* far better parents for you. That won't fix your childhood, but your adulthood will be filled with joy. Of course, I'm saying that because I have every intention of making it so. Who knows? Maybe they'll even find their way into *His* heavens after they realize the drivel their church fed them was lies and blasphemy rather than the real deal. However much it pains me, I can recommend a few churches that do walk the straight and narrow."

"Put the addresses in a card for them as part of their Christmas present," I ordered.

"I can do that." Lucifer snickered while watching Darian work on dinner. "As for you, how are you liking my ultimate Christmas present to you? Isn't she magnificent?"

"Don't call her a Christmas present. She wasn't a present. I'm her present, a present she gave herself, and it wasn't for Christmas." Darian shook his head and gave one of his soft, patience-tested chuckles. "I do love her, and she needs to hear it early and often. She's getting her scheduled dose of adoration after we've evicted all of our guests."

The patience-tested chuckle always intrigued me, as he'd somehow transformed his general frustration into amusement. He claimed he wanted me to see how people could be with a little effort, and he loved me too much to get mad at me for struggling to accept affection.

It had taken a few months for me to get used to the idea, as I'd discovered I had no idea how to handle people openly loving me. I responded better to gestures rather than words, but the instant Darian had figured out I had no idea how to process spoken affection, he worked to acclimate me to the idea—or at least numb me due to frequency. "You just had to start, didn't you?"

"Always. It's a joy in my long life." Lucifer slid off the counter. "Try to act surprised and delighted about the fish, Diana. Darlene spent a chunk of the morning crying that her little children were going to a new home. I escaped here because I can't tell her she shouldn't cry because Ruby's babies are all grown up, but she's redefining what it means to be hormonal. I had to make Ruby's girlfriend immortal, which is why she only gets to keep one. And I told her that she can only breed Ruby to his new beloved girlfriend. I had to sit down and have a talk with the fish so they could share the same aquarium. Normal bettas would kill each other given half a chance and any excuse. They're only allowed to fight when it's time to breed, and they've been told they're only allowed to breed once a year at most. They can be freeloaders the rest of the time. Then I made sure that's the case by fiddling with them."

Ah. "She's in the fertility stage of her cycle?" I'd learned succubi, much like humans, had cycles, and when a succubus hit the peak of her fertility, she became a hormonal mess, needed to be fed more often than usual, and wanted to be around babies or make a baby—or several babies, depending on the length of her cycle.

Darlene, much to everyone's relief, tended to have a short fertility stage of her cycle, only running Lucifer ragged for two to three weeks out of each year, as measured on Earth.

The Devil, who enjoyed being run ragged, grinned. "She sure is. The children will help tone her down, but I figured I'd let her work that out of her system. I'm not going to be available tomorrow, as she'll need a lot of tender, loving care to bring her back to an almost-sane state."

"She's showing her wings and spots, isn't she?"

"Every single one of them," Lucifer replied in a rueful tone. "And she's at the stage she couldn't hide them if she tried. *He* is going to meddle slightly over dinner so she's somewhat sane, but the instant *He* leaves, I'll have to take her home, else she'll start a hell-wide party."

"I'd feel sorry for you, except I really don't. You'll have a good time tonight, just make sure you give *Him* a hug."

"However much I loathe and abhor the idea, I shall."

Liar, liar. Rather than call Lucifer out on his bullshit, I smiled. "Your cindercorns are playing in the snow. I thought they hated the snow?"

"Well, normally, that's the case, but *someone* can't keep her hands off my nephew, so she only has herself to blame for her current situation—or her soon-to-be current situation, as I *am* the Devil, they *did* agree to stay at my house tonight, and it's Christmas, and I want more little cindercorn foals to spoil. Those ones are old enough to handle some additions to the family."

I glanced out the window at the pair of fillies who were determined to catch their father and the Four Horses of the Apocalypse in a convoluted game of chase while their mother whinnied her laughter. One day, both would fly, although their stubby little wings didn't do more than flap ineffectively, covered in down and baby feathers. "How old until they start flying?"

"They won't until adulthood, much to their future annoyance. They'll take their first short flights in their late teens. The next pair won't have wings. Initially, this will come as a relief to their beleaguered parents, but they'll learn looks are deceiving."

"Setting them up for another set of twins?"

"It's payback for the quadruplets they inflicted on a family friend," Lucifer replied. "I very clearly heard Bailey claim she wanted more children. Very clearly. I also heard Sam state the same thing where Bailey couldn't hear him. As such, they are getting precisely what they want for Christmas. Again. Anyway, the foals will go to the kids' dinner, so you won't have to worry about them being underfoot, and the Four Horses will keep an eye on the kids, so security will be good. I mean, add in the congregation of devilish and demonic babysitters, and there's no safer place to be than in hell right now."

"No kidding. I assume they'll shift to human eventually?"

"Soon. Ra is bringing your parents now, so I'll send them around front. Honestly, they're cindercorns at my request—and the standard unicorns are around for the same reason. We want to convince your parents to change their ways, not fully traumatize them. I mean, when *He* reveals who *He* is, it'll be a little traumatic."

"A little trauma will not hurt them," *He* said, poking his head into the kitchen. *He* had chosen the form of a willowy black man, not much taller than me, possessing an almost feminine air. *His* mischievous smile both warmed and worried me. As warned, *He* wore one of his fallen son's suits, pitch black with a red tie. "Could I bother you for an extra layer of shroud? I usually shroud completely to avoid any chance of an accident."

I'd learned from the archangels *He* was still fairly young, and *His* mortal personality still thrived. According to everyone I'd asked, they hoped that never changed.

Sliding off my stool, I smiled and concentrated on *Him*, narrowing my eyes until I pierced through the barrier safeguarding mortals from *His* visage. Any other day, I wouldn't have been worried, but when in hell in what could become a family feud, I understood *His* concern. I reached out and touched *His* brow between his eyes, drawing a circle with the tip of my finger.

My shroud encapsulated *His*, and as *He* worried, I drew a second, larger circle around the first to layer on the protections.

Before conversion, it would have taken a great deal more work and effort than simply willing the shroud into being—and nobody could erase the tracing of my finger from *His* skin.

"Come see me when you want that removed," I replied, allowing myself a satisfied smile.

"Thank you. I will after your parents leave and there are no mortals underfoot." *He* smiled at Darian. "You have been working with your mate long enough he would survive seeing my face."

"I throw him into lava pools for fun," Lucifer announced with pride. "She's done excellent work with him. She's at least two or three years ahead of schedule. Of course, he has been an active participant on that front.

In some ways, I think he wants to be converted even more than she wants to convert him, and that says a lot."

"I would say they are about equal on that score," *He* replied with a chuckle. "Easter was entertaining, but I have to say, this is something else. I added gifts to the living room, although I'm concerned we will run out of space. Attack and Snack are rather displeased their domain has been filled with presents."

"They will survive. They'll just curse at us a little," I replied with a chuckle of my own. "We can put more gifts in that sitting room thing Darian wanted."

"It is a cigar parlor," my husband-to-be announced in a solemn tone.

"You don't even smoke. Or drink. Yet you have boxes of cigars and a ridiculous number of Scotch bottles in there. There *are* liquors other than Scotch, Darian."

"I haven't bought all of the Scotches I want yet."

"You don't even drink."

"They're pretty, and I like the bottles. And if someone comes over who likes Scotch, I will be prepared."

Men. "We can put any extra gifts in the cigar parlor."

"We can also put them in the billiard room if needed."

That room would be the death of me—

or the ultimate destroyer of my lingerie. For some damned reason, I couldn't resist when he challenged me to a game of pool, but I couldn't play the game to save my life—or keep my panties. "No. The overflow can go into the family dining room because we're using that damned hall Lucifer insisted we have."

There was no way in hell I'd be putting any gifts in that room, especially not when I had to look my parents in the eye and pretend we spent most of our time playing pool instead of me paying out the consequences of my inevitable losses. At the rate we went, I would have to buy new lingerie soon, as Darian left no survivors in his wake.

Darian snickered, then he dared to leer at me. "I wonder why."

"Evil," I hissed at him before marching for the front door, where chaos brewed in the form of my parents discovering that holy hell would forever have a new meaning for them.

I SUSPECTED Lucifer had gotten to Ra and dressed him up, as the divine wore a suit that made it clear he was a prime specimen. The petite woman hanging off his arm, with pale hair and darker skin, wore a buckskin dress decorated with silvery symbols of the moon in all of its phases.

Menily. I'd heard about Bailey's divine mother, a moon goddess worshipped by the Cahuilla. At least one Cahuilla band still existed in California, although I had no idea if they still believed in her.

My mother and father gaped at the divine pair with wide eyes, and to add to the fun, we had an unexpected guest in the form of the pastor of their church and his wife. I raised my hand and covered my mouth, wondering how I'd handle that.

I bet the pastor had come to crash the dinner party and try to save my soul. Again. Probably through drowning me. Turning, I called, "Lucy?"

The Devil strode through my home and joined me. "Don't worry about it. Darian knows they're coming, so there's enough food for everybody. To keep my father happy, I'm skewing to slightly good splashed with a little evil today. I'll handle this part of the introductions."

He walked out and stood beside me, *His* stance relaxed, although something in *His* eyes warned me trouble brewed on the horizon.

"Ra, it's nice to meet you again," Lucifer said, before turning on the charm and smiling at Bailey's mother. "And you are just radiant as always, Menily. I am delighted to welcome you to my home—and the home of my esteemed secretary."

It amused me the Devil opted to go for our usual introduction routine, which we used to put those new to us at ease. I waved. "I'm Diana, but I've learned to respond to esteemed secretary as needed. I'll also be the one who responds to the various calls for help if you become overwhelmed. I regret to say we're a little short on soot and lava today." I held out my hand I giggled at the falling snow. "I hope a winter wonderland doesn't bother you. This is actually *my* home, but you know how Lucifer gets."

Menily's laughter chimed, similar to an archangel's, but somehow brighter and more soothing, as though she could heal the entire world of all its sins with the power of her joy alone. "You are Lucy's precious new filly!"

Well, that was a cat out of the bag. "I'm more of a nightmare, but precious new filly sounds so nice, gentle, and sweet."

My parents spluttered, and the pastor made choking noises.

The pastor's wife smirked, and when I glanced her way, her smirk eased to a knowing smile and a shrug.

How interesting. I made a mental note to ask Lucifer about the pastor's pretty wife, who fit the general trophy bride stereotype to a disturbing degree.

Lucifer joined Menily in laughing. "Your daughter and granddaughters are in the back playing with the horses, so if you want to go see them, you have time before dinner."

Ra held onto his beloved long enough to give her a kiss before sending her off with a rumbling chuckle. I pointed to the most direct path to get to the back of the house, and Menily ran off with the same general enthusiasm as the fillies romping in the snow. "Please forgive her. We rarely have a full day with our daughter and our grandchildren, so she's been very excited about this visit. This is one of the few places where our lights always shine together."

Well, well, well. "You have my phone number, Ra. I have to goose Lucy for a guest house, anyway, as I keep getting unexpected guests. If you need some time to see your wife, you can come visit."

Ra's smile matched the brilliance of the sun. "There are few presents Menily would enjoy more than that. Thank you."

One Egyptian contained, the entirety of the Christian pantheon to go. "The grandchildren might learn some bad habits from the Four Horses they're currently playing with. Kanika is attempting to supervise, but it's fairly chaotic back there. You might want to go join them."

Ra's smile broadened to a grin. "I shall

do that."

He disappeared, and it intrigued me he did so without any light at all.

"He caught a sunbeam," Lucifer explained. "It's a different sort of teleportation, and it doesn't have bursts like the rest. Sunlight is reflecting from the windows of your home, so he transferred himself through those beams to your backyard."

"Damn it, Ra!" Menily burst out.

"He opted to manifest in front of his wife so she ran right into him, and now he is rolling her in the snow, as he caught her around the corner and there aren't many watchful eyes." Lucifer smirked, and he gave the pastor his undivided attention. "In case you haven't figured it out yet, *pastor*, I'm Lucifer. You may have heard of me. The Lord of Hell. The Lord of Lies, the Fallen One."

He snorted, stepping beside me and leaning over to whisper, "The most annoying yet somehow most loved of my sons, but there is no telling him that for some reason."

I loved the Christian pantheon's delightfully twisted family. I whispered back, "You had something to do with that, you know."

"I love those who have the courage to actually *talk* to me rather than just confess their sins or act like I only exist to forgive them." *His* words, while spoken in a whisper, somehow captured the attention of my parents and the pastor.

The pastor's wife stepped up to the devil, smiled, and dipped into a curtsy.

How very interesting.

Lucifer held out his hand, and when she took it, he kissed the back of her hand. "Don't you just have the prettiest manners? Is it not amazing how such a pious woman can lead the so-called devout straight into temptation?"

"Lucifer," *He* warned. "We are trying to be polite hosts today. You can be an impolite host to that one later. Little one, do go to the main house and see Darlene. She can take care of you before dinner, and I will attend to some of your problems personally."

"Off you go," Lucifer murmured, and he touched the woman's cheek in a gentle caress, and she vanished in the brimstone I associated with the Devil utilizing his power. "As it seems I'm not going to be permitted to eviscerate you at my leisure, welcome to my many hells. You'll get to enjoy your stay today, but should you ever raise your hand to one of mine ever again, your soul will never leave the darkest pits of my many hells—and I will let Diana have a turn with you. Let me tell you there is little worse than the pain of the most holy of fires eating away at your bones here." With fire dancing in his eyes, the Devil gestured to his father. "This is my father, and I will *not* mind my manners should you upset *Him* today."

The pastor's eyes bulged at the disappearance of his wife, but upon hearing who the Devil introduced, he paled to a ghostly white.

He chuckled. "I come here for Christmas once, and you are out to scare the sin right out of the future residents. This is a time of celebration and family. They are guests."

"For the moment," Lucifer growled.

He smiled at my parents. "Please do not mind my son. He has a difficult time accepting my fatherly love, and your lovely Diana has forced him to show his better side, more than he is comfortable with. He is even at high risk of liking it. While this is your daughter's home, allow me to be the one to welcome you inside and wish you a most merry Christmas."

"Who *are* you?" my mother blurted.

"I am who I am," *He* replied, "But you may call me YHWH." *He* paused, and with the faintest of smiles, he spelled it as modern humans might, as Yahweh. "I am the Lord your God, who brought you out of the land of Egypt to give you the land of Canaan." I remembered YHWH from the scripts, spelled in only consonants in the original Hebrew version of the bible, a key foundational difference in the forbidden lore I'd read versus the bible most people read—and worshipped. When *He* spoke *His* name, he did so with a slight emphasis on the final sound, as though implying *His* name might be short but it would endure.

Before the pastor or my parents could recover, *He* said, "Four of you came, but only one is worthy to stand before me, sacrificing so that others would not be sacrificed. Of the three of you who remain, two might find a way back into my light. One of you walks through the valley of the shadow of death, but *I* will not be with you, for I do not forgive the unforgivable."

My eyes widened, and Lucifer met my gaze and lifted a finger to his lips. Then, the Devil turned his stare onto my parents. "Your future son-in-law works in the kitchen. Perhaps it would be wise if you were to go see if he needs any help. You have seen what you need to see this day."

My father, as though in a trance, headed for the door. I worried at his jerky stride, but I said nothing.

The Devil never acted without reason.

My mother lifted her chin. "Is it true, what I believe?"

With a softening expression, Lucifer regarded my mother while *He* engaged the pastor in a staring contest. "You would ask the Lord of Lies for the truth?"

It took courage to face a divine and bear the burden of his full attention, and my mother erased my misconceptions of her strength when she stood taller in the presence of the Devil. "I saw your kindness. So yes, I would ask the Lord of Lies for the truth."

"What you believe is true."

Fury turned my mother's face red, and she turned to the pastor of the church she'd dutifully obeyed all of my life, slapped the bastard so hard his head snapped to the side, and drove her knee directly into his groin before palming her fist and driving her elbow into the back of his neck.

My mouth dropped open in the time it took him to collapse.

"Go to hell and stay there," she snarled before storming into my house after my father.

I stared at the man who'd taught me to fear the water, and he groaned on the ground.

"You might translate that to mean 'have a merry Christmas' if you think about it," Lucifer stated, his amusement brightening his eyes. "Isn't it funny how the start of redemption is as little as bringing a lost sheep home?"

"His wife?" I asked.

"A succubus he bound with magic he had no business wielding. Saving you allowed me to save her, too. Darlene will put her into her brother's care. He's an incubus with a gentle touch, and she has not been properly fed in a long time. All that is left to do is break the bonding, and that means dealing with the man. You may have dabbled with forbidden magics, but you did not do the forbidden. He has."

I contemplated transforming and incinerating the bastard with holy fire.

"With my son's blessing, I will handle this matter," *He* announced.

Lucifer's grim smile chilled me. "You have my blessing."

"*Come*," *He* ordered, and his sole command rattled the ground beneath my feet. From around the house came a white horse who bore no rider, his head held high and his eyes burning with an unholy light.

Conquest, the first of the Four Horses of the Apocalypse, came to a halt and waited for *His* command.

"*Come*," *He* ordered once more, and the rattling strengthened, although my home seemed immune to the power of *His* voice. A red horse cantered into view around the corner of my home, and with him came the cindercorn fillies and their parents, who flanked Lucifer and observed with fire and smoke trailing from their mottled coats.

War stepped on the pastor on his way to join Conquest, and the man screamed.

Bailey snorted flame at the man, and she nosed her fillies until the pair headed for the opened door of the house, which Lucifer closed behind them.

Some things young children did not need to see, and the darker nature of the Four Horses of the Apocalypse counted.

Sam, however, remained, and his ears turned back, and he lashed his tail.

"Don't fuss," Lucifer scolded. "It's not like the bastard hasn't earned *His* ire. Just observe, or you can go into the house, too."

To make sure the pastor stayed put, *He* rested his foot on the asshole's neck. "*Come,*" *He* ordered.

A black horse walked over, his head held high in equine pride, and his fiery eye focused on the man who'd face a fate worse than mere death. On silent hooves, much like when famine crept into the world to do its dark workings, the Third Horse joined the line.

Death scared most, and the pastor came to his senses enough to realize the identity of the final horse. The confessions fell from between his lips, beginning when he was but a child without mercy, drowning a puppy merely because he could. None of the pastor's sins seemed to surprise *Him*.

From theft to rape to murder, and even a confession he'd hoped I would drown because he didn't appreciate how he felt my eyes could see right through him. I put more thought into transforming and becoming the pale horse to bring death for his crimes.

"You are the nightmare that becomes his

end, and the daydream that becomes the beginning for many he made suffer," *He* said. "Unbeknownst to you, you have already played your part in his trial and execution. Because you suffered, others will not, and you will reap your rewards over your long life. When it is time for you to walk through the valley of the shadow of death, I will be with you, and you will find the journey is not dark and cold, but filled with light, warmth, and love, much as your life will be."

I was grateful Lucifer had sent my parents away to meet Darian, who would charm them with his wit and his kindness. Some things would have left scars, and I worried my mother's beliefs had done enough damage, in that she had never acted on what she had suspected.

"She acted once she learned the truth," *He* reminded me. "And she sought the truth much as you do. That is something you learned from her. This one has a serpent's forked tongue without my son's refined sense of justice. I will say this much, and may your mother one day forgive me for these words. She brought this sinner in the hopes you, with your contacts she does not approve of, might see his sins and make them known. You were her last hope—and you, because I *do* listen to the prayer that is life, would have seen what she had feared. You would have acted, and this same moment would have come to pass but in a different way. Your mother was willing to pay the price of your love for another's salvation."

"I mean, I literally brought her to hell on Christmas to tell her I've become some devil-demoness horse, so it's not like I'm winning any good daughter awards."

Sam headed for my house, and Lucifer opened the door for Bailey's husband. He disappeared inside, and the Devil closed the door. "Don't mind him. Things like this trip his trigger, and his first instinct is to check on his precious cindercorn and their children. After, he'll probably shift and have a talk with your parents about any investigation that'll need done. Justice will be served."

"Yes, justice *will* be served," *He* said. With a heavy sigh, he ordered, *"Come."*

The pale horse, the one most feared above all others, trotted around the corner with his ears pricked forward, wearing a bridle and saddle, although he carried no rider. Instead, an archangel strode beside the animal, and he carried a scythe, much as the visage representing death might.

"I will not walk this one through the valley, my father," the archangel announced, and the pale horse stayed close as though to support his claim.

"I do not expect you to, for this one sinned using my name to do so. No, I would not ask you to provide companionship for this one. He is undeserving," *He* replied. "I would not ask this of any facet. He can wander through the cold dark and find his way alone, until my fallen son retrieves the soul himself."

I clacked my teeth together in an attempt to hold my temper, but the thought of some spirit sticking around annoyed me into saying, "There will be *no* creepy ghosts of pastors haunting *my* house, Lucifer. You will retrieve that asshole and *promptly* toss him in a dark dungeon somewhere."

The pale horse joined the rest waiting for *His* command.

He stepped away from the pastor and said, "Do with him as you will, and may those of Earth remember why the End of Days should be feared."

The Four Horses of the Apocalypse converged, and the instant they touched the man lying prone on the ground, they vanished, taking their victim with them. *He* dusted off his hands. "Now that is finished, how about we rescue that young man from the kitchen and open some presents before we have dinner? We have a lot to celebrate today, all because some idiots stole the wrong lady's cat."

"Whatever you say," Lucifer grumbled, heading inside.

He waited until the Devil disappeared inside. "He gets easily confused at times. I should get him a dictionary. 'Whatever you say' is not how 'I love you' is pronounced, but that is what he means."

The archangel groaned and vanished, too.

"Please do not mind Azrael. He is just grouchy because he knows I am right."

"You'll get some attention later, I'm sure. You'll survive until then."

"But are you really sure?" *He* asked.

His question startled me so much I tripped and fell into the snow, spluttering. "You are something else, Yahweh!"

"I am what I am. I also happen to be an asshole sometimes, and I really hate when people sin in my name."

"Is that your version of 'I said what I said' but with a twist?"

"It is."

"You're the reasons angels are assholes, aren't you?"

"As a matter of fact, yes," *He* replied before walking into my home and leaving me to think about his words in the snow falling over the Devil's many hells.

THE NEXT BOOK in the Magical Romantic Comedy (with a body count) series will be Plaidypus, releasing in December 2021.

DEAR READER,

I hope you enjoyed Catnapped!

I wanted to take a moment to thank all of the wonderful readers who have reached out to say how much you appreciate reading my books over the course of this past year. I'm sorry I haven't been able to reply to all of you, but I'm so glad you're finding some joy and escape through reading.

For those of you new to the Mag Rom Com series, here's a brief guide to several of the reoccurring characters featured in Catnapped, including the character's name and which books you can find them in. (I have been informed this book may trigger binge re-reading.)

Please note that this is a quick and incomplete list.

Lucifer (AKA Satin, Lucy, the Devil, Darlene's Pet Toy…) was introduced in Whatever for Hire, and he can also be found in Burn, Baby, Burn, Grave Humor, A Chip on Her Shoulder, Double Trouble, and The Flame Game.

Darlene (The Devil's wife) was introduced in Whatever for Hire and can also be found in the Flame Game, Grave Humor, and A Chip on Her Shoulder.

Michael and Gabriel were introduced in Whatever for Hire and show up throughout the series. They had more major roles in Grave Humor and A Chip on Her Shoulder.

Unicorns: Bailey (and Sam) can be found in Playing with Fire, Burn, Baby, Burn, and the Flame Game. The standard unicorns are in Double Trouble. The celestial unicorn has made a single appearance as a side character, and she will be the star of a future book entitled On Point.

Belial was first introduced in A Chip on Her Shoulder.

He shows up whenever ***He*** feels like it, but you can get a hefty dose of ***Him*** in A Chip on Her Shoulder.

Happy reading!

~R.J.

About R.J. Blain

Want to hear from the author when a new book releases? You can sign up at her website (thesneakykittycritic.com). Please note this newsletter is operated by the Furred & Frond Management. Expect to be sassed by a cat. (With guest features of other animals, including dogs.)

A complete list of books written by RJ and her various pen names is available at https://www.thesneakykittycritic.com/complete-list-of-books-by-year-of-publication/

RJ Blain suffers from a Moleskine journal obsession, a pen fixation, and a terrible tendency to pun without warning.

When she isn't playing pretend, she likes to think she's a cartographer and a sumi-e painter.

In her spare time, she daydreams about being a spy. Should that fail, her contingency plan involves tying her best of enemies to spinning wheels and quoting James Bond villains until she is satisfied.

RJ also writes as Susan Copperfield and Bernadette Franklin. Visit RJ and her pets (the Management) at thesneakykittycritic.com.

FOLLOW RJ & HER ALTER EGOS ON BOOKBUB:
RJ BLAIN
SUSAN COPPERFIELD
BERNADETTE FRANKLIN

Printed in July 2023
by Rotomail Italia S.p.A., Vignate (MI) - Italy